The Conscious Teacher

By Deborah Nichols Poulos

The Conscious Teacher is about strategies and techniques educators might employ to become more effective teachers. In an accessible, conversational style, Deborah Nichols Poulos presents unique approaches to teaching that will inspire new and veteran teachers alike.

She begins with her personal story of not learning to read all through elementary school. Her early failures convinced her she was dumb. At first, she struggled, but when she still failed, she adopted an *avoidance strategy* that served her well until junior high. An experience in the seventh grade flipped a switch and started her on a journey to becoming an outstanding student and, later, to applying the lessons she learned as a child to her own teaching

What makes *The Conscious Teacher* unique are the inspirational lessons that are unlike what most teachers get in their teacher-education courses or student teaching. Ms. Nichols Poulos points out, for example, that from the very first day, it is important that students learn they will be treated with dignity and respect no matter what. And especially helpful are the steps Ms. Nichols Poulos employs to set up a behavior management plan that works.

She explains the strategic steps she takes before school starts—how essential it is to get to know each student before they walk into class on that first day. She also illustrates how setting up classroom routines helps students know what to expect and how to make the best use of every minute. And she emphasizes the importance of the *parent-student-teacher team* and includes many examples of how to communicate with—and involve—parents, even those who may be difficult.

Foundational to her program are reading and writing. Among other things, she lays out the steps for students—even as early as fourth grade—to write five paragraph essays and their own student-authored books, and to research and write reports that include bibliographies. When she differentiated curriculum to support all students' needs, she found their learning accelerated.

All teachers will appreciate her ideas about how to teach the basics of math, as well as advanced math concepts. And her ideas for teaching the arts are inspirational, as she describes in detail how her fourth graders performed Shakespeare's *Hamlet, Macbeth, King Lear, Julius Caesar,* and *A Midsummer Night's Dream.* She also shows how to integrate social studies with literature and writing. Her experiences taught her that young students are much more capable than many people realize.

The Conscious Teacher is an indispensable guide for all new teachers. Many of the ideas Ms. Nichols Poulos provides will also be an eye-opener for parents and experienced teachers as well. *The Conscious Teacher* is simply a *must have* for anyone truly interested in giving young children a positive and solid foundation for their later schooling.

Praise for Deborah Nichols Poulos' *The Conscious Teacher*
What Educators, Her Former Students, and Parents of Her Former Students Say about Ms. Nichols Poulos and *The Conscious Teacher*

What Educators Have to Say

There is no occupation that is more important and less appreciated than that of a teacher. So many of us who succeeded did so because of a conscious teacher. I am thrilled that a Conscious Teacher has written this important book. Too many teachers have not taken the time to share their amazing insights. I am grateful that Deborah Nichols Poulos has written **The Conscious Teacher** *to make new teachers aware of the ideas and techniques that well-prepared and truly conscious educators can employ to improve the lives of their students. Bravo Deborah!*

Delaine Eastin, Former State of California Superintendent of Public Instruction, 1995-2003

––––––––––

The Conscious Teacher *is a superb resource for educators, parents, and school administrators seeking tried-and-true advice on teaching. Written by a teacher with many years of experience, this book covers a range of topics from how to set the stage for effective learning to how to provide differentiated instruction within the classroom. All of this is done in a very accessible and engaging manner that leaves readers feeling inspired and eager to employ the book's techniques.*

Cynthia L. Pickett, Ph.D., Associate Professor of Psychology, University of California, Davis

Ph.D., Social Psychology, Ohio State University, 1999

M.S., Social Psychology, Ohio State University, 1996

B.A., Psychology, Stanford University, 1994

––––––––––

Deborah Nichols Poulos' remarkable book, **The Conscious Teacher,** *grew, as she describes, from her early humiliating academic experiences. It's a deeply personal and passionate depiction of all she learned that led her to teach and share. We owe her a debt of gratitude for sharing her personally derived wisdom. I was moved in so many ways on each page.*

As a social psychologist and participant in the "human potential" movement of the 1950's-1970's, I am particularly impressed with her focus on establishing a social system, a culture based on a set of clear values:

- *respect for individual differences.*
- *individualized, personally meaningful, learning goals.*
- *clear behavior standards with agreed upon consequences.*
- *a team approach: teacher-parents-child engaged in open discussions of all issues, negative and positive.*
- *an open learning environment that is caring and personal, where continuous feedback is given.*

As I write this, one word jumps out: "loving." I wish I'd had such an early education. To read her wisdom is a revelation in enlightenment.

Vladimir Dupre, AB (History and Political Science) Oberlin College, 1943.

Ph.D. (Human Development) University of Chicago, 1956.

Hanover & Grinnell Colleges, Assistant & Associate Professor, 1948-64, &

University of Kansas, Associate Professor of Psychology, 1965-68.

National Training Laboratories in Applied Behavioral Sciences,
Director, Regional Office, 1968-70, President 1970-76.
Private Psychotherapy Practice in Family Therapy, 1976-2002.

———————

Debbie Nichols Poulos was one of my students in education courses at the University of California at Davis. I have followed her professional career since that time. I know she looked at each individual student and evaluated their strengths and weaknesses, providing individual and group activities to address their unique needs. She was a TEACHER, not a 9-4 sort of person. She was always on the lookout for ideas that would be meaningful for each student. Debbie kept in mind the subject that the students needed to master. She worked hard to integrate subjects into meaningful educational experiences. Debbie continued to experiment and grow every year. She continued to grow as a teacher and as a woman.

When she retired, she turned her creativity to quilt making. She visualized what the quilt would look like, and used colorful fabrics and designs to create unique finished projects. The same was true of her teaching. She knew what she was trying to accomplish in one year with her students. She created unique plans for them, helping each to progress through individual and group activities as far as they could go.

The Conscious Teacher *is easy to read and understand, giving teaching techniques for the novice as well as for the experienced teacher. It is broken down into short precise examples that can be adapted to an individualized teaching approach. It is both a practical and a visionary book. I would recommend it be given to each beginning teacher or teacher at any level.*

S. JoAn Skinner, Supervisor, Dept. of Education, 1962-1990, University of California, Davis.
Lecturer: Introduction to Education; Reading; Early Childhood Education;
Creative Problem Solving; Seminar with Student Teachers
Director of the original Head Start Training Program for the State of California

———————

Teaching the whole child is the way to describe Debbie Nichols Poulos—she truly saw the whole child and "Walked the Talk." Our daughter was so lucky to land in her 6ᵗʰ grade class when we moved to Davis. She made a difference in her life that year and in many years to come. She was an exceptional teacher and person. **The Conscious Teacher** *is truly a valuable addition to teacher education literature.*

Carole Plack, Yolo County (CA) Office of Education, Teacher Evaluator and Parent

———————

The Conscious Teacher *is written by a brilliant educator who has spent a lifetime seeking to help children achieve their full potential. I recommend it highly.*

Madhavi Sunder, Professor, Senior Associate Dean for Academic Affairs, UC Davis School of Law.
President (2016), Davis Joint Unified School Board
AB (magna cum laude Social Studies) Harvard, 1992; JD Stanford, 1997

———————

The Conscious Teacher *should be required reading for any new teacher at any grade level; it can also be an invaluable resource for even the most experienced teacher. Ms. Nichols Poulos offers detailed and specific suggestions for creating a*

classroom of mutual respect and high expectations by teachers in varied circumstances from elementary through high school. She offers advice from her own experiences. Her comprehensive examples of what to do and her respect for students, teachers and parents create a handbook of useful plans and, even more important, a framework for how to nurture students so that real learning can happen.

Naomi Feldman, BA Bard College (History, Economics and Political Science)

MAT Northwestern University

Teacher, Evanston Township High School 1972-1995 (Combined Studies-History and English-Humanities, AP European History)

When Debbie read the first chapter of the yet unnamed **The Conscious Teacher** *to the memoir writing group that I facilitate, comments ranged from: "I wish you had been my teacher!" to from other teachers in the group, "I'm sorry I didn't have your book when I was teaching. Such innovative and inspirational ideas." It has been a joy for us to share this writing journey with Debbie.*

Joan Callaway, Author: *It's an Ill Wind, Indeed; The Color Connection: From a Retailer's Perspective; Invisible to the Eye*

My first teaching assignment was at Fairmount Elementary School in the outer Mission District of San Francisco. Except for two short student teaching assignments in the spring of 1960, I had basically no clue as to the unlimited number of dimensions that were involved in teaching. My education classes in college had focused on curriculum with very little attention paid to the interpersonal, interactive aspects of teaching. What an incredible first day of school when I stood in front of 42 fourth graders of mixed cultures and realized that I was their "teacher"! And, not only that, but I was responsible for modeling characteristics that I wished them to learn—respect for others, kindness, caring, sharing, curiosity, love for learning …

At that time, the SFUSD did not have teachers' aides, so it was just me and the kids—those beautiful, expectant faces of all shades and colors. It's been many years since that memorable day, and the details have faded, but I would like to think that I did some of the things that Deborah Nichols Poulos suggests in Chapters One and Two of her book—get acquainted with your students, have them get acquainted with one another, learn about their families and cultures, and above all practice respect and caring for all. For me, those first two chapters lay the groundwork for being a successful teacher. The remaining chapters are filled with rich nuggets of excellent techniques in the various subject areas. The author did an outstanding job in these chapters as well.

The Conscious Teacher *should be required reading at the college level for all students preparing to be teachers and distributed to all first year teachers before that momentous first day of school.*

Patricia McCallister, B.A. (Education/Psychology), 1958 & General Elementary Teaching Credential, 1960. California State University, San Francisco.

Teacher Grades 1-4, San Francisco Unified School District—1960-69

Teacher Grades 1-6, Siskiyou County, California—1969-79

The Conscious Teacher *is a valuable guide for anyone considering the teaching profession as well as those already in the classroom. The sections on behavior management and differentiation will be helpful for parents as well as teachers. Nichols Poulos writes with compassion and the kind of understanding that comes from experience. I wish I had read this practical yet inspiring guide as a young, inexperienced teacher. It would have made a world of difference!*

Ann Martel-Corley, BA (European History & Elementary Credential), UC Berkeley.
Teacher Grades K-3, Mt. Diablo Unified School District, CA

What is striking about Deborah Nichols Poulos, her insights into herself and her teaching methods is her transparency. She aptly describes her own academic struggles and isolates the critical teacher interventions that assisted her in becoming a highly successful student. Her approach to teaching consists of methods, but underneath her techniques are critical beliefs in students' abilities and acute observations about how underachieving and gifted students act and how to identify their needs for optimum student success. She is concerned about the progress (or what prevents it) of every student.

Her belief in the power of the engaged parent-student-teacher paradigm is critical for student success. Detailed appendices present a gold mine of student and classroom assignments, grade rubrics for subject areas, grading and reporting standards, sample forms and letters which address multiple tasks teachers must master to be effective. Her love and respect for all children illuminates the very heart and soul of Deborah herself—a teacher with knowledge which she graciously shares and a very kind person with a gigantic heart for children and their well-being.

Darell J. Schregardus, Ph.D.
Ph.D. University of California, Davis
M.A. Roosevelt University, Chicago
Certified Psychologist - State of Michigan
Licensed Marriage, Family & Child Counselor - State of California

What Former Students Have to Say

As an elementary school student in the 1980s, I experienced a number of different teaching styles and philosophies, ranging from the laid-back to the authoritarian. I have mostly positive memories of my early education, but Deborah Nichols Poulos stands out as truly exemplary. I am now a parent and fellow educator myself, and have spent considerable time reflecting on those teachers whose practices most effectively supported and developed each student's potential.

Debbie's fourth-grade class offered a unique dynamic, emphasizing a commitment to mutual respect, shared discovery, individual freedom of creativity and exploration, and clear and appropriately challenging expectations. She encouraged us to be independent thinkers and to take intellectual risks. This was most evident in her emphasis on the value of perseverance and how she created an environment that pushed us to experiment with different problem-solving approaches and learn from our mistakes. In a "gifted" class of mostly over-achieving nine- and ten-year-olds, many of whom had up until this point taken academic achievement somewhat for granted, learning how to fail—and then try again—was one of the most important lessons Debbie taught us, and one I wish were more commonly prioritized in American education.

Furthermore, she emphasized the process of learning as much as its product, as well as the more elusive social-emotional skills students develop when they learn how to work with others and navigate academic struggles and challenges. Too often, these so-called "soft" skills are placed in opposition to academic success, but Debbie demonstrated that empathy, fortitude, and curiosity were necessary—not incidental—to intellectual rigor. I am so grateful to have had the opportunity to be in her class, an opportunity that helped to build a foundation for future academic achievement and, more importantly, instilled a commitment to lifelong learning.

I wish I'd had a college version of **The Conscious Teacher** *years ago when I started teaching First-Year Composition. Having real-life, pragmatic examples of how people move through and structure their teaching responsibilities would have been so very helpful. My textbooks were more abstract and theoretical in nature, which would have been fine for an experienced educator, but were not as useful for someone struggling to imagine just "what" it was I would do in the classroom, let alone "how" and "why" I would do it.* **The Conscious Teacher** *blends teaching philosophy and practical application in an accessible, exciting way; I can't wait to buy a copy once it is out.*

Karen M. McConnell, Teacher of composition and poetry, University of Michigan

BA 1999 and MA (English) Boston College, 2006

PhD (English Language and Literature) University of Michigan, 2013

———————————

Deborah Nichols Poulos was my 4th grade teacher, and my favorite throughout all of elementary school for the lasting positive impacts she instilled within me. There are three areas that come to mind most when thinking about that year. The first is how she helped me to discover my love of performing. She helped the class to develop a quality production of Shakespeare's Julius Caesar, and recognized my budding talents by giving me the role of Cassius. Discovering a love of acting gave me a concrete passion (I wasn't an athletic kid) and helped develop my confidence and public speaking skills, which have been lifelong assets.

Also, her method of teaching writing, especially during the Student Authored Book Contest process, instilled a love of storytelling. I told my Mom that it felt like I was learning to write all over again, but in a way that made sense to me and made it interesting and fun. And lastly, I feel Ms. Nichols Poulos helped to develop the beginnings of critical thinking, which was something I built on throughout my academic years, and what I credit as being the single most important trait that has helped me succeed in my career.

I'm excited for the students who will learn in these same ways from teachers who read **The Conscious Teacher**.

Jennifer Wilson Owens, Senior Strategy Consultant, Kaiser Permanente

BA (Media Studies and Communication) Scripps College, 1997

———————————

One of the best things about Ms. Nichols Poulos was her high expectations for all students. She believed in every child's capacity to learn and access high-level material (novels, plays, math concepts), even if the way a child learns is different. Just by being a student in her classroom, Debbie taught me about differentiation before I had ever heard it used by professors in my education classes. Now, as a teacher myself, I still find inspiration from my memories of Debbie and the projects we did in her classroom. My own students are reaping the benefits of Debbie's teaching, almost a generation later.

Molly Shannon, 4th grade teacher, Lafayette School District, Lafayette, CA

B.A. in English, UC Berkeley, 2002

St. Mary's teaching credential, 2007

———————————

In the 4th grade, school was for real, for the first time in my life. It was because Debbie Nichols Poulos was my first teacher to take students — and our effort — seriously. We were expected to read, to write, and to study math seriously. She devoted class time, every day, to "silent sustained reading": reading, in class, quietly, for long enough periods to actually get into and enjoy long books — real books — with chapters and everything.

And writing in her class was serious as well. She got us to write our own books, and it was real writing that she expected. She made time for us to write drafts of our books, to write improved revisions, and to illustrate them — I remember it being a long and involved process — and then we entered them into a citywide book contest. When I won an award in that contest, Debbie's pride made me feel like I'd won a gold medal in the Olympics: she was so excited, and I felt like a hero. Debbie had high expectations – of herself and her students – and rising to the challenges she posed was a turning point that made a difference in my life.

She was a serious teacher; I became a serious student. I learned a lot that year about reading, writing, and math, but I also learned about the value of focusing and working to get better. In her class, I discovered that effort matters, and the accompanying feeling has stuck with me for several decades so far.

Now many more students will have the opportunity to learn from the ideas Debbie shares in **The Conscious Teacher.**

Vinci Daro, PhD, Director of Mathematics Learning, Understanding Language/Stanford Center for Assessment, Learning, and Equity, Stanford University, Palo Alto, CA.

BA 1995 (UC Santa Cruz), PhD 2006 (UNC Chapel Hill)

What Parents of Former Students Remember

Ms. Nichols Poulos was my son's 5th grade teacher and, although a bright child, he had certain behavior issues which created challenges in the classroom. Debbie was the only teacher my son had throughout his schooling that I felt really understood him. She knew how to work with him to help him achieve his best potential; to feel cared about and accepted at school. Her skills, knowledge and abilities, along with her compassion for her students, made her an outstanding teacher. She was unforgettable to her students and their parents alike.

The Conscious Teacher *is a treasure trove of information new, as well as veteran, teachers can use to achieve the same success with their students.*

Sue Woods, Mediator/Facilitator; Center for Collaborative Policy, CSUS

BA (1975) Social Welfare, San Diego State University

———————————

Kindness contributes to the birth of all possibilities! Debbie Nichols Poulos carried her innate kindness of self into her classrooms where her students, my daughter, Jenny, among them, were enthusiastically encouraged to be curious, learn about themselves, and delve into things all new and exciting. She lent her gentle voice and smile in uplifting support whenever needed by energetic fourth graders striving to be independent and competent learners. It is gratifying that her experience and insights are in **The Conscious Teacher** *to teach others to be better than they expected to be! Thank you for the profound lifetime work that produced such a legacy.*

Evelyn Buddenhagen, Former Program Director, Explorit Science Center, Davis, CA

———————————

Despite it being over 30 years since my daughter was in the fourth grade, I have fond and vivid memories of an extraordinary year with two devoted teachers, in tandem, who provided an enriching and respectful experience. One of the teachers was Deborah Nichols Poulos.

My daughter Jenny, at that point in her life, had no idea that school could be a place of challenge. But with encouragement to reach her potential, using step-by-step instruction, she flourished under Ms. Nichols Poulos. She remarked to me one day, several months into the school year, that she felt like she was learning everything for the first time—how to write, how to think critically, how to work in groups, how to read for comprehension, as well as enjoyment, and how to assess her individual strengths and weaknesses.

And now Ms. Nichols Poulos has written **The Conscious Teacher** *to help other teachers to engage students the way she did. How fortunate they are to have an opportunity to learn from her years of experience.*

Barbara Wilson, Mother of Jennifer Wilson Owens, Davis, CA

Debbie was a profoundly sensitive teacher who had a talent for inspiring her students to do things that they (and their parents) might never have guessed possible. A Shakespeare play—memorized and performed by her Fourth Graders! What a special evening that was. Thank you, Debbie. Your students and their parents will never forget you.

Every teacher, aspiring teacher, and parent should read **The Conscious Teacher**. *Deborah Nichols Poulos has distilled her years of experience in teaching elementary school into a readable and moving blueprint for educational success.*

Tim Shannon, Shannon Government Relations, Sacramento, CA.
Father of Molly Shannon

The Conscious Teacher

*What all teachers and engaged parents
need to know to be more effective*

DEBORAH NICHOLS POULOS

PAGE PUBLISHING, INC.
Conneaut Lake, PA

First originally published by Page Publishing 2019

ISBN 978-1-68409-558-2 (pbk)
ISBN 978-1-68409-559-9 (digital)

Printed in the United States of America

Dedicated to
John, my children, and my grandchildren

Contents

Part I: My Own Story

Part II: Before You Decide to Become a Teacher...

...You should realize that teaching is a time-consuming career

Part III: How to Get the Job You Want: Consider Substitute Teaching

Part IV: First Things First: Set the Stage for Effective Learning

Part V: Instruction in the Classroom

Part VI: Teaching Gifted Students

Foreword

The Conscious Teacher, by Deborah Nichols Poulos, is more than a comprehensive 'how to' guide for both future and veteran teachers. It is an up close and personal look into how she became the teacher she describes for her readers. In many ways the book is a memoir of how she became the premier master teacher she models.

Throughout, however, *The Conscious Teacher* provides a wealth of resources valuable to any teacher who strives to be effective in meeting the diverse needs of K-12 students. It also serves as a helpful resource for parents engaged in their children's education.

The book is divided into six parts with subsequent sections:

In Part 1, Section One, *On Not Being Able to Read,* Deborah recounts her struggles with reading and the impact this had on her own education trajectory. She reminds us of the struggles faced by many of our students who fall through the cracks even when teachers and parents are well intended.

In Section Two, *On Not Being Able to Do Math,* Deborah recounts her frustration with math content, and we cheer when she finally has a teacher who makes a difference. She calls her story with math a "cautionary tale" that we should all take to heart.

Sections Three and Four, *College* and *After College,* lead us through Deborah's decision to become an elementary school teacher and give us glimpses into her personal life from the early years through her retirement.

In Part II, *Before you Decide to Become a Teacher,* Deborah provides valuable advice for anyone considering entering the teaching profession. Her insight offers readers a realistic view of the hard and often unseen and unrecognized work that it takes to be an effective teacher. From explaining that teaching is not an 8 am to 3 pm job, to sharing that some school issues are bound to keep you up at night, Deborah walks us through the commitment necessary to truly master content and know your students.

In Part III, *How To Get the Job You Want: Consider Substitute Teaching,* Deborah presents us with advice about becoming an excellent substitute teacher and the value of that experience when seeking a full-time teaching position. She explains that substitute teaching allows you to get an inside look at schools where you may want to teach and also for you to become known, giving you a step up when it comes to applying for jobs.

In Part IV, *First Things First: Set the Stage for Effective Learning*, Deborah shares time-tested strategies for creating an inclusive classroom culture, as well as for establishing classroom norms with high expectations for learning. She shares specific strategies for working with parents that join the teacher and parents as partners working toward the shared goal of supporting each student. Deborah also reminds teachers of the need to prepare ahead for when a substitute teacher is needed and the importance of making that process as smooth as possible for all involved.

Part V, *Instruction in the Classroom*, gets right to the core of how to teach the content areas of the curriculum. Deborah walks us through her teaching "gems" across the content areas: reading, language arts, technology, math, social studies, the arts, and physical education. This part is the equivalent of being given access to the file cabinet of a veteran teacher where all the best of the best information about content and strategies are kept.

Part VI, *Teaching Gifted Students*, addresses a student population too often overlooked in our teacher preparation programs and in professional development in our K-12 schools. Deborah discusses how she met the academic and socio-emotional needs of her gifted students. And she advises us how to deal with the transition for students from regular self-contained classrooms to self-contained gifted and talented education (GATE) classrooms. Furthermore, she shares strategies for meeting the range of multifaceted needs of gifted students, including intra- and interpersonal giftedness.

As the Director of Teacher Education at the University of California, Davis, I am honored to be asked to write the foreword for *The Conscious Teacher*, by UC Davis alumna Deborah Nichols Poulos. Throughout her 27 years of teaching, she impacted hundreds of lives and created learning communities within her classrooms that appreciate, respect, and meet the needs of all learners. We are proud to call her one of our own. We look forward to sharing her experiences and time-tested strategies with new and veteran teachers in our programs.

In my work to prepare new teachers, I draw heavily from two equally important sources: 1) research focused on issues of teaching and learning, and 2) experienced preK-12 educators from diverse content areas, communities, and educational settings. While we can teach pedagogical approaches and have student teachers learn about and practice specific strategies, what we can't teach is what Deborah defines as being a *Conscious Teacher*. We indeed want all of our educators to be thoughtful and to consider the impact that each and every decision has on each and every student. She calls for us to move away from a one-size-fits all perspective and, instead, to consider the needs of the struggling reader or the gifted student in our classrooms. Deborah also reminds us that effective teaching is grounded on universal principles that include kindness, integrity, and consciousness.

As the head of teacher education at UC Davis, I have to look at the big picture. We are currently experiencing a critical teacher shortage in our country (Castro, Quinn, Fuller, & Barnes, 2018). Persistently lower salaries (Miles & Katz, 2018), increased teacher certification requirements (Shuls, 2018), and the low status of the teaching profession (Skaalvi & Skaalvik, 2015) are leading many teachers to leave or not enter the profession. In my two decades in teacher education, I have become convinced that the most effective recruiters into education are teachers like Deborah who look back at a career in education and speak to the power and joy of shaping their students' lives. The many praises from community leaders, the countless testimonies of her impact from former students, and the endless praise from parents of former students, individually and collectively, speak to her influence as a conscious teacher. Each and every student deserves a teacher like Deborah.

Many have argued that teacher retention presents an even greater challenge than recruitment. We know that a significant number of teachers leave the profession within the first five years. Nieto, in her book *What Keeps Teachers Going?* (2003), writes about teaching as evolution, as autobiography, as love, as hope and possibility, as intellectual work, as democratic practice, and as shaping futures. Nieto discusses how, in spite of all the challenges inherent in teaching, teachers who persevere do so because they are able to embrace these various aspects of teaching. In this book, Deborah speaks to each of these areas through her reflections and the resources she shares with both those preparing to enter the classroom and those who are experienced teachers.

Deborah, in concluding her book with *Final Thoughts*, reminds us of the many rewards inherent in a teaching career. It is evident throughout the book that she embodies what it indeed means to be a Conscious Teacher. Her call to action for all teachers to "be creative, to work hard, and to see that every single student benefits from his or her year in our care" is one that is timeless and that reminds us of the great responsibility and privilege it is to teach.

Dr. Margarita Jimenez-Silva
Director of Teacher Education and Associate Professor
School of Education
University of California, Davis, CA

B.A in Liberal Studies and Early Childhood Education,
    Concordia University, Irvine, CA
M.Ed. and Ed.D. Human Development and Psychology,
    Harvard Graduate School of Education
California Multiple Subject Credential
Teacher Educator Since 1997
Taught in K-9, 1991-1997

References

Castro, A., Quinn, D. J., Fuller, E., & Barnes, M. (2018). "Addressing the importance and scale of the U.S. teacher shortage." *UCEA Policy Brief 2018-1.*

Miles, K. H., & Katz, N. (2018). "Teacher salaries: A critical equity issue." *State Education Standard*, 18(3), 18.

Nieto, S. (2003). "What keeps teachers going?" *New York, NY: Teachers College Press.*

Shuls, J. V. (2018). "Raising the Bar on Teacher Quality: Assessing the Impact of Increasing Licensure Exam Cut-Scores." *Educational Policy*, 32(7), 969-992.

Skaalvik, E. M., & Skaalvik, S. (2015). "Job satisfaction, Stress and coping strategies in the teaching profession—what do teachers say?" *International Education Studies*, 8(3), 181-192.

Preface

The ideas I share in *The Conscious Teacher* have been in the back of my mind for a long time. They have germinated since I retired from teaching in 2000. My husband had been telling me for years that I needed to publish my teaching experiences so others could learn from them.

It was in my memoir-writing group, however, that the project gathered momentum. I had joined the group in 2013. At first, like the others, I shared the writing I was doing to tell my life's story. But when the group learned I had written about my teaching, they wanted me to share that work instead. Once I read the first excerpt, they urged me to set aside my autobiographical memoirs and focus instead on putting my teaching ideas into a book before it was too late.

Having people enthusiastically support my work and say it was important enough to be published was in itself extremely encouraging. But their saying "before it is too late" made me realize that they were right on point, bringing a sense of urgency to the task that I hadn't felt before. The fact is that I am living with an incurable illness that is going to take my life sooner rather than later, and I needed to prioritize.

I have ALS, amyotrophic lateral sclerosis (Lou Gehrig's disease). It has slowly taken away my ability to control my muscles, and it will, before long, take my life. My illness required me to retire early, and now I suddenly realized I shouldn't delay any longer in writing the book and getting it published.

It wasn't as if it were a difficult task. I didn't have to study or do research. All I had to do was reflect on my 27 years of teaching and write about what I had learned and put into practice. In the fall of 2015 I picked up what I had begun a few years earlier and started writing in earnest

To show what can happen when teachers allow students to slip through the cracks, I begin the book with **Part I—My Own Story**, about not really learning to read until I was in the 7th grade, and how I overcame this devastating failure and became a strong student. (Not until after college did my Mom tell me that—as a five-year-old—I'd been tested as gifted. I had gone through my first six grades not learning to read, thinking I was stupid. Evidently my parents thought I was just lazy. And no teacher ever looked into why I couldn't read.)

There is no doubt that my early experiences in school gave me an insight into what can happen to bright students (or any student) through no fault of their own. But these experiences were also behind my developing many of the ideas I later used in my own teaching. I didn't want any of *my* students to languish as I had with unaddressed issues, and I wanted *all* of my students to be taught in ways that allowed them to enjoy learning.

The main part of the book, however, is what I learned from teaching: **Part IV (First Things First: Setting the Stage for Effective Learning)** and **Part V (Instruction in the Classroom)**, in which I discuss a variety of practices educators might use in each curriculum area to become more effective teachers.

These are unique approaches that are not normally found in teacher education courses, and many of which may even be new to veteran teachers. Much of what I share was developed during my longest single teaching experience—eight years teaching a fourth grade gifted class. But the methods that I learned there work just as well when teaching *any* students.

First there are the general practices that are useful in all classes. High among them are the importance of "knowing" each student before the first day of school, always treating students with dignity and respect, and using differentiated approaches to address all students' unique learning needs. I also describe my behavior management plan that works.

And I emphasize why it is important to involve parents. I provide a variety of examples of how to work with them (even those who challenge you or your methods), and I stress the importance of establishing a *parent-student-teacher team.*

I also suggest what I have found to be effective for teaching each standard subject in the elementary curriculum. For example, basic to all teaching are reading and writing, and I show how even fourth grade students can learn to write five-paragraph essays, student-authored books, and research reports that include bibliographies. Another example: by integrating writing with social studies (i.e., by requiring good writing when working on reports and journals), a teacher can reinforce the principle that following established writing conventions is important across all subjects of the curriculum. I have also expanded upon what is usually taught for art and drama. For example, my fourth graders have performed Shakespeare's *Hamlet, Macbeth, A Midsummer Night's Dream, Julius Caesar,* and *King Lear.* Young students are much more capable than many people realize.

With the ideas I share in *The Conscious Teacher* as a foundation, I hope to inspire and empower other teachers to trust their insights and to confidently develop their own methods of engaging students in ways that both support and challenge them to reach their full potential.

I hope *The Conscious Teacher* will become a guide for all *new* teachers, and I believe it will be an eye opener for many *experienced* teachers *and parents* as well. In the end, this book is directed at all who are truly interested in giving children a positive and solid foundation in their elementary years.

It took a year to write, and three years for what I needed to correct, change, and add. And now it is finally finished. It has been worth every minute.

Deborah Nichols Poulos
September 2019

Acknowledgements

First of all, I must thank my memoir-writing group for encouraging me to share what I had learned from my years of teaching. This was the motivation and inspiration I needed to renew my work on a project that had lain dormant for far too long. Thanks to these friends—and the leadership of Joan Callaway—I got going again. Over almost a year, at each meeting the group made their comments about what I had just written and continued their encouragement and critiques. This group primed the pump so that this book began to be fleshed out and, for the first time, vetted by others.

One member, however, took it on in detail. I owe a huge debt of gratitude to my friend, Judy Wydick, who copy-edited and helped to organize the manuscript. She is a former English teacher, and her background in writing vastly improved *my* writing. This included paying close attention to how each chapter was organized. She went through the entire manuscript over and over again, offering her enthusiastic encouragement and insightful critiques.

And thanks to Katie Jeannerett and her team at Page Publishing for shepherding the book throughout the process, from editing to publication.

I am grateful, too, for the loving support of my many women friends. Many of these women I've known for almost fifty years: Marlene Bell, Dawn Daro, Ginny Heitz, Gail Johnson, Jan Jursnich, Pat McCallister, Elinor Olsen, and Sue Woods have supported me in countless ways through the years.

Then there is my quilt group, which has maintained our connection through monthly gatherings since 1999: Cynthy Bissell, Ann Driemeyer, Cindy Finley, Bobbie Hewell, Deborah Kitchens, Debbie Perry, Heather Roemer, Sherri Wallace, and Louise Zabriski. I also must mention another friend, Robbi Henle, who is extended family of the quilt group. And at University Retirement Community, JoAnn Diel, a special friend and supporter, stands out among many friends here because she has become much more than indispensible in working on my quilting projects.

I have been especially buoyed by any time I get to spend with my four adult children and thirteen grandchildren, even though they are not directly related to writing this book. They are John Stewart Poulos and his children Kady (23), John Michael (21), Lindsay (19), Nicholas (16), and almost five-year-old twins Wesley and Kennedy; Alexandra Poulos Fullerton and Michael, and Elsie (26), Graham (23), and Annie (20); Matt Taggart and his children Samantha (13) and Jack (11); and Kelly Taggart Scavullo and Andrew, and Azalea (11) and Oscar (8). I am especially grateful for the efforts Kelly makes to bring Azalea and Oscar for overnight visits from San Francisco every few weeks. I hope for many more years to interact with all my grandchildren and watch them grow.

Foremost, I thank my husband John, who has always believed I offered a unique perspective that I should share, and who was the first to encourage me to write this book. He has been steadfast in his support for me and for this project. None of this would have been possible without his help. His love sustains me.

Introduction

A great deal of time, energy and creativity go into teaching

Teaching elementary school children is an incredibly rewarding career. Teachers truly change lives. But it does not happen easily. A great deal of time, energy and creativity go into classroom teaching, and many people do not realize that it is also an incredibly *demanding* career. Anyone who is thinking of becoming an elementary school teacher has much to learn beyond what is taught in teacher-education programs.

The first thing an aspiring teacher should know is that being an elementary school teacher isn't easy simply because the subject matter is "elementary." And these teachers do not have short workdays with weekends and summers off. To be successful, classroom teachers should expect to be at school from 7:30 to 5, to take work home each night, and to plan a summer that includes in-service training to expand and improve their teaching skills. Learning to teach effectively is an ongoing process that never really ends.

Teacher training falls short of truly preparing teachers

Even more important is recognizing that they can't achieve success by passively going through the motions of giving routine textbook and workbook assignments. Standard texts and traditional approaches generally do not do a sufficient job of *engaging* students in learning. In order to address the diversity of needs in any elementary classroom—and truly engage students in the learning process—teachers must seek and develop their own curricula.

Further, I don't believe standard teacher-training courses and student teaching go far enough to provide essential guidance for *beginning* teachers. This is especially true in the area of classroom management. The result is that many teachers meet their first classes without being properly prepared. By default, they tend to engage in an authoritarian relationship with their students in order to control their behavior and to tell them what they should learn.

It took me several years of teaching and a variety of *experiences* to realize that there are many strategies that are *not* taught in either teacher education courses or student teaching that are invaluable when working with young children. I devised my own effective organizational and student behavior management systems, created a unique learning environment, and developed my own curriculum to address students' individual needs. Seeing how well the children responded, I learned to trust my insights and instincts and slowly developed confidence in my own ways of teaching. I found these to be *far* more effective, and these are the ideas I present in this book.

Why I take elementary education so seriously

The main reason quality elementary education became so important to me was that I had a reading disability that affected my entire education, and when I became a teacher, I had a keen interest in seeing that none of my students experienced what I had.

Though my teachers taught as best they could at the time (I entered kindergarten in 1950), I never learned to read in elementary school—primarily due to my moving from one school to another at a critical time in first grade. But not only did my teachers not try to find out why I was having problems, my parents—both loving, thoughtful, college-educated teachers—did not intervene when it was clear that I wasn't doing well.

I detail my own story in the first part of the book. You will see how my personal experiences taught me the significance of getting to know each child and the importance of learning different approaches to dealing with *all* children—not only those at grade level but also those who struggle and those who are far ahead of their classmates.

My background also helps explain why it has been so important for me to **work** *with* **my students**. When I first began teaching, I felt the approaches I'd been taught separated me too much from my students. Rather than being above them, *dictating* to them in an authoritarian role, I wanted to be on a more even footing where we would *work together*, where they would participate more in the learning process. In this book, I discuss the many ways I learned to make this happen.

Two factors that may explain why I was so successful as a teacher

It wasn't until I was writing about intra- and inter-personal intelligences in the last chapter of this book that I realized that these two intelligences applied to me. To explain briefly, a person who is intra-personally gifted has a strong sense of self and is adept at knowing and managing himself. A person who is inter-personally gifted has a strong sense of others and is adept at relating to, understanding and interacting with others. And I believe that knowing myself well and being able to relate well to others in large part facilitated my teaching. These characteristics and how I used them inform all of what I have to say throughout the entire book.

I discuss these more fully and suggest that if you aren't familiar with these attributes (or don't naturally have the advantage of possessing them), you should learn about them, as it will make reading this book much more meaningful. And that is because much of what I say in the book teaches how to employ characteristics like these to better address the needs of students.

Why it is important for parents to be engaged in how their children are taught

Parents are in the best position to be advocates for their children's academic and social-emotional needs. And more than ever before, they must be engaged in how their children are taught. This is true for all parents, but especially for parents of students whose work is generally *below* or *above* grade level.

Given my own early school experiences, I've always been especially concerned about the children at both ends of the spectrum. Many of the ideas in this book apply directly to them, for teachers should be taking care that students who may be struggling get the kind of help that will work for them, while at the same time challenging those students who are working above grade level.

If a parent sees something in this book that might assist her child, she might mention it to the child's teacher. Parents, in fact, may be the best ambassadors for introducing teachers to this book. At the very least, they can supplement their children's education at home with many of the ideas presented here. Parents may also find behavior management ideas that are helpful to them.

With this in mind, I have comments directed to parents at the end of each chapter, suggesting ways they can help their children or ways they can work with the teacher to help them.

Why I chose this title for the book

I have deliberately called this book *The Conscious Teacher*. When it was in draft form, a friend asked if I didn't mean *The Conscientious Teacher*. After all, a teacher *should* be conscientious, working hard to do everything in her power to help a child learn and develop a good sense of self. But that is not what I wished to write about.

Instead of following standard norms, I want teachers to self-critically *think* and *consider what to do* rather than act out of reflex or commitment to pedagogy that might be outdated.

What I present here diverges from many of the norms teachers learn in teacher-training programs. I attribute my own success to approaching teaching differently. To be a truly effective teacher, a person must *consciously* think *beyond* what she has been taught. I believe incorporating the following elements leads to truly effective teaching:

1. *Kindness.* Zen Buddhism teaches a doctrine that enlightenment can be attained through direct intuitive insight. It emphasizes **ethical actions, charity, tenderness, benevolence, and sympathy.** These ideas resonate with me. The approach to teaching I present in this book comes from several years of direct intuitive insights that are embodied in the Zen approach (something I had not realized at the time I was learning to teach), in which one must *consciously* make choices—choices that include these traits. And I believe my approach relies on all of them, as well as **empathy**— essential elements for both relating to others in all settings and to good teaching.

2. *Integrity.* Operating out of integrity means that you make a personal choice to hold yourself to a consistent standard of honesty and fairness. When you model these characteristics to your students you send a powerful message.

3. *Consciousness.* This is defined as having "an executive control system of the mind." Being truly *conscious* enables one to have an "awareness, subjectivity, the ability to experience or to feel, to have a sense of self." These qualities enable a person to be confident about her perceptions. In the realm of teaching, rather than simply following rules learned from textbooks and a master teacher, I developed the confidence to evaluate for myself what are the best approaches for my teaching, what works for me—through *consciously* making choices based on my everyday experiences.

In the end, I learned that truly effective teaching is an ongoing process of *actively thinking about* what is best for each student (and working with each one to bring out his/her full potential), *carefully including* new, effective approaches and ideas that have evolved from my experiences. I am *always thinking about and improving upon* the systems and techniques I am developing in the classroom—a constant work in progress that calls for *consciously* observing, and applying, what works best. Thus the title: *The Conscious Teacher*.

Part I
My Own Story

On Not Being Able to Read
How not learning to read in the first grade affected me throughout all the grades

One of my main motivations for writing this book came about because of my personal experience of being unable to read as a child. So before I go on to talk about teaching, I want to share my own experiences as a student.

You see, when I was in the primary grades, through a series of misadventures that no one recognized, I didn't learn to read; and as I advanced to the intermediate grades, I tried to hide my failure. My inability to read dominated my life between the ages of six and twelve—almost all of my elementary school years and into the beginning of seventh grade.

Reading failure is one of the most debilitating failures one can experience. (Those who cannot read at a time when *everyone else can* would call it *the* most debilitating!) And for all too many children (and adults), it is a failure from which it is difficult, if not impossible, to recover.

I came to believe that my reading failure story—along with the "*aha*" experience that came to me subsequently—offers a new perspective to this old problem. Friends, mostly fellow teachers, say it is a compelling story, and the theory it spawned is worth telling to a wide audience. I begin by telling my own story.

The following experiences are drawn entirely from my own recollections, and we all know that memories can be flawed or inaccurate. All I can say is that this is the story as I remember living it. Though some of the elements were told and retold as a part of family lore, most of what I experienced has remained vivid in my mind over the subsequent years.

Ultimately, it is a story about overcoming failure and becoming successful. I believe it is a cautionary tale.

1. What happened in the early grades

Kindergarten—a happy time

We lived in San Diego, California, and I went to Andrew Jackson Elementary School for kindergarten. In 1950, five-year-olds were not taught to read in California. Kindergarten was a year to learn socialization skills and to engage in imaginary play.

I remember kindergarten as a happy time of building castles of large cardboard blocks. We pretended to be the attackers or defenders of the castle. We built an airplane the same way, positioning chairs within the airplane structure. We played all kinds of games out on the playground.

I don't remember learning letters of the alphabet and numbers, but I suspect we did do some of that. Teachers read to us from illustrated storybooks, and we talked about what these stories were about. We learned songs and played different simple instruments. Kindergarten was a year of exploring and making new friends.

In any case, reading instruction did not begin until the first grade.

First Grade—We move from California to Tennessee

When I started first grade, I was still in San Diego, not far from San Diego State where my dad was a chemistry professor. My classmates and I were still working on reading-readiness activities when, in October, our family moved to Oak Ridge, Tennessee, for a year where my dad was to work at the National Radiation Lab.

A miserable first day in a new culture

I vividly remember that first day in a new school, in a new town. I knew no one, but I had been looking forward to this adventure, meeting new people and making new friends.

Instead, I remember feeling an intense sense of being studied by everyone in this new classroom—by both the other children and the teacher. I may not have *looked* any different from the other kids, but here in Tennessee I sure must have *sounded* different. (*They* certainly talked funny!) I also quickly realized that everyone else knew each other well. After all, they had been together since the beginning of the school year—and probably the previous year as well. I was new, different, arriving late, coming all the way from California. I realized that I was "the stranger."

It wasn't long before I was asked to join a small group of children, sitting like birds on a wire on the vinyl floor tiles in front of a *Big Red Storybook* that was propped on a tall easel in front of us.

I was very familiar with books. My parents had read to me often. I enjoyed listening to the stories and loved to examine the illustrations, picking out details that were referred to in the words read by my mom or dad. After the reading, usually at bedtime, I'd "reread" the stories by myself, turning the pages and looking at the pictures for the clues I needed to retell the stories, sometimes over and over again. But I hadn't linked the words I heard with the words printed on the pages. I don't know that I even thought about the printed words as the source of the stories.

In any case, I thought the teacher was going to read to us. Instead, she stated that each of us was to take a turn reading from the book. And I realized that when it was my turn, I was expected to do the same!

A rude awakening

Being asked to read in front of classmates was an intellectual and emotional awakening for me. Not only did the Tennessee children in my new school speak in what seemed to me like a foreign language—they were already *reading*! I had no idea what to do, as I *didn't know how to read!*

Now, in a room full of strangers waiting for my turn to *read*, I knew that I would be revealing something to everyone about who I am. I was about to experience what I later realized was my first memorable failure.

I was near the end of the line. My attention was focused intently on the words I heard coming from my classmates and the words printed so boldly under the colorful illustrations of Dick, Jane, the red wagon, and their dog, Spot.

And then it happened: "Debbie," I heard the teacher say. "It's your turn." I had been concentrating so hard on listening to the other children read that I had not noticed that the child just to my right had finished her turn.

I took a breath and began to attack my sentence, one word at a time. Of course, I don't remember the sentence, but I do remember the *excruciating* anguish, frustration, embarrassment, and humiliation I felt as I struggled along from word to word—sometimes guessing right, sometimes guessing wrong, and sometimes having no idea what to say. The teacher corrected me or filled in the correct next word, and the next, until I had made it to the period at the end. I knew this little dot marked the end of my turn.

There were two more readers after me, but I no longer paid any attention. I didn't look at the book, and I didn't listen to the words. All of my attention was inside my own head. And the sound inside my head was like that of ocean waves crashing on a sandy beach, the scene before my eyes like the snow on an old-fashioned television screen.

Soon my distraction was interrupted by the teacher's voice dismissing the group. It was time for our little group to return to our desks, while another group of kids positioned themselves in a line in front of the book. I watched from my desk as student after student read a sentence from the book. It was clear to me that I was the only one in the class who had so much trouble completing the sentence correctly. I was in pain, and I didn't know what to do about it. I felt helpless and alone.

I can't know whether I hid my feelings, but I didn't tell anyone at school. Even when I went home, if I shared what had happened that first day of school, it apparently didn't register with my parents that this was a problem they needed to address. But *I* knew there was a problem, and I knew it was *me*.

The scenario of the first day was to repeat itself again and again. The second day I was called to the firing line with the low reading group. Again, I was unable to read my sentence, and this continued day after day.

When and how reading was taught in the 1950s

At this time, I need to talk about when and how reading was taught in the 1950s. I have since learned there was no single approach.

First was the issue of *when* to begin teaching reading. Some schools—like mine in San Diego—postponed actual reading instruction in favor of reading-readiness activities. Students learned to recognize letters of the alphabet and engaged in other non-reading activities. Other schools, like in Oak Ridge, began actually teaching reading at the very beginning of first grade. By the time I arrived in late October, they had learned enough to read from the *Big Red Story Book*, the first real reading text children were exposed to in that era.

It's not that the words in this text were so difficult; it was just that I had never been exposed to any of them. Had I been taught just these few words before joining that reading group on the first day, I would have been off to a good start. I would have learned these words quickly and been able to concentrate on learning the other words. This little bit of instruction could have made all the difference for me as a first grader. Without them, I was at the mercy of luck and chance. And being *expected* to read when I'd never been taught any of these words was traumatic.

Then there was the issue of *how* to teach reading. Some teachers used a *phonics* approach, which taught children how to sound out words. Others relied on teaching a *sight* vocabulary—later known as the *whole language* approach, of teaching children to memorize words then recognize them when they appeared on a page. This second technique was used in Oak Ridge; but if you didn't know the word in the first place, there was no way to figure it out. And I don't remember *ever* being taught the strategy for sounding out words I didn't know.

Some words were impossible to remember

At first I worked very hard, trying to find the key to unlock the mystery of the words. I paid close attention as my classmates read. And because I would associate the words with illustrations in the book, I slowly began to identify and remember *some* of them. Yes, it turns out I was picking up the big **content words**: **picture words** like *wagon, house,* and *dog*; **name words** like *Dick, Jane and Spot*; and **color words** like *white* and *red*, ones that had meaning to me and made sense because of the pictures.

But my luck with reading was no better on these later occasions than it had been the first time because of all the words with which I could make *no* connection: words like *were, went, with, want, when, where* and *them, these, those, this, they, than, then*—they were a complete mystery to me. No matter how closely I paid attention, no matter how hard I tried, I could never remember which word was which. How was I to know one from the other? They were all just a mess of letters that looked too much the same.

Years later, as a teacher, these were the words I would call the "glue words," without which the sentences would not hold together. In that sense, try as I might, the sentences I was asked to read always fell apart. The teacher and the other students tried to help me as I stumbled through my sentence, but their efforts lasted only as long as it took for me to get to the end of the sentence. I simply couldn't remember all the new words. Each time I was presented with these mysterious glue words (and many other words), I failed.

I also remember what I'd call "reading lessons." We would sit on the floor in front of an easel on which the teacher had written a couple of columns of words. The little group would read the words along with the teacher, and the teacher talked about the words. Sometimes the words rhymed. Sometimes the words began with the same letter, or were spelled the same in different parts, or had some other common element, like they were all used in the same story. But even though I could follow along with the group to repeat the words as the teacher recited them, I didn't come away from those little group lessons with any sense of *how* to unlock the mystery of the words. When I came upon those words again, on my own or when I was asked to read in front of the group, I just couldn't remember which word to say that was a match for the word on the page.

When my teacher asked me to read, she simply assumed I could. And as a child, I figured that if an adult asked me to do something, I was supposed to know how to do it, so it was obviously *my* fault that I couldn't read. Further, I feared that all these potential new friends now knew I was stupid; there was no other explanation to my six-year-old mind. They were expected to read, and they could. I was expected to read, but I couldn't.

Things only got worse

Even worse, I couldn't read to myself either. I couldn't—as I was asked to do so many times—go back to my desk and read the story silently to myself. So when told to do this, instead of reading, I'd look out the classroom windows and daydream about what I would do when the reading period ended or when the bell rang and we would go outside for recess. My only comfort in these silent reading sessions was in knowing that *no one but I knew* that I couldn't make sense of the words on the page, didn't know the story as it was written.

I knew I had to hold the book as if I were reading it. I became good at looking at it and turning the pages, but I no longer really saw what was printed there. Finally, I'd close the book and set it down, as if I were doing what I'd been told to do. Now I could go on to something that I enjoyed doing, something that I was good at.

I couldn't answer oral questions about the story unless the answers were revealed through the illustrations, though fortunately—at least in the simpler early stories—they often were. At first, I actually got enjoyment out of "reading" the pictures for meaning and at least telling myself the picture story. But the pleasure in this diversion soon disappeared. So before long, although all my senses were on high alert during my reading circle's oral reading sessions, when I returned to my desk, my strategy was *avoidance*.

The pain and humiliation of my reading failure was so intense that I had no incentive to continue trying to read when I had time on my own. My survival skill—when not in the reading group—was to do anything other than try to read. Avoidance kept me from having to confront my failure.

Second Grade—and a move back to San Diego

The summer before I started second grade, we moved back to San Diego and my former elementary school, Andrew Jackson, but my experience in school was much the same as in first grade. Although I learned a lot of things, reading was not one of them.

In those days, there were no reading specialists to diagnose students with reading problems and help the teacher develop strategies for working with each of them. So my teacher was on her own to figure out what to do with me. The only help I remember ever receiving, however, came during oral reading to get me through my sentences—but I didn't learn from it. And my parents still thought it was just my lack of effort, not something in which they should intervene.

As I recall, there were three levels of reading groups—Redbirds, Bluebirds, and Yellowbirds—and the teacher moved students from one group to another according to how well they read. If I was lucky and I guessed right in my group, I might be bumped to a higher group. But no sooner would that happen than I would guess wrong and be dropped back down to the low group. Evidently, it wasn't easy for Ms. Bain, my second-grade teacher, to determine where I belonged.

This year, we carried our chairs into a circle for reading lessons. As early fall faded into Halloween and Thanksgiving, the groups became static, and everyone knew his or her assignment for the rest of the year. By then I had taken my place as a regular member of what I knew was the low group. Regardless of what the group was called to disguise its rank, I knew I was in the dumb group. I knew I was dumb.

Each time I joined a group and received a reading assignment, I became intensely anxious, but not as anxious as when I knew I would be called upon to read out loud in front of the group. And this, unfortunately, was destined to happen at least once every day.

My strategy

It didn't take me long to realize that Ms. Bain usually had the group read in order, starting with the child seated at her left. But occasionally—at least often enough to keep us a little off balance—she would begin in the opposite direction. And then there were those times that put me into high panic when she would skip around the group, calling on each of us at random and asking us to read aloud. Although I knew I could do nothing to prepare for this last eventuality, my usual strategy was to sit somewhere in the middle of the circle, usually a child or two closer to Ms. Bain's right side than her left.

My seating strategy was the only one I put into practice as I joined the reading group. I had no strategy for the task of reading itself, for which the operable system was luck or chance. On any given day, for any given story, for any given reading group, the scenario was essentially the same. I would use the time before being called on to read aloud to listen intently to my group mates and to look intently at the words and pictures printed on the page in front of me. As students closer and closer to me took their turns to read, I even gauged which sentences would be mine.

It was always difficult to strike a balance between using the reading knowledge of the kids who read before me to teach me the words I didn't know, or to try to jump ahead to find and practice the words in the sentences that would be mine to read. But regardless of how I calculated this equation, I usually failed to garner enough information to succeed with even one sentence, let alone two or more.

I might get off the first word or two with a speed and confidence that belied my knowledge of the certain doom that would follow. Then I'd stumble, be interrupted with corrections, wait eagerly for someone to supply the word I didn't know, or simply give up in total frustration and shame, as my sentences were picked up and read by the next kid in my group. Even though I knew I had been revealed once again as the poor reader (reading failure that I was), at least I had survived yet another turn in the reading group. And with any luck at all, the group's time with the teacher would run out before that indignity would pass to me again. And tomorrow would be another day.

I am aware that it was sometime during my second-grade year that my reading failure became a fact of life. I knew I couldn't read, that I had little hope of ever learning to read, and I knew that all my peers and my teacher knew this too. I accepted this ignominious fate as fixed, and I had no clue of any other approach. Had I seen any way out of this terribly painful reality, I certainly would have jumped at it—but the fact is, I didn't. The tenacity that was second nature when it came to physical tasks was nowhere to be found when it came to reading.

There must have been other kids in my class who had trouble reading too; after all, I was always in a group with other kids. But I was certainly too occupied with my own troubles to give much thought to others.

Summer school after second grade—another move in San Diego

In the summer between second and third grades, we moved again, but this time staying in San Diego. My parents had bought a lot closer to the college campus where my dad was teaching. The new house they were building was not yet finished when we had to move, so we moved into an apartment nearby.

That summer I attended summer school at the San Diego State Campus Lab School, the school where teachers received much of their training. It was thought to be of a higher caliber than the public schools and was highly sought after; most students who went there had been put on the waiting list right after they were born.

They had an opening in the following year's third grade class, and my going to the summer school program was to give them an opportunity to decide whether to admit me for third grade. As it turned out, they decided not to. This was another disappointment due to my reading failure: I knew that it was because I was not a good reader.

Third Grade—my third new school in three years

That fall I began third grade—this time at Montezuma Elementary School. And even this teacher did not wonder at my inability to read.

I distinctly remember the times we would have to read a story to ourselves. I would sit there at my desk with my book open, but all I *really* did was look out the classroom windows at the sky, the clouds, or the birds, or I would simply turn my face toward the book and let my mind wander. Just as I had so often done, I would turn page after page, mechanically, simply making a show of reading.

There still was nothing in this routine to help me figure out words I didn't know—not in the special vocabulary list, textbook story, workbook, or worksheet pages. Yes, I had memorized *some* words and was aware that my bank of *known* words was growing, but these helped only if they were the words I had to read. Unfortunately, there were many *more* words that I had not yet learned, and this number was growing all the time.

In any case, I still had no idea how to figure out words for myself.

Briefly, a tutor

My mother must have realized I was having trouble reading (either from my low grades or from my teacher), because that year she hired a tutor who came to our house once a week to help me with my reading—an old lady who brought lavender sachets she had made. She asked me to do exercises in workbooks in which I was to choose—from a few options—the correct word to complete the sentence. These were primarily grammar exercises in which the answer to the question was grammatically correct.

Since I couldn't read the sentences, I asked her to read them for me. When she did, I could easily tell her the word that correctly completed the sentence, because I learned proper English from my parents. I enjoyed working with her, but she apparently didn't know how to provide the help I really needed. I don't remember how long she came or why she left, and, unfortunately, she was never replaced.

Fourth through sixth grade

By fourth grade my reading failure wasn't so painful. Rarely were we asked to read out loud unless we volunteered. When the teacher chose kids to read aloud, he chose the good readers. So I began to relax and not worry so much about my failure. As long as my inability to read was not on public display, it was not so much of a problem. It became easier for me to hide in plain sight.

Since I had been with the same kids since the third grade, my classmates already knew I was one of the dummies. No amount of effort was going to change that.

Of course, over the years my skills and vocabulary grew, but, unless I was required to read aloud, I didn't choose to read. I may have given it a haphazard effort from time to time, but I never read for pleasure. Why would I voluntarily subject myself to the emotional pain of confronting my failure? As long as I didn't try to read, I didn't have to face the humiliation. Avoidance worked. My survival strategy was intact, and I continued to use it.

I suppose, to be fair to my teachers and parents, I did well enough in school that they didn't see my difficulties as the handicap—both educationally and emotionally—that I knew they were. After all, my motivation was to hide my failure as much as I could.

Those were the days of E (Excellent), S (Satisfactory), and N (Needs Improvement) grading. I got mostly Ss and a few Ns. The common refrain on my report cards was that my effort was lacking. Well, that was certainly true. But it was equally true that no one had ever tried to teach me the key to unlocking words I hadn't memorized.

I had heard the refrain "Sound it out" until I thought I would scream. But these words meant nothing to me. No one had ever demonstrated what it meant. Or at least I couldn't figure it out reliably. And I certainly wasn't putting in the effort to try to figure it out on my own.

I was able to contribute to class discussions because I was a good listener. I was okay in math as long as I had help reading word problems. I was great at any activities requiring visual/spatial aptitude, good at sports, and good at making friends. And on the playground, it didn't matter who could or couldn't read. I was a happy kid, and the trauma of having to read aloud in front of my classmates had faded—or so I thought.

Seventh Grade—and Horace Mann Junior High School

It never occurred to me that my avoidance would *not* be a successful long-term strategy. All I was concerned about was the present, the short-term; the future did not enter my mind.

Then came seventh grade—the transition to junior high school—not only a new school, but mostly new students coming from about eight elementary schools.

Suddenly, the tables were turned. Within the first week or so of my English class, the teacher brought in a class set of *Time* magazines, and announced that we were going to learn to *read for understanding* in this standard periodical. He said we would start reading with the student closest to the door and continue until everyone had a chance to read a paragraph or two. We would stop occasionally to discuss the meaning of what we read.

I always sat in the desk closest to the windows in the back of the room, figuring it was the best place to hide. Now I realized I was about to be found out. Today there was no seat in the class that would be safe. Further, these were *not* the students with whom I had gone through elementary school—except for three or four from my former school who already knew of my reading failure. So my anticipation of hiding my failures from all these potential new friends was suddenly at risk. My avoidance survival strategy was about to be turned on its head.

As soon as the first student began to read, my attention became riveted on the text of the magazine. I tried to track the words on the page with what I heard. Word by word, sentence by sentence, paragraph by paragraph, my fellow students read down the columns of text, progressing down the columns of desks toward me. There would be no hiding for me today.

I listened intently, trying to match the words on the page with what I heard my classmates read. My attention had never before been so tightly focused. As my turn to read drew closer, I skipped ahead to anticipate which paragraph would be mine. I scanned that paragraph for the same words a classmate had already read, and if there were new words, I worked quickly and intently to try to figure them out. Listening to the discussion of the article's meaning helped me to figure out words that fit the context.

I hoped that the class period would end before my turn came, but as the reading moved into my column of desks, I knew I would not escape. I had to skip down to different paragraphs a few times, but I was gaining confidence.

Aha!

Finally, it was clear exactly which paragraph I would have to read—thankfully, a short one. I had time to work on it and figure out all the words, associating the words in my paragraph with the ones I had heard. Now all I had to do was read them "calmly and fluidly," as I'd heard my teacher say so many times, as if it were no big deal.

As the student in the desk in front of mine finished reading, I took a deep breath and began to read. I read slowly, but deliberately. I tried to remain calm and reached the end of the paragraph without stumbling or missing a single word. I slumped in my seat as I breathed a huge sigh of relief, absolutely amazed with myself. I had actually fooled my teacher and all the students in my class into believing I knew how to read.

The biggest feat by far, however, was that I had fooled myself. This experience forced me to reevaluate my strategy. If I could succeed in reading a paragraph in *Time* magazine in just one class period, just think what I could do if I worked on reading on my own time!

2. Suddenly, Everything Changes

This experience flipped a switch, and I was suddenly motivated to work on reading. As never before, I focused my attention on school assignments that required reading. I don't recall how long it took, but it wasn't long before I was reading everything I was required to read. Somehow I finally understood what "sound it out" meant, and I figured out how to use context clues. I still did not read anything that wasn't required, but I did put a great deal of effort on all my assigned work.

I become a good student

It seemed like almost overnight I was becoming a good student. My writing and spelling improved, and my reading just seemed to take off. By eighth grade, I had become a better-than-average student, and in ninth grade, I was getting mostly A's. In the tenth grade, as a student in the academic track at Crawford High School, I was one of only two students in a class of over 700 to get straight A's.

My high school principal sent a letter to my parents congratulating them on my achievement. When I saw the letter, I was *outraged!* My *parents* had *nothing* to do with my achievement! Why wasn't *I* being congratulated? But my outrage didn't dim my satisfaction. I understood the irony of the situation. It wasn't until years later, however, that an even greater irony came to my attention.

Once I learned to read and began to apply myself, I became a serious student. I went straight home each day to work on my homework, and after dinner each evening I went right back to work on my assignments. Still being a slow reader, I took longer than most students at my level to read and comprehend the work.

There were no distractions. Boys weren't interested in me, so I never had a boyfriend in high school (though I would have liked to have had one). And I wasn't a member of clubs or social groups, as I spent most of my time studying. I had a few girlfriends with whom I got together for movies or high school football or basketball games, but my focus was on getting good grades and being admitted to a well-respected college or university. and this would extend through the rest of high school.

My older cousin had gone to Stanford, and as an eighth grader I imagined going there—until I learned it was too expensive. That was when I set my sights on the University of California, an almost-free university, respected as outstanding around the world.

We move to Santa Rosa for my junior and senior year

The summer of 1961 we moved from San Diego to Santa Rosa in Northern California, where once again I would be the new kid in school—this time Montgomery High School. But by this time, I was doing well and taking all the toughest classes, so it didn't matter. Although my new high school was smaller, by the time I graduated, I ranked eighth in my class of just under 400.

It is interesting to note that as a high school student, I was asked to write only two book reports. Though I was in the academic track that emphasized reading and writing, we didn't otherwise do the book reports that were a big part of the *non*-academic-track classes. I selected *Kon-Tiki*, by Thor Heyerdahl, and *We*, by Charles Lindberg. (*Kon-Tiki* chronicled the story of Heyerdahl and a group of men who sailed on a large raft from the west coast of South America across the South Pacific to the Tuamoto Islands, in what was French Polynesia. *We* told the story of Lindberg's epic solo flight from the United States to France.)

But I didn't actually read either book. Instead, I constructed my book reports from the fly leafs on the books' covers, and found selected passages within the books from which to quote. I didn't have the time it would have taken me to read these books—I needed to focus my energy on all the other assignments I had to work on.

It wasn't until years later, however, that I realized that I had chosen books that illustrated the classic struggle of man against nature. Perhaps these adventures resonated with my own individual struggle to survive despite what seemed like insurmountable odds.

The Scholastic Aptitude Test (SAT)

I had never been good at standardized tests, and the SAT was no exception. Taken during the spring of my senior year, it was timed and required reading for comprehension and answering questions, defining vocabulary words, and solving math problems. Timed tests always made me highly anxious, and on these high-stakes tests, this anxiety interfered with my ability to concentrate and slowed me down.

The reading comprehension and vocabulary test frightened me the most. Though I'd vastly improved my reading skills and speed, I was still a very slow reader with a limited vocabulary, and it took me a lot of time to figure out answers. Requiring less reading, the math section was not as challenging, but several parts of the test contained word problems that slowed me down.

I ended up scoring only 1005 out of 1600, with 465 in reading comprehension and vocabulary and 540 in Math, scores that were not competitive. Fortunately, colleges took into account grade point averages (GPAs) as well as SAT scores, and my high school GPA was close to a 4.0 (the highest GPA possible in those days).

The Subject A Exam

I passed the Subject A exam—the test given in California (and administered separately) to make sure students are adequately prepared for college-level writing. My results demonstrated that I was prepared.

I remember going down to UC Berkeley to take it. We were asked to write the ubiquitous five-paragraph essay, a task my senior English teacher, Mr. Coresberg, had had us practice over and over again. We'd had that structure drilled into us during our entire senior year.

I had not been as anxious about this exam, because in Mr. Coresberg's class I had received mostly As and some A+s on my essays and other written assignments. I was very proud of my success in his class, as he had the reputation of being the toughest English teacher at my high school.

And I felt good about how I'd done on the exam. When it was known that students had received their results, Mr. Coresberg called me at home to ask how I'd done. When I told him I had passed, he said, "I'm just tickled." I was excited too. This meant that I would not have to take Subject A English as a freshman, a "makeup" class for which I wouldn't have earned any units.

3. Looking Back Years Later—Two Revelations

I realized I probably had had ADHD

I didn't learn about ADHD (Attention Deficit Hyperactivity Disorder) until 1967-68 when taking classes for my teaching credential. Several of the characteristics matched my early school behaviors to a T. I was a daydreamer, easily distracted, fidgety, had trouble sustaining attention and finishing work, and interrupted others—not waiting my turn. These are just a few of the common characteristics of ADHD that I could see described me as a young child. It was easy to see why I'd had so much difficulty in school. I'd had ADHD at a time when it had not yet been recognized or defined.

I was too busy teaching and taking classes to really think about this at the time. But later, upon reflecting, I could see how I had eventually recovered and learned the tools that enabled me to do well in high school and college. And I could clearly see what a huge advantage it is now for teachers and parents to understand the learning issues confronting a child with ADHD. My life would have been far easier had this information been available to my teachers and parents when I was in the early grades.

I learned that I'd been tested as gifted—as a young child

It wasn't until after college that I learned from my mother that I had been tested as gifted when I was five years old. (Five is the best age to test kids, as it relies simply on aptitude—rather than what a child has learned or his ability to read.) One of my dad's colleagues in the education department at San Diego State wanted guinea pigs for giving intelligence tests, so my parents volunteered me.

I vaguely remember the experience as being like a game, as he asked me questions, had me copy shapes and designs with paper and pencil, and asked me to identify different arrangements of shaded shapes. The results of the test were given to my parents.

I seriously doubt whether my knowing I was gifted would have made any difference in my experiences when I was in elementary school. It was clear, however, that my parents were not particularly concerned about my school performance. They apparently believed it was a matter of effort on my part, not aptitude, and that my achievement—or lack thereof—was entirely up to me. I guess they reasoned that eventually I would do well. I suspect that since I had adopted an avoidance strategy toward reading, I didn't ask them for help. And they must not have asked me to read for them, or my difficulties would have been obvious.

I can't explain why they weren't more involved, however. It is a mystery to me still. My mother had been an English major in college, and she had taught fourth grade for two years before getting married. She certainly could have—or should have—taken a more active role in determining what was going on with me and worked to remediate it. She was aware enough to hire a tutor for me in the third grade, but apparently, after that, figured that I'd manage all right when I made the effort.

Even gifted kids may have trouble learning to read

The main point I want to make here, however, is that even gifted kids may have trouble learning to read. And I'm a perfect example of that.

I've also realized in my seven years of teaching gifted children in the GATE program that being gifted doesn't mean simply that a child is especially smart. Being gifted covers a huge range of abilities—from being especially capable in one area while having difficulties in others, to being extraordinarily bright overall.

I discuss this subject in "Part VI; Teaching Gifted Students." Given my personal history, I have strong feelings about this subject, one that many teachers do not fully understand. But it is behind the reason I wrote this book.

A positive outcome

Having learning difficulties wasn't all bad. These early experiences with failure eventually turned me into a hard-working student and, in the end, a better teacher. I believed I had to try harder than others to succeed, and I did. In so doing, I developed the ability to persist in overcoming obstacles that lay in my path. I would use these qualities of perseverance again and again throughout my life.

Later, after going into elementary education, I realized that my difficulties with learning to read would be an advantage in teaching children who were struggling to do so. In the chapter on reading, I share the techniques that I found worked so well with young, developing readers. Needless to say, I did *not* make assumptions about their potential abilities based on their difficulty reading.

And though teaching reading was one area of the curriculum to which I brought a unique perspective, I also developed other teaching techniques that I believe are unique. So in addition, I will share other important things I learned from teaching that were never included in my own education.

For Parents

My parents, though well educated and loving, did not fully understand their role in the process of my education. Despite their background and experience, I think they felt that all they had to do was send me off to school each day for my teacher to educate. (After all, I was young and bright; I'd pick things up quickly.)

I would have been a much more successful student if my parents had paid closer attention to the effect the move from California to Tennessee might have on me in school. They should have anticipated that I could well experience considerable challenges—going to a distinctly different part of the country, after the school year had started, during this critical, formative period. They should have immediately met with my Oak Ridge first grade teacher to make sure the transfer would go smoothly. There is no doubt in my mind that had they talked to her before my first day there, the fact that reading instruction had not yet begun in my school in San Diego would have come out, and she would then have been prepared to help me. This simple bit of information would have made a *huge* difference. In other words, conscientious parenting could have prevented me from being put on the spot to read on that first day of school.

Or, when this didn't happen, they should have paid closer attention *during* the transition—been more attentive to my reaction to the first day or two, perhaps just asking me more questions, listening closely to how I responded. And then they could have—and should have—intervened early on, especially when it became clear that I was having problems. As loving as they were, **they were not the kind of engaged parents I hope readers of this book will be.** Perhaps these parents will discover ideas for more effectively helping and supporting their children.

In the end, I did recover, and I even became a teacher myself. Given the experience I had, however, I believe I offer a unique perspective that will help new teachers before they step into the classroom for the first time—and perhaps even cause experienced teachers to *rethink* how they interact with their students.

On Not Being Able to Do Math
How not being taught math visually affected my ability to advance in arithmetic

My primary struggle was with not being able to read, since reading is the basic skill for all learning. My secondary struggle, however, was with learning math. Though I was doing fine with addition, subtraction, multiplication, and simple division, when long division was introduced, I was lost. I also couldn't understand how to make equivalent fractions for adding, subtracting, reducing, and comparing.

1. The Struggle Begins

Fourth Grade—and my frustration with algorithms

Long division was part of the fourth grade curriculum. It was taught as a series of steps, an algorithm that we had to follow, making correct calculations along the way. I remember challenging the teacher with questions about the sequence of steps and trying to find a better way to understand what we were doing. I also remember her being very impatient with me. All she could offer was the algorithm that we had to memorize. It was only much later that I realized she didn't know any other way. By then it was too late to forgive her.

I was able to memorize—or remember—things that made sense to me, but I couldn't remember what, for me, were a series of random incomprehensible steps. So I was at a loss. When we did our classroom or homework assignments, I could follow the example of steps, but for tests I couldn't remember what to do.

One day, in prepping for a test, I asked my good friend, Donna Musil, who sat next to me, if she would let me copy off her paper. She agreed, so I was all set.

Unfortunately, after the test was over, I was found out. I don't recall exactly why that happened. I just remembered that Mrs. Youngblood called both of us up to her desk and reprimanded me for cheating. It was embarrassing. But I was not about to cringe under her humiliation of me. By then I was beginning to find my own voice.

I complained to her: "What do you expect me to do when you won't teach me in a way I can understand?" I shocked myself with my boldness, but I was really frustrated with her, and I felt it very unfair that I was being called out for something I thought was primarily due to her failure, not mine.

This was one of many "aha" moments when I learned something I would later use when it came to my own teaching: **you are not teaching if your students don't understand, or learn, what you are trying to teach.** It's axiomatic. (I didn't learn the meaning of that word until my eighth grade math class.) But Mrs. Youngblood didn't get it. She thought she was teaching, and that it was my problem that I didn't get it, not hers.

Fifth through Seventh Grades—the struggle continues

I continued to struggle with math. I had trouble converting fractions to lowest terms and creating equivalent fractions so that I could add and subtract. Again, all of this was taught as a series of steps, an algorithm that I couldn't remember. We weren't provided with visual/spatial clues or manipulatives to give us a concrete/real-world relationship between the symbols/formulas and the meaning of the concepts taught.

I still remember a test in seventh grade on which we were expected to put a series of fractions, all with different denominators, in order from least to greatest. I had no idea how to do this.

2. Eureka!

Eighth Grade—everything comes together

Eighth grade was the turning point for me in school. As I look back now, I remember how dramatically everything changed for me. Ever since my seventh grade reading epiphany, I had worked really hard on all my classes. As a result, I began to get A's in English, social studies and speech. I had already been getting A's in Home Economics and PE, but this was the first time I had received them in any academic classes. And the same thing happened with math.

The right teacher made all the difference

My eighth grade math class was taught by Mr. David Jones and was based on Max Beberman's University of Illinois' Committee for School Mathematics (UICSM) Program. It later came to be called "The New Math." Pay attention, Mrs. Youngblood: this is what I was talking about back in fourth grade.

The UICSM program taught axioms and theorems, set theory, algebra, and geometry. It taught everything for basic understanding visually, spatially, and in a way I would call "organic," as it made sense to me organically. This is exactly what I needed to understand math. This was real *math*, not algorithmically-based *arithmetic*.

Our one class of approximately 30 students was evidently experimental. Mr. Jones had attended the UICSM summer course in order to be trained to teach the program. We were told at some point that those in the class had been selected randomly. But I, in my efforts to raise my academic image, decided I had been specially selected for the class. Oh, the tales we tell ourselves to get by in life! At any rate, I did do well; in fact, I did *very* well. In this one year I made up for all my previous years of failure in math. On my daily assignments I was getting A's, and I got my first A in math on my report card. That also meant I was getting straight A's.

I remember only too well the difficulties I had had with math just the year before! I had failed the test in seventh grade that focused on identifying equivalent fractions, sequencing fractions with different denominators from least to greatest, and adding/subtracting non-equivalent fractions. It had been a bunch of mumbo jumbo as far as I was concerned. But in the UICSM class, we drew pie charts to actually *show* what equivalent fractions were, and it became refreshingly clear to me. Now—after "seeing" it—I was finally able to understand the steps and remember them for tests. Wonder of wonders, miracle of miracles—it finally made sense to me.

My attitude toward school completely changed. Now, schoolwork was all I focused on. I came right home after school, started in on my homework, and didn't do anything else until it was done. And I studied hard for tests. Being able to read and do math had not only meant that I was able to learn, but that I loved learning. I became highly motivated by the improvement in my grades. It was as if I had become a different person.

This was also the year that my cousin Dick Nichols went off to Stanford University. I knew Stanford was a top-drawer university that was difficult to get into, but now that I was quickly remediating my academic flaws, I set my sights on attending that school.

Ninth grade, then sophomore year at Crawford High School

The math class that started in eighth grade went on together to ninth. The core of that curriculum was geometry, which I loved. It was visual and spatial—right up my alley.

The following year Mr. Jones moved on with the class to Crawford High School. That year the primary focus was algebra. I really loved math the way Mr. Jones taught it—the UICSM way. It was fun and easy.

Junior and senior years at Montgomery High School

After moving to Santa Rosa, I discovered how lucky I'd been to have Mr. Jones as my teacher those three years, because he had set me up to be successful in math. He not only did an excellent job of teaching algebra my sophomore year, but he'd actually introduced me to some advanced algebra. Therefore, as a junior taking advanced algebra/trigonometry (one of just three girls in the class), I was ahead of the game and found it was easy to follow the new concepts.

Further, my new teacher, Mr. Gyving, did a great job of teaching these advanced math subjects. I really loved advanced algebra; it was fun, fairly easy, and very clear because we were using logical steps to manipulate equations and to solve for the variables. It was like playing a game. Trigonometry was more difficult, but I worked at it and did well.

Senior year, however, I didn't even consider taking calculus, as it had a reputation for being very difficult—and different from algebra and trig. It didn't help that with so few girls taking these classes, I was starting to believe that girls couldn't do as well as boys. Besides, I'd already taken the math I needed to apply for college, so I didn't have to take calculus.

3. Looking Back

What if I had taken calculus in high school?

Eventually, long out of college, I *had* to take calculus as a requirement for a master's degree in business administration. And to my great surprise, it turned out to be easy and very straightforward—a matter of simple manipulations of numbers in patterns. It was like learning how to add and subtract, and it drew upon my knowledge of algebra and graphing equations in the four quadrants.

Clearly, I shouldn't have been scared off by calculus in high school. Had I taken it then, my attitude toward math probably would have been quite different.

And why didn't anyone notice my tested strengths?

There's also the matter of my having been identified as gifted at age five when I took the Stanford Benet intelligence test. I believe my giftedness was in large part due to my visual/spatial abilities. These parts of the test had been easy for me. (This probably was why my favorite pastime as a child was drawing house plans: I loved poring over my mom's *Sunset* and *House Beautiful* magazines and had designed many rooms and houses for fun.) I'd like to think that if I had been told I was gifted in this way, it would have improved my attitude toward math, making me more confident of my math abilities.

Even though neither of my SAT scores was stellar, my math score was 75 points higher than my English score. So I certainly should have had more confidence in math than in English.

It's clear, in retrospect, that I might have done well as a math or engineering major in college, and that, if I had done so, I might have gone on for a degree in architecture, which had always fascinated me.

The moral to the story

I tell this story about my early years—not because I am unhappy about how things turned out, but because I don't want the same thing to happen to another student because she mistakenly lowered her sights due to a lack of confidence. As the old saying goes, "Better to have tried and failed, than never to have tried at all."

I tell my story as a cautionary tale. We all have insecurities and doubts about our abilities. That's why it is so important for parents and teachers to look out for us when we are still in school, to help us to make the best decisions. I'm sure they will discover other girls, and perhaps boys, like me, who doubt their abilities and talents despite their successes.

My life really did turn out all right—in fact, it turned out great.

For Parents

The troubles I had with math were similar to what I had with reading. Like me, many children need spatial/visual cues to help them understand math. Fractions are a good example. I explain all this in the chapter about teaching math.

When teachers don't pick up on this, parents may be the only ones around to help their children understand math. There are many charts available to help students visualize math, so if teachers aren't using these, parents can introduce them to their children. This is why I have said that this book is also for **engaged** parents.

Section Three
College

I was confident enough about my qualifications for college (and all too cognizant of the high $25 cost of each application) that I applied to only two universities: the University of California at Berkeley and at Davis. I was admitted to both. And although I was attracted to UCB for its beautiful campus and stellar reputation, I ultimately decided that its more rural counterpart, UCD (located in a small town with around three thousand students) was a better fit for me. In the fall of 1963, I began my freshman year at UC Davis.

Deciding on a major—ironically, it wasn't math

My high school teacher had encouraged me to major in math in college since I had done so well in advanced algebra and trig. I enjoyed math, and though I wouldn't say it was all easy, I worked at it and it made sense. And my SAT test scores clearly showed that I was stronger in math than in English skills. So why didn't I major in it?

Primarily, it was my lack of confidence. College math classes, like higher math in high school, were mostly all men. The prevailing wisdom at the time (though not necessarily stated) was that men were better at math than women, and I lacked the confidence in myself to be competitive with them. Despite knowing I was good at math, I simply doubted my abilities at the college level. It doesn't make any sense, but it's what I believed at the time, and there was no one around to dissuade me. So despite strong evidence to the contrary, I didn't go the math route.

And that's a shame. I didn't realize that my natural talents lay in visual/spatial reasoning and I didn't have confidence in my math ability.

So what then?

At first I thought I would be a home economics major focusing on clothing design—I had been designing and sewing my own wardrobe since I'd taken a Singer sewing course the summer after sixth grade. But when I learned that the home economics department was in the Ag School and that I would have to take a bunch of science classes, I quickly changed my mind, as I had no interest in science.

(What I actually was most interested in in college was having a boyfriend and finding a husband. I figured I'd be a stay-at-home homemaker and mother like my mom had been. Any career plans were only a backup in case I didn't find a husband before I graduated.)

Next I considered being a PE major since I was good at sports and could see myself as a PE teacher. But PE, too, required a number of basic science classes. I had taken physiological psychology and was *not* looking forward to taking two required courses with reputations for being tough—organic chemistry and kinesiology. So I dropped PE as a major, though I did end up with it as a minor.

I finally settled on English as a major—as had my mother. This was an odd choice, given my lack of a reading background and the fact that I'd faked the only two book reports I'd ever had to write. And though I had improved my reading and writing skills through my hard work, I was still a far cry from being as well prepared to be an English major as were other students who'd grown up as avid readers. I was diligent in my studies, however, and did well enough in the end, but I did not distinguish myself.

The decision to teach elementary school

Half way through my senior year, and not having found a husband, I realized I would have to get a job and support myself after I graduated. (I had a boyfriend; in fact we dated for three years of college but had not yet talked of marriage. It's a good thing I was looking ahead, because my boyfriend broke up with me in the spring of my teacher-credential year.)

It was 1967. In the 1960s it was common for English majors to go into high school teaching; but since I still looked so young that I could have been mistaken for a student, I decided not to pursue a secondary credential. The other common options for women at the time were to become a nurse or a secretary. I fainted at the sight of blood, so I knew nursing wasn't for me. And, although I'd taken shorthand in high school and was an excellent typist, I wasn't interested in being a secretary either.

So I decided to become an elementary school teacher. I applied to the UCD Internship Program, which would enable me to have a full-time, paid, teaching job during the fifth year while taking courses at night needed for the credential. I was excited when I was accepted to the program.

The Internship Program and Elementary Teaching Credential

Soon after being accepted to the program, I applied for a job in Fairfield. I met with the superintendent there, and he offered me a choice of teaching third grade or fifth grade at Anna Kyle Elementary School. I took the third grade opening, as I believed it would be the easier of the two grades.

That summer all the internship teachers did their student teaching during the six-weeks of summer school while taking education classes on two afternoons. I taught in a second grade classroom under a master teacher. Besides the education courses, one afternoon each week the interns met with our UCD teaching supervisors.

Then, during the internship year, we took the remaining credential courses at night on campus while at the same time teaching full time. I taught at Anna Kyle Elementary. At the end of my year as an intern teacher, I qualified for and was granted an elementary teaching credential. It was a Life credential that I didn't have to renew.

I loved that first experience teaching in Fairfield and never looked back. I received my elementary teaching credential in 1968 and taught for 27 years, grades 1–6, mostly in Davis, California. I've never regretted a moment of it.

Section Four
Life after College

Teaching in Santa Rosa—for one year

Once I had my credential in hand, I decided I wanted to move back home to Santa Rosa where I could live with my parents, as I didn't want to live in an apartment with no roommates to help pay the rent. So I applied for a position teaching first grade there at Spring Creek Elementary in the Rincon Valley School District and was hired.

I appreciated this opportunity to be a teacher in the grade in which I'd had so much trouble, and it was very satisfying to teach as I wished I had been taught as a first grader. In many ways it was like coming full circle regarding my reading difficulties.

I found, however, that teaching in this small town and being in a classroom all day severely limited my chances of finding a husband. In fact, it seemed in many ways as cloistered as being a nun in a convent, and I decided that if I continued as an elementary teacher, I was not going to find a husband.

Therefore, when friends living in San Francisco encouraged me to move down to join them, I decided that living in the City would not only be exciting, but it would provide the kind of social environment that I wanted.

A Move to San Francisco

In July 1969, I moved in with three friends, one of whom had been a classmate at UCD. The apartment was at 2299 Sacramento on the corner of Sacramento and Buchanan Streets, across the street from Octavia Park and just two blocks up from Fillmore Street, a "happening" area of San Francisco.

My first task was to find a job. I'd taken typing in ninth grade and was a very fast typist. I'd also taken shorthand stenography in high school and, although I was rusty, I knew that with use I would soon be back up to speed.

After a short search, I was hired as the secretarial assistant to the facilities manager at Commonwealth National Bank (CNB) at Sacramento and Montgomery Streets in the heart of San Francisco's financial district. The location of the building was perfect, though the location of my *desk* left something to be desired: it was on the second floor in a non-descript, linoleum floored, wide-open space with just a few desks.

Going to work each day was fun—a complete change of pace from teaching. Instead of being limited to the four walls of my classroom, I was out and about in a beautiful city. The work was a simple, undemanding, 9 to 5 job. No work to take home. No working weekends. I got to interact with a lot of people and move freely around the city. It was a breath of fresh air, and I found it exciting to go to work each day.

Although I had a metallic blue 1967 Camaro, I left it parked on the street by my apartment and each day rode the Sacramento Street bus straight down to Montgomery Street. I usually took my lunch, as I couldn't afford to eat out and preferred to spend my money on my wardrobe rather than food.

I frequently spent my lunch hour shopping at the nearby J. Magnin or I. Magnin stores, as I really enjoyed dressing up for work. Those were the days of Twiggy (the skinny British model) and mini-skirts. But even though at 5' 10" and 120 pounds I had the body and look of a model, I remained dateless. Actually I was too skinny. Maybe that was the reason I was dateless.

Then, after a few months working in the nether reaches of CNB, I was promoted. I became a secretary for John Barclay, the Vice-President in charge of foreign dealings, who at that time was arranging shipments of goods to Seoul, Korea. *And,* his desk was on "the platform," the first floor area where the bank officers were located. My desk was right in front of Mr. Barclay's, facing the tellers' windows across the wide-open lobby. Being on the main floor was much more exciting, as it was where the action was.

I meet Dick Taggart—again

The new location, however, did not bring me a new boyfriend right away. But perhaps it was the new atmosphere that changed my luck in that department, because after several months I did meet up again with someone of interest. It happened as a result of my having attended a New Year's Eve party in San Francisco at end of 1968, while I was still living in Santa Rosa.

At that party, I had run into Dick Taggart. I had first met him in 1965—in the spring of my sophomore year when we were taking the same physiology lab. His girlfriend had gone to high school with one of my roommates. He had left UCD after his junior year to attend the UCSF medical school, and when we met at the party, he was in his third of four years there.

His ex-girlfriend (from our time at UCD) was one of the co-hostesses of the party at their Webster Street home near Union Street. Dick and I ended up sitting on a small bench, talking until it was time for me to head home. I appreciated his interest in me. In fact, I thought I might hear from him after we had had such a good time together at the party, but I didn't.

Then—out of the blue—he called me in November of 1969—after I'd been in the City for four months. He'd just heard from the same ex-girlfriend that I was now living in San Francisco, and he asked her for my phone number. By then he was in his last year of med school. We went on a few dates before he moved to Denver for winter quarter so he could ski in the Colorado Rockies while he took classes at the University of Colorado Medical School there.

We kept a stream of letters going back and forth. Our interest in each other became more serious as we got to know each other better. I joined him at the end of the quarter for skiing in Aspen, and then we drove home together. We ended up having a terrific time during that week, and we both knew by then that we wanted to stay together. On our way back to San Francisco we stopped in Sacramento to see his parents. It was there that we began talking about marriage. It was already April, and we wanted to plan our wedding for that summer.

Marriage and children

Right after he graduated from med school that June, we moved to Santa Ana, as his internship started then at Orange County Medical Center. We were married August 29, 1970, and during that year I taught fourth grade at Heim Elementary School in Orange.

Once he finished his internship, he was drafted, given the rank of captain, and assigned to serve at Shepard Air Force Base in Wichita Falls, Texas. It was there during our second year that our son, Matthew David, was born. In the summer of 1973 we moved back to California—to Davis, as he was to start his residency at the UC Davis Med School in Sacramento that fall.

Then, over the next several years, our marriage faltered. We went to marriage counseling, but it didn't work. It began to look like we were headed for divorce, so I started substitute teaching, hoping it would lead to a full time job. Our daughter, Kelly Elizabeth, was born when we lived in Davis, and I was thrilled to have a son and a daughter.

I substitute taught for the next few years, during which time I got to know the district and its teachers. (I talk about this period later in the book when discussing how substituting can help you get a job.) We finally separated, and I filed for divorce in 1978. Although this was a difficult period for our family, I knew it would work out for the best in the end—and it did.

Teaching Again—for 24 years

In 1978 I finally got a full-time teaching position. By then I had substitute-taught for four years, so I was well known to teachers in the district. I was hired just before Halloween to teach a second grade class at West Davis Elementary (WDE).

Because I was new and had the least seniority, over the next few years (1978-82) I was laid off each June and rehired *just before* school started in the fall. After second grade at WDE I was hired to teach a 4/5 combo at West Davis Intermediate (WDI). Then it was a sixth grade class at WDI, then a fourth grade again there, then a fourth grade at Valley Oak. Each year, the inevitable layoff, the period of uncertainty, and then rehired to teach a different grade, in a different classroom, often at a different school.

You might think that all of this uncertainty and change made for a lot of difficulty. True, it wasn't easy, but it was because of this that I became adept at being flexible and getting up to speed on the job, skills that I highly value. (Many of the ideas I share in this book were developed during these years.)

Starting in 1983, however, I had seven years of experience teaching fourth grade in the self-contained GATE program at Valley Oak Elementary—until 1991 (with the 1988-89 year off for a sabbatical). When I arrived there, the program was expanding to serve fourth, fifth and sixth grades, so my first year's class was a fourth/fifth combination, but after that my classes contained only fourth graders. This is the experience that taught me the most about how to differentiate to meet students' individual needs, given that there was such variety among the GATE students. Obviously, it was also where I learned about the needs of gifted students.

After seven years teaching GATE, I left the program because I didn't like the new principal who had been hired the last two years I was there. I requested a transfer back to WDI, and I was hired to teach fifth grade there.

The following year a brand new elementary school, Patwin, opened, and I requested a transfer there. It was at Patwin that I was to teach my final eight years: the first four teaching fifth grade, then a year of a 5/6 combo, and—finally—three years of sixth grade.

Although I didn't think of it when I first decided to go into elementary education, I ultimately realized that my difficulties with learning to read were an advantage in teaching children who were struggling to do so. In the chapter on reading, I will share the techniques that I found worked so well with young, developing readers. Needless to say, I did *not* make assumptions about their potential abilities based on their difficulty reading.

And though teaching reading was one area of the curriculum to which I brought a unique perspective, I also developed other teaching techniques that I believe are unique. So in addition, I will share other important things I learned from teaching that were never included in my own education.

I loved the challenges and diversity of my various teaching experiences with different grades, different schools, and different communities. These experiences challenged me to learn and to develop my own approaches to students and the curriculum. I wouldn't change anything. And it was through all of these experiences that I developed the ideas I share in this book.

I was very happy to have found a career as a teacher. It turned out that I was good at it and that I enjoyed it. I feel as if I made a difference in the lives of many of my students, and they enriched my life as well. I know I worked to teach students in ways that encouraged them to overcome their insecurities and doubts about themselves, as I didn't want them to experience the kinds of school experiences I had. I am just glad that I was able to put my own experiences to good use on behalf of my students.

Politics helped me find love—with John Poulos

Seven years after my divorce, I met my current husband. Our meeting occurred because of an interesting choice—this time an excellent one.

I was approaching the age of 40 and still wanted to find love. Again, I knew that since I was spending all day in a classroom, a truly cloistered setting, I was unlikely to meet any eligible men. So what did I do? I decided to enter local politics. Rather than choose another career this time, I chose something that really put me out front in the community!

Three seats were up for election to the Davis City Council. Though I had followed the local political scene with great interest for many years, I had not been active. Now, suddenly, I came out of nowhere, a single, divorced mother, an elementary school teacher with no political alliances, vying for a seat on the City Council. I gathered a group of women friends around me, mostly fellow elementary school teachers, and launched my campaign—advertising myself as the candidate with the 3Rs who would Respond, Respect, and Represent.

It turned out that being a teacher was good preparation for being a candidate. I was detail oriented and certainly very experienced at planning and preparing. Further, having taught in Davis for 11 years, I was well known by the families of all of my students. Although I am a Liberal and fit right into the values of this liberal community, my opponents in the campaign, also Liberals, actively sought to undermine my candidacy by characterizing me as a Pro-Growth Conservative. But that's a story for another book. Despite their efforts, when the votes were tallied, I had gotten the most votes, and, also of note, with by far the least amount of money spent.

And it was through my choice to run for a seat on the City Council that I met my husband, John Poulos, a law professor at UC Davis's King Hall. John had two grown children, and his ex-wife, a former Davis mayor, had supported my campaign. John had seen my photo in the newspaper and had cut it out and pinned it to his bulletin board. He told me later he'd "fallen in love at first sight." He also appreciated what he'd read in my campaign literature and what he heard about me from colleagues and friends.

I didn't meet him till our first date, a truly blind date, in December 1984. I knew he was a professor at the UCD Law School, but I'd never seen him. I opened my front door to see a tall, dark, and handsome man standing there. We went out to dinner and talked and talked. We were both surprised and delighted at how much we had in common—what we wanted in a relationship, politics, books, skiing, theater, food, and more. We didn't waste any time. We were married the next summer on July 7, 1985. I can tell you now that I did meet the love of my life, and he was definitely worth the wait!

Realizing a dream—several times over

I mentioned at the beginning of this section how, over the years, I had wished I had been an architect, as I loved the idea of designing and building my own home. I first realized my dream the summer of 1981, two years after my divorce. That was when I acquired a lot in Davis in Village Homes, a new and, at that time, unique solar home community. I then designed the 2500 sq. ft., three-story home, and, as the general contractor, began the process of interviewing and hiring the subcontractors.

Construction began in late May just before the end of school and was finished in mid-September, just after the beginning of school. I rented a house just down the street from the construction site so that it would be easy to supervise construction during my summer break from teaching. I must say, I was really quite proud of myself for this accomplishment. It was something I'd dreamed of doing since I was a little girl.

Then, after John and I married, we wanted to have a home that was truly ours. So we bought a lot, and I began to design the 3,600 sq. ft. home we would build the following year. It turned out beautifully. I was the architect, and we shared the job of general contractor.

But that's not all. In 2006 I was again able to call upon my architectural skills to design a major remodel of our house at Alpine Meadows in the Sierra Nevada Mountains—changing it from an 1100 sq. ft. cabin, on three levels, to a 3000 sq. ft., handicapped accessible, home. Again we both worked as the general contractors. I truly was delighted to have been able to design and build *three* of my own homes.

My Life Takes a Dramatic Turn

I had to retire from teaching in 2000—a tough decision for me, as I was only 55. But the previous year I had been diagnosed with primary lateral sclerosis (PLS), an incurable progressive degenerative neuromuscular illness. I knew I would eventually lose my ability to walk, but did not know how quickly the illness would progress. In the meantime, I wanted to use whatever time I had left to do things with my husband before I became unable to do so.

We felt so fortunate that we'd been able to see a great deal of Western Europe together—on our honeymoon in 1985, on his sabbatical in 1988-89 when we lived in France, and on the sabbatical I was granted in 1997 to study the ancient civilizations of Greece and Rome.

Having had these opportunities to travel—before my illness progressed too far—made it much easier to deal with my limitations later on. And we still managed, with careful planning, to go on his last sabbatical in 2001 for six months around both Western and Eastern Europe, plus an amazing cruise in South America from Buenos Aires, Argentina, to Santiago, Chile, in early 2003.

Later that same year I began to use a power wheelchair full time (which necessitated our buying a handicapped-accessible van to accommodate my heavy power wheelchair). Unfortunately, my deteriorating condition put an end to our travels together, though since my husband retired in 2004, he has been able to continue taking one or two trips a year, which I have been able to enjoy vicariously.

Then, in 2006 I was diagnosed with a more serious progressive degenerative neuromuscular illness, *Amyotrophic lateral sclerosis* (ALS), Lou Gehrig's disease. This was a more dire diagnosis, but I am fortunate that its progression has been slow. In the face of these illnesses and their effects, I've learned to value what I *can* do and not dwell on or bemoan what I can't do.

Our move to University Retirement Community

In 2011, to better provide for my needs as my illness progressed, my husband and I moved into University Retirement Community (URC). It provides many interesting activities for residents; and given my ability to zip around by myself in my power wheelchair, I can take advantage of whatever I want. I've never been able to relate to the phrase "confined to a wheelchair" because *my* wheelchair gives me the freedom to get around independently.

I continue to pursue activities that please and sustain me and to feel good about my life. I am an avid reader and participate in two book groups that meet monthly. Before my fine motor coordination became compromised, I did watercolor painting, and through email, I enjoy keeping in touch with everyone who doesn't live nearby.

Quilting

My favorite pastime now is quilting—the endeavor that saved me when I retired, and that has given me the main creative outlet I needed. It began when nine teacher friends started a quilting group in 1999. We meet once a month and have become very close friends in the years since we started.

I have made over 160 quilts, and a few wall hangings, for family, friends, and myself. Although I now need help to cut fabric and sew, I still create each original design myself. I've created a design that I believe is unique to me that results in a spiral, or maze-like, pattern. Starting with a focus fabric, I select light and dark fabrics from my abundant stash. (I haven't bought fabric in over six years, and I'm making 10 to 20 twin, queen, and king sized quilts a year.) We cut 9.5" squares of the lights and darks, pair them, sew diagonal lines, cut them apart, and get two light/dark half square triangle blocks.

Once all the blocks are sewn we are ready for what I call the "quilt dance"—arranging the squares on my living room rug. It's when the magic happens. That's the first time the quilt top is revealed by how I choose to arrange the different half square triangle squares. It's a fluid creative process that isn't complete till I've reviewed the arrangement, made adjustments, and finalized how the blocks will be sewn together. I send these labeled stacks of blocks off to my quilter to sew together and quilt.

I've made many new friends at URC who, though not quilters, have helped me continue to make quilts. It's been fun to include them in the process. One friend in particular, JoAnn Diel, has done the lion's share of work on the quilts I have designed in the last three years. I still have an abundant stash of fabric so there are plenty of options for future quilts. I love the fluid creative process I have developed.

Children and Grandchildren

Thanks to my two marriages, I now have four children, and they have given us 13 grandchildren, all of whom make me very happy. Below are sketches of our children and *their* children:

Alekka, John's daughter, met Michael Fullerton when she was in college at UC Davis. They married in 1989 after graduation and settled in Petaluma on property his parents owned. Alekka then commuted to UC Hastings in San Francisco to attend law school.

While in Petaluma, they had Elspeth Joan. The family then moved to Davis for the next 20 years where Alekka had a family law practice. There they had two more children: Graham Edward and Annelise Carol. In 2015 Alekka, Michael, and Annie moved to Haines, Alaska, as Alekka had grown weary of law practice, and they'd found property there and wanted to start a new chapter in their lives.

The grandchildren now: Annie, who finished high school in Haines in 2017, is going to the University of Alaska in Fairbanks. Elsie graduated from UC Davis in 2015, and she has been working in the medical field in Alaska and is applying to medical school. Graham, who graduated from Claremont McKenna in May 2018, plans to work for a while before applying to medical school.

John, John's son, met Michele Granger soon after graduating from Claremont McKenna and starting law school at the University of Arizona. While Michele was still a student at UC Berkeley (where she was an outstanding softball pitcher), John transferred to UC Berkeley's Boalt Hall Law School. They were married soon after he moved to Berkeley. When Michele graduated, they moved to Anchorage, Alaska, where John had a clerkship with a member of the Alaska Supreme Court.

Michele was on the 1996 Olympic team that went to Atlanta, Georgia, where she pitched the gold medal winning game. They had recently moved to Granite Bay, CA (just east of Sacramento) when John began to practice law in a large firm's Sacramento office. They had four children: Kady Joan, John Michael, Lindsay Grace, and Nicholas.

The grandchildren now: Kady is attending the University of Washington in Seattle, and John Michael is at the University of Montana in Bozeman. Lindsay and Nicholas are finishing high school.

John and Michele divorced in 2012. John then met Stacy Lumadue, and Stacy had twins: their son Wesley and daughter Kennedy.

Matthew, my son, went to UC San Diego and graduated in 1994 with a degree in French. He spent a year at the Sorbonne in Paris where he earned a master's degree in French language and literature. He worked for several years in the governor's office in Sacramento and went to McGeorge School of Law part-time, before transferring to Boalt Hall Law School at UC Berkeley.

He went to work for a large law firm's Los Angeles office, and he met Lauren Yeschin in LA. They married and have two children: Samantha Kate and Jack Hayden. They have been divorced for several years.

Kelly, my daughter, went to UC Santa Cruz and graduated in 1997 with a degree in Environmental Studies. At Santa Cruz she met Andrew Scavullo, and they were married in 2003. Kelly teaches in San Francisco, and Andrew is a civil engineer supervising construction projects. Their two children are Azalea Evelyn and Oscar Ambrose, and they live in the San Francisco Presidio.

I am very proud of my children and grandchildren, and I appreciate any time I have with them.

Memoir writing

In 2013 I began attending a memoir-writing class to provide my family with a history of my life. When this group saw some of what I'd written about my teaching, they urged me to share that instead, insisting my ideas were worthy of publication. Their interest gave me the impetus I needed to forge ahead, and *The Conscious Teacher* is the fruit of that labor.

Conclusion

It is comforting now to realize the extent to which my difficulties learning to read and do math resulted in my becoming perseverant. I learned resilience from surviving the trauma of these persistent early failures. I no longer feared failure.

In my adult years I learned to make my own way, becoming more and more independent. Through my teaching experiences I learned to trust my own judgment and make things up as I went along. It didn't hurt that my first eight years of teaching, every single year, I had to get up to speed from scratch before facing a different grade in September.

I continued to gain confidence in myself when I set out to design and build that first house during the summer of 1981. Some wondered whatever possessed me to think I could do such a thing. But I had worked through all the steps required in my mind. It was an audacious aspiration, but I knew I could do it, and I did.

And what on earth possessed me to think I could mount a successful bid for a seat on the Davis City Council? I had no experience, no experienced workers, and nothing in my background that would suggest I would ever be interested in such a thing. But I had learned from my early failure experiences not to fear failure as an adult. And wanting to expose myself to a wider audience in an effort to find a husband made perfect sense to me. What did I have to lose?

As it turned out, nothing. I not only won the election, but I drew my husband to me. He is the love of my life. We have now spent 33 happy years together.

My resilience has certainly served me well in dealing with my illness and the disabilities it has brought with it. From the very beginning I made the choice not to let my illness keep me from enjoying life.

Now I have written this book. It has been a satisfying journey to discuss my early failures and my later successes. Putting together all the ideas I used in teaching, in the hope that they will help other teachers, has been an enjoyable process. In doing this I've been able to relive much of what made my years of teaching so gratifying.

I believe my early struggles taught me the lessons that have served me well in all the years since, especially in my adult years, as I learned to integrate these lessons into my life. I continue to live a full and rich life. I feel extremely fortunate to have realized so many satisfying accomplishments

My Education and Teaching Experience

Education

1967: B.A. English, University of California at Davis, CA.

1967-68: Completed education courses through the UCD Internship Program.

1968: California Elementary Teaching Credential for Life.

1975-77: Completed one year of coursework for a Master's Degree in Business Administration, California State University (Sac State), Sacramento, CA.

1990-92: Completed all coursework for a Master's Degree in Gifted and Talented Education at California State University, Sacramento, CA.

Teaching Experience

1967: Summer School: Second grade practice teaching at Bransford Elementary, Fairfield, CA.

1967-68: Third grade at Anna Kyle Elementary School, Fairfield, CA, while in the UCD Internship Program earning a credential.

1968-69: First grade at Spring Creek Elementary, Santa Rosa, CA.

1970-71: Fourth grade at Heim Elementary, Orange, CA.

1971-72: Reading teacher, grades 4-6, Guadalupe Catholic School, Wichita Falls, TX.

1974-78: Substitute teacher, grades 1-6, Davis Joint Unified School District, Davis, CA.

1978-79: Second grade at West Davis Elementary, Davis, CA.

1979-80: Fourth/fifth grade class at West Davis Intermediate, Davis, CA.

1980-81: Sixth grade at West Davis Intermediate, Davis, CA.

1981-82: Fourth grade at West Davis Intermediate, Davis, CA.

1982-83: Fourth grade at Valley Oak Elementary, Davis, CA.

1983-84: Fourth/fifth grade GATE class at Valley Oak Elementary, Davis, CA.

1984-88: Fourth grade GATE at Valley Oak Elementary, Davis, CA.

1988-89: Sabbatical year in France

1989-91: Fourth grade GATE at Valley Oak Elementary, Davis, CA.

1991-92: Fifth grade at West Davis Intermediate, Davis, CA.

1992-95: Fifth grade at Patwin Elementary, Davis, CA.

1995-96: Fifth/sixth grade class at Patwin Elementary, Davis, CA.

1996-2000: Sixth grade at Patwin Elementary, Davis, CA.

Part II
Before You Decide to Become a Teacher …

... You Should Realize That Teaching is a Time-Consuming Career

In the Introduction I pointed out that teaching is a demanding career, but I didn't go into detail. I feel it is necessary to explain this, as some who go into elementary school teaching think it will be easy.

Compared to 9 to 5 jobs with only two weeks off each year, teaching can seem like an attractive alternative. But teaching requires a lot of work that can only be done after the school day ends. It takes a great deal of time to plan and prepare for what you will teach; to master subject matter content; and to review, correct, give feedback, and grade students' work. And, though teachers don't teach during the summer, they need this time to become more proficient in the subject area curriculum and processes for teaching it.

The following are points that anyone going into teaching should realize.

1. Teaching students is just part of your workday

To explain this statement, I'll describe my school in Davis, CA, where the school day for various ages of students is anywhere from 8:15 am to 3:10 pm. Kindergartners attend only three hours, the older students up to six and a half hours.

Teachers, however, are required to be on campus a half hour before and after school each day. They are also required to be on campus a week before school starts in the fall and several days after the end of the year.

Then there are the after-school staff meetings, meetings with parents, and discussions with other teachers regarding how to handle various issues (whether they be with discipline or teaching techniques). None of these activities can be done during the teaching day while the students are in the classroom.

2. You must spend considerable time planning what you will teach

Teachers need time outside of class to plan for *in*-class time. Let's look at the requirements for the youngest and the oldest students.

First look at kindergarten. Imagine being faced with 20 to 30—or more—wiggly, unfocused five-year-olds in school for the first time. Kindergarten teachers must know minute to minute what they intend to do to keep them occupied and help them become socialized with their classmates, as well as plan for many variables.

Sixth grade is at the other end of the spectrum. Imagine 30 pre-pubescent, hormone-raging 11- and 12-year-olds. To keep them interested in subjects that are much deeper and broader, you need even *more* time to plan your lessons so you will constantly be on top of things. For example, the social studies curriculum for sixth graders includes history from early humans through the ancient civilizations of the Fertile Crescent, Egypt, Greece, Rome, India, and China. And the math curriculum content is much more advanced. Planning how you will cover all the content in the time in which you have to teach it takes a great deal of careful thought.

No matter what grade you teach, you have to plan a week at a time for each subject, as well as for the long term. Your daily plans are your guide for what material will be taught each day, so you need plenty of uninterrupted time to plan for *everything*.

3. Time-consuming preparations can only be done after the school day

To prepare for the next day's activities, kindergarten teachers have to set out materials and directions for multiple stations every day of each week—preparations that can't be done from the comfort of one's home. Given the short attention spans of five-year-olds, they require consistent attention. Therefore, kindergarten teachers must know minute-to-minute what they will teach so they can keep our youngest students focused on learning the basic skills needed for academic achievement.

First through sixth grade teachers have all kinds of preparations, too, though most of them can be done at home. The only thing teachers need to do while the students are still in the classroom is write notes to individual parents about behavior or academic issues that must be sent home with these students at the end of the day.

Below are three kinds of preparations that take considerable time. Since I'm more familiar with the intermediate grades, my first two examples apply more to what those teachers must do, though the other one certainly applies to all grades:

- Preparing weekly assignment sheets. These show what work is due in each subject area for each day of the week.
- Preparing worksheets for each area of the curriculum. In the content areas of the curriculum, you must prepare worksheets for vocabulary and comprehension in reading; grammar, usage, capitalization, and punctuation in language arts; math exercises to learn and reinforce concepts and facts; and social studies vocabulary and content information.
- Preparing flyers or notes to send to all parents about general activities. For example, this must be done regarding Back to School Night and Open House; grading standards; how to help their children with homework, including how to use proofreading symbols when correcting their children's written work; and parent/student/teacher conferences.

Each of these activities takes considerable time outside of class, and there are certainly others. Yes, teaching is *much* more time-consuming than most full-time jobs.

4. It takes time to master the curriculum content you will teach

You must have knowledge of the subject content before you start to teach it. After all, you cannot learn the content at the same time you are teaching it. So you have to spend time out of class reading and studying to be sure you are knowledgeable before you present lessons to the students.

Once you master the subject area, you must figure out the processes you will use to teach the content to your students. Take social studies, for example: Will you read to them from the textbook, or a literature book based on the subject area? Will you create games that help students learn the content? Will students meet in small groups to read and discuss the content, and then complete worksheets that highlight the main ideas you want students to retain?

You need to learn or create different kinds of processes depending upon what subject area you are teaching. For math, for example, you will have to create a large number of processes so that students learn the concepts and number facts. For literature/language arts/reading you will use a different set of processes that are specific to teaching reading and writing. The same is true for science, P.E., art, drama, and music. All this preparation takes time.

5. Thoroughly correcting your students' work daily is critical to their learning—and to your "knowing" them

The task of correcting students' work and providing detailed feedback is essential to their learning. Yes, correcting is time-consuming, but that is what makes for good learning—and good teaching. A teacher's corrections—and explanations about why they are necessary—not only help students learn the subject content, but also help them improve their writing skills. Developing a student's writing skills in the early grades can make a huge difference later on.

And as students are required to write longer papers in fourth, fifth, and sixth grades, the time required for a teacher to correct their work increases tremendously. For example, they may well be writing daily descriptive-writing paragraphs, as well as drafts for book reports, five paragraph essays, stories, and social studies journals and reports, just to name a few.

To help them with their writing, you must correct spelling, capitalization, punctuation, and grammar, as well ask questions so students will pay attention to details in their writing. And you need to make suggestions about what you think will *improve* their work. After you provide carefully detailed editing assistance, students are expected to incorporate these corrections into their next draft or their final products—which you also need to read and correct. All this makes for considerable extra work on your part, but the end result is extremely gratifying.

Not so incidentally, **your individual attention to students' written work is a large part of what grows your relationship with each student.** Through your feedback, you are engaging and supporting each student in the learning process. You are also relating to them on an individual level that communicates to them how much you care. The significance of your role in relating to students through their writing cannot be overestimated.

6. Maintaining a successful behavior management plan takes time

No matter what grade you teach, you will have to establish a management plan that works to keep things running smoothly. This is no small feat. Maintaining order among students from kindergarten through sixth grade is challenging— an "all day, every day" necessity to manage students so that all runs smoothly, and students are working productively.

Classroom management may, indeed, be the most important skill any teacher must have. Without this as a foundation, all of your best lesson plans, knowledge of content, and processes won't go anywhere.

7. Summers include teacher training

To keep up with new trends and techniques, teachers are required to "upgrade" by taking certain classes during the summer. You may also want to take classes to earn units so that you can advance on your district's salary schedule. Summers are the only time teachers are free to take classes that will advance their teaching abilities.

Summers also give you time to read in your field to improve your knowledge of content and processes. And you may want to teach summer school to get experience with a different grade level, or to earn additional income.

In any case, this is a time rich in possibilities for making you a better teacher.

8. School issues will keep you awake at night

Each night when I lay my head on the pillow to go to sleep, I would start to think about specific students who had learning or behavioral issues to solve. I'd think about the curriculum and how I might adjust it to better meet the needs of my students. There was always something my mind began to churn on when I began to relax and try to go to sleep. I think my mind even worked on these issues while I slept.

Summary

Clearly, a great deal of a teacher's time is spent after the school day is over. Planning and preparing for classes, becoming proficient in the subjects you teach, correcting students' work and providing feedback, meeting with other teachers and administration on a professional level—*all* take your time after the students go home. To get everything done you must stay late and take work home.

Teaching is an all-consuming career choice that, if you are not careful, will take over your life. Even when I had a very young family, and later when I was divorced and my kids were still young, my time, energy, and attention was always being pulled away from my family and toward teaching concerns.

Then, during the summer break, upgrading in your field and enriching your repertoire through taking classes on your own, and reading in your field are critical to advancing your competence as a teacher. These are the reasons teaching is a much more demanding career than most people realize.

Part III
How to Get the Job You Want:
Consider
Substitute Teaching

Substitute Teaching
And How It Can Help You Get a Full-Time Job

Although this book is about regular classroom teaching, I felt it wouldn't be complete without talking about substitute teaching. **Whether you want only to substitute, or whether you want to substitute just until you can find a full-time position, there are things you can do to make subbing more rewarding for yourself, the students, and their teachers.**

In my case, I had taught several years before moving to a new city where teaching jobs were scarce. So though I will talk about how substitute teaching can provide you with an advantage when full-time teaching positions become available, the techniques I will be discussing apply to anyone who wants to substitute.

My situation

In 1973, my husband, one-year-old son, and I moved from Wichita Falls, Texas, to Davis, California. There were few teaching positions open at the time, and I knew there would be a great deal of competition for jobs in this University of California town. I reasoned, however, that if I could get my foot in the door, I might improve my chances.

Indeed, I discovered that substitute teaching was a good way to get a full-time position in the district where I most wanted to work. Even more important, however, was that I realized that to be seen as a desirable substitute, I had to do more than simply register on the substitute list. I have several suggestions that worked for me, but it definitely takes homework.

Of what follows, points #1 and #2 below are especially important if you are new to the area.

1. Lay the groundwork

Beginning teaching jobs are more available now than they have been in the recent past, but you still must carefully prepare for the job you want. The following are steps you might take to make it easier to do so.

Familiarize yourself with the district

Check out the schools where you might like to substitute. This is particularly important if you aren't familiar with the district. Go to the district office to find out where the schools are located. Decide which schools are most conveniently located for where you will be living.

Prepare your resume and application

Next, prepare your resume and application. This is a straightforward process, but you must create it in such a way that you stand out among the other applicants.

For the resume, refer to online resources to learn different ways to create a resume that highlights your education, talents, interests, and abilities. Then make sure it is neat and well organized in the standard form so those reading it can quickly identify your strengths.

The same is true for completing the district's application. Be sure to give specific details that show your unique preparation.

Note: You will not need the application if you are intending only to substitute. But if your primary objective is ultimately to obtain a teaching position, you want to give them an application as soon as possible. You then go to the district's personnel office to submit the application and resume. If there are no positions open, they can tell you where to go to get on the substitute list.

Prepare a "Notice Advertising Yourself"—your secret weapon!

This notice is something that you will place in all the teachers' boxes for whom you would like to substitute to detail what you will do for them and to give them your qualifications. This is something most people don't think to do that can make all the difference in becoming a sought-after sub. And it is something you will spend as much time preparing as you did your resume and application. It is, in essence, **a description of what you will do—as a substitute—to assure that the class will be well run in the teacher's absence.** It should contain the following:

1. **What you are prepared to do as a substitute:**

   The notice may include the kinds of things I included in my own advertisement (which I discuss below), such as being prepared to teach my own lesson plans in all the subject areas. Showing that you are prepared to teach lessons and manage the class, whether or not the teacher has left lesson plans, gives you a big advantage.

2. **A description of your strengths:**

   Just as each teacher has his/her strengths, some of them unique, you may well want to describe yours—showing techniques or talents you are prepared to use to make a particular subject more interesting or engaging.

In the end, this advertisement should make the teacher feel comfortable knowing that whenever she has you in her classroom, she can be assured that her students will benefit from the experience, that the class will be well run in her absence.

How I did it: The Bicentennial Substitute

In 1975, when I first started subbing in Davis, I advertised myself as "The Bicentennial Substitute." I prepared a red sheet of paper, my notice advertising myself, that described the kinds of activities I would provide.

On this sheet, for first grade through sixth grades, I let the teachers know that I had prepared myself to teach "stand alone" lessons for each of the content areas of the curriculum. This is especially important for a teacher to know in case she needs a sub at the last minute, and doesn't have time to do detailed lesson plans. It helped that I had had some teaching experience in several grades; but even without this advantage, I could have researched what was being taught in each grade.

With my red-sheet advertisement, I included my resume so teachers could see my experience, and I stated that they could rest assured that their students would be well managed. I then put one of these packets in each of the teacher's boxes at the schools where I wanted to sub.

Note: My notice advertising myself is in Appendix A, p. 208.

Why these preparations are important

You need to think about this from the point of view of the teacher. When a teacher knows she will be absent, planning for a substitute can be a lot of work and trouble. Therefore, you must show that when *you* are the chosen substitute, you can make it easy for her to prepare. You also need to show that when you are the sub, the students will get the kind of behavior management that will keep things running smoothly.

When I provided teachers with information about what I would do as a substitute, I enabled them to see that, if I were their sub, they wouldn't have to leave detailed lesson plans. Believe me, this is a big relief for teachers—both when they have little notice before they have to be absent, and—especially—when they don't have *any* warning, such as when they suddenly become sick. Even when they *do* know ahead of time, it is comforting to know the kind of teacher who will be taking over their class.

2. Become known

Give teachers your information

To become a substitute, the first step—getting yourself *known* as a substitute—is extremely important, particularly if you are new to the district. These are the things you should do:

1. Prepare a packet of your notice advertising yourself and your resume.

You will want to get this to teachers for whom you will want to substitute.

2. Visit each school in which you want to teach.

If there is a district office, you might go there first to get general permission to visit the various schools, as you want to begin the process of getting yourself known as a desirable substitute.

3. Place a packet in the teachers' boxes.

Go to the school's office and speak to the secretary to get permission to put this information in their boxes. Show her one of the packets so she will be comfortable with what you want to do. She may ask you to speak to the principal as well.

- **If you are a regular elementary school teacher,** you should place the items you prepared in *all* the teachers' boxes.
- **If you are a specialist** (e.g., reading, math, bilingual classes, etc.), ask the names of these teachers so you can give them only to the teachers who specialize in your field.
- **If you are a high school teacher,** you will put the packets only in the boxes of teachers in whose classes you are qualified to substitute.

4. If possible, time your visit for the lunch hour when you might meet the teachers.

I suggest going to each school during the lunch hour when teachers are most likely to be out of their classrooms and in the teachers' room. Ask the school secretary if she will take you in to introduce you. You can take this opportunity to tell the teachers that you have just put packets of information about you in their boxes. Just say a few words about yourself—*keep it really brief*—so teachers see that you are eager and energetic. This way they will be able to put a face to the printed information they will find in their boxes.

5. See if you can observe some grade levels you are interested in teaching.

I go into this topic more thoroughly in the next section, but it is something to consider: it would help you get a feel for the school—and the teachers would get to know you. It would take some work, however: the school might well require you to provide your resume and application to learn more about you, and they will probably have you talk with the school's principal so she can evaluate whether to give you access to their classrooms.

You want teachers to know who you are *so they will request you* (so you won't be just a name on a list of substitutes). Otherwise, it will be left up to the sub caller to make a random call off her list.

Observe classes where you might like to teach

There is another technique that I didn't use, but which could also be useful: observing in classes where you would like to teach. This might well be in the school closest to where you live. Or it might be where bilingual classes are taught that you would like to learn about, or perhaps an inner-city school or a laboratory school where you have a particular interest.

Your motives could be two-fold: to learn how particular teachers handle their classes, or to learn useful techniques should you substitute there. And not only would the teachers get to know you and feel more comfortable about having you substitute for them, but you would find substituting easier as you would be more familiar with the classes. In any case, making a personal connection with the teachers is a big step in getting more jobs substituting.

As I mentioned before, when you go to the school to ask about observing, the secretary will probably ask you to talk with the principal of the school so that she can evaluate whether to give you access to classrooms. You should be prepared for this. Be sure to point out that the main reason you are doing this is so that you will be better prepared to substitute in their classes.

On the other hand, if you are able to establish a good connection with the secretary, you might tell her about your interest in observing some of the classes (explaining why), and ask if she could take you to meet a teacher whom she thinks would be willing to let you observe. If the teacher is willing to let you come that day, excellent! Chances are, however, that she would prefer that you come at a pre-arranged time. But let her know that you would like to spend several hours in her classroom so you have a full opportunity to observe what she does.

Let her know that you are willing to help out in any way she would like while you are visiting. It would be to your advantage if she can see you in action, working with her students. If she takes you up on this offer and assigns you some tasks to perform while you observe, both the teacher and you will have the best opportunity to evaluate your participation. Then take a seat in the back of the room so you can easily see the whole class. Keep a notebook so that you can record your observations and feelings.

Before you leave each classroom, write a note to the teacher saying something positive and specific about what you observed during your visit. Sign your name, and give your phone number so the teacher can contact you directly. This way the teachers whose classrooms you visit will be able to let you know in advance when they will be absent and when they will be requesting you as their sub.

If things go well, you might ask her to introduce you to another teacher (or several). Through this initial process, you will begin to get a feel for the school. If all goes as planned, you will be successful in getting across this first threshold to gain access to the classrooms you may want to observe.

After you visit other schools and grade levels, you should discover several options of schools and grade levels in which you are interested. By the time you are finished with your observations, you will have enough information to help you decide which grade level suits you best and whether this is a school at which you would like to work.

When openings occur, you will be ready to apply. In the meantime you will have an advantage when the teachers you visited need a sub.

It will also be to your advantage to have watched how the various teachers approach their work. And if you have taken good notes, you will be one step ahead should you end up substituting in that teacher's class.

3. Be prepared to be an excellent substitute

If the teacher I'm subbing for leaves specific lesson plans, of course I follow them. If, on the other hand, she has not left detailed lesson plans, I come prepared to present my own lessons and activities. In this way the students get a change of pace, and the teacher doesn't have to worry about leaving detailed lesson plans—particularly if she gets ill after leaving school and is unable to prepare them.

Note: Substitute teachers can refer to Part V, "Instruction in the Classroom," p. 111, for the subject area chapters of the book to help with ideas for these lessons.

What I do for students when subbing

1. **Introductions.** The first thing I do is to introduce myself to the class. Then, while I take the roll and do the lunch count for the day, I ask students to read silently from a book they are reading. (If they don't have a book, I ask them to choose a story from their reading textbook.)

2. **Descriptive Writing.** I bring laminated photographs from nature calendars to class for these exercises and ask the students to describe what they see. This exercise can be modified depending on the grade level. If the students are in first or second grades, I may ask them to write just two or three sentences. If they are in third through sixth grades, they should be able to write an entire paragraph. For the higher grades, I add a lesson about including a simile and a metaphor in the paragraph.

3. **Spelling.** It should be easy to follow the teacher's plan for the week's spelling lesson. If this isn't clear, I ask the students about their spelling work for the day. This work is usually straightforward with a specific assignment for each day of the week.

4. **Reading.** For the reading period, I ask students to read the assigned story to each other, or to take turns reading aloud to the class. This will take care of helping the students who may not be able to read the story on their own. Then I will work with students who need help on the follow-up exercises from the reading textbook.

5. **Math.** I use the math textbook pages to determine what activities I will ask them to do. I either teach the lesson from the textbook, or I teach my own lesson that targets the skills identified in the textbook. It is easy to create a lesson and write problems on the board for students to work on.

6. **Social Studies and Science.** For these classes I follow the assignments from the pages the teacher has left. I usually read the selections to the class, stopping frequently to ask questions to discuss the content. In this way the whole class is engaged in the lesson. I may ask if any students want to read sections of the text. Depending on the grade level, I may help the students to take notes on, or outline, what they are learning from the textbook.

7. **P.E.** P.E. is easy. I usually ask the students to pick their favorite playground game—for example, dodge ball, kickball, softball, or whatever they choose. Before we start to play the game, I ask them to run a lap around the field. I use my stopwatch to help motivate them to run as fast as they can.

8. **Art.** I bring my own art activity. This is usually a simple contour drawing lesson—for example, drawing their own shoes, or drawing a still life I arrange at the front of the class. Most students enjoy these kinds of lessons.

What I do for teachers when subbing

1. **I always correct all the student work I assign.** For example, if I have them write descriptive paragraphs, I correct their papers for spelling, punctuation, capitalization, and grammar, as well as for the content ideas, and I also provide suggestions about improving the paragraphs. (It is also possible that you will be providing the teacher with an effective new model for correcting his students' written work. Even many experienced teachers don't realize how important it is to thoroughly correct and give feedback on everything students write.)

   I also correct any worksheets or other assignments students turn in to me. In this way I make sure I've corrected all the work students complete on the day I substitute, leaving none of this work for their teacher to do when she returns.

2. **I always leave a detailed note telling exactly what I did.** At the end of the day, after I have subbed for a teacher, I always do this so that she will know what I have done with her students. *This is very important*, as such a note will go a long way toward giving teachers confidence in you—and in their feeling comfortable about recommending you to their colleagues.

How I benefited

Before long, I was subbing almost full time at my favorite school, the one that was closest to where I lived. I ended up getting two long-term subbing jobs there—one for two months in a fifth grade, and one for three months in a sixth grade. (Long-term jobs are the best because then you don't have to wait to be called early each morning and scramble to get where you need to go.) And as soon as there was a full-time job available, I was hired.

How you can benefit

1. **You can set yourself up to get the subbing jobs you desire and quicker consideration for a full-time job.** All teachers wish for a good substitute when they are absent, and subs who are dependable and highly regarded will get called first. If you earn this reputation, you, too, could find yourself in an excellent position to garner desirable, long-term subbing jobs and, ultimately, a full-time position. Superintendents are more likely to hire teachers full-time who have been observed teaching as substitutes. This applies to anyone who is new to a school district and wants to be hired full time.

2. **Subbing in different classrooms can help you decide what grades you would most like to teach.** Though you could teach summer school or be a teacher's aide, those activities generally require a longer commitment. Short-term subbing experiences in kindergarten through sixth grade classes can help you determine the student age that best meshes with your personality and skills.

   There is a good reason for this. **Teachers are often best suited to teach children of a particular age.**

   For example, I never could imagine teaching kindergarten. It is the only elementary grade I have never taught and never wanted to teach, as it was always just too intimidating for me. I take my hat off to all the kindergarten teachers out there who meet these little bundles of energy each day and get them socialized and ready for first grade. But you may find you prefer these younger, unmolded children.

   And I know many teachers who say they would never teach sixth graders. These older children, who have a reputation for being rowdy and difficult to manage, and who study a more advanced curriculum, are just too overwhelming for them.

   I, on the other hand, really liked working with sixth graders: I've found them lively, quirky, funny, and—most of the time—fun to be with; my personality and sense of humor meshed with theirs. (Perhaps I was just an overgrown sixth grader!) They certainly challenged me, but I was energized by how they tested me, enjoyed figuring out ways to work with them, and always looked forward to being with them. However, I didn't teach sixth grade until I was a seasoned veteran, having already taught many years at the fourth and fifth grade levels.

   In any case, before you settle into teaching a particular grade, it is simply wise to work with children of different ages. Short-term teaching, particularly substituting, will give you an opportunity to experience what it is like to teach different ages without your having to do it for a whole year.

Summary

Good subs are hard to find. Great subs are few and far between. By marketing yourself in the ways I have suggested here—and by preparing appropriate lesson plans—you enable teachers to know ahead of time that you will be a *great* sub, guaranteeing that you will be at the top of the list when subs are called.

The ideas I share here will make your subbing job easier. Instead of always having to figure out the assignment and get up to speed on what the class is studying, you can bring your own lessons. Best of all, preparing in these ways makes it much easier for the teacher for whom you are subbing.

Substituting will give you valuable experience that will aid you in discovering what age students you are most interested in teaching. Using these strategies will bring you to the attention of administrators as the substitute so many teachers are requesting, and may well pay dividends when the district has full-time teaching jobs available.

Part IV

First Things First: Set the Stage for Effective Learning

CHAPTER 1

Take Strategic Steps before School Starts

Well before your students arrive at their new classroom, you need to think about some important policies or practices you want to set into motion once school starts. These are strategies and techniques you should not leave until after school begins, believing you can figure them out as you go along.

Preparing thoroughly for any new class of students well before the first day of school is essential. The best teachers don't leave anything to chance. As soon as the Conscious Teacher has access to information about her students, she should plan everything from her classroom setup to the various ways she will interact with her students. "Forewarned is forearmed!"

Of the following guidelines, the first, "Determine to model a culture of respect," is the most important: the others in the rest of the book all evolve from and depend on it. Creating a classroom in which mutual respect is the standard—expected of everyone—is essential to establishing a comfortable and safe place for students and teacher alike. Once the standard of mutual respect is established, truly successful learning is more likely to follow.

1. Determine to model a culture of respect

The foundation for any teacher's relationship with her students is *respect*. If a teacher doesn't establish a relationship of respect between her students and herself, how can she expect to be respected by them? From the very first day a teacher lets her students know whether or not they can trust her by watching her behavior.

- Does she lead through the power of her authority?
- Does she intimidate and threaten?
- Does she raise her voice and display anger?

or

- Does she establish reasonable behavioral ground rules and then repeatedly reinforce them through teaching strategies that model respect?
- Does she always maintain an affect of calm and support?
- Does she demonstrate an attitude of mutual respect?

The most successful teachers take the second route. I will be mentioning throughout this book how the teacher always models respect, particularly in difficult situations.

The Three R's: Respect, Responsibility, and Resourcefulness

In my school (West Davis Intermediate, WDI, in Davis, California), the teachers worked together to develop the following guidelines to help both the teachers and the students understand how to behave respectfully, and why it is so important. I feel the concepts are so important that I am including them here:

> School climate directly reflects the extent to which students practice **respect, responsibility,** and **resourcefulness** in the classroom and on the playground. We at WDI are committed to helping students understand the importance of these behaviors and practice them in their daily lives. It is our goal that these "Three R's" will be the behavior norm for our school community, and we are actively engaged in bringing this goal about.
>
> We have focused our attention this fall on respect, with teachers and support staff helping students become more conscious of ways that they can demonstrate respect in their interactions with adults and peers. By clearly identifying examples of respect or disrespect, adults and students alike have been able to practice more effective ways of relating to one another.
>
> While we cannot expect change overnight, building a climate of tolerance and respect will be the key to realizing the rest of our goal—fostering responsibility and resourcefulness as well.

The ideas come from "The Three R's of Self-Esteem" by John K. Rosemond (Hemispheres, January 1993). Rosemond also brings up what he had noticed when talking to parent and professional groups as he travelled across the country. Seeking out teachers who had taught 30 years or more, he asked them how they would compare children of 30 years ago with those of the '90s, and it sounded like what I have been hearing these days:

> Their words, of course, are different, but their answers are always the same. Today's children, these teachers tell me, are lacking in respect, responsibility, and resourcefulness. As a veteran North Carolina teacher recently told me, "Today's child is self-absorbed, often does no more than it takes to just get by, and gives up almost immediately if a problem even looks hard." In other words, we abandoned the Three R's of child rearing to our peril."

Does this sound familiar? Given that it does, I feel strongly that we need to go back to some basic ideas, beginning with this: True self-esteem develops as a child discovers that despite frustration, failure, fear, and other adversity, he is capable of solving problems on his own and can stand successfully on his own two feet. Parents can, and should, provide the opportunity, support, and guidance the child needs to make this discovery, but they cannot guarantee the discovery itself.

Thomas Jefferson said pretty much the same thing when he said we have a right to the pursuit of happiness, but that the outcome of the pursuit is a matter of individual responsibility.

Along those lines, many parents fail to realize that by trying to make their children happy, they end up with children who cannot make themselves happy; by protecting their children from any and all frustration, they end up with children who cannot tolerate frustration; by solving problems for children that they can solve for themselves (albeit with struggle), they end up with children who give up quickly when the going gets tough. In short, you do not help children learn to stand on their own feet by letting them stand on yours.

Assisting children towards the discovery of true self-esteem requires that parents create family environments that communicate the Three R's of respect, responsibility, and resourcefulness. In the family, parents, not children, should command center state.

Children should have a daily routine of chores for which they are not paid; they should do their own homework, find the majority of their own after-school recreation, and not be allowed to waste great amounts of time in front of television sets and video games. (**Note**: In this day and age we know all too well how much cell phones, computers, and other tech devices have added to the diversions for our kids.)

A child who is respectful of others will conduct himself with a sensitive regard for other human beings. A child who is responsible will do his best, regardless of the task or the situation. A child who is resourceful will try and try again until success is at hand.

Out of these strengths gradually emerges a genuine sense of self-worth and self-respect. In other words, a child who possesses the Three R's has been prepared as well as possible to stand on his own two feet and discover that which brings true satisfaction to his or her life.

Is that old-fashioned? Absolutely, as in tried-and-true.

How we encouraged respectful behavior at my school

The following are the definition, language and modeling behaviors the staff at West Davis Intermediate has developed to use consistently with our students. Parents can support our focus on the value of respect at home by discussing and using these guidelines with their own children.

Respect means accepting and honoring others in a way that indicates that they are valued. It means that we make a conscious attempt to show consideration to others.

Helping students to act more respectfully

These requests should be made in a gentle, but firm, way using a positive tone of voice. After requesting, wait for the change before proceeding:

Be respectful.

Be courteous.

Please change that body language.

Please treat him/her kindly.

Please be polite.

Can you show that you care?

Can you show some polite consideration to him/her?

Stop the arguing. It will not get you what you want.

What do you need to do to be courteous?

Please change that comment to a positive one.

Please make a helpful comment.

Behaviors that should be modeled and reinforced whenever possible

Saying thank you.

Monitoring the tone of voice.

Modeling how to make an apology after a mistake.

Being respectful and sensitive to differences.

Being honest.

Being helpful.

Reporting chronic disrespect.

Listening attentively.

Taking turns.

Using eye contact when talking to another.

Asking non-respectful people to stop the behavior.

Following the Golden Rule.

Caring for property.

2. Use the CUMs to learn about your students—before you ever meet them

Preparing to meet a new group of students must involve getting to know them even before the first day of class. Every teacher is provided with the means to do this—in the **Cumulative Record Folders (CUMs)** that they receive for each of the students in their class for the coming year.

CUMs are full of valuable information

The CUMs tell when a student has had behavioral issues, learning disabilities, or family challenges, or if he uses English as a second language. They contain teachers' assessments of students' achievement with 1) comments about effort from report cards, and 2) notes from reading specialists, psychologists, parents, and others about particular issues relating to the child. The CUMs also provide test information from the previous spring that shows each student's grade level achievement in reading and math.

I wasn't doing this when I first began teaching. As a beginning teacher I didn't realize the significance of the CUM-record information. It took me a few years to realize the importance of delving into these files for information that would help me to "know" my students before they stepped into my class. The CUMs turned out to be a gold mine.

Were it not for the CUMs, some of this information would have taken me a long time to discover; other information I might never have figured out. Knowing critical details about each child beforehand meant that I was much better prepared to meet all of his needs from the very first day.

CUMs enable you to intervene before disruptive students act out

Knowing about students with behavioral issues means you are better able to intervene before they act out. I find that meeting with these students—and their parents—before school starts helps immeasurably.

We talk about difficulties these students have had in the past. Usually the students are easily frustrated, which is why they become disruptive. I explain that I am there to help them. I tell them that they can give themselves a "time out" and go outside if they feel they need it.

Whereas in the past their disruptive behavior had gotten them into trouble, they now know we will work as a team to learn how to manage their behavior. For example, I tell them that if they are feeling upset or roiled inside, they can give themselves a "time out" and go outside. Our conversations before school starts help them to trust me, to understand that I am on their side.

CUMs make clear which students need buddies

Knowing in advance which students are new to the school enables you to assign a "buddy" to partner with each of those children until he feels comfortable in this new environment. You can also assign buddies for students who are English-language learners, those who are below grade level in reading or math, or students who are facing other challenges that the CUM information tells you about.

CUMs enable you to help each student from the very beginning

Knowing about your students before the first day of class means you are prepared from Day One to help and support each one—the beginning of what is an ongoing process of "getting to know each student." It's like having a magic wand. This knowledge is essential for motivating your students to do their best and to continue to progress. No student will do his best work unless he feels the teacher truly knows him and is there as a positive supporter.

I can't say enough about how important it is to know as much as possible about each child. After all, we are teaching the whole child. Every detail available to help us understand and support each of our students is critically important to increase the chances of their success.

3. Become aware of cultural and ethnic differences

Students who are in the minority in a classroom need special thought and attention. These are individual students, or groups of students, who are different from, or feel they are different from, most of the other students in a classroom. Examples are students of a different social/economic status, ones who may have only one parent or be adopted, racial or ethnic minority students, or students for whom English is a second language. Then again, *you* may be in the minority, in which case you will have to do a great deal of work so your class will learn to trust you.

Kinds of challenges you may encounter

Davis is a mostly Caucasian, middle to upper middle class community. Even so, I had students from minority communities: African Americans, Hispanics, and other foreign nationalities. I had some students from migrant worker families. Some of my students were English-language learners, whose parents didn't speak English, and some whose parents were illiterate.

I had many students from single-parent families, some who were adopted, and some who were in foster care. To my knowledge, I never had a student who was homeless. I had students with various learning disabilities and behavioral disorders, such as attention deficit disorder (ADD), attention deficit hyperactivity disorder (ADHD), oppositional defiant disorder (ODD), and bipolar personality disorder, to name just a few. Some of my students were physically disabled. I had one student with Down Syndrome and one with autism.

Each of these students requires special understanding and attention, but I treated *all* of my students with individual attention (an extremely important point to keep in mind). In order to be engaged in learning to the optimal degree, all students need to be "known" and understood by their teachers. That means each student must *feel* that her teacher truly understands her. **This is why a thorough study of the CUMs before the first day of school is so important.**

What if you are in the minority in your classroom?

I know there are many communities that are more diverse and may be more challenging than mine. If you are Caucasian and teach in a predominantly African American, Hispanic, Chinese, or other population that is racially or ethnically different from you, it is paramount that you take steps before the first day of school to introduce yourself and to ask questions of the parents of the students you will teach.

Many ethnic groups that may formerly have been in the minority are becoming—or have become—majority communities. For example, in California the Latino population is a growing segment of the overall population. Wherever you teach, and whatever your racial or ethnic relationship is to your students, **it is paramount that you reach out to get to know them.**

This will be just the beginning of the dialogue that you must keep open and active throughout the year. It is only in this way that these children *and* their parents will learn that you want to understand them and that their best interests are first and foremost in your mind as you work to advance students' learning. This is an essential element of establishing trust in you among these families.

If you are racially, ethnically, or culturally different from the students you teach, you are going to automatically be perceived as an *outsider*. **It is only through conscious and deliberate steps that you will begin to break down the barriers that separate you from your student population and their parents.** This is critical and essential to your success in educating these students. If you remain an outsider, your students will not be motivated to take the steps necessary for them to learn.

You must respond to the needs of racial or ethnic communities

Taking these steps to truly get to *know* your students before the first day of school is just the beginning of the process necessary to engage students who are from different populations. Two other steps are essential: 1) you will need to look at the grade level curriculum through their eyes, and 2) **you must find and use literature that is by and about people from the same racial or ethic communities you are teaching.**

Taking these steps to truly get to *know* your students before the first day of school is the genesis of the process necessary to engage students who are from different populations.

4. Create a strategic seating chart

Once you have information from the CUMs about each student, you are ready to create your seating chart. The seating chart should not be left to chance. It is the first strategic plan any teacher will create, and it will set the groundwork for the first day of school. A thoughtfully prepared seating chart will help set the stage for success.

A wise teacher will keep the following in mind:
- Mix girls and boys throughout the room.
- Seat students with behavior or learning issues near the front of the class.
- Seat students with behavior issues near students with histories of being well-behaved.
- Seat students with learning issues next to students who can help support them.
- If there are students new to the school, seat them next to students who will be their "buddies" as they become acquainted with their new school environment.

Once you have created the seating chart, do the following:
- Affix nametags to the desks so students can find their desks.

- Next to the desk nametag, place a stick-on nametag on which you have written the student's name.
- Provide a set of colored marking pens for each student.

Plan to change the classroom seating arrangement every four to six weeks, while keeping in mind the above issues.

5. Be prepared to welcome each student by name

Another advantage of reviewing the CUMs before the first day of school is to associate each student's name with his/her photograph. A wise teacher memorizes the names and faces of each student. Doing so will enable you to stand at the door and greet each of your students by name as they enter their new classroom—a powerful tool. The students feel recognized, important—*respected*. The significance of this step should *not* be underestimated.

6. Plan to use humor whenever you can

A part of preparing to welcome students is not only to smile and be friendly, but also to use humor often. Your being humorous helps students to relax and feel comfortable, while at the same time they realize that their teacher can be fun, i.e., can be human!

I always mixed humor into whatever we were doing—and found it to be especially effective with sixth graders. (Who knows: perhaps that is because I have a sixth grader's sense of humor.) In any case, when you act dopey and make fun of yourself, students realize that learning can also take place in a more relaxed atmosphere, and humor simply makes being in class more enjoyable.

Keep in mind that you will have already set up a behavior management system that clearly determines the behavior that is expected of them. That includes the fact that they cannot act up and get out of control just because the atmosphere is more relaxed. You are always in charge, but that doesn't mean you can't also relax and have fun.

7. Determine which pairs of students will interview each other

Starting on the first day of school, the students will begin to introduce one another. Part of your before-school preparation will be to put pairs together to do this. As you develop a sense of each student's strengths and weaknesses (from studying the CUMs), try to match those who may lack skills with those who have stronger skills. This way, on the first day of school, you will already have a prepared list, and you can simply announce who will introduce whom.

8. Prepare for students with special needs

Over my 27 years of teaching, I had three special-needs students. (These were in addition to the many students with Individualized Educational Plans [IEPs], and, of course, other students with *individual* needs.) I felt it vital to integrate each of these students into the entire class. Even though they may have stood out from their classmates in some ways, it was imperative that they be treated like everyone else.

At the beginning of each year when the special-needs student was not in class, I talked to the other students about his coming. I explained that despite the fact that he has special needs, he shouldn't be treated any differently than anyone else in the class. I made it clear that it is really a two-way street: each special-needs student needs to feel he is part of the class, and at the same time the rest of the class needs to learn how to be comfortable with someone who seems different.

By having this talk ahead of time, my students learned about each of these students' special needs and the importance of treating him like anyone else. It turned out to be a wonderful experience for all of the students.

Please look at Appendix M (p. 362-363), in which I describe each of the three students and discuss the benefits of this learned behavior, which I think are extremely important.

The teacher as a model of desired behavior

A teacher can teach about empathy and actively help students understand how they should behave around students who have special needs, but the biggest teaching device is modeling appropriate behavior. She can set the stage so the students become more empathic by observing how she demonstrates it, something all teachers should strive to do. The teacher's behavior has a huge effect on the students.

The importance of integrating

Students working together to help someone less fortunate than they become a powerful force, and, when they are thoughtfully guided regarding a special-needs student and see how the teacher behaves toward him, the experience can make a major difference—in *their* lives and in the lives of the student with special needs. When the teacher sees this happening, there is a great sense of satisfaction.

Given my experience, I generally believe that it is best if special-needs students can be integrated into the regular classroom. But that belief is based on the teacher's using these or similar techniques with the rest of the class. *Everyone* can benefit in the end.

But do look at p. 362 for more explanation of the benefits.

Summary

If you determine early on that you will establish a culture of respect, it will be a part of you before you ever begin to teach. That attitude will affect everything you do, beginning with your preschool preparations. Then from the day you meet your students, when they sense that you respect them, they are more likely to relax and trust that you have their best interests at heart. More importantly, when you model respectful behavior, you are more likely to see it in your students than if you rely on an authoritarian approach.

Even before the first day of school, it is important to get to know your students. Learning about their academic and social-emotional needs before meeting them is essential. Then being able to greet them by name that first day will be a delightful surprise, making each student feel important. On top of that, your thoughtfully devised seating chart will go a long way toward managing—and responding to—your students' needs and behaviors.

For Parents

Parents too have a role to play before the first day of school, and their children usually enjoy this period when working together with a parent to prepare for the excitement of the beginning of a new school year. Here is what your child will need most:

- **Basic school supplies.** Some teachers send out a list of what they want their students to bring.
- **A sturdy backpack** in which to transport books, notebooks, and other school supplies each day. If the parent cannot afford these school supplies, she should let the teacher know. Most schools have access to these supplies from their local philanthropic and service organizations.
- **A designated place at home to do homework**—very important.

If there are things the teacher should know, meet with her before school starts. Let her know if there have been any recent changes, or traumatic episodes, in the child's life, e.g., death of a close relative, a new baby, a chronic illness in the family, an illness that has affected the child's life—or even a recent move!

It is equally important for parents to be willing to maintain an open dialogue with their child's teacher throughout the year.

Parents may learn from the section on modeling a culture of respect as well. They, too, may want or need reinforcement on how to manage their children's behavior in ways that are appropriate and respectful—ideas that are as applicable to good parenting as they are to good teaching.

CHAPTER 2

Get to Know Each Other Right Away

1. Have the students personalize their nametags

Students already feel welcome as they enter the room, put away their backpacks, and find their names on their desks.

Once they are seated, ask the students to use the colored pencils or pens to decorate (i.e. personalize) the stick-on nametags, then put them on. These will last only the first day of school, but the nametags will help students learn one another's names, and decorating them is a fun first activity.

Then ask them also to decorate the *desk* nametags. The desk nametags will stay in place until the seating chart changes and new nametags are made.

Having students create and decorate their own nametags gives them a chance right away to express their individuality—"I am my own person. I am unique."

2. Tell the students about yourself

Once the nametags have been decorated, briefly tell the students about yourself, providing just enough to give students a peek into who you are. You might include your teaching history, family information, and hobbies—whatever you think would interest the children. This will model for students what they might like to share about themselves, something they will be doing shortly.

At some point after my first few years of teaching, I asked my students to call me by my first name "Debbie." Some parents objected to this at first, but eventually supported it. I wanted to be approachable by my students. Even though I was the one in charge, I also wanted them to view me as another member of the team. I nurtured a cooperative rather than a competitive classroom climate.

3. Have students interview and introduce each other

Sometime during this first day, you will begin the process of explaining how the students will interview and introduce one another to the class. Students will help determine how this is done. Having students participate in the process of how they will introduce each other should make them more comfortable and less nervous.

Together determine the interview topics

First have the whole class think about topics on which to interview classmates: interests, favorite/ least favorite subject(s) in school, family, summer activities/trips, where they are from, how long they've lived in town, pets, and anything they wish to add. Explain that this process is called brainstorming—suggesting a lot of ideas that will be refined later.

Develop standards for public speaking

Then ask them to brainstorm standards for introductions. After this you can create a poster listing the expectations for class oral presentations.

>   Standards for public speaking
>   1. Look at the audience.
>   2. Speak loudly and clearly.
>   3. Stand still.

Tell them who will be partners

Once the students have learned about interviewing and introducing a classmate, announce the partnerships you have planned. Though one of the pair may be more skilled at doing this, the concept of introductions will probably be new to both students.

Make it clear that they are expected to help each other throughout this process. Then give the students time to interview their partners.

Student partners will then

- meet one-on-one to learn about each other,
- take notes in preparation for introducing the student partner in front of the class,
- convert their notes into the text of their presentation.

The first homework assignment should be converting their notes into what they will be reading or saying when they introduce their classmates. On the second day of school, ask for volunteers to go first. Both students will stand or sit side by side while introducing each other. You can decide how much time to allow each day for these introductions. It will take several days for everyone to be introduced.

By partnering students for introductions, you are introducing a cooperative model from the very beginning. Students are

- using their listening and writing skills while interviewing each other,
- practicing their writing skills by turning notes into the texts for their introductions,
- employing their speaking skills while introducing their partners.

Note: In Appendix B (pp. 209 & 210) are two documents to help students become acquainted with each other and you with them:

"Making New Friends"—encourages them to talk to their classmates to find out more about them.

"About Me"—helps them think about themselves and will provide valuable information for you as you get to know your students.

4. Discuss cultural differences

Most classrooms are made up of culturally and ethnically diverse populations. Talk about how such diversity enriches our lives and how it provides us with opportunities to learn about—and better understand—people who may be different from us. In fact, this is an opportune time to teach that the United States was founded by immigrants and has a proud tradition of welcoming people from all over the world.

Cultural and ethnic information should be included when students introduce one another. This experience gives everyone an opportunity to share and learn what makes them who they are.

Summary

Introductions all around early on help the students learn about you and one another and help them feel more comfortable in this new setting. You want to engender a feeling of community right away so that each student begins to feel known and as an important member of the group.

For Parents

Whenever your child brings home an assignment in which he will have to speak in front of the class, it would be very helpful if you have him practice with you beforehand. For fun, he could first introduce his sister to you—or you to your spouse! Then he could practice his school introduction, using the notes he has prepared about his classmate. You can go a long way to help your child gain confidence in carrying out such an activity.

CHAPTER 3
Make Behavior Standards a Priority

1. Involve students in creating behavior standards

Now it's time to establish class behavior standards. Students should be involved in suggesting standards that make sense to them. And having had an earlier experience brainstorming, they will probably be much more comfortable sharing their ideas.

As they make their suggestions, have them phrase their points in positive terms. For example, they should say "Raise your hand and wait to be recognized before you talk," rather than, "Don't interrupt." (As their teacher, you should always make sure you use positive terms when correcting students' behavior, consistently modeling this important standard and how you want them to think.)

Record ideas as students suggest them, using the overhead projector or the chalkboard/whiteboard. Involving them in this process shows you respect their opinions.

Once you have listed a number of ideas, ask students to help refine them, reducing them to a few key standards. You can always guide and suggest ideas during the refining process. For example:

Standards for Behavior
1. Enter the classroom quietly and ready to learn.
2. Raise your hand and wait to be recognized before you talk.
3. Listen respectfully to each other.

(NOTE: Always phrase behavior expectations in positive terms. For example, say, "Raise your hand and wait to be recognized before you talk," rather than, "Don't interrupt." Respond in a positive way to students' misbehaviors at all times. Your modeling of this behavior can't be emphasized enough.)

Keep classroom standards simple and to a minimum. Add to the list as the need arises.

Make a poster of the standards, and keep it displayed at the front of the classroom. Make it clear that these standards are established for everyone's benefit.

2. Establish consequences for when behavior standards are not met

Behavior is always a work in progress, so students will need to be reminded of expectations from time to time. Therefore, the class should discuss what should happen when students don't follow the established behavior standards.

These ideas should also be recorded for all to see during the brainstorming process. After students have shared a number of their own ideas, the teacher should add hers. Once again, these ideas should be refined and consolidated onto a poster displayed in front of the classroom.

For example:

Consequences For **Not** Following Behavior Standards

1. Warning
2. Time-out
3. Loss of recess or other privilege
4. A note sent home
5. A talk to a parent on the phone
6. Student-parent-teacher conference

In this way the students themselves are involved in creating what they think are appropriate behavioral standards and what the consequences should be when those standards are not met. From the very beginning, you are demonstrating your respect for their ideas. And in so doing, the students are far more likely to follow the rules they have set for themselves.

3. Give students a "Behavior Standards and Consequences Agreement"

Once the students have completed creating a list of the expected behavior standards and consequences for when these standards are not met, give each student a copy of a "Behavior Standards and Consequences Agreement" to sign and turn in. You will write this from the standards and consequences you and your students create. In this way students affirm their commitment to their "Behavior Standards and Consequences." You should collect and keep a file of all these signed agreements.

4. Discuss bullying

Bullying is an especially serious kind of bad behavior that needs particular attention after the basic standards and consequences have been discussed.

Start by giving a few examples of bullying. Ask students to give examples of bullying they have seen or experienced. Ask for a show of hands for students who have been bullied. Ask for volunteers to tell how being bullied made them feel. Talk about how unacceptable it is for anyone to experience being bullied.

Discuss how students should respond when they see a student (or students) being bullied. Talk about different scenarios and how students can support each other when confronted by bullies.

Role-play different bullying situations. This will help students learn how to respond if they are bullied, or what to say if they observe someone else being bullied.

Insist there is zero tolerance for bullying and bullies. Make every effort to assist students in standing up to bullies and in stepping in when they see bullying. And make it clear that when students are bullied—or see another student being bullied, they need to report it *immediately* to the teacher on yard duty and to their classroom teacher. It is not up to just the student who is being bullied to stand up to bullies; **it is up to every student to reject bullying and to report bullies.**

5. Reinforce behavior standards

Over the years, I have developed a routine way of handling students when they disrupt the class or don't follow the established classroom behavior standards. After students have finished setting consequences for not following behavior standards, I say something like this:

> My goal is to help each of you to be responsible and in charge of your own behavior. If you behave in a way that disrupts the class or doesn't follow our established behavior standards, I will give you a warning. If the inappropriate behavior persists, I will ask you to take a "time out" outside until you feel you are ready to be in control of yourself and abide by our standards.
>
> We can have a silent signal (e.g., finger to my nose or to the side of my head), or I can ask you by name to take a "time out" until you feel you are ready to return to class.
>
> I want you to return to class as soon as possible—hopefully in no more than just a few minutes. I will then discuss the issue with you during recess.
>
> If this becomes a persistent issue, remember the consequences: you will have to stay in for recess, and, if that isn't enough for you to improve your behavior, I will have to involve your parents in what is happening.
>
> I'm so glad you all helped set up the consequences, for you know the kinds of things that will motivate you to follow the standards you have set.

It is essential to remain calm, confident, and respectful in the face of disruptive behavior. As I said before, appropriate behavior is a work in progress. It is critically important that you never lose your cool in responding to students who misbehave and disrupt the class. (Expressing frustration or anger is not an option. You may feel frustrated or angry, but expressing them is a choice. You must model appropriate behavior at all times.) The consequences have been established and posted, and there is an escalating response as needed to address persistent disregard for the class's behavior standards.

It is through your calm and respectful modeling that students will learn respectful behavior. This is especially important for those students who persistently need help in learning how to manage their behavior and follow the class's standards. Over time, using these techniques, students will become better at taking responsibility for and managing their own behavior. These standards—and the way consequences are handled—reinforce that each of us can count on being treated with dignity and respect.

6. Recognize good behavior frequently

It is also important to recognize when students *are* following the standards—when the class's behavior standards are being met. For example, "I like the way you all came into class this morning and quietly got to work on your SSR" or "I appreciate how you are being supportive of one another and working together." You should make a point of acknowledging appropriate behavior—catching students being good—several times each day. **Positive reinforcement for appropriate behavior is a powerful tool.**

An especially *strategic* time to do this is when inappropriate behavior occurs. Students who have had habitual difficulties behaving properly often act out in order to get negative reinforcement, i.e., they like getting the negative attention. It is for this reason that **it is especially important not to buy in to a student's efforts to get attention for misbehaving.** The silent signal is an important element of helping a student correct her behavior without calling it to the attention of the whole class.

Thus, when a student is being disruptive—*that* is a strategic time to recognize and praise the *other* students who are following the behavior standards. For example, it is at this time that you might say to the well-behaved students, "I really appreciate how you are quietly concentrating on your work."

Another response is to simply *ignore* the misbehaving student while continuing with the class. What is *most* important is not to give attention to the misbehaving student. You decide whether or not to ask the student to take a time-out or to ignore her. If necessary, you can quietly move to the misbehaving student and indicate she needs to take a time-out without calling it to the attention of the whole class.

Incidentally, when you are recognizing good behavior at the same time someone is misbehaving, it is generally best not to identify any students by name, as you don't want to pit individual students against each other. You should nurture a culture of cooperation, not of competition.

7. What if your behavior-management system doesn't work?

I prefer to deal with behavior issues myself rather than send students to the principal's office, a consequence many teachers rely on more than their own techniques. But sometimes, even with well-developed classroom behavior-management plans, some students aren't responsive.

In a handful of cases, the above-described techniques haven't been sufficient for me to deal with some persistently disruptive students. Therefore, in order to be prepared for when a student doesn't make progress in managing his/her behavior, **you must have a backup plan.**

When students aren't able to control themselves using the sequence of consequences in our classroom plan, I may send a student to the **principal's office** to calm down. If repeated trips to the principal's office aren't effective, I set up a plan for **parents to come to school to pick up their child.**

Some students may need to be referred to the **school psychologist,** who can provide assistance with those students who may have personality disorders. Students diagnosed with these disorders behave in ways that require additional interventions. I consider such cases to be extreme.

In the most severe cases, a **suspension** may be called for. Suspensions usually last for just a few days. And if that doesn't work?

Once with a first grader, I found that none of these techniques was effective in managing his behavior. He was continually disruptive in the classroom and on the playground. He was referred to the school psychologist, but that didn't help. His father, a psychiatrist, wasn't able to modify his behavior either. One day he went into the girls' bathroom, locked the door from the inside, and climbed out the window, resulting in some girls' wetting their pants when they couldn't get into the restroom during recess. He stood nearby and laughed. After this incident, he was suspended.

Later, he pushed girls over onto the wood chips in the play structure area and onto the asphalt on the playground. By this time, we had run out of ideas to help him—school officials, his parents, and I had tried everything with no success. After the last incident, the student was **expelled**. Of course, this was the most extreme consequence of all, and it was used only as a last resort.

Summary

Involving students in establishing behavior standards—and establishing consequences when standards are *not* met—sets the groundwork for a classroom managed with democratic principles in mind. A teacher who works *with* her students to establish rules of behavior is more likely to see her students follow those rules. These guidelines will help you get the year off to the best start possible.

For Parents

Parents, too, may want or need reinforcement on how to manage their children's behavior in ways that are appropriate and respectful. It may help parents to remind them to involve their children at home in creating standards of behavior and establishing consequences when behavior standards are not met.

CHAPTER 4

Establish Your Routines from Day 1

Establishing activities that are routine help students know what to expect and what to do. Routines help the classroom to run more efficiently and effectively with less time spent on giving directions. Students can then work independently because they no longer have to wait for the teacher to tell them what to do.

1. SSR (Silent Sustained Reading)

The first academic routine to establish is a **Silent Sustained Reading (SSR)** period at the beginning of each day. Some years I called it **Daily Independent Reading Time (DIRT)** because my students loved to say that. So feel free to use **DIRT** in place of **SSR.** Students are expected to enter the classroom quietly, go to their desks, open their chosen SSR books, and start reading.

Students choose these books for themselves. They can read their own books from home, or books from the public library, the classroom or the school library. It is important, however, that the books be at the appropriate reading level for each child. I teach students **The Five Finger Rule** to help them learn to select books at the appropriate reading level for them.

The FIVE FINGER RULE—how students self-select SSR books:

- Open the book to a random full page (no illustrations).
- Start to read at the top of the page.
- Put down a finger for every word you can't figure out.

— **If you put down five fingers before you get to the bottom of the page**, the book is probably too difficult for you.

— **If you get to the bottom of the page and you haven't put down any fingers**, the book may be too easy for you.

The SSR reading allows and encourages students to read at the level that is most comfortable for them. It is essential that students reading below grade level have this opportunity—and encouragement—to read at their natural reading levels. The same is true for students reading *above* grade level.

It is important for the teacher to use SSR book selections to help support students' natural reading abilities. It is through these book selections that students reveal their reading levels and book subject preferences. You can also use the information you get from their SSR choices to guide students' future reading.

The routine of students doing SSR as soon as they come in to class each morning means that **every minute at the beginning of the day is used productively.** There is no wasted time while you take roll, do lunch count, read notes from parents, or meet with students who need to talk to you.

You can determine how long this reading time lasts depending on what you need to do before beginning the day's lessons.

2. SSR bookmarks

To keep track of what the students are reading, prepare **Bookmark Reading Logs**—slips of paper containing a grid for recording the number of pages read each day. On the top of each slip, the students write their name, the book's title and author, and the number of pages in the book. Below is an example of the information students are expected to fill in on these bookmarks.

Name:	
Title:	
Author:	
No. Pages:	
Date:	Pages Read:	

Note: A full page of "SSR Bookmarks" that can be copied is in Appendix C (p. 213).

3. Daily SSR at home

Students should be required to read at home at least fifteen to thirty minutes a day. They can choose to take their SSR book back and forth between school and home, or they can choose a book dedicated to home reading only. The same bookmark reading logs should be used for books students choose to read at home.

The students should indicate on the log the number of pages they read each night. When the book is finished, the bookmark log should be turned in to you. It is through the act of reading that students grow their vocabularies and their comprehension skills—skills that are the basis for all learning.

Furthermore, research has shown that children who read twenty minutes a day *every* day make tremendous strides in development of their reading skills/comprehension, as compared to those who don't do this.

4. Asking students to grade each other's papers

Having students grade papers is especially helpful for math, spelling tests, and grammar assignments, where future learning is built on the skill that has come just before. Grading such work immediately allows you to catch students' errors right away and reteach before moving on to the next day's assignment, therefore avoiding having their problems compounded. As you read, or display, the correct answer, students should mark the paper he/she is assigned to correct.

Using ID numbers to report scores

Each student should be assigned an ID number. Using a standard grade book with numbered spaces, write the students' names in alphabetical order: "1. Anderson, Betty" to "30. Zender, Jim." This way, to get scores into your grade book, you will be calling out numbers, not names.

Next to the list of names is an empty grid in which you will write students' scores for each different assignment. Use a separate page for each subject or type of assignment. At the top of each column is a place to enter the date and the description of the assignment.

Converting number scores to percent scores

Each student should have a calculator at his desk. Once papers have been corrected students should convert the raw scores to percent scores. Divide the number correct by the total number of items. Move the decimal point two places to the right. That number gives the percent score. For example, 20 correct out of 40 possible yields a score of .50 or 50%.

Determining the "Class Curve"

For some assignments you will want to determine the class curve. Ask for a show of hands as you say each possible score. Record the number of students with each score. From this distribution of scores you can create a Normal Curve.

Determining a grade for each score

If you wish to, you can use this information to determine the grades for each score. For most of these kinds of assignments I use number values instead of letter grades. For example, an A grade converts to a 5, a B a 4, and so on. The number grades seem to be less emotion laden than letter grades.

Recording scores in the grade book

Record scores immediately after the class has finished correcting the papers. As you read each ID number—in order—from your grade book, the student who corrected the paper with that student's ID number will call out the score. You then write the reported scores next to the numbers as you proceed down the list. Through this quick process, you know right away who needs help.

The benefits of having students grade papers

The first benefit is to enable you to **record this type of routine class work in a timely manner.** Many assignments and tests can be corrected at the same time by the whole class, with students correcting either their own paper or that of a classmate.

A more important benefit, however, is that **immediate feedback about a student's performance on a particular assignment allows you to intervene right away**—while the assignment is fresh. For example, sometimes I ask for a show of hands, as we are correcting, to find out how many students missed each item. If enough students have missed something on the daily assignment or test, I will reteach right then; otherwise, I will invite a small group to meet with me later. In any case, this enables me to identify which students to group for re-teaching *right away*. Immediately after correcting each day's assignment, I teach the lesson for the following day. While the rest of the class begins to work on the next assignment, I work with the students who need re-teaching.

This technique is especially helpful for math and grammar assignments, when future learning is built on the skill that has come just before. It is important to catch errors and reteach before moving on to the next day's assignment—to avoid compounding students' errors and misunderstandings.

Hearing scores reported is not an issue

Although individual scores are reported for everyone to hear, the students are taught to be respectful of one another with regard to their scores. They soon learn that although they may do well on one assignment, they may do poorly on another. And since no one wants to be made to feel embarrassed about a low score, all students need to treat others the way they want to be treated when they don't do well. They eventually realize that they are all in this together.

They also learn to appreciate that correcting papers and reporting scores right away allows them to be retaught before their mistakes and misunderstandings confuse future learning. If they want to get the kind of help they need to be more successful students, they have to acknowledge when they need help. Making mistakes is just a normal part of the learning process for everyone.

Having students correct each other's papers and reporting each other's scores, makes it difficult to know whose score is being reported when a number is called out. In the end, reporting scores on a daily basis becomes so routine that, before long, students don't even pay attention to who is reporting or what other students' scores are.

5. Spiral notebooks

Each student should have a separate spiral notebook for subjects in which there are regular daily or weekly assignments, the front of each labeled with the subject and the student's name. A Language Arts notebook would include assignments for spelling, reading, writing, and other language arts. A Math notebook would be for regular math assignments. The same would be true for Social Studies or Science.

There are at least three advantages to keeping each subject's assignment in its own spiral notebook:

1. Assignments are organized in one place where they are unlikely to be misplaced or lost.
2. They are kept together over time so that it is possible to track progress.
3. They are available for parents to use to hold their children accountable *and* —because they can track their progress—be more supportive.

This type of historical record makes it much easier for students, teachers, and parents to assess the quality of a student's work over time.

6. Folders with pockets

Students should also have a folder with pockets to keep work that is not done in their spiral notebooks. Students should have a different colored folder labeled with the subject and the student's name, just as noted above for spiral notebooks. This will include tests students take, as well as work the teacher wants to collect from time to time.

7. Weekly assignment sheets

I use a five-day calendar grid to create a place to record weekly assignments. At the top, I write "Assignments for the Week of September 7." Just above the grid, I leave a blank for Name, where each student will fill in her/his name. I label each of the five columns with the date. Within the grids, I fill in the specific subjects, page numbers, or assignments that are due on each day. Across the five days, I always write, "SSR 20 to 30 minutes each night."

At the bottom of the page, I label a blank for Parent's Signature. Students are required to take the form home for parent signature on Monday and return the signed form on Tuesday. Students use the form for the rest of the week to keep track of when each of their assignments is due. The assignment sheet goes home every night so parents can hold their children accountable for work that is due each day.

You should decide on a reward for returning the signed form, or a consequence for not returning the signed form. My consequence is to keep students in the classroom for the lunch recess if they don't return the signed form. I call this the Lunch Club. I hold a Lunch Club just one day a week. It is usually effective. After missing the longest recess of the day, students usually make sure they get the forms signed and returned on time.

Note: Two examples of Weekly Assignment Sheets are in Appendix C (pp. 211-212).

8. Assignment notebooks

I ask students to use Steno notebooks to record all their assignments on a daily basis. This includes all assignments whether or not they are completed in class. Students are expected to record each day's date, as well as list the textbook title, page numbers, and item numbers they are expected to complete. If the assignment doesn't come from a textbook, students are expected to describe the assignment: "Descriptive writing paragraph" or "Math problems from chalkboard."

I periodically check assignment notebooks, then initial, and date them. I also ask parents to check them periodically and initial and date them. These notebooks help students learn to keep track of work they have to do and to stay organized. This expectation sets the groundwork for practices that will help students throughout their school years.

Summary

The following classroom routines help to simplify regular classroom activities so that students can anticipate what is expected of them and be more independent:

- **Specific times for regular SSR reading practice**
- **Specific techniques for immediate feedback on their daily work**
- **Regular times when they work independently** (so they don't have to wait for you to give them directions)
- **Clearly designated ways for them to organize their work** (so they, their parents, and you can easily see where help is needed or where they have made progress in their learning)

For Parents

Establishing these classroom routines allows parents to know what is expected of their children. Several of these routines help parents to hold their children accountable for what is expected of them in the classroom and at home.

Parents must establish routines at home as well. Some of the most basic are the most important, but overburdened parents sometimes don't have the energy to think about them till the night before. If, however, you can talk with your child ahead of time while they are excited about the upcoming school year and plan these routines together, both you and your child will benefit.

- **Set a regular bedtime.** Make it a given, and see that the child(ren) adhere to it. If lights-out is at eight, start the routine at seven with bath, then a quiet time of reading or being read to, moving the time later as they get older. Whatever the routine is, stick to it. It is imperative that students arrive at school well rested and ready to learn.

- **Provide a healthy and nutritious breakfast—every morning.** Set up for it the night before if necessary, but make it a given. Children need this to have the energy to pay attention in class.
- **Establish a homework routine.** Work this out with input from your child(ren), then be consistent.

Parents demonstrate by these actions that they value and support their children's education. As much as the children might grumble, they realize that their parents care about them.

CHAPTER 5

Create a Plan for
Parent-Student-Teacher Teams

For a child's education to be the best it can possibly be **teachers, students, and parents must operate as a team.** The relationship of one to the other is like the legs of a three-legged stool. If any one of the legs is missing, the stool falls over and fails to do its job.

All three elements of the educational team are extremely important. Parents and teachers must have open communication: the parents need to learn how best to help and to support the education of their child, and the teacher needs to learn of any special circumstances regarding the child, or the home, that might influence the child's performance. The child's job is to pay attention in class and to conscientiously complete all her assignments, and, of course, she needs to trust that both the teacher *and* her parents are there to help her learn. Positive interaction between all three is essential for the child's success.

1. Communicating with parents

In order for parents to be able to play their role as members of their child's team, you need to make clear to them the importance of communication—both when you meet with them individually and when talking with them at Back-to-School Night.

But it is your responsibility to keep the parents in the loop about what is going on in the classroom and what is expected of their child. Seeing the weekly assignment sheets enables them to hold their children accountable for their regularly assigned work, but they also need to know about any special projects and ways they can assist their children with these projects. The more parents know about what is expected of their children, the better they will be prepared to help and support them.

2. Main points to keep in mind

To keep communication flowing with the parents, keep these points in mind:

1. Discuss the importance of open communication and the Teacher-Student-Parent team when you meet with parents before school starts or at Back-to-School Night in the fall.
2. Make sure the parents **sign the weekly assignment sheets** to know what is expected of their child.
3. Make sure all **written communications to the parents are clear and concise.**
4. Keep the parents **informed about any special projects** and suggest ways they can help.
5. Send a **personal note to the parents** when their child does something that should be commended.

These kinds of interactions between you and parents are critical in order to optimize the child's potential and to create the most favorable circumstances for his learning. **Just make sure before school starts that you have a plan on how you will communicate with the parents!**

Note: Below are the kinds of notes I send to parents—placed in Appendix D. Over time you will develop your own notes and ways of communicating with parents, but my notes may give you some ideas. Also, parents may find here some specific steps to take to support their child. (See p. 214 for page numbers.)

1. Back-to-School-Night notes.

Back-to-School-Night agenda.

Parent Information Packet to read before "Back-to-School Night:
Home/School Communication, Homework, Backpack Rule, Progress Reports, Evaluations, Behavior Expectations.

"Back-to School-Night Questionnaire" & "Student Goals"— two forms to get information from parents about their child.

STUDENT GOALS—form parents fill out to help teacher to get to know students

Weekly Schedule—example for 6th grade.

Back-to-School note describing what is expected of the students:
School/Home Communication, Assignment Notebooks, Homework, Study Time, Student Behavior, Student Assessment.

Back-to-School Night Information Packet:
Description of daily classes, Homework, Behavior Expectations, Evaluation & Grading, Working with Child at Home in all subjects.

Back-to-School Night—Math: information packet and Homework, Behavior expectations, Working with Students at Home.

2. Notes about the curriculum

Sixth Grade Curriculum letter—what to expect in each class.

Fifth/Sixth Grade Combination Class Curriculum letter (Sep 7)—what to expect.

Beginning of school letter (Sep 6) to 6th grade parents describing what they can expect.

Math Information Letter (Sep 20).

Letter (Oct 21) alerting parents to 6th grade math being taught, introducing them to a math aide.

Curriculum Information Letter to Parents, Oct 5—bringing parents up to date describing what children are studying and what to expect.

3. Homework plan that works

Homework Policy Plan.
Homework Plan.

4. Notes about meeting students' individualized learning needs

November letter to parents of children producing consistently above-grade-level work in reading and language arts skills—about new modifications in teaching Spelling, Grammar, and Spotlight reading.

5. Notes about parent-student-teacher conferences

Fall (Oct 21) pre-Parent-Student-Teacher Conference letter.
Untitled note about Gates-McGintie Reading Test results and Parent Volunteer Survey.
Updated Reminder Letter to Parents, (Jan 7)—second trimester note reiterating importance of having correct Classroom Supplies for organizing things, Complete/Incomplete Assignment and study habit expectations, Conferences, Parent Meetings, Teacher Bulletins, and Current Bulletin.
Letter (Feb 23) describing class work that has been done in the 2nd trimester.
Winter (Feb 26) pre-Parent-Student-Teacher Conference letter

6. Other single documents:

Working with Your Student at Home.
Classroom Management Plan and Evaluation Plan.
"50 Ways to Volunteer in the Classroom."

CHAPTER 6

Report Cards and Conferences

Report cards and conferences are standard for all teachers. Although all elementary teachers fill out report cards and usually schedule conferences with parents twice a year, I have three practices I want to share.

1. Two significant elements to provide in report cards

Although it is acceptable to write just a brief comment for each subject on the report card, I suggest that teachers should provide more details in their comments. I recommend that for each subject, teachers comment about both 1) what the student is doing *well* and 2) an area in which he/she might *improve*.

Although including these details can take considerably more time, they give parents concrete information they can use to focus attention on their children. In my experience, parents appreciate being able to assist their children using this information, and both parents and students appreciate receiving written acknowledgement of their successes.

2. The importance of including students in parent/teacher conferences

I strongly suggest including students in the parent/teacher conferences. After all, these meetings are *about* the students, so why shouldn't they be at the center of them!

Having the student present means he is listening when I tell his parent(s) about his accomplishments, which confirms up front that we both recognize what he has done well. He is usually quite pleased when his strengths are pointed out—especially when he has improved in a problem area. It boosts his confidence—and helps to make the changes more permanent—when he hears this kind of message conveyed.

At the same time, I take this opportunity to discuss areas where he needs improvement, whether in academics or behavior: you'd be amazed at how carefully a student pays attention at such a time! Even when he doesn't especially appreciate having to talk about any weaknesses, the conversation can always be handled in a way in which he can be encouraged to see how improving on shortcomings can lead to a strength.

Also, conferencing with the parent and child *together* gives me a glimpse into their relationship. When I have this opportunity to see them interact, it sometimes helps me understand how to intervene or facilitate these relationships.

Occasionally a parent will ask to speak to me without the student present. In these cases I simply ask the student to step outside. I do the same if there is something I want to discuss alone with the parent.

The Parent-Student-Teacher Team

This is a good time to reiterate what I presented in the previous chapter, that **for a child's education to be the best it can possibly be, teachers, students, and parents must operate as a team.** The importance of creating this team cannot be overstated. Parents and teachers must have open communication so that the parent can know how best to help and support the education of her child, and the teacher can know of any special problems the child has or circumstances at home that might influence his performance. And the child must realize that her teacher and her parents are working together—with her—to see that she is supported and helped as much as possible. Positive interaction between all three is critical to fully developing the child's potential and creating circumstances that are optimal for his learning

Note: See Appendix E (p. 253) for page numbers of examples below of what I used regarding student evaluations:

1. **Form for students to use to evaluate themselves:**

    "Student Self-Evaluation"

2. **Letters I have sent to parents:**

    3rd trimester parent-teacher conference note, March 4

    Spring Parents-Student-Teacher Conference, March 9-16

    Progress Report—January 28

    Letter to Parents about Fall Progress Reports—regarding student evaluation practices

    Mathematics Third Trimester Grade Report

    Fifth Grade Parent Feedback Form

3. Dealing with critical parents

No matter how well you do your job, there will always be some parents who will challenge your approaches or criticize you. When a parent is critical, I've found that the best response is *not* to be defensive. Parents want to know that they have been heard and that their concerns are taken seriously. It is important for you to take in the criticism, think about it, and respond thoughtfully.

No matter how conscientious you are, you are going to make mistakes. If a parent points out something you've done that you agree was a mistake, accept it and apologize. None of us, no matter how hard we try, is above making mistakes. If you are criticized for something you *don't* agree was a mistake, take in the critique, and then explain why you did what you did.

Whether the parent agrees with you or not, you are ultimately in charge of what you do. You and the parent may have to agree to disagree. The bottom line is that you, not the parent, are in charge of how you deal with students' behavior and their educational experiences while they are in your class. Hopefully, despite disagreements, you will continue to have every parent's support.

Summary

Report cards and parent/student/teacher conferences are not just end points in evaluating a student's work for the past grading period, recognizing their achievement level for each academic subject and behavioral standard. Conferences are also an opportunity—in front of the students and their parents—both to recognize their successes and to discuss areas in which improvement is needed. I do this for both academics and behavior. And should a parent not agree with some of your assessments, teaching techniques, or course content, it is important to remain calm and confident in the event of such criticism.

For Parents

Parents should be aware of the standards by which their children are being graded and evaluated. It is therefore important for them to participate actively in the teacher-student-parent team. A strong teacher-student-parent team is necessary to help the student reach his full potential.

CHAPTER 7

Prepare Ahead of Time
for a Substitute

The regular classroom teacher should have available *all* information a substitute needs to know when she must be absent—both routine activities and special circumstances. Some of the following are standard, expected of all teachers, but others are common sense ideas that I developed. You might keep these in mind so the substitute doesn't waste time getting up to speed, and your students don't waste a day of learning.

1. Standard procedures

To prepare for a substitute, you must have the following standard items at your desk. All teachers should prepare them at the beginning of the year and *update* as needed as the year progresses:

1. A clear seating chart for the classroom;

2. A daily/weekly schedule of when each subject is taught; and

3. The times for recesses, lunch period, and end-of-day class dismissal.

4. A note containing any special information a substitute should know to do her job well.

It is critical, for example, to know the names of any students who have special needs or who exhibit behavior challenges—and perhaps a suggestion of how you deal with these students. This information could be in an envelope attached to the seating chart with "Confidential information for the substitute" written on the outside.

2. "Forewarned is Forearmed"—keep important information for subs updated

The following is critical for the substitute so she can keep the students on track to learn what you are currently teaching:

1. Keep your Lesson Plan Book updated daily.

If you develop a *routine* of keeping notes (in your Lesson Plan Book) of what you are currently teaching and *update each day's plans*, your sub will be better prepared to pick up where you left off. This way, when you unexpectedly get sick, you don't have to worry about not having left detailed plans.

2. Keep an updated note on the skill your students are working on.

Examples:

In math we are working on adding and subtracting decimals.

In language arts we are learning about adjectives and where they go in sentences.

3. Leave bookmarks in books you are using.

For the curriculum from textbooks, simply put a bookmark where you left off. If you are reading aloud to the class, leave a bookmark in that book as well.

If you *routinely* prepare all of the above information, you will not have to do any additional work for a specific time you need a sub. Keeping these notes should be easy and minimally time-consuming. Of course, when you do know in advance that you will be absent, it is always most helpful to a sub if you are able to leave more detailed notes.

Summary

These simple steps make it easy to be sure your sub will have sufficient guidance to teach and manage your students when you are absent. It should be a big relief to both you and your sub to know that you have left everything a sub needs to do the best job possible.

Part V

Instruction in the Classroom

The information I share in this part of the book is not comprehensive curriculum information. It contains curriculum ideas that I developed to fill in for what I believed was missing from standard content. So in a way this is supplementary content, but I consider it to be essential to effective teaching and learning in each subject area.

CHAPTER 1

Reading

The foundation of learning is reading, so time spent on reading must be a classroom priority. We have already established the reading routines of SSR in the classroom and at home every day. Now it's time to discuss **direct instruction** of reading skills.

1. Identify students' reading levels before school starts

As I said earlier, I make a point of getting to know as much as I can about each child *before* the first day of school. From the CUMs, I know what grade level each child has tested at the previous spring, information that prepares me for organizing reading instruction to meet students' individual needs.

But I still need to meet individually with students whose tests show they are reading below grade level. I do this during the very first days of the school year. In this way, I can assess for myself the level at which each of these children is reading, and I can determine the kinds of help they will need.

2. Help students who will need support

Meet individually with these students

Because of my own reading failures, I am acutely sensitive to the needs of students who have difficulty reading. I intervene with them one-on-one so they don't have to suffer in front of their peers. It is key that the teacher knows all the students' reading strengths and weaknesses before she puts them into situations that may be embarrassing or uncomfortable. This can be as true for students reading far above grade level as it is for students reading below grade level. I do not make assumptions about their potential abilities based on their difficulties reading.

I meet with individual students during the SSR period, using the books each student has selected as her SSR book. Since I've already taught the Five Finger Rule, these books are at each student's reading level. And because I have met with these students individually, they don't have to be embarrassed about reading below grade level when they have to read in front of their classmates. I do this in the back of the classroom so it receives minimal attention from the rest of the class.

Once I determine which—and how many—students need reading support, I explain what they can expect during whole-class reading lessons. I reassure them that I won't ask them to read aloud unless they volunteer. I also share my own personal difficulties learning to read, and I tell them that I want to be sure they feel comfortable about the ways I will teach them reading.

My struggles learning to read have served me well as a teacher. Those early difficulties certainly resulted in my developing sensitivity to the feelings and needs of the students I would later teach. My students have expressed appreciation for how I work with them, and they have been able to relax when working in the reading group, whether it has been as a whole class or a small group.

Pair students so those who need help have it nearby

When reading from a grade-level text, students who are reading below grade level will need help and support. These students should be paired with students reading at or above grade level. The seating arrangement should be adjusted so that these partners sit next to each other.

I advise setting up partners for every student in the class. In this way, no student will stand out from anyone else. I tell students that they all have the option of reading with a partner at any time. (Some like to read together for social reasons rather than because they need help.)

I suggest that students read silently together until one needs help with a word or phrase or with comprehension. Then the student needing help can get it from her partner.

I train everyone to work on how to **sound out words** and **use context clues** to figure out words they don't know. Students are asked to speak very quietly so as not to disrupt others. In good weather students can go outside to read together, although in this case I only allow those to go outside who I know need help.

When students are grouped by reading levels to read classroom literature books, they each partner with another student from this group. From time to time I meet with these groups, especially those who need support, to teach lessons and assess progress.

3. Make sure all students know the basics of reading

Before you begin having students read, it is important to review the basics to be sure *every* student has mastered the basic reading skills and strategies. You never know whether students who currently read below grade level have *missed* certain lessons in the earlier grades, or if they *never understood them in the first place* and may now be ready to take in the concepts. My own experience—of moving from one school to another without being assessed, and never having been taught basic phonics—has definitely informed the practices I employ with my students.

So that no one starts from behind, I reteach **short and long vowels**, **consonant blends** and **digraphs**, as well as other word elements that teach students approaches to figuring out words they don't know. My lessons focus on a phonics approach so that students learn how different letters sound together—how to "sound out" new words. (See "Tools for Sounding Out Words," the first document in Appendix F, p. 262.)

Through these lessons, I begin to see students who have been struggling, sometimes for years, relax, and even smile, when they participate in reading sessions. They are so relieved to learn to unlock clues to overcoming their difficulties.

4. Make reading assignments more effective

Teachers in most classrooms are required to use a reading textbook. These texts provide not only grade-level reading selections (with accompanying vocabulary and comprehension exercises); they also provide an opportunity to expose all students to the same material for whole-classroom discussions and lessons.

Early in the year I use the reading textbook four days a week as explained below. (One day a week the students participate in Literature Discussion groups, as explained in #9 below.)

Reading from the textbook

In the beginning of the year we spend two days a week reading selected stories from the textbook. The whole class reads the story aloud together, stopping to discuss while targeting **vocabulary** and **comprehension**. It is during these discussions that I teach a story's **literary devices**: **story themes**—man vs. man, man vs. nature, man vs. himself; and **plot structure**—setting, character development, obstacles or conflicts the character confronts, climax, and resolution.

As the year progresses I let those who want to read the selection independently to do so, while I meet with a small group that wants and needs support. I may need to meet a second day with the students who need support.

Working on textbook exercises

Two days a week students work on exercises from the textbook, or I teach other lessons that build reading skills. I decide whether the vocabulary and comprehension exercises accompanying a textbook selection will be done orally with the whole class or individually in students' spiral notebooks to be corrected the next day.

When students complete these textbook assignments, they know to use this time to read books that have been assigned for their Literature Discussion Groups or their SSR books.

Note: In Appendix F (p. 280) is an assignment called **"Literature & Weekly Writing II, 'The Dragon Doctor,'"** which I created based on the reading textbook.

5. Differentiate to meet the different needs of students

Reading is one area of the curriculum that must be differentiated to address the different learning needs of all students. Because the students vary so widely in reading abilities, you need to decide ahead of time which selections from the reading textbook will be read by the *entire class*, which will be read by only *some* of the class, and which will be *skipped*.

Challenging and supporting the more able students

As the year progresses, I often decide that the more able students (this includes students who read at grade level) don't need the textbook reading or exercises. It is then that I assign them to read from one of the sets or individual literature books at their reading level. I prepare vocabulary, knowledge, comprehension, analysis, synthesis, and evaluation exercises specific to these books. (In #9, below, I discuss these concepts more fully when students use Bloom's Taxonomy to write questions for their Literature Discussion Groups.) These lessons provide more challenging learning experiences for students working above grade level.

Freeing the better readers to work independently allows time for me to meet with the students who need support to read the textbook selection.

Note: In Appendix D (p. 242) is a **November 5 letter to parents of children doing above grade level work**—about new modifications in teaching spelling, grammar, and *Spotlight* reading. (*Spotlight* is the title of the reading textbook.)

Supporting the less able students

When the textbook is too difficult for some students, I assign them to read from one of the literature book sets at their reading level. Whether they are reading from the textbook or a literature set, I meet with these students in a small group.

I may ask them to read a particular chapter or a set number of pages before we meet. We may read the assigned pages together aloud, or they may read silently in the small group and ask for help when they need it.

Sometimes, as I said above, I pair less able students with more able students to read the selection together, providing another opportunity for students to help one another and to be respectful of their learning differences.

During our group meeting, I ask questions about the story. Those who want to respond volunteer. If no one volunteers, I answer the question.

I ask students to read orally *only* if they volunteer. If no one volunteers, I read and ask them to follow along with their fingers, tracing under the words as I read them. When I come to words that I think may be difficult, I sound them out, showing students how to combine the sounds that each letter makes.

6. Employ the support of a reading specialist

Some students qualify for help from the school's reading specialist. These students are excused from class each day to meet with the reading specialist, either individually or in small groups. It is up to the teacher to decide what part of the regular classroom program these students will miss.

I usually prefer to keep these students in class for the daily reading period—unless their skills are so low that this work is too difficult for them. Some students—even if eligible for the reading specialist's support—are better served by remaining in the classroom. This is best determined by the classroom teacher, parents, and reading specialist together.

7. Read to the class regularly

I read to the whole class, usually right after lunch each day—always for at least ten minutes. How long I read depends upon how much time we have in our schedule.

Reading orally to the whole class gives me the opportunity to teach new vocabulary as I read, to discuss comprehension, and to discuss ways the author develops her **dramatic structure.** Discuss setting the stage by introducing **setting** and **main characters**; the **rising action** during which the main character(s) encounter **obstacles**; leading to the **climax** when the character(s) overcome the obstacles; the **falling action**; and, finally, the **resolution** when the story comes to an end.

Discussing these elements when you read to the class reinforces the lessons taught in the literature discussion groups. It is a simple and direct way to teach these concepts to the entire class using a story they are all exposed to, and also to model the importance of time spent reading.

Note: A diagram of Dramatic Structure is in Appendix F (p. 274).

8. Create vocabulary development exercises

Dictionary Searches

Each week assign students to use their dictionaries to look up a word that begins with each of five letters from the alphabet. For example, start with A, B, C, D, and E. Ask students to find a word that begins with each of these letters. They should write the words, their parts of speech, their definitions (in students' own words), and use them in their own sentences in their spiral notebooks. Each week go to the next five letters of the alphabet, and so on. When you finish the alphabet start again. This activity should continue all year.

Once the students have finished this exercise for five words, ask students to share their words, parts of speech, definitions, and sentences in front of the whole class. I would assign students by creating a pattern down columns or rows of seats in sequential order. Each week the next five students, in order, will share their "Dictionary Search" work. You can decide whether to do one a day, or all five on one day.

This activity serves three purposes. It allows students to become more familiar with dictionaries, it provides them with an opportunity to learn and share new vocabulary that is of particular interest to them, and it gives a very brief, structured, experience speaking in front of the whole class.

Textbook and Literature book exercises

Another vocabulary development exercise uses the textbook or literature books. Select vocabulary words from any books the whole class reads. Teaching students new vocabulary from their reading assignments should be an integral part of all reading lessons. You select words from literature books. And you can either select your own words or use those provided for the textbook.

9. Ask students to respond to questions about literature they read

It really is important to teach children how to think critically about what they read—and to begin when they are still young. I used two particularly useful techniques: Bloom's Taxonomy and suggested interpretive questions from the Junior Great Books Program.

Bloom's Taxonomy

Bloom's Taxonomy is a framework for categorizing educational goals. The framework consists of six major categories: **Knowledge, Comprehension, Application, Analysis, Synthesis**, and **Evaluation**. In other words, students must first have the basic *knowledge* in order to *comprehend* what they are learning, then *apply* and *analyze* it, *think about it creatively*, and *evaluate* it.

Bloom's Taxonomy
Action words for inquiries

Knowledge—The student recalls and recognizes information.

Define	Narrate	Relate
Label	List	Name
Report	Recall	Tell
Repeat	Memorize	Locate
Record		

Comprehension—The student changes information into a different symbolic form of language.

Identify	Restate	Express
Explain	Discuss	Review
Describe	Recognize	Report

Application—The student solves a problem using the knowledge and appropriate generalizations.

Demonstrate	Interview	Illustrate
Dramatize	Schedule	Translate
Practice	Apply	Interpret
Operate		

Analyze—The student separates information into component parts.		
Debate	Question	Criticize
Distinguish	Inventory	Solve
Diagram	Differentiate	Experiment
Compare		
Synthesis—The student solves a problem by putting information together that requires original creative thinking.		
Compose	Arrange	Assemble
Design	Plan	Prepare
Catalog	Formulate	Construct
Propose	Organize	Classify
Evaluation—The student makes qualitative and quantitative judgments according to set standards.		
Select	Predict	Assess
Measure	Rate	Estimate
Judge	Choose	Evaluate
Value		

Under each category are subcategories, each lying along a continuum from simple to complex, and from concrete to abstract. These sub-categories are the practical applications for dealing with each category—designed to help students think about and question what they are reading and learning.

A full page of "Bloom's Taxonomy" is on p. 266.

If you have any doubts about how to use Bloom's taxonomy, there is considerable help on the internet for suggestions in how to use it. An example is *The Best Resources for Helping Teachers Use Bloom's Taxonomy in the Classroom.*

The following are the authors' brief explanations of these main categories:

- **Knowledge** "involves the recall of specifics and universals, the recall of methods and processes, or the recall of a pattern, structure, or setting." [This is listed first because it contains "skills and abilities," with the understanding that knowledge is the necessary precondition for putting these skills and abilities into practice.]
- **Comprehension** "refers to a type of understanding or apprehension such that the individual knows what is being communicated and can make use of the material or idea being communicated without necessarily relating it to other material or seeing its fullest implications."
- **Application** refers to the "use of abstractions in particular and concrete situations."
- **Analysis** represents the "breakdown of a communication into its constituent elements or parts such that the relative hierarchy of ideas is made clear and/or the relations between ideas expressed are made explicit."

- **Synthesis** involves the "putting together of elements and parts so as to form a whole."
- **Evaluation** engenders "judgments about the value of material and methods for given purposes." [1]

By the time the parent volunteer is involved, the students will have learned how to compose their questions. They know to take one of the "action words" they see listed in each category, from which they create a question that will help provide ideas for discussion.

For example, under "**Knowledge**" (which a student must have before he can recall and recognize information), the student might select "Define," i.e., "Define what is meant by _____." Or "List": "**List** the characteristics of the main character." Such questions will help all the students think more about what they read.

Over time, the questions go from simple, knowledge-based questions to (eventually) comprehension, application-, analysis-, synthesis-, and evaluation-based questions following Bloom's Taxonomy.

Note: For more support information regarding Bloom's Taxonomy, see Appendix F (pp. (265-268).

Junior Great Books' Interpretive Questions

Another way I prepare students for literature discussions is to show them a variety of ways to think about what they are reading. An excellent guide is "Seven Types of Interpretive Questions" from the Junior Great Books Program:

1. **Meaning**—"What did the author mean when he/she said …?"
2. **Use of language**—"Why did the author say _____ instead of _____?"
3. **Character Traits or Motives for Actions**—
   "Why did _____ act in a particular way…?"
   "Why did the author give _____ a particular characteristic?"
4. **Purpose**—
   "What was the author's purpose in choosing _____?"
   "Why was a particular passage included in the story?"
5. **Connections**—These questions should ask about relationships and connections between elements of the story.
6. **Sequence of Events**—These questions should ask about the significance of a particular sequence or the reason for a particular sequence.
7. **Overall problem of meaning**—This would be a suggested interpretation of the overall meaning of the story. What message did the author want to impart?

10. Use parent volunteers for literature discussion groups

One day a week I plan for parent-led small-group literature discussions. It is ideal if a teacher is able to recruit four or five parents who are willing to come in to class one day a week to lead these 30- to 40-minute literature discussion group meetings. In communities where parents aren't available, perhaps other volun-

---

[1] From the appendix of *Taxonomy of Educational Objectives*.

teers can be recruited. (A senior-living complex or a senior center can be an excellent place to start. The school's PTA could also be helpful.)

These small literature discussion groups allow students of very different abilities to read selections at their optimal reading levels *with others of similar ability*. A class of 30 students can be divided into five or six groups of five or six students each.

This is another setting in which the teacher employs the sets of literature books at varying reading levels described above.

Note: My "Guidelines for Literature Discussion Leaders" is in Appendix F (pp. 275-276).

How students prepare for literature discussion groups

Students use Composition Books as their Literature Notebooks. For each meeting, all students are required to complete three tasks:

1. Read the assigned pages or chapters, and be prepared to discuss them at the next group meeting. (The number of pages assigned depends upon the books and reading levels of each group.)

2. Write ten words from their reading that are new, difficult, or have some other interesting characteristic. (They aren't required to look up the words or write definitions; all they have to do is write them in their notebooks.) Students' doing this helps them to focus on the vocabulary of the stories they are reading.

3. Write two questions about what they read for that week's meeting from either Bloom's Taxonomy or the Junior Great Books Program's "Seven Sources of Interpretive Questions," both described in # 9 above. These questions are meant to stimulate conversation in the discussion group. (I always let the parent volunteers know ahead of time when I want the students to use each of these two types of questions.)

For any one of the six areas in Bloom's Taxonomy, the students use one of the words to begin an inquiry—e.g., "**List** the characteristics of the main character," is from the **Knowledge** section. The questions go from simple, knowledge-based questions to (eventually) comprehension-, application-, analysis-, synthesis-, and evaluation-based questions following Bloom's Taxonomy. (I teach students how to formulate all of these types of questions earlier in the year before we begin the parent-led Literature Discussion Groups.)

How parent volunteers lead literature discussion groups

The format for each discussion group is the same.

1. The leader asks students if they want to share any of the words they listed in their notebooks. (This is entirely voluntary; students are not required to share.)

2. The leader then asks if students want to share any of their questions. (She decides how much time to allow for sharing of these questions, expecting students to share them.)

3. *If the students don't share their words or questions*, the leader begins the discussion using questions she has prepared using Bloom's Taxonomy or the Junior Great Books format. Questions should focus on the specific part of the book assigned for that week's discussion. The discussion leader may also focus questions on the story's dramatic structure: setting, characters, plot, and so on. (The teacher presents lessons on these ideas at a separate time.)

4. The discussion leader tries to draw each member of the group into the discussion.

5. At the end of the group meeting, the leader assigns the pages or chapters to be read for the next week's meeting.

6. See #4 below in particular.

Note: In Appendix F are all the documents I prepared to help students and parents understand reading expectations: (See p. 261 for page numbers.)

1. **Guidelines specifically to help parents evaluate their child's reading at home**
   Form to be used at home by parents to evaluate their child's reading.

2. **Information to help students improve their reading skills, as well as help parents know how to support students in developing these skills**
   "About Reading and the Development of Strong Reading Skills at the Intermediate Level"
   Bloom's Taxonomy documents:
   "Background of Bloom's Taxonomy."
   "Bloom's Taxonomy—Action Words for Inquiries."
   "Bloom's Taxonomy—detailed explanations of the six categories."
   "Bloom's Taxonomy—The building blocks of knowledge extending students' thinking."
   "Class Discussion/Participation Rubric"—for students, parents and teachers.

3. **Documents that stretch students' ability to think about what they have read—and help them write thoughtful book reports**
   "Thinking about My Reading": Fiction Books, Level I."
   "Thinking about My Reading": Fiction Books Level II."
   "Thinking about My Reading": Informational Books, Level II."
   Dramatic Structure Diagram.

4. **Information to help Literature Discussion Leaders (Many of the documents listed above will also help Literature Discussion Leaders)**
   "Guidelines for Literature Discussion Leaders."
   "Response to Literature Checklist."
   "Responding to Errors in Reading"—suggested for when a child is reading out loud.

5. **Examples of assignments for students**
   Form for "STUDENT BOOK REVIEW"
   "Literature & Weekly Writing II, "The Dragon Doctor"—example of a literature assignment based on textbook reading.
   The Egypt Game, The Golden Goblet, and *Journey to Topaz*—questions about reading comprehension from literature books the whole class reads.

6. **Examples of book reviews written by students:**

4th/5th Grade	5th Grade	6th Grade
Tuck Everlasting	*The Watsons Go to Birmingham*	*The Bronze Bow*
	The One-Eyed Cat	
	Kokopelli's Flute	

If you are amazed at the quality of some of the papers, be aware that not one of these examples is from a student in my GATE classes. They are all from students in regular classes who have learned what I have been telling you about. (Some of these show grades and my comments.)

7. Books that are appropriate for each grade

"Literature list for 4th, 5th, and 6th grades." I have put asterisks in front of titles I think are the most important to read in conjunction with the social studies curriculum for each grade.

11. Stock the classroom library

In most classrooms, the students' reading achievement levels (as determined by the previous spring's standardized testing) range from a year or two *below* grade level to several years *above* grade level. It is not unusual to have—all in the same class—five or six students reading below grade level; a good number of students reading at grade level, yet with some struggling; and several reading *above* grade level. For this reason, using exclusively a grade level textbook for reading instruction is not the best approach.

The "Goldilocks Principle"

The best way to boost students' reading skills is to provide them with books that are *neither too hard nor too easy, but are just right* for their individual reading achievement levels. This is something Goldilocks would have understood!

We've already discussed how the **Five Finger Rule** (p. 95) helps students select books at their appropriate reading levels. So that my students can *easily* learn to make selections using this technique, I provide—in the classroom—a library of both individual books and *sets* of books.

Selecting literature books for the classroom

Students in every classroom should have easy access to literature at their individual reading-comfort levels, while at the same time literature that challenges them and expands their vocabularies and reading comprehension skills.

The wide range of literature books should

- match the maturity and interest of the students, and
- be at reading levels ranging from 1-2 years *below* grade level to several years *above* grade level.

They should include the following:

- **sets of six-to-ten books of one title** as well as **individual titles**.
- **fiction** and **non-fiction** books;
- **books that integrate the social studies content for the grade level** so students will learn more on those topics while reading literature selections.

Having a carefully-selected classroom library of both *sets of one title* and *individual titles* will enable you to provide reading-level-appropriate alternatives to the textbook and to reinforce information the students are learning in social studies. These books will also be a rich source for exercises you might create. Such a variety in reading materials and instruction is far preferable to relying solely on grade-level texts.

Note: "Literature list for 4th, 5th, and 6th grades" is in Appendix F (pp. 313-317).

Summary

Reading should be a daily priority. It is important for you to differentiate reading instruction to meet students at their individual reading levels, and to provide a wide variety of books in the classroom for them to read when the regular reading textbook is either too difficult or too easy.

I found that the more I was able to relate one-on-one and understand each child, the more effective I was in teaching him or her. This was true not only with those who found reading difficult, but with all children. I was able to identify students whose abilities were off the charts as well as those who struggled, so I could tailor activities to meet each student's unique needs. Gifted students, those of very high ability, need reading and writing activities that address their unique needs as well.

Having weekly literature discussion group-meetings for students at each level enables them to read and discuss books comfortably. As students are challenged at their *own* levels, they gain confidence in their reading abilities, and their skills grow and grow. Reading orally and discussing the story with the entire class adds another layer to helping build students' vocabulary, comprehension, and literary writing techniques.

Not being able to read truly affected my life. In the end I *did* learn, but given what a long time I had this disability, I knew that these experiences would help me to teach children in ways that would prevent them from experiencing what I had.

For Parents

My most important message to parents is to be especially alert to any problems your child might have with reading. Then work with her teacher to be sure she receives appropriate intervention as soon as possible to remediate areas of weakness.

Parents can also use some of my ideas to help support their child at home. Within the list of my handouts at the end of the chapter, three in particular were for my students' parents:

- **Form** parents can use at home to evaluate their child's reading (p. 263).
- **"About Reading and the Development of Strong Reading Skills at the Intermediate Level"**—a note reminding parents that my students must always have a literature book to read during SSR time, **discusses how to find the appropriate-level book for each child**, and gives a list of required reading that year (p. 264).
- **"Response to Literature Checklist"**—asking students to respond to prompts about their reading in the following categories: Enjoyment/Involvement, Making Personal Connections, Interpretation or Making Meaning, Insight into Elements Authors Control in Making Story (p. 277)."

CHAPTER 2
Language Arts and Writing

Writing is a skill students learn in tandem with their reading skills. The combined skills of reading, writing, speaking, and listening should be nurtured throughout the school day. A variety of strategies should be employed to build writing skills.

1. Using language arts textbooks

Most grade levels have language arts textbooks that focus on teaching language, grammar, and writing skills. Rather than using the textbook assignments in sequential order, I pick and choose lessons as they apply to those on which I want to focus. I use these textbook lessons along with exercises I have developed, and I adapt the textbook lessons to allow for differentiation.

2. Using spelling textbooks

The only textbook I use in its entirety is a grade-level spelling book, which most districts provide. Monday students use each word from the spelling book in a sentence, which I grade. They take a *trial* test Wednesday, the *final* test Friday, correcting each as a whole class, exchanging papers or correcting their own. Immediately after correcting the tests, students write each misspelled word correctly five times and turn in to me. Students do spelling *exercises* from the textbook, due Tuesday through Friday, then correct them in class. When tests and exercises are corrected in class, scores are reported using student ID numbers.

Bonus words

For many students, the weekly textbook spelling words are too easy. So each week I add 10 bonus words that are more difficult, usually from either the social studies lesson we are working on, the literature book the class is reading, or the book I am reading to the class.

Almost all my students enjoy the opportunity to learn to spell more challenging words. They are excited when they meet the challenge and succeed with even a *few* of these bonus words.

I may choose words with interesting characteristics (e.g., *alluvial, sedimentary, volcanic*) or ones that are a particular part of speech (e.g., *lovingly, grudgingly, frugally, sparingly, sprightly*). Any student has the option of including these bonus words on her spelling test. Students receive extra credit for spelling any of these words correctly.

The challenge of the bonus words seems to motivate even students who may be working just at, or below, grade level to work harder on the textbook spelling list. Motivation is the key to learning, so anything that motivates is helpful.

3. Teaching sentence elements and parts of speech

Although below I discuss parts of speech and other sentence elements separately, I teach them in tandem. And one of the best techniques I've found for teaching them is called the sentence-building strategy.

The Sentence-Building Strategy

The **sentence-building strategy** is just what it says—building a sentence, starting with only two words (a subject and predicate), and—word by word—creating a sentence.

A. Use the sentence-building strategy to teach sentence elements
Subjects and Predicates

The **subject** is what the sentence is about.

The **predicate** is what the subject does; it shows the action of the subject.

Use the sentence-building strategy to teach **subjects** and **predicates**. To begin, write a simple sentence on the board consisting of just two words, labeling them as subject and predicate (with one line under the subject, two lines under the predicate—*even though the publisher is unable to do it here*).

Whales swim.

After you have a subject and a predicate, ask students to suggest other words that fit the sentence to build it to be longer and longer. When students participate in this process, the learning process is more organic. Rather than being presented with sentences that are already prepared, students get to participate in the process to better understand how to create sentences for themselves. They might look like this:

Big whales swim.

Big gray whales swim quickly through the water.

Big gray whales swim quickly through the water on their way to the feeding grounds.

Once the students have learned the process, you can give them a sheet of 20-30 sentences, where they have to identify the subject and predicate of each sentence. Do the first 5-10 together as a class so they get the idea. As they learn how to do this, ask them to complete the exercise on their own. Correct these together as a class, asking different students to share their answers. By putting one line under the complete subject and two lines under the complete predicate, it's quick, easy, and fun.

Objects—and the object of a verb

Another important sentence element is the **object**. When you introduce objects, I would keep it simple by first discussing the **object of a verb**.[2] Since you have been teaching subjects and predicates, and since the object of a verb appears in clauses (which have a subject and a predicate), use as an example a simple sentence such as "John hit the ball."

An **object** is a noun, pronoun, or noun-like element representing a *receiver of an action*. The **object of a verb** receives the action of the verb.

In the sentence "Tom hit the ball," *ball* is the object, receiving the action of the verb *hit*. Tom *hit* (his action) the *ball* (what was hit). In this case, "hit the ball" is a complete (entire) predicate. The *object* is a part of the predicate.

As they will shortly learn about nouns (and as an object is a noun, pronoun, or noun-like element), they can learn to spot the object by answering the question "what." John hit "what"? John hit "the ball." Betty saw "what"? Betty saw "the movie." Ask the students to give other examples.

Just as you did with subjects and predicates, you might give them a sheet of 20-30 sentences where they have to identify the subject, verb and object. Have them put one line under the <u>subject</u>, two lines under the <u>verb</u>, and circle the object, e.g., <u>Johnny</u> <u>hit</u> the (ball). Waiting expectantly with squinting eyes, <u>Jane</u> then fiercely <u>hammered</u> the speeding (baseball). ("Ball" and "baseball" are the objects, so each should be circled.)

Note: See Appendix N, p. 364, for some "Common errors in written and spoken language."

B. Use the sentence-building strategy to teach parts of speech

I've found that students learn parts of speech best when they participate in the process of thinking of the words and helping to place them in sentences, rather than being presented with a completely didactic lesson from a textbook. **Using the sentence-building strategy, students participate in the process of learning the function of each part of speech and where it goes in a sentence.**

To begin the sentence-building exercises with parts of speech, write a sentence on the board consisting of just a noun and a verb. Explain these parts of speech and label them. Explain that the noun is the subject of the sentence and that the verb is the predicate. Underline the subject once and the predicate twice.

As you proceed to build the sentence, add a blank before the noun, writing "adjective" under it. Explain the adjective, and ask students to brainstorm examples. Then write the sentence again leaving a blank before the verb, writing "adverb" under it. (You can also leave a space for the adverb *after* the verb, showing that an adverb can come after the verb.) In this way you build the sentence as you introduce each new part of speech.

Have the students copy these lessons into their Language Arts spiral notebooks. Then ask them to complete exercises you prepare that use the kinds of words the class has been working with. By correctly doing these exercises, they demonstrate that they understand each part of speech and how to use it. (You decide how many parts of speech to teach each day.)

---

2   You can discuss the **object of a preposition** later after they have learned what a preposition is. If a student brings it up, however, you may have to start before then—or tell them you will get to that shortly.

Parts of speech

NOUNS: Explain that a word that identifies a person, a place, or a thing is a **noun**. Create three columns on the board, one for each type of noun. Then ask students to brainstorm examples and place them in the correct column.[3]

    After collecting a wide range of examples on the three lists, ask the students if they see any examples that stand out. A student will probably point out that some of the nouns are *capitalized*. Explain that these are **proper nouns**—the *names* for an individual person, place, or organization

PRONOUNS: At this point you can introduce **pronouns** that are used in place of nouns, such as I, you, he, she it, him her, they, them. You might show a sentence with a pronoun instead of a noun. Because some pronouns like "I" and "me" are often misused, I have created a document ("Pronouns") in Appendix G, p. 330, which you may find useful—to learn about these and other pronouns.

VERBS: Now create a new list to brainstorm *action* words—**verbs**, putting them on the board as the students suggest them.

ADJECTIVES: Next ask students to brainstorm words that *describe* the whales. Explain that words describing, identifying, or further defining a noun are **adjectives**. They will suggest words like *huge, gigantic, gray, killer.*

ARTICLES: Now may be the time to introduce **articles**. Explain that an **article** (a, an, the) is used before a noun to identify it, as in "The whales swim," "A whale swims," or "He ate an apple." And, if appropriate, you can point out that "the" is a *definite* article, while "a" and "an" are *indefinite* articles.

ADVERBS: You may then ask students to brainstorm words that describe *how* whales swim. Students will suggest words like *fast, slowly,* and *gracefully.* Once students have suggested a list of these words, explain that words that describe more about the verb (or an adjective or another adverb—"modify" them) are **adverbs**. Adverbs tell *how, when,* or *where* something happens.

CONJUNCTIONS: Explain that a word that joins or separates two parts of a sentence is called a **conjunction**. *And* and *but* are conjunctions. Other conjunctions will be taught as they appear in students' writing.

PREPOSITIONS AND PREPOSITIONAL PHRASES: Ask students to expand the sentence further. They will provide phrases such as these: "The enormous whales / swim gracefully "through the ocean," "under the water," "against the tides."

    Explain that these are **phrases**—groups of words that don't have a subject or predicate. These phrases begin with a **preposition**—a word that explains the relationship to an object, and they are called **prepositional phrases**. In this case, they tell more about *how* or *where* the whales swim—*under* the water, *against* the tides.

    An easy way to illustrate prepositions (showing the relationship to an object) is to draw a simple vase on the board, then draw a line showing *through* the vase, a line *over* the vase, *under* the vase, *on* the vase, *beside* the vase, and so on. This works very well as a basis for learning prepositions. Or hold a glass and use a ruler to show *over, under, through,* and *beside* the glass.

---

[3] While going through these parts of speech, keep in mind that you may want to transfer the suggested words to a poster. I discuss that topic on the next page.

The object of the preposition

Explain that the rest of the phrase is the **object of the preposition**. In the phrase, "under the water," *under* is the preposition and *water* is the object of the preposition (*"water"* is the object, telling *what* is under). *Against* is the preposition and *tides* is the object of the preposition (*against* <u>what</u>?—*against* the tides).

These phrases, as a whole, function as adjectives (to tell more about a **noun**) or **adverbs** (to tell more about a **verb**). Example:

<u>"On the field</u>, the baseball player ran <u>past third base</u> and slid <u>into home plate</u>."

<u>On the field</u>" tells more about the noun "player" (i.e., *modifies* "player") and—as a whole—acts as an adjective; <u>past third base</u> tells more about the verb "ran" (i.e., *modifies* "ran") and—as a whole—acts as an adverb telling *where* he ran; and <u>into home plate</u> tells more about the verb "slid" (*modifies* "slid") and—as a whole—acts as an adverb telling *where* he slid.

A prepositional phrase can be either in the subject or in the predicate. Example: "The enormous whale *on the horizon* / swam gracefully *toward the ship*."

These lessons go on and on, as they add to the students' arsenals of writing skills and knowledge of the elements of the English language. The Language Arts textbook will provide a basis for appropriate grade level grammar lessons. You will decide how far to go with grammar lessons, depending on the grade level of your students and your assessment of their needs and readiness.

C. Create word bank posters

While doing the brainstorming activities above (i.e., getting suggestions of whatever part of speech is being studied and then writing them on the board), you create **word banks**—a collection of these groups of words. Throughout the process of creating these word banks, transfer all or some of the words from the board onto **posters.** These posters display examples of each part of speech. Students can refer to these posters later when they write sentences.

At the top of the posters, put the definition of the part of speech: "Verbs are action words: *run, build, write, play, scream, throw.*" Select new words to add to the posters each day.

These word banks provide **scaffolding** (supporting students while they are learning new skills) to help those whose vocabularies and spelling skills are low. Displaying posters that define and give a number of examples of the parts of speech help support students while they are learning. The class can add to these posters at any time.

D. Write sentences using what they have learned

Each day, as these lessons progress, ask students to write five sentences using the parts of speech you are teaching that day. They should label
- the **subject** and **predicate** of each of their sentences
- any **objects**
- **all the parts of speech** they have learned so far
- **each new part of speech** as it is taught

They can use words from the word banks or any words that are the focus of that day's lesson. Give them just five-to-ten minutes to write their sentences, and then ask for some of them to volunteer to read a sentence so you can see the extent to which they understand the exercise.

When students complete this assignment, ask them to turn in their papers to your desk. Those who need more time can complete the assignment later, but all papers should be turned in before the end of the day.

As students expand their knowledge of parts of speech by using the sentence-building strategy, they demonstrate this new skill by labeling the parts of speech in the sentences they write. In this way students learn what part of speech each word is playing in their sentences. I have found that employing this technique enables students to learn parts of speech easily and naturally.

Note: Examples of worksheets (from a literature book all students read) I used to help students learn about words and sentences are the **"Banner in the Sky" exercises** in Appendix G (pp. 332-337):

    1) for learning the sentence-building strategy and parts of speech.
    2) for labeling parts of speech and placing words in context.
    3) for vocabulary development.

4. Writing a paragraph

Introduce students to paragraph writing by demonstrating on the white board or the overhead projector. Explain that the paragraph is about one topic (or idea), and that everything in a paragraph should be about that topic.

Begin by explaining the important elements of a good paragraph:

Indenting the first line. You indent the first sentence about one-half inch, so the paragraph (which introduces a new topic) will be clearly set off from the paragraph that precedes it. A paragraph indentation *signals* that the writer is going to introduce a new topic.

Topic sentence. This sentence is the first sentence, and it introduces the topic so the reader will know what the paragraph is about.

Supporting sentences. Supporting sentences give more information about the topic. A strong paragraph will usually have at least two supporting sentences.

Closing sentence. This is the last sentence that concludes (closes) the paragraph.

Then ask them to copy the paragraph below and the labels you use to indicate its elements.

(Indent) (Topic Sentence) The trees looked bare and cold. *(Supporting Sentences)* Their trunks and branches stood out against the rugged rock wall in shades of pink and orange. Leaves from all these trees must have blown away, for there were none to be seen. *(Concluding Sentence)* It would be a long harsh winter for these lonely trees, hidden away in this desert canyon.

Point out that **a paragraph should be at least two or three sentences long,** and reiterate that it should **focus on just one topic**. Even if they have done this before, it is wise to review the elements of a paragraph.

5. Writing descriptive paragraphs—and doing so each day

Five-sentence descriptive paragraphs

To become good writers, students should write every day. Early in the year, once they have learned the basic elements of a paragraph, I ask them to write descriptive paragraphs every day. We continue these daily lessons for several weeks. Eventually I use these exercises a day or two a week.

They really enjoy describing what they see. To help them, I laminate nature photographs from calendars, set one on the chalk ledge, and ask students to write a descriptive paragraph.

The first day I ask them to describe the photo using five sentences. I don't provide a lesson, other than to remind students that they should describe what they see so that it conveys the picture to someone who can't see it. This is when I point out that what they write should **show, not tell**—**show** the details, not just **tell** about what you see: "The trees without leaves are bare and cold" rather than "The trees look as if winter has come." After students have time to write, I ask for a few volunteers to read their paragraphs. On the same day, they turn them in to the **In Basket** on my desk.

Over time, students improve the quality of their writing for the targeted lesson, as well as on their spelling and grammar skills. They seem to be more motivated and involved when the writing lessons focus on their own creations, rather than on exercises from a textbook. I do find the textbooks handy, however, when I want to follow up with a text lesson to test students' grasps of specific skills.

Providing these open-ended, student-centered writing activities, rather than relying on those in the language arts textbook, **allows the teacher to differentiate her writing curriculum.** Students are then able to express themselves at their own levels, rather than be limited by the structure of a textbook lesson. It is just as important to help pull up students as it is to expand the challenges for students who are performing above grade level.

Once the students have the concept of writing a descriptive paragraph, you can then go on to ways to make the sentences more interesting. I create word bank posters, like the example below, to help students to be more descriptive in their writing.

Similes

On the second day of descriptive writing, I explain a simile. "A **simile** is a figure of speech that compares one thing to another using "like" or "as" to make a description more emphatic." For example, "crazy like a fox" or "as brave as a lion."

We brainstorm different similes on the board, using one of the calendar photos. After brainstorming several examples, I ask students to write their five-sentence descriptive paragraphs using at least two similes. After students have time to write, I ask for volunteers to read their paragraphs. As always, paragraphs are due before the end of the day.

Metaphors

On the third day of descriptive writing I explain a **metaphor**, which is a figure of speech that identifies one thing to be the same as another unrelated thing. For example, "The stormy ocean was a beast devouring the shoreline." Or, "The sun was a golden globe, almost blinding us as we walked." As was done with the similes, have the students use metaphors in that day's descriptive writing paragraph, after which you might ask students to volunteer to share their paragraphs.

My students enjoy learning how to use these figures of speech in their writing. They like to create unique similes and metaphors that express their own personal perspectives, and they also are excited about sharing these orally with the rest of the class.

Varying the beginnings of sentences

As descriptive writing lessons progress, I point out how students can **vary the beginnings of sentences so that they are more interesting.** At first, students will usually write sentences that follow a predictable pattern of Article-Adjective-Noun. For example, "The bare trees stood out from the mountain." Brainstorm some ways of varying sentence beginnings.

Use the calendar photo of the day to explore ideas. "Bare-branched trees seem to huddle in the shadow of the mountain behind them." "Speckled flakes of gray dot the darker charcoal-colored rocks." Once this characteristic of students' writing is pointed out to them, they will usually do a better job of varying sentence beginnings. Ask students to volunteer to share examples of their writing before collecting them.

Students seem to appreciate lessons that help them to write more than basic sentences. They quickly move from "The lazy dog sleeps all day," to "Sleeping all day, the lazy dog missed all the fun." It is fun to see them excited about and engaged with their writing.

All of these writing exercised improve students' reading skills as well.

Correcting and grading descriptive-writing paragraphs

I thoroughly correct spelling, grammar, punctuation, capitalization, etc., on all the students' papers, but I evaluate (grade) based only on their use of the target skill taught that day. Depending on the quality and quantity of similes, metaphors, or other features of the students' writing content, I grade using a plus (+), a check (/) or a minus (-). Sometimes I will use a "check plus" or a "check minus."

In the beginning, I use few minus grades—and then only for papers on which very little effort is evident, or ones that are incomplete. I want to encourage students as much as possible with my evaluations, so I write encouraging comments on each paper. I might also make suggestions of how to improve on sentences students have written. I return papers the next day.

When a teacher is grading individual writing papers, it is important not only to reward a student for work well done, but to challenge her to improve her work. When the teacher is determining grades for report cards, however, it is important to evaluate each student based only on the grade level standards.

Students' descriptive-writing folders

Students are expected to keep a collection of all their paragraphs in a Descriptive Writing Folder. Occasionally I ask students to choose a paragraph to rewrite, making the corrections and improvements I suggested on the first drafts. These rewritten paragraphs have to be stapled to the original assignment so that I can easily compare the two for improvements. I usually ask for one rewrite a week.

6. The five-paragraph essay (FPE)

This basic essay is a standard essay form traditionally taught in high school. The Subject A Exam administered to entering college freshman to assess their writing skills uses this standard form.

But there is no reason much younger students shouldn't be taught this form of writing. Students can learn to write a five-paragraph essay as early as third grade. I have routinely taught the FPE to elementary school students with great success. However, I don't usually start teaching the FPE until later in the year.

It's a good idea to point out that the structure of a FPE follows that of a well-constructed paragraph: an introduction, supporting elements, and a conclusion – all about one topic.

The FPE follows a set formula:

The introductory paragraph sets out the main subject of the essay along with three subtopics, providing just a little bit of information about each of these. This paragraph ends with a sentence that provides a transition to the first subtopic paragraph.

The three subtopic paragraphs each use the same form. They begin with a general topic sentence about the subtopic. Then the next four or five sentences provide details about this subtopic. Each paragraph concludes the point, ending with a sentence that provides a transition to the next paragraph.

The concluding paragraph wraps up each of the subtopic paragraphs and concludes the essay.

7. Poetry

Students can learn to write simple poems in the early grades. The following are three kinds I teach. Quite simple in form, they introduce students to the basic elements of poetry. You can find others in any of the many books about writing poetry. These are good sources for learning about **rhyme**, **meter**, and other poetic elements.

Name poems

Students write the letters of their names in capitals in a vertical line (one above the other) on the paper. Each capital letter will be the first letter of a word or phrase that describes the student. For example, for "Tanya" the poem might be: "Tall, Athletic, Natty dresser, Young, Attractive." They might also enjoy working in pairs, writing the words or phrases that describe their partner.

Haiku

Haiku, a traditional Japanese poem, has three lines with five syllables in the first and third lines, and seven syllables in the second line. This form of non-rhyming poetry is often about nature, frequently juxtaposing one element against another.

Limericks

Limericks are traditional Irish poems that I teach before St. Patrick's Day. Kids really enjoy learning this humorous poetic form that emphasizes meter and rhyme.

Poetry books

Students create 20 poems in the styles of poets we have studied in our Poetry Unit and then put them together to make their own poetry books. Their original poems include both rhyming and non-rhyming poems, limericks, haiku, and any other forms they choose to emulate, and I emphasize using metaphors and similes. Their book should also include two poems they have selected to copy from a poetry book.

The following is the set of directions I hand out to the students:

Poetry Book

You will be writing poems to be published in your own personal poetry book. Poems may behand-written or word-processed. I will provide you with blank books in which to write.

Required Poetry Book Contents:
1. Cover design and title
2. Dedication page
3. Table of Contents (title of each poem and page number)
4. 2 poems copied from a poetry collection
5. 20 original illustrated poems using a variety of poetry forms and techniques
   - Topics can be humorous or serious, but should be appropriate.
   - Include rhyming and non-rhyming poems.
   - Use vivid, descriptive language, similes and metaphors.
   - Each poem should be written on a separate page (or pages).
   - Each poem must be accompanied by an illustration or decoration.

Due dates:

Jan. 12—Turn in all poems for editing/revising suggestions no later than Friday, Jan. 12.

Jan. 19—The completed book is due on Friday, January 19.

Be creative, and have fun. Use the classroom poetry resource box, dictionary, thesaurus, and any other personal or library resources available.

---

8. Letter writing

Students should learn the **basic format for a formal letter**, including return address (their address), date, inside address (the address of the person to whom they are sending the letter), greeting/salutation, and closing.

To put this to use, I ask them to write a letter to a relative, such as a grandparent, aunt/uncle, or cousin. I explain that personal letters don't require including return or inside addresses (a format used only for formal business correspondence), but I ask them to do so here for the practice.

After the initial letter-writing assignment I ask students to participate in **pen pal writing** activities. These letter-writing activities are continued through the year. Your students can write to students in another classroom in your school or another school in your district. If you know a teacher in another city, state, or country, you can arrange pen pal writing with those students.

I also ask students to **write letters to fictional characters** in books they are reading, as well as to **real historical figures** from the social studies curriculum.

9. Book reports

As early as third grade, students can learn to write book reports. **These can follow the format of a FPE.** The first paragraph introduces the title, author, setting, main character(s), and plot. The next three or four paragraphs provide details about the setting, characters, and plot of the story. The last paragraph wraps everything up to conclude the report.

Students should be expected to write as many as six-to-eight book reports a year. I introduce them to different literary genres and ask them to write book reports about books they've read. Some of the fictional genres for which I ask students to write book reports are **science fiction, drama, action and adventure, travel, poetry, comics, art, diaries, journals, series, trilogies, fantasies, mysteries, realistic fiction,** and **historical fiction**. I also ask students to write non-fiction reports for an **autobiography**, a **biography**, and a **book about a particular era of history relating to the grade level social studies curriculum**.

Note: In Appendix F are documents useful for book reports: (Previously referenced in Chapter 1 on Reading, they also apply to writing.)

1. **Documents to help students write their book reports (pp. 270-279):**
   "Thinking about my Reading": Fiction Books, Level I."
   "Thinking about my Reading": Fiction Books Level II,"
   "Thinking about My Reading": Informational Books, Level II."
   "Student Book Review"—a form I created for book reports.

2. **Examples of students' book reports (pp. 284-312):**

6th Grade	5th Grade	4th/5th Grade
The Bronze Bow	*The Watsons Go to Birmingham*	*Tuck Everlasting*
The Egypt Game	*The One-Eyed Cat*	
Kokopelli's Flute		

10. Student-authored books

In my district, the head librarian for the elementary schools established the **Student-Authored Book Project** for all the elementary-aged students in the district. This is a wonderful program that encourages creative writing. Students can approach the task from whatever skill level they possess, as it is a project that allows for differentiation among students.

The following shows how you can have students writing books in your class—or how you might introduce the project to your school:

The elements of plot and dramatic structure

In my classroom I take this opportunity to teach the elements of plot and dramatic structure. I begin by discussing the three main conflicts employed in fiction writing: **man against man, man against nature,** and **man against himself**.

The first element of dramatic structure, the **exposition**, introduces important background information about the **setting** and **main character(s).** Then I teach students to create what's called **the rising action**—at least three minor related events, conflicts or obstacles the character(s) have to overcome on their way to solving the overall obstacle/conflict. I explain that the entire **plot** depends on these events to set up the **climax**—the main obstacle or turning point—of the story.

I explain that the **climax** is when the main character(s) overcome the primary obstacle, and ultimately leads to the satisfactory **resolution** of the story. The suspense has been building to the **climax**, the turning point of the story. Following the climax is the **falling action** during which the circumstances of the main character(s) return to normal. The **resolution** of the story comprises events from the falling action to the end of the story itself. Any obstacles or conflicts have been overcome, and the reader senses a relief of tension or anxiety.

Note: A diagram of Dramatic Structure is in Appendix F (see p. 274).

Why students are able to grasp these literary concepts

These ideas may seem too complex for elementary students. However, students can more easily grasp these ideas if the teacher points out and discusses these characteristics in the stories he reads aloud to the entire class, or that the students read on their own in literature discussion groups. By spring, when I teach the Student Authored Book project, students should be ready to use this information to create their own stories.

How students benefit from becoming authors

Once students begin writing, I ask them to turn in sections of their rough drafts as they write. This way I can help support them as they continue to write. I correct spelling, grammar, and punctuation, and I make suggestions about what to expand or add. Students use these ideas as they continue to build their stories. This kind of work is tremendously time consuming for the teacher, but it gives students essential support. When they write their next draft, they incorporate these corrections and ideas.

Once their final draft is complete, I do a thorough editing. Students use these edited final drafts to write the final versions of their stories, and they add illustrations. Students also create hard covers for the stories to complete their books. Inside the front flyleaf, they write a brief summary of what the story is about. On the back flyleaf they write "About the Author." On the back cover of the book they create five brief "Reviews."

In my experience, students write stories that range from six or seven hand-written pages to 40 or more pages, engaging in this project at their own levels. Whether students write a short simple story or a long complex story, they all feel excited by their accomplishments. Further, as they will have written a book just as real writers do, they unconsciously develop a greater appreciation for the books they read. This project has always been a very satisfying endeavor for both my students and me.

11. Integrating writing with social studies topics

Social Studies is a perfect area in which students can work on their writing. It also helps them understand that good writing is not only for writing class, but also for communication in general. It doesn't hurt to let them know that if they learn to write well in all situations, their writing skills will be appreciated by all the other teachers—now, in high school, and in college, and by employers when they are trying to get a job. And the more they write, the easier it will be.

Journal writing

I ask students to write papers using information we are studying in social studies. For example, I ask them to write a journal pretending they are sightseers in ancient Egypt traveling along the Nile River, Pilgrims traveling from England and settling in the New World, or pioneers traveling on the Oregon Trail in that era of our country's history. These are social studies curriculum areas for fourth, fifth, and sixth grades, respectively.

For each assignment, I provide them with outlines indicating what information I want them to include in their journals. Their journals integrate factual content with creative writing.

Report writing

I ask students to write traditional reports about different parts of the social studies curriculum. After I create a list of report topics, students decide what to write about. It is within the context of these reports that I teach how to write **footnotes** and entries in the report's **bibliography**.

Note: The document in Appendix J entitled "Examples of Bibliographic Citations" (p. 347) is what I used when students were writing Social Studies reports to teach them how to cite sources. You will need to point out the elements so they will know how to write a bibliography correctly.

12. Two sets of "Fives" for students to keep in mind when writing

1. The Five Ws: To make sure students include all the necessary details when writing, I teach them to ask themselves the "Five Ws:" Who? What? When? Where? and Why? For example, have they made clear WHO was involved, WHAT happened, WHEN it happened, WHERE it took place, and WHY it happened? You might also add a sixth question, "How" (HOW did it happen?), but "How?" can also be covered by "What?" "When?" or "Where?" In any case, these questions are basic in gathering information or solving problems, and they also apply to clear writing.

2. **The Five Senses:** Also, when they are writing stories, I remind them to think of the five senses: sight, taste, touch, smell, and hearing. Including details about the senses helps bring readers into the story as they have a clearer feeling about what is happening. I suggest you Google "Using the five senses in writing" for excellent examples.

13. Guidelines for parents helping students revise and edit story projects

When students are working on a major writing project such as the Student-Authored Book project, parent involvement is tremendously helpful. The teacher can also be a great help to the parents by sending out a note with the guidelines listed below.

When I write such a note, I further encourage the parents by letting them know how much I appreciate their providing revision and editing assistance on the stories, given what a time-consuming process it is.

Be aware in the first point below that my students always do their work in pencil so they can easily make changes.

1. **The writing tools parents should use when helping a student with his story project:**
   1. When the student is writing a rough draft or revising it, write suggestions and corrections in ink because ink will stand out better from their handwriting.
   2. When a student gives you his final copy, use a pencil so he can make the corrections easily without having to rewrite it.

2. **When revising, focus on the elements of the story. Look for the following:**
   1. Ask questions about story parts that are not clear or that could be clarified by adding detail. Suggest possible solutions.
   2. Look for passages that could be shortened or expanded.
   3. Look for passages that could be made more interesting through the addition of descriptions. Using words that "show" and "paint pictures," rather than "tell" has been one of our goals.
   4. Even fantasies and science fiction stories need to create events that make sense and that are logical within the story's make-believe reality. If a story progresses as an illogical sequence of disjointed events, not held together by a clear context, provide suggestions to help fix the problem.
   5. Each story should develop character and setting descriptions, a plot structure that leads to the climax, and a resolution.

3. **When editing, focus on the writing mechanics of the story. Include the following:**
   1. Write in the correct spelling of misspelled words. Requiring students to correct spelling in a lengthy project is too time consuming and frustrating.
   2. Mark incomplete and run-on sentences. Show what changes will correct the problem. For example, add a missing verb, or break a run-on sentence into two or more shorter sentences.
   3. Provide assistance with capitalization, commas, apostrophes, and ending punctuation.
   4. Paragraphing: Use editing symbol for a new paragraph whenever needed to break up long paragraphs. Editing symbol sheets are in story folders.

5. Dialogue: Each new speaker's words must begin a new paragraph. The proper punctuation for dialogue is as follows:

"Let's go to the store," Kate suggested.

Ben quickly responded, "Please wait until I finish making my list."

If dialogue dominates the story, suggest cutting some dialogue and replacing it with narrative.

Note: In Appendix G (beginning on p. 318) are examples that I prepared for writing instruction:

1. Notes for students, parents, and parent volunteers

"The Elements of the Writing Program for Grades 4, 5, and 6"

"Story Project Revision and Editing Guidelines"

"EDITORS' MARKS" to use when correcting writing

Rubrics used to evaluate students' written work:

"4th GRADE RUBRIC for WRITTEN LANGUAGE"

"5th GRADE RUBRIC for WRITTEN LANGUAGE"

"6th GRADE RUBRIC for WRITTEN LANGUAGE"

2. Notes for parents and parent volunteers

"Parent Volunteer Mini-Workshop"

"Guidelines for Correcting Written Work"

3. Examples of exercises for learning about words and sentences

"Banner in the Sky"—for learning the sentence-building strategy and parts of speech

"Banner in the Sky"—for labeling parts of speech and placing words in context

"Banner in the Sky"—for vocabulary development

4. Example of a student writing assignment

"The Pet" (Weekly Writing I)—an exercise in creative writing (writing a three-paragraph essay from the point of view of a pet).

Summary

Students in my classroom engage in daily writing activities. Reviewing and providing feedback on students' writing is the most demanding and time-consuming element of teaching. But it is also the best way to help students grow their writing skills.

I employ all of the techniques I discussed in this chapter to engage students in writing. I find that engaging them in the writing process, rather than simply asking them to respond to prepared lessons, is very rewarding both for the students and for me. In this way, students learn that their own voices have power. Their writing becomes an expression of who they are, not just of what they are learning.

For Parents

This chapter helps parents to understand the concepts and methods their children are being taught in school. Further, they can effectively use these techniques when they work with their children at home. Within the documents listed above, parents will see examples of the kinds of notes I give to students and parents. These will help them understand what their children are learning about writing.

CHAPTER 3

Handwriting and Computer Skills

Manuscript handwriting instruction used to begin in first grade, but with the advancement of skills to lower levels, in many schools it is now taught in kindergarten. Cursive handwriting, on the other hand, has been abandoned altogether in many school districts, thanks to the wide use of computers, with students using them instead of learning cursive. I believe, however, that students should continue to be taught both manuscript and cursive, as well as computer skills.

1. Manuscript handwriting

Many manuscript-teaching guides are commercially available. Special-lined paper should be used so that students have a guide for the height of different letters. Letters are grouped by common shapes so that instruction proceeds logically from one letter group to another. Students should have daily practice in order to become proficient.

Once students have been taught all of the lower-case and uppercase letters, they should be expected to write these correctly in all their written work. You will need to monitor and correct students' use of manuscript writing regularly to assure that they are held accountable for the correct letterforms.

2. Cursive handwriting

Cursive handwriting instruction used to begin in third grade; now some schools don't teach it at all. I believe these skills should continue to be taught for two main reasons: 1) not *all* work is done on computers, so students should know how to write quickly and legibly; and 2) they also need to be able to *read* cursive writing, not all of which will be well executed. Unless students are taught cursive in school, they are unlikely to pick it up on their own.

Cursive teaching guides are commercially available. Special-lined paper should be used, just as with manuscript writing. As with manuscript writing, students begin by practicing letters with similar forms, and gradually learn to link letters together correctly to form words and phrases. Upper case letters are the last to be taught, as they are the most complicated forms.

As students become proficient, they should be expected to use cursive for all of their written work. If cursive instruction begins in the fall and continues on a daily basis, it should take just a few months for students to become proficient. Even so, you will have to monitor and correct students' use of cursive handwriting in order to hold them accountable for the proper letterforms.

3. Computer skills

Teach computer skills as early as kindergarten

Students should be taught correct keyboarding skills as early as possible. Kindergarten is not too early to begin. Nowadays, even very young children are using keyboards, so the sooner they learn proper keyboarding, the better. Since it is harder to correct bad habits than it is to learn correct keyboarding from scratch, it is important to begin this training in kindergarten.

You can create your own images of the computer keyboard by copying it, duplicating it, and laminating it so that each student can have her own copy for keyboarding practice in the classroom. If you don't want to create your own, there are copies on the Internet you could use.

Students should have their own computers

Some school districts even provide all of their students with laptop computers for use while they are enrolled in their schools. These programs provide equal access to computers so that students who cannot afford their own computers are not left out. If some districts do not have the funds to provide laptops for everyone, perhaps they can at least provide computers for those students who cannot afford their own.

Have students do some homework on the computer

Once students are proficient in using proper keyboarding skills, they should complete some of their written assignments on the computer.

Keep in mind, however, that most word processing programs automatically correct spelling, grammar, punctuation, and capitalization. Therefore, you should teach the students to be on the lookout for such corrections—and to understand why the corrections were made. Using a computer can then not only help with their computer skills, but it can also help them with their overall writing skills.

Summary

It is important that the elementary school curriculum continue to include teaching manuscript and cursive handwriting skills in the early primary grades. Once cursive instruction is complete in third grade, students should be taught computer-keyboarding skills. By fourth grade all students should have achieved competence in manuscript, cursive, and computer writing skills.

For Parents

Parents can support their children in using proper manuscript and cursive handwriting skills. When their children have the use of computers, parents can assist them in mastering proper keyboarding skills as well.

CHAPTER 4

Language Arts and Public Speaking

Presenting information orally to the rest of the class helps students gain confidence in their public speaking skills. I have them do this on at least four occasions during the year. I've already mentioned the first assignment—having students introduce each other at the beginning of the school year. Over the rest of the year, they do public speaking in these other—quite different—exercises. The assignments are generally suitable for students in the fourth through sixth grades.

1. Family histories

The second public speaking assignment is to research their family history, which requires them to interview family members: parents, grandparents, aunts and uncles—anyone from whom they can gather this information. Because some extended family might live a distance away, I start on this early in the year. Each of these presentations will be from three to five minutes long.

Family histories are often considered enjoyable, inspirational and sources of pride. A child whose family may have its origin with the Mayflower will enjoy the exercise. Someone who has recently crossed the border, however, may be reluctant to share. Adopted or foster children face challenges, too. Consider options for children whose family histories may bring more pain than joy. In these cases you can work with them to develop alternatives. This is a delicate topic that can be handled sensitively to meet each child's needs.

Before the interview

Before interviewing, the students brainstorm the kinds of questions they might ask, using *who, what, where, why, when,* and *how* to help remind them of basic information they need. For example, "Who were our first ancestors to come to the United States?" "When did they come here?" "Why/how did they come here?" "What kind of work did they do?" "Where did they first settle?" Some students may be unable to learn information beyond two or three generations, but even in that period they will have plenty to talk about.

Family tree diagrams and rough drafts

Once students complete their interviews, they prepare family tree diagrams and write rough drafts of their oral reports. The format for these presentations will vary, as each student decides what parts of their family history are most interesting to share with the class. After I correct these rough drafts and make suggestions about how students might improve their presentations, they create the final drafts.

They also learn to create note cards on which they write the main ideas of their presentations.

Standards for giving a speech

The next step is for the class to review the standards for speaking in front of their classmates, standards they already established when they began to introduce each other. For example, "Speak loudly and clearly." "Stand still and make eye contract with your audience."

Practice

The students then need to **practice delivering the information orally**. I suggest that they do so at home in front of their family or in front of a mirror. About this time I have them sign up for when they will deliver their family histories.

We hear five or six presentations a day for a week. I evaluate based on the quality of the information in the report and how well they used the presentation standards the students brainstormed.

2. Pretending to be a story character

As a bit of a change to the ordinary book report—and to provide another opportunity to speak before the class—I ask students to **present a book report orally to the class** in which they pretend to be a character from one of the books they have read. These presentations always include the kinds of information required in book reports. But in these oral reports, after stating the title of the book and author, each student will assume the role of the first person narrator. He will even create his own costume for the presentation.

First, students prepare a rough draft of their presentations, following the same book report standards brainstormed earlier in the year. Their oral presentation will be different, however, in that each student decides the *order* in which to present the information about the story's character, setting, and plot. Needless to say, they can be very creative—and I encourage their creativity! Then I correct their drafts and provide suggestions for improvement. And on the day of their presentation, they wear the costume they have prepared.

Just as before, I evaluate based on the quality of the information in the report and of the presentation itself.

3. Reciting poetry

During our unit studying poetry, I ask students to select a poem to memorize and present to the class. They can find a poem in one of the sections of the reading or language arts textbooks, which always contain units on poetry, or in books of poetry in the school and classroom libraries. The poets whose poetry the students seem to like the most are Shel Silverstein, William Blake, and Edgar Allen Poe.

The students should memorize a poem that is at least ten lines long. Other than that, there is no specific requirement. If they like a poem that is too long, I can help them select a section of the poems that could stand alone. Or they can choose to read the rest of the poem, rather than having to memorize it.

Students follow the standards they set for oral presentations, and I grade based on the quality of the content and presentation.

Summary

Providing various opportunities for students to speak to the entire class helps them to gain confidence in themselves and in their public speaking skills. The content of these presentations helps students to get to know each other better. These experiences also reinforce reading and writing skills.

For Parents

It is important for parents to know what their children are expected to do for oral presentations. It would be a big help to their children if they would set aside time at home to support them in rehearsing for presentations they will do in class.

Furthermore, parents can then encourage their children to use the public speaking standards when the family gathers to talk about their day's activities around the dinner table. Family involvement is tremendously significant in reinforcing the importance of activities at school.

CHAPTER 5

Math

Math is a unique element of the elementary curriculum. Like reading, it is an essential foundational skill, but it stands alone as the only element of the curriculum that deals with numerical content and concepts. Fortunately, the teaching of elementary math has vastly improved from the days when I was in elementary school.

Grade level math textbooks provide the content of the math program for each grade. To bolster their math skills, students can go online to find programs that also do that. What *I* find most helpful, however, are readily available in most classrooms—manipulatives (objects students can count and move around) that can greatly help students to visualize math operations.

In this chapter I am simply sharing some of the ideas I have found useful in helping students to learn math skills and understand math concepts.

1. Math vocabulary—even young students can learn proper terms

Although most of my experience is in intermediate grades four through six, I believe that even at the earliest level, students can—and should—learn the true vocabulary of math. I see no reason to dumb it down.

Even first graders can learn the terminology that applies to their level of math. If they can learn the names of dinosaurs, such as Tyrannosaurus Rex and Brontosaurus, they can learn the correct names for parts of equations.

Young students actually enjoy being challenged to learn the accurate terminology that applies to their level of math. Furthermore, the sooner real mathematical vocabulary is introduced, the easier it is for students to begin to understand not only the words, but also the concepts they represent/describe.

For example, I believe that when addition problems are first introduced, they should be called **equations**. The same should be done for subtraction equations.

Other words they should learn:

An **addend** + an **addend** = a **sum**.

A **minuend** - a **subtrahend** = the **difference**.

A **factor** (times) X a **factor** = a **product**.

A **dividend** (divided by) ÷ a **divisor** = a **quotient**.

Make a poster to illustrate these equations.

I discuss other vocabulary as I go through this chapter.

2. Algebra at the primary level

I start teaching algebraic concepts and its vocabulary as early as first grade. For example, when students learn sums, I use the word **equation**: "In the *equation* ___ + 2 = 6, we are solving for the **unknown** number represented by the blank." Since the blank could just as easily be represented by x, I say so: "We will call the blank space, the **unknown**, X."

You can teach even young students to subtract 2 from both sides of the equation to get the **value** of X: _X_ + 2 - 2 = 6 – 2, then X = 4. All of these concepts, and their vocabulary, should be displayed on posters positioned for all to see.

3. Manipulatives

Thank goodness manipulatives are now used commonly in all grades. If I could design them for my classroom, I'd have a set of at least 20 unmarked blocks, 6 decahedron (ten-sided) blocks marked with numerals from 0–9, and 6 octahedron (eight-sided) blocks marked with the signs **+ - ÷ x =** and the signs **≠** (not equal), **>** (greater than) and **<** (less than).

Teachers can use whatever is available to create manipulative sets. Checkers or pennies, for example, can be used to represent the number of items to be added or subtracted, and the signs and numerals can simply be written on squares of paper.

Each student should have her own set of manipulatives to use for "acting out" math problems so she can more easily learn numbers and establish a number sense. For example, children learn to understand the numeral 4 by using and manipulating four of the blocks. Manipulatives are also helpful for learning beginning addition and subtraction equations, both visually and spatially. I know they would have been a great help in my own beginning math education.

Students should be encouraged to use their manipulatives to solve equations when they work on their own. Before long, they will have their number facts so well established that they no longer need to use manipulatives.

4. Numbers and place values

Give each student a two-foot section of **sentence strip** on which to create a **place value chart**. (Depending on the age of your students you may want to make these charts for your students.) Each place value location should be about an inch and a half wide. There should be room for at least 13 places on the chart, including room for commas, a decimal point, and a label for each place value. Cut ten cards, each about an inch and a half wide, that you have labeled with the numerals 0 through 9 for each student.

Draw a horizontal line to indicate each **place** on the line. There should be space for three numeral cards to the right of the **decimal point** (for tenths, hundredths, and thousandths) that marks the division between **whole** and **fractional** numbers. To the left of the decimal point make spaces for 1s, 10s, 100s, 1,000s, 10,000s, 100,000s, and millions.

Put a comma after each three places on the number line to the left of the decimal point. Each three places is called a **period.** These are the **ones period, the thousands period, the millions period,** and so on. Each of the place values should be labeled. Duplicate and laminate the finished **place value charts** so there are enough for every student.

The first period (to the *left* of the decimal point) is the **ones period.**   1,000,000,**000**.000

The second period (to the left of the ones period) is the **thousands period.**   1,000,**000**,000.000

The third period (to the left of the thousands period) is the **millions period.**   1,**000**,000,000.000

These periods continue to the **billions, trillions, and so on.**

To the right of the decimal point, do the same with horizontal lines and label. Label tenths, 100ths, and 1000ths.

Practicing reading numbers in place values

I begin by reading simple numbers, then higher numbers, and asking students to use their number cards to place in the correct place value locations. For example, "1,349 is 1 thousand, 3 hundreds, 4 tens, 9 ones." Be sure not to say *and* unless you are indicating the decimal point. **The term "and" should only be used to indicate the decimal point.**

These exercises should be repeated, with students taking turns to give numbers for the rest of the class to show on their own number lines. Students can also work on these in partners, taking turns being the one to give the numbers and follow the directions. Each time students finish placing the numerals in the proper places, they read the resulting number. In this way they practice placing numerals in the correct place value locations and in reading the resulting numbers.

These exercises should be repeated for 10–15 minutes or so each day for several days, so that students receive enough opportunities to learn these place values and to practice reading the resulting numbers. Numbers should be read into the *millions*. Once decimal places are introduced, include them in the practice as well.

5. Grids

All of the grid activities described below use 10"x10", one-inch-square grid papers usually available to all elementary school teachers.

100s grid

Using 10"x10" (one-inch-square) grid paper, students should fill in the grid with numbers from 1–100, with 10 numbers in each row and column. We use a **base 10** number system made up of **10 digits** from **0–9**. These digits are used to create **numerals** that stand for **numbers.** These grids reinforce students' familiarity with their numbers, and you can begin using them as early as first grade and continue through sixth.

We adults take for granted much about our number system, but students are just learning this. The 100s grid *shows* students how our number system is made up of groups of 10 numbers. The first row shows the numbers from 1–10; the second row shows 11–20. Organizing the numbers from 1–100 on the grid helps students to *visually learn and understand* the relationships among the numbers. Counting is usually the way children first learn their numbers, but counting doesn't teach the *structure* of our number system like the 100s grid does.

Math grids aren't new to elementary classrooms. I just think they should be used more often.

Addition grid

Teach students how to create an addition grid. Use this grid to illustrate all the addition equations from 2 to 10 or 12. Show how these math grids duplicate all the equations for each combination. For example, 2 + 4 = 6 is duplicated with 4 + 2 = 6, so there are only half as many combinations to learn as are shown on the entire grid. Students use these grids to help them memorize these addition equations.

Subtraction grid

Teach students how to create a subtraction grid. Use this grid to illustrate all the subtraction equations from 2 to 10 or 12. Show how the math grid duplicates all the equations for each combination (the same as with the addition grid above) so there are only half as many equations to learn as are shown on the entire grid. Students use this grid to help them memorize subtraction equations.

Multiplication grid

Set up the multiplication grid as you did for the other grids.

Among other reasons this is useful, the multiplication grid can be used to help students memorize the times tables, learn about **square** numbers, count by 2's, 5's, and 10's, and recognize special numbers like the two-digit products of the 9s all adding up to 9.

After my students fill in their multiplication grids from 2 x 2 to 12 x 12, I ask them to draw a red outline around each of the *square* numbers shown along the diagonal of the grid. Then I ask them to fold the paper along this diagonal line. I point out that the products on one side of that line are exactly the same as the products on the other side, so there are really only half as many equations to learn.

Then we circle the products of 2's, 5's, and 10's in different colors to highlight the fact that they can learn these products by counting by these numbers.

Highlighting these characteristics of the multiplication grid helps to show students that **the number of facts they have to memorize isn't so daunting**. I find this always helps to motivate those students who otherwise may feel overwhelmed. All students are then able to view the task of learning their multiplication tables as a task about which they feel more confident.

Times Table - 12x12

	1	2	3	4	5	6	7	8	9	10	11	12
1	**1**	2	3	4	5	6	7	8	9	10	11	12
2	2	**4**	6	8	10	12	14	16	18	20	22	24
3	3	6	**9**	12	15	18	21	24	27	30	33	36
4	4	8	12	**16**	20	24	28	32	36	40	44	48
5	5	10	15	20	**25**	30	35	40	45	50	55	60
6	6	12	18	24	30	**36**	42	48	54	60	66	72
7	7	14	21	28	35	42	**49**	56	63	70	77	84
8	8	16	24	32	40	48	56	**64**	72	80	88	96
9	9	18	27	36	45	54	63	72	**81**	90	99	108
10	10	20	30	40	50	60	70	80	90	**100**	110	120
11	11	22	33	44	55	66	77	88	99	110	**121**	132
12	12	24	36	48	60	72	84	96	108	120	132	**144**

Vaughn Aubuchon at *www.vaughns-1-pagers.com*

Division grid

Use the multiplication grid in reverse to show division. Use the interior number and divide by one of the numbers at the top. The answer is the number on the side. Or divide by one of the numbers on the side. The answer is the number at the top.

Prime number grid

A **prime number**, or **prime**, is **a number that is greater than 1 that has no positive divisors other than 1 and itself.**

When introducing prime numbers, I ask students to fill in a 10"x10"grid with all the numbers from 1–100. Once the grids are filled in, I ask students to find the prime numbers. Do this as a whole class activity. Students will discover that 2 is the only **even prime**, as all other *even* numbers can be divided by 2. Circle the 2 in a colored pencil as the only even prime.

Ask students to identify *other* prime numbers by encircling them with a *different* colored pencil. Then go through the entire chart together circling *all* the prime numbers. They will be able to see how the 2 stands out from the rest.

Identifying prime numbers helps students learn what numbers will never be the products when multiplying factors. This is another way of supporting students' learning of factors and products for the multiplication tables.

6. The "10's Rule" for adding and subtracting

As students begin to learn sums and differences past 10, I introduce what I call the 10's Rule. For example, when presented with the equation 7 + 4 = _____, they can convert the larger of the two addends to 10 by adding 3 from the 4, turning the equation to an easy-to-solve 10 + 1 = 11. They do the same with differences, so that 11 – 4 = ___, becomes 10 – 4 = 6 + 1 = 7. **The 10's rule simplifies all equations with sums and differences greater than 10.**

7. Division

Basic division can be broken down so that students can see <u>dividends as products</u>, and <u>divisors and quotients as factors</u>. Dividing whole numbers should be well established before introducing long division. For example, 12 ÷ 4 = 3. In this equation 12 is the **dividend**, 4 is the **divisor**, and 3 is the **quotient**. Students can see that 4 and 3 are both **factors** and that 12 is the **product**. Using the multiplication grid, as described above under "Division Grid," helps students to learn both their multiplication facts and their division facts.

Long division

Long division is taught so that equations that involve large numbers can be solved. Long division is the process of successively dividing the **divisor** into the **dividend** to get the **quotient.**

The first problems should be fairly simple. The **dividend/product** and its **divisor/factor** are used to find the other **factor** or **quotient.** Then they can subtract the resulting product from the dividend to get the remainder. This will illustrate the first major concept of long division, i.e., that you **divide** the **divisor** successively into the **dividend**, each time recording that **product** under the **dividend** and subtracting it from the original **dividend**. This succession of steps ultimately leads to a **quotient,** and a **remainder** or a **decimal remainder**, if the **dividend** can't be **divided** evenly.

Divide:	$3\overline{)75}$ 3 goes into 7 — 2 times... with some extra!
Multiply:	$3\overline{)75}$ 2 X 3 = 6
Subtract:	$3\overline{)75}$ -6 1
Bring Down:	$3\overline{)75}$ $-6\downarrow$ 15
Repeat:	$3\overline{)75}$ -6 15 -15 0 $15 \div 3 = 5$ $5 \times 3 = 15$

Pinterest.

Long division with decimals

I will discuss decimals later. For now, I just want to mention that the decimal place in the quotient is in the same place as in the dividend.

Long division and mixed numbers

When dividing numbers that solve to a quotient with a **remainder,** teach students how to express the remainder as a **fraction.** Expressing remainders in this way, *rather than as decimals,* results in a **mixed number** quotient.

8. Fractions

These exercises should be repeated for 10–15 minutes or so each day for several days, so that students receive enough opportunities to learn these place values and to practice reading the resulting numbers. Numbers should be read into the *millions*. Once decimal places are introduced, include them in the practice as well.

I begin teaching **fractions** using pie charts. In this way they can be taught sooner than most curricula suggest.

Define **fractions as equal parts of a whole**. A poster should show the definition with examples. Simple examples will be eighths, sixths, fourths, thirds, and halves. Shade in the fractional parts and label them with the corresponding fraction—1/8, 1/6, 1/4, 1/3, 1/2.

Students should be given construction paper pie charts with the above, and other, divisions.

Adding and subtracting fractions

You should provide students with pie charts for different fractional numbers: thirds, fourths, fifths, sixths, etc. Using the pie charts demonstrate for students how to add and subtract fractions.

Write equations on the chalkboard, white board, or overhead projector. Students cut the pie charts apart and manipulate the pieces to show how to solve fractions equations.

The Giant Inch

I have students create a "giant inch" to discover (in an easy-to-work-with form) how an inch is divided into different parts—halves, fourths, eighths, and sixteenths.

Give each student a 12" x 5" piece of white drawing paper. (These are cut from standard pieces of 10" x 12" drawing paper.) Ask students to use their rulers to draw a line across the 12" length of the paper. Then ask them to copy the way the lines are drawn between the end of the ruler and 1". These lines are different lengths to show the fractional divisions of the inch. The line to indicate the ½" is the longest. The lines are progressively shorter to indicate 1/4", 1/8", and 1/16".

Then ask the students to label each of the fractional parts of the ruler. For example, 1/2" is also labeled 2/4, 4/8, and 8/16. All the 1/4" marks are labeled, as well as the 1/8s and 1/16s.

Using the giant inch, students can see the equivalent fractions for a 1" strip. This is a visual way to help students understand **equivalent fractions**.

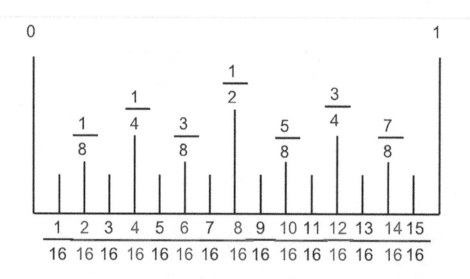

Reducing fractions to their lowest terms

Demonstrate how, by dividing the numerator by itself, and dividing the denominator by the numerator, fractions can be reduced to their lowest terms. Use the number lines to illustrate this.

Students have already labeled equivalent fractions on their Giant Inch and their number lines. Now you can show them how each of the fractions under ½ can be reduced to their lowest terms by dividing denominators by numerators. It is easiest for students to understand this concept, and how it operates, after they have worked with their pie charts and labeled their Giant Inch and number lines.

9. Decimals

Dividing fractions to create decimal numbers

Demonstrate how fractional numbers can be converted to decimal numbers by showing a few examples. For example, show how 1 divided by 2 becomes .50. Ask students to follow what you do by recording it in their Math spiral notebooks. Continue to give examples of a series of fractions converted to decimals while they record your examples in their own spiral notebooks. In this way students learn how to convert fractions to decimals.

Rounding decimals

Demonstrate how to round numbers to a particular place value. Show how decimal numbers of 4 or lower are rounded down, and that numbers of 5 or greater are rounded up. For example, 4.235, rounded to the *ones* place, becomes 4, and that 4.235, rounded to the *hundreds* place, becomes 4.24. Give students experiences rounding numbers to different place values.

Converting a decimal number to a percent

Students in my class first learn how to convert a decimal number to a percent when they are correcting papers. They divide the number of items they got correct by the total number of possible items. For example, when someone gets 18 out of 20 questions correct, they learn that they must divide 18 by 20, which is .9 correct. **To convert a decimal number to a percent,** they must **move the decimal point two places to the right: .9 = 90%** correct.

In this particular example the denominator, 20, is a multiple of 10, so if you reduce the fraction from 18/20 to 9/10 it is easy to see that the result is .9 or 90%.

Similarly, 17 correct out of 20 [17/20] converts to .85—or 85% correct.

Or, 21 correct out of 26 [21/26] converts to **.8077—or 80.77%.** In this case I teach students to round to the nearest whole number, so 80.77% converts to 81%. Therefore, 21 correct out of 26 = 81% correct.

10. Using calculators

Most school districts provide calculators for intermediate grade classrooms (4th-6th grades). Some teachers believe that calculators are a crutch, but I have found that instead they reinforce the learning of number facts—especially times tables and percents, and they give a quick and easy way to auto-correct mistakes. **Calculators help to reinforce learning how to solve equations correctly.**

11. Translating mathematical questions into equations

I teach how to convert sentences, or questions, into equations. I point out how the words of these questions are easily translated into equations: **what** becomes a blank __ or X; **of** translates to the multiplication sign x; and **equals** is obviously the = sign.

The question "25% of 80 equals what?" converts to the equation **.25 x 80 = ___.**
(Remind the students that instead of a ____ to show "what," the **unknown** number, use X.)
.25 x 80 = X.
Multiply .25 x 80 to get X, and X = 20.
Therefore, **.25 x 80 = 20.**

The question "What percent of 60 equals 20?" converts to the equation **X% x 60 = 20** (or __% x 60 = 20).

I explain that in order to get the X (or blank) *alone* on one side of the equation (so that you can solve for the **unknown** number), you have to divide the number next to the blank by itself. But you also have to divide the number on the other side of the = sign by the same number. (If you don't divide by the same number on both sides, the two sides won't be equal!)
In the equation X% x 60 = 20, dividing 60 by itself changes it to 1, so (60/60 = 1), which eliminates it from the left of the = sign. But on the right side you have 20/60, and *that* is what you are going to work with.

X% x 60/60 [1] = 20/60   X% x 1 = 1X%   1X% = X%   X% = 20/60
20/60 (20 divided by 60) =.3333.
Convert .3333 to a percent by moving the decimal point two places to the right, so
.3333 = 33.33%.
Round to the ones place to simplify: 33.33% = 33%. Therefore, X = 33%, or **.33 x 60 = 20.**

And finally, the question "60% of what equals 25?" becomes the equation .60 x X = 25.
Divide both sides of the equation by .60 to get X alone on one side of the equation.
.60/.60 [1] x X = 25/.60
so X = 25/.60.
Then 25/.60 = 41.666

Round to the ones place to simplify: $41.666 = 42$

12. Geometry

Students who are visual/spatial learners will be pleased to be introduced to concepts that address their strengths if they have been struggling with the computational elements of math. These lessons will eventually involve some computation, but this will be scattered among the visual/spatial parts of the lessons. What follows is not comprehensive. Refer to a geometry textbook or manual to get all the information you will need to teach these lessons.

Plane geometry

Provide students with all the basic plane geometry information. Teach them about all the basic shapes: squares, triangles, rectangles, parallelograms, trapezoids, rhombuses, pentagons, hexagons, septagons, octagons, and decagons. Teach students how to use protractors and compasses to measure angles. And teach them basic geometric terms such as parallel, perpendicular, right angles, acute angles, and obtuse angles. These are all important lessons that most students will enjoy.

Solid geometry

Solid geometry is the study of three-dimensional shapes such as spheres, cubes, blocks, pyramids, and tetrahedrons. Teach your students the characteristics of these and other solid geometric shapes. My students always enjoyed learning about them, and they especially liked using construction paper to build models of some of the geometic shapes, after which they learned how to calculate their volume.

13. Graphing

Another area of the math curriculum that appeals to visual/spatial-talented students is graphing. I often used the following to make sure everyone in the class understands the concepts.

Give your students graph paper and have them draw and label the X-axis horizontally across the middle of the paper, then draw and label the Y-axis vertically through the middle of the paper. They should label the intersection of these two axes with zero-0.

To the right of the zero, have them label the numbers for each of the next grid lines 1, 2, 3, 4, and so on to the edge of the paper; and above the zero and the horizontal axis, have them label the vertical axis the same way. They should then label the remaining two axes with negative numbers: -1, -2, -3, etc.

Last, they need to label each of the four quadrants. Starting at the top right, label that quadrant 1. Then proceed clockwise to label quadrants 2, 3, and 4.

Once students have created these grids, you can teach them to graph coordinates. Coordinates are always written as (x, y). Therefore, the first coordinate is the location on the X axis, and the second is the location on the Y axis. Where these two meet is the location to be marked. When X and Y are both positive, it will be in the first quadrant. When X is positive and Y is negative, it will be in the second quadrant. When X and Y are both negative, it will be in the third quadrant. And, when X is negative and Y is positive, it will be in the fourth quadrant.

After students are comfortable graphing specific coordinates, you can teach them to graph algebraic equations. If you are unfamiliar with the process, you can learn how to teach this by using either the math textbook or a supplementary resource about graphing equations.

14. Teach problem solving strategies

Learning problem-solving strategies is an important part of studying math. Ask students to consider the following as they try to figure out the answers:
- Look for the important words in the question.
- Look for a pattern.
- Try an easier problem following the same pattern.
- Work backwards: try an answer and see if it works.
- Draw a picture of the problem.
- Create a table or chart based on the problem's elements.
- Make a model of the problem.
- Think logically.

Learning various approaches helps students to become better at solving problems.

Note: In Appendix H (pp. 339-340), I included the following examples of math activities to show how I ask students to demonstrate their understanding of math:
1. A house-design project
2. A math concept review

Make sure they tie in such projects with why it is they have to learn math in the first place.

Summary

Most of the ideas I share here are about helping to make math more visual and conceptual, rather than primarily a matter of rote memorization. In my experience, involving students in creating their own materials helps them to better understand concepts as they are presented.

Instead of listening and watching the teacher write numbers on the whiteboard/chalkboard or overhead projector, students are engaged with the immediacy of their own materials right in front of them. They are demonstrating their understanding of what the teacher is presenting by following her directions as they create their own pie charts, number lines, and other materials.

Using manipulatives is an integral part of making math concepts more concrete and less abstract. Posters that illustrate the various math vocabulary and operations help reinforce students' learning. These kinds of activities help engage all of the students' learning modalities, not just memorization.

For Parents

The information about math activities in this chapter can help parents know how to support and reinforce their children's math learning. The chapter also may contain material some parents didn't learn—or might have forgotten! Understanding the approaches the teacher uses in the classroom helps parents be more effective in helping their children. That is why this book is as much for *engaged parents* as it is for *conscious teachers*.

CHAPTER 6

Social Studies

Social studies is an important content-based area of the elementary curriculum, and it is an area of the curriculum that can easily be integrated with reading and writing. Students learn about social studies topics when reading both fiction and non-fiction literature books. And they write about social studies subjects in a traditional report format, as well as when writing journals pretending to be people who lived during different historical periods. The primary resource for teaching social studies is the textbook, which contains all the grade level topics students should learn about.

1. Using the social studies textbook

Each grade level is provided with a social studies textbook with a specific curriculum subject matter to be taught. For example, in California the fourth grade social studies subject is California history and geography. Publishers are expected to create these textbooks at the reading level for that grade. However, so many students are reading below grade level that it doesn't work to ask students to read this material by themselves. I handle this in a variety of ways so that students of *all reading levels* have access to the information in their grade level textbook.

Whole-class oral reading

Probably the most common way to enable all students to have access to information in a textbook is to read and discuss the text orally with the entire class. Sometimes I read while the students follow along, and sometimes I ask students to volunteer to read to the class. As the text is read aloud, either I pause, or I ask the student to stop, at which time we talk about the main idea(s) or main points being made in the text. If a student is doing the reading, I support him by paraphrasing the main ideas from the textbook.

Outlining

An excellent time to teach students how to outline is while reading the textbook together as a class. Using the overhead projector, I demonstrate how to convert the information in the text's paragraphs into an outline. As we read, I ask students to identify specific facts or ideas that are important enough to put into the outline under the headings. My students are then expected to copy the outline into their Social Studies spiral notebooks. Once they have had outlining modeled for them, they usually are able to outline on their own or with partners.

Small-group oral reading

After teaching the whole class how to read, discuss, and outline information from the textbook through modeling these activities, I break the class into small groups to do the same thing. The amount of time it takes to make the transition from whole class to small group oral reading varies from class to class, as it is important that each small group be made up of a diverse cross-section of students in the class—from above to below grade level performers. The numbers of above-grade-level readers will determine the number of small groups. In a class of 30 the optimum number of small groups would be five or six.

I assign each small group a section of the chapter to read, discuss, and outline, and then allow time for all the groups to complete this assignment. While they are doing this, I circulate among the groups to assist and support where needed. I also monitor the timing of the groups so that they all try to complete the task in the time allowed. Supporting the students in this way helps them become autonomous in their approach to the assigned reading.

Small group presentations to the whole class

Once the small groups have completed reading, discussing, and outlining their assigned part of a chapter, the students discuss how they will present their information to the whole class. One member of the small group will use the overhead projector to show the rest of the class the main points made in that section of the text. Others in the group will present the main ideas of the text. Some may summarize the main ideas in their own words, while others may read from the text to illustrate the main ideas.

The group will decide what role each member feels comfortable playing, but I expect each member of the group to participate. If a student does not feel comfortable, however, that is okay. Over time, everyone in the class usually finds a role she is willing and able to play.

The amount of time it will take to complete these activities will vary from chapter to chapter in the book and from time to time throughout the year. As time goes by, however, students will be expected to complete these tasks in shorter and shorter times. Usually it will take at least three class periods to read, discuss, and outline a section of a chapter; to plan how the chapter will be presented to the class and to prepare that presentation; and to present the information to the rest of the class. I continue this process until students demonstrate that they can complete outlines independently, in partners, or with a small group.

I usually prepare supplementary information about the chapter. This may include any number of possibilities—from emphasizing vocabulary words to using word-search puzzles, map exercises, or fill-in-the-blank, knowledge-based worksheets related to the chapter. Most textbooks provide a variety of these supplementary exercises; but when they do not, the teacher should create them.

Presenting chapter reading and group work in this way provides students working *below* grade level with the kind of support (scaffolding) they need, while providing students working *above* grade level with opportunities to express their unique abilities. This entire process involves *all* students in reading, writing, speaking, and listening, and each student is encouraged and supported while participating in all phases of the task at a level with which she feels comfortable.

Reading and outlining the chapter independently

At some point in this process, some students will prefer to read and outline the chapter by themselves rather than in a group. It is up to you to decide when to introduce this option. You may decide to wait until the first student asks for this option, though your decision will depend upon how many students are ready to continue this work independently. You might decide to give all of these students a section of the next chapter to outline independently before letting them continue in this way. It would probably be best if at least *half* the students in the class were prepared to work on their own

Then you have to decide if there are enough students left who are capable of leading the small groups that will continue. Some of the more able students are likely to want to continue with the small groups because they prefer to have social contact with their classmates. Depending upon the number of students still working in small groups and their skill levels, you may be required to lead one of the small groups.

The motivation for some students to decide to read and outline independently is that this way they can complete the work more quickly and will, thus, have more time to work on something of their own choosing. Seeing this option, other students may be motivated to work harder so that they, too, will be free to work on something they would prefer to do. These kinds of teaching strategies, therefore, show all students how to take advantage of opportunities to work on tasks they most enjoy.

Testing on social studies text content

At the end of a chapter or unit, students take a test to see how well they have mastered the information. Most textbooks include chapter tests with their materials. Occasionally I make up my own test, combining **true/false, multiple choice, fill-in-the-blank,** and **short written answers**. Regarding the latter, I usually include a choice of questions to be answered in a paragraph.

Note: In Appendix J (starting on p. 341) are the following:
- Two examples of tests I used:
    Mesopotamia—test key and test
    Ancient Greeks—unit test key
- Two examples of sixth grade students' responses to tests:
    Early Humans
    Archaeology

2. Using literature books

I use both fiction and non-fiction individual literature books to supplement the social studies textbook. **Novels** related to the social studies topics provide an excellent way to immerse students in the historical period they are studying. **Non-fiction books** about historical characters and content can contribute a deeper understanding of these topics than what is presented in the textbook. Students enjoy reading these books as an alternative or supplement to the text.

Note: The Literature List for 4th, 5th, and 6th Grades appears in Appendix F (pp. 313-317). I have included fiction and non-fiction titles that integrate with the Social Studies curriculum at each grade level.

3. Special projects

Five-paragraph essay on a social studies topic

Near the beginning of the year **when my sixth graders study Early Humans**, I divide them into groups and give them materials about Homo habilis, Homo erectus, Neanderthal, Cro-Magnon, and Homo sapiens. These materials tell about each of these early humans, where/when they lived, and other characteristics. They read these materials together in small groups, and use the content to write the first five-paragraph essays of the year.

I model how to write the introductory paragraph that tells what will be in each subtopic paragraph. Then I show how each subtopic paragraph gives the details about where they lived, food, shelter, or other characteristics. I show how the last paragraph concludes with a summary of the information in the subtopic paragraphs.

Journals

At least once a year I include a special project that asks students to write a journal while playing the role of a person from the historical period we are studying. Students write journals in fourth grade about following the Oregon Trail; in fifth grade about living during colonial times; and in sixth grade about traveling among the sites along the Nile in ancient Egypt. They **learn to use first person narrative** to write about their experiences as if they had lived during the historic period they are studying. These journals integrate factual knowledge about the period they are studying with creative writing.

Research papers

Students also do traditional research projects on a topic of their choice from the social studies curriculum. They turn in outlines of their research papers; they learn how to use footnotes and bibliographies to show the sources of research information; and—through these research projects—they continue to work on writing well-organized papers. Research papers help them with their spelling and other language arts skills. I thoroughly correct all students' outlines, rough drafts, and final reports.

Note: Examples of Social Studies activities I prepared for my students are in Appendix J (see p. 341):

"Native Americans Long Term Project."

"Early Humans Research and Report" note that goes home to parents explaining expectations for research report.

Letter to students and parents reviewing instructions for the Early Humans Research and Report— to guide them as they complete their project.

Country Report—Directions for report.

Two examples of student responses to questions about Early Humans and Archaeology units.

Bibliographies—two examples illustrating how to create bibliographic references.

Summary

Social Studies is a major area of the curriculum that is largely textbook-dependent. The textbook contains all the content required by each grade level, and I use it in ways that help students who may not be able to read it independently. Many students, however, also enjoy being able to read novels and non-fiction stories about the people, places, and events of the historical period they are studying.

Whenever possible, I also integrate the social studies curriculum with activities such as learning how to do outlines, cooperative work in small groups, and practice in oral presentations, as well as with writing exercises through five-paragraph essays, journaling, and research papers.

For Parents

The content information and the kinds of activities students are assigned to do for social studies may be as new to parents as they are to their children. This is an excellent opportunity for real dialogue with one's child, asking about what is being taught, really listening, and then learning from him, i.e., let the child teach the parent.

A parent who shows genuine curiosity may encourage the child to articulate what he has been learning; and when the child has trouble explaining what he's learning, he will go back to clarify what he is supposed to know. Such talks could be the basis for interesting dinnertime conversations—as well as for clarifying some of the concepts the students are learning.

CHAPTER 7
Science

My school had a special teacher for science, so I didn't teach it. For those teachers who *do* teach science, I would suggest techniques similar to what I used for integrating Social Studies with the rest of the curriculum.

CHAPTER 8
The Arts

Once a week, I present a different art activity to my students. It is important to add art lessons to expose the students to different art mediums, but it also gives them a break in the academic program. My lessons progress from simple drawing to more complex lessons, most using standard art materials available in any classroom.

1. Drawing and painting

Contour drawing

I ask students to draw one of their shoes using a pencil on a 10" x 12" drawing paper using contour drawing. This technique requires them to begin by drawing a continuous line to complete the *outline* (or contour) of an object. They should keep their eyes on the shoes while drawing this outline, as focusing on the lines of the shoe, rather than on the drawing itself, results in a more accurate drawing.

Once students complete the exterior contours of their shoe, they can fill in the interior details. Amazingly, the result is a very accurate rendering of the shoe. This technique is surprisingly successful in showing all the students that they can create an accurate drawing of an object—even those who lack confidence in their artistic skills.

Self-portraits

Drawing self-portraits is an interesting exercise in learning to draw a face, and the students will be amazed at what happens when they follow the required steps.

But first, if you don't feel confident about carrying out the steps I outline below, either 1) find a basic drawing book with a detailed illustration of the steps necessary to create the self-portrait, or 2) look online for a tutorial that uses the following basic technique.

Also, ask the students to bring a small mirror from home so they can actually study themselves as they are drawing.

To begin, students can use a 10" x 12" sheet of drawing paper or a standard 8½" x 11" sheet of paper. Have them fold it four times into sixteenths to create sixteen equal-sized sections (four columns of four squares). In the top half of the page, *lightly* draw a horizontal line (across the page) half way between the top fold and the center-fold; do the same on the bottom half (between the center-fold and the bottom fold).

These are the instructions I give them:

The head. Draw an oval for the head, with the top of the oval starting in the middle of the top fold, following around on the right to the vertical fold, down to the middle of the bottom fold, and up again on the left through the opposite vertical fold, to the starting place in the middle of the top fold.

The eyes. On the horizontal crease across the middle of the paper, inside the oval, *lightly* draw four dots, so you have *five equidistant spaces*. On the 2nd and 4th spaces (between dots), draw ovals for eyes, leaving a space between the eyes and a space on either side of the eyes. They may add eyelids if they like.

The nose and eyebrows. Draw the bottom of the **nose** on the line below the centerfold: it will be as wide as the inside-corner of each eye; and as you go up (drawing the nose), it will be narrower between the eyes. **Eyebrows** are the continuation of an arc from the top of the nose, but you do not actually keep a line between the upper nose and the eyebrows. Remember to draw what *your* eyebrows look like, as everyone's eyebrows are different.

The lips and ears. Draw the **lips** halfway between the bottom of the nose and the bottom of the oval, and they are as wide as the distance between the eye pupils. The **ears** are roughly between the eyebrows and the bottom of the nose.

The hairline is at the line above the centerfold, and some hair will be in front of the ears.

The neck and shoulders. Draw the **neck** starting below the ears on a line down from the outside corners of the eyes. The neck curves down into the shoulders, which are as wide as the paper.

Then personalize your self-portrait. Add a **hairstyle**. Draw the **collar or neckline** and **top of the clothing** you are wearing (or what you *wish* you were wearing). Use colored pencils to fill in the color of the eyes, hair, skin tone, and clothing.

Watercolor painting

We first talk about color itself—which are the primary colors, and how mixing them creates secondary colors, then ever new and different hues. It can be helpful to have a color wheel or to have the students create their *own* color wheels. I teach them how the depth of color is changed by using less water or by adding more. Eventually, I teach how the juxtaposition of various colors intensifies or mutes their effects.

Throughout the year I provide students with a variety of watercolor painting activities. When learning about colors, they paint various examples, or they can paint their own drawings, like the sunflowers in their van Gogh sunflowers below. But once they have a better understanding of how to use watercolors, they do activities such as, for example, painting a sketch of a vase of flowers I place in the front of the room, or what they envision would be a beautiful sunset.

I use a basic watercolor book to help me with these lessons and suggest you do the same for further guidance in teaching watercolors.

Copy the style of well-known artists

My school library has large color prints of art/paintings of famous artists. I use these to teach about artists as well as to ask students to copy their styles.

Vincent van Gogh's sunflowers. I first place a large painting of Van Gogh's "Sunflowers" at the front of the room where everyone can easily see it. On a 10" x 12" piece of white drawing paper, they first sketch the flowers, using the contour drawing technique, then paint their copy with water colors.

Matisse's cut paper collages. Select a Matisse example that shows his cut-paper collage designs. Provide 10" x 12" white paper, a variety of 6" x 10" colored construction paper options, and rubber cement or white glue. After presenting a lesson about Matisse's art, ask students to create similar original designs of their own.

One of the techniques I present is how to cut the paper in shapes so that each cut "echoes" the cut before. Students should use all of the colored paper so no pieces are left over.

Braque's collages. Select a Braque example that uses cut paper to make collages. Provide 10" x 12" white drawing paper, black marking pens, glue, and magazines. After discussing the characteristics of one of Braque's collages, ask the student to create original similar designs by cutting and pasting from the magazines. Once the glue dries, have the students use a black marking pen to draw over the collage like Braque did on his collages.

Picasso's Cubist paintings. Select an example of one of Picasso's cubist portraits. Provide 10" x 12" white drawing paper and a set of colored marking pens. After discussing the elements of Picasso's cubist portraits, ask students to create their own example of a portrait in this style.

2. Drama

I discovered a book called *Shake Hands With Shakespeare*, by Albert Cullum. It includes several of Shakespeare's classic plays, maintaining his original dialogue, but cut to lengths that make them more manageable for children to perform.

The spring of each year, I ask my fourth, fifth, or sixth graders to perform a play. They have performed *Hamlet, Macbeth, King Lear, Julius Caesar*, and *A Midsummer Night's Dream*. Each production was developed in the following way:

Scripts

I ask a parent to type up a copy of the script and to reproduce and bind enough copies for each student.

Before we begin to read the script, I ask several students to take a classroom dictionary to their desks so we can periodically use them to look up difficult vocabulary words. I then ask students to volunteer to read aloud, and the whole class works on reading the script together. We stop to discuss the action in each scene.

Preparing for auditions

I ask for several volunteers to stand in front of the class and read a scene, as I like to have students take turns participating. During these readings we work on **volume, enunciation, pronunciation, inflection,** and **emphasis** as students read the lines. I ask several different students to read the same parts of the same act of the play so I can get a feel for which students might best play which part. We continue to discuss the meaning of the scenes, and I encourage students to ask questions, both of me and of the students playing the parts.

Students take scripts home to prepare for auditions. They turn in papers indicating, in order, their preferences for the parts for which they want to audition. In this way I know how many parts each student is interested in, and I can figure which role I think will be the best for each student—even if it isn't his/her first choice.

Auditions

I ask students to bring their scripts to the front of the class to use when auditioning. I don't expect students to memorize lines for these auditions, but some students do. Everyone who wants to audition for a part is asked to read from the same scene or act. I audition the main characters first and then go on to audition secondary characters. I don't always choose the student with the best audition to play a part (and I am careful to let the students know this). I take into consideration other factors, such as who needs a boost by playing a particular character, even though his/her audition isn't the absolute best.

As soon as everyone trying out for a main character has auditioned, I make my choices. Students then readjust to try out for other parts. We go through this audition process until I have selected students to play every part. I also assign understudies for each part.

Select students for off-stage roles

I explain that students who do not have acting parts may apply for off-stage responsibilities. These are the stage manager, stage hands, head prompter, prompters, set designers, costume designers, and others. Understudies are chosen from among these students.

Rehearsals

There are two venues for rehearsing. They are used in this order:

In the classroom. I ask students to take their scripts home to memorize in preparation for rehearsals. The first rehearsals take place at the front of the classroom. The rest of the class can work on class assignments, read silently, or watch the rehearsals. As these rehearsals progress, we discuss **facial expressions**, **gestures**, and **actions** that go with the dialogue. I use these rehearsals to help me map out the actors' movements for when we go on the stage.

On the stage. Once I determine that rehearsals have progressed far enough that we need to use the stage, we move to the auditorium. I will use my diagrams to direct characters on, off, and around the stage. By this rehearsal, actors are expected to have their parts fully memorized. I ask students to rehearse different acts of the play on different days, so that each of our stage rehearsals does not take longer than 30 to 40 minutes.

Sets

My class keeps sets simple and to a minimum. We have sometimes created a large backdrop by painting on butcher paper or large slabs of cardboard. If we need a forest, we may have two or three painted trees standing up on cardboard. If we are in a castle, we may have a backdrop of painted stone walls or a stack of painted blocks. I remember for a production of *Hamlet,* we hung a curtain from a rod supported by block walls for the scene when Polonius is stabbed to death.

Costumes

Most characters create their own costumes, with advice from the costume students. Other students share items they have that help with completing costumes. When necessary, some parents may assist in making elements of costumes. When we did *A Midsummer Night's Dream*, the donkey's head was made out of paper-maché.

Dress rehearsals

Our final rehearsals are done with full stage settings and characters in costumes. We work out any wrinkles in our production and made sure each character has mastered his/her lines.

Programs

I prepare a program for each of our plays, listing each act and noting the role each student plays, from on stage roles to behind the scenes workers.

Note: An example of a program from a production of *A Midsummer Night's Dream* is in Appendix K (p. 358-359). The pages, reduced to fit here, were originally done on one sheet of 8½" by 11" paper that was then folded.

Performances

We invite other classes at our school to two daytime performances, and we hold an evening performance for parents and families.

3. Music

I have no musical talents; I cannot carry a tune, nor can I play any instruments. For music in my classroom, I have relied on records, cassette tapes, and CDs. I have also employed the musical talents of some students. Though my students haven't learned some things a teacher with musical abilities might have taught, they did learn that even those without musical talent can learn to appreciate music!

The following are some of the music activities I have done with my students:

Singing along with an autoharp

In my early teaching years, I used an autoharp to strum the tunes as the kids sang along from a music textbook. I learned to play it, and several of my students already knew how to play it as well. I don't even know if autoharps are used anymore, but that is something to think about if you want to try something students really enjoy.

Using records, tapes, and CDs

Students enjoy singing along to popular recordings, especially learning the songs of the current top singers and bands. When the Beatles were popular, my students loved to sing "We All Live in a Yellow Submarine." Some students who enjoyed singing together would practice in duos or groups, then perform for the class. These experiences were fun and relaxing interludes from the regular classroom routines.

Using students as performers

Many students are accomplished musicians who enjoy bringing their instruments to school, telling about them, and playing a tune or two. The classroom is a comfortable place for students to share their musical talents with their classmates.

Using CDs of classical composers

I use CDs of classical composers as background music during art activities. From time to time during the activity, I talk about the composer, give some of his background, and perhaps play another of his well-known compositions. It's amazing how later they will identify some compositions that they heard and discussed in the classroom.

Summary

I find that students really enjoy these art activities. They learn specific art skills, as well as information about artists in a way that is accessible to them. Sometimes I have been able to show several slides of an artist's work before our class lesson, and on our classroom world map we locate where the artist is from. Students who felt they had always lacked artistic ability gained considerable confidence after using the contour drawing method to draw their own shoes. It is always gratifying to see students feel good about themselves as artists.

And as for the plays, each year I run into students who recall their experiences producing a Shakespeare play as one of the highlights of their elementary years. They tell me how much they enjoyed their participation—including both the boy who played *Macbeth* and, in *Julius Caesar,* the young woman who played Cassius. Theirs were memorable performances, even from 30 years before. I can't recommend this endeavor for students highly enough, and it was a profoundly satisfying experience for me as well.

Even though I have no musical talents, I figured out ways to bring music into the classroom. Others can use these ideas as well. Using popular recordings with which the students can sing along is an easy strategy. Listening to classical music as a background to doing art activities is also an easy way to include music. And talented students enjoy teaching their fellow students about the instruments they are learning to play.

For Parents

Parent involvement in dramatic arts activities is especially important. I rely on parents to help with costumes and sets, as well as to assist with performances. Not all parents are available during the school day, but most parents can help their children rehearse at home. Information in this chapter helps parents learn what they can do to support their children.

CHAPTER 9
Physical Education (PE)

Physical education (PE) is an area of the curriculum that may be easy to short change, but it is important to put careful planning into how it is taught. Every school, neighborhood, or teacher may have favorite games and sports, but there are some basic elements that should be a part of every classroom's PE period.

1. Physical fitness and learning PE skills

Endurance running

I begin almost every PE period having the class run around the field. For most schools, this is the perimeter of the playground. I use a stopwatch to time how fast the class can run one lap around the playground, then record the date, the time in which the first runner finished, and the time in which the last runner finished. I also write these times, not only in the PE section of my class record book, but also on the whiteboard/chalkboard. As the class improves its speed for first and last finishers, I keep the fastest times recorded on the board. Using the stopwatch seems to help motivate students to pick up their pace. This daily running activity contributes to everyone's fitness.

Relay races

I divide the class into relay teams so that I can try to balance skill levels on all the teams. Five teams of six students each usually works well. There are all kinds of relay activities you can ask students to do, such as running, jumping, skipping, and hopping, that don't require any equipment. Over the years, I've found that many students haven't ever learned to skip, and this is a great time to teach it.

More complicated relays involve throwing beanbags, balancing something on their heads, and running an obstacle course around plastic cones—plus ideas the students think up. Relay races are a fun and creative way to build coordination skills, physical fitness, and team spirit.

Round-robin activities

Round-robin is a series of activities through which teams rotate. For example, I might set up four or five stations from among the following: tetherball, foursquare, two-square, the horizontal ladder, tossing back and forth a softball, kickball or basketball, pitching and kicking the kickball, pitching and batting the softball, throwing baskets, guarding and throwing baskets, dribbling a specified distance, chin-ups, sit-ups, pushups, and running the obstacle course through the play structure. You and your students will have fun thinking of activities that can be learned/practiced in this way.

For round-robin activities, I choose the teams so that students on the team have very similar skills. In this way, each team's members are fairly evenly matched. So when they play each of the games, there isn't a big difference in the ability levels among the students on that team. The reason for this is analogous to why I group students by reading levels—so they aren't embarrassed about their skill levels.

I assign each preselected team a starting place and tell everyone the order by which they will rotate through the activities. Depending on how long the period is and how many stations are set up, I decide on how long teams will stay at the stations. If I have a thirty-five-minute PE period and five activities, I set my timer to rotate every seven minutes.

Organizing teams in this way allows students to improve their skills while competing with other students at similar ability levels so that no particular students can dominate. Students who are less physically able appreciate being able to build their skills while competing with classmates at their own level.

2. Sportsmanship

In addition to developing physical fitness and PE skills for games and sports, students learn sportsmanship during the PE period. There is nothing unique about what I teach about sportsmanship. In addition to the climate of respect that is already a part of our classroom environment, I teach students to be supportive of each other during competitive PE activities. For example, when students make mistakes, get tagged out, or slow their team down, I emphasize that classmates should be encouraging, not discouraging. They should say "Nice try" or "Better luck next time." There is no place for behavior that puts students down in the PE period any more than there is in the classroom.

3. Group PE

One day a week, all the teachers of the same grade level at my school planned for a PE period at the same time. We regroup our classes so that there are students from each classroom on the same teams. In this way, we provide opportunities for all the students of our grade level to get to know one another. We believe that mixing the students adds a positive dimension to our grade-level activities.

4. Games and sports

At the schools where I taught, students played all the standard games and sports. They played games such as kickball and dodge ball, as well as sports such as softball, soccer, volleyball, and basketball. Each school and area of the country has its own favorite games and sports that students play during PE periods. The activities described in numbers 1–3 above are intended to improve students' fitness and skills so they are better prepared for any of the games or sports that make up their school's PE programs.

Summary

Each classroom's PE period should be a time when students have an opportunity to improve their PE skills and physical fitness, while they play any of the games and sports that are standard at their schools.

For Parents

PE is an area of the curriculum in which parents are already involved, such as with Little League, soccer, and other children's sports activities in their communities. Many of the activities described here would be fun for families to do on weekends. The section on sportsmanship helps to remind parents of ways their children need to be treated and how they should treat others.

Part VI
Teaching Gifted Students

CHAPTER 1

Teaching Gifted Students in a Self-Contained Class

1. Understanding gifted students

How I learned about teaching gifted students

My main teaching experience took place in Davis, California, which has had classes for gifted children since the 1960s. The program began with just one class, but by the early 80s it had grown to two combination classes (a three/four and a five/six). When I started teaching in the program in 1983, it became three self-contained, gifted classes for grades four, five, and six, all at one elementary school. Then, in the late 1980s, California provided state funding to local school districts for gifted classes, and that is when the Gifted and Talented Education (GATE) program began.

In the early years of gifted classes, the students in the class were usually ones recommended by parents and teachers. To acquaint families with the program, the school began holding a Parent Night in the spring of students' third grade year, with students welcome to attend. Ultimately, state funding for GATE allowed the district to test all third graders each spring to identify gifted students. This universal testing meant many more gifted students were identified. Some parents of students who tested into the program decided to keep their children at their neighborhood schools, but that didn't happen as much after the program expanded to more schools.

I taught the fourth grade gifted class from 1983-91.

There are huge differences among gifted students in a class

What struck me the most about my gifted classes was that although all the students had been tested as gifted, the range of abilities among them was huge.

To begin with, their IQ scores ranged from 130 to as high as 180. But there were other major differences. Some students were highly motivated; others seemed to lack any motivation at all. Some students showed advanced skills in reading and writing; others showed advanced skills in math. So even though all

176

the students were highly intelligent, their needs were also very diverse. I quickly realized that a differentiated curriculum was critical if they were to be challenged as individuals.

In fact, the span of abilities in my GATE classes was at least as wide—and sometimes wider—than in classes I had taught in the neighborhood classrooms. I had developed my own methods for addressing different needs in the regular classroom, and now I needed to do the same thing, but even more so, with my GATE class.

Teaching gifted students was a tremendous learning experience for me. It was through teaching this class that I learned to do the kinds of curriculum differentiation I describe in each of the subject areas of this book. I enjoyed the challenge, and this experience vastly improved my skills in teaching students with a wide range of abilities.

What makes a student gifted

The main characteristic that makes students gifted is that they have a *high potential for learning rapidly*—much faster than the average student. This fact is critical for understanding why the gifted benefit from being taught in a specialized, self-contained, program. It is also critical to note that gifted children fall within the category of "**special needs**" students. So in order to properly engage and support them in learning, these students **need** specialized approaches and programs.

Since gifted students are so quick to learn, meeting their needs in a regular classroom setting can be extremely challenging. And when teachers have several gifted students in a regular class (bright students whose needs vary greatly, but who can learn faster than the rest of the class), a teacher can be overwhelmed and severely challenged! That is why it is better for both students and teachers to have the gifted students taught in their own separate classroom if at all possible.

The fact that gifted students have this potential for learning rapidly is often not understood, and conversations about GATE focus too much on *achievement* and not enough on *learning styles*. Yes, gifted students are frequently high achievers, but so are many motivated regular students who work hard. Gifted students, by contrast, become high achievers *because* they are rapid learners.

Research about the characteristics of gifted learners

To understand the need for special programs for gifted students, it helps to be familiar with the research done on the subject. Researchers generally agree that gifted children are developmentally and cognitively different from the general population. And as a result, they have different educational needs.

The following research findings explain why gifted children need to be identified and provided with differentiated programs to meet their unique needs:

Susan Winebrenner[4] (2000) argues that gifted students learn differently compared to their peers in at least five important ways.

1. These children need less time to study new material.
2. They remember better what they have learned, which makes repeating previously mastered concepts unnecessary.

---

[4] Winebrenner, Susan, "Gifted Students Need an Education, Too," Educational leadership: journal of the Department of Supervision and Curriculum Development, N.E.A. January 2000.

3. They perceive the learning material at a more abstract and multifaceted level than do their classmates.

4. They become passionately involved in specific topics and find it hard to move on to other topics until they feel satisfied that they have mastered them as much as they possibly can.

5. Gifted children can operate on several levels of concentration at the same time, meaning that they can monitor classroom activities without paying direct or visual attention to them.

Recognizing Winebrenner's points is important for understanding what makes gifted learners different. I consider her basic ideas critical for teachers who work with gifted students.

Jean Sunde Peterson[5] (2009) warns that *positively stereotyping* gifted children can cause under-identification of the gifted child's problems. That is, gifted children may not expose their vulnerabilities to parents and teachers, preferring to maintain a positive image instead. Other obstacles to identifying social–emotional problems in gifted children are their ability to compensate for, or mask, concerns, and their belief that they must solve their problems autonomously.

The most positive results are found in full-time grouping and in programs with curricula that are the most adapted to gifted children. When offered more complicated knowledge and skills, gifted children develop significantly more than children who are not gifted. Gifted children need to be challenged, which necessitates some form of regrouping, whether for an entire class of gifted children or a cluster group.

Karen B. Rogers[6] (2002) reports that an average of one-third to one-half an additional year's achievement growth should be possible within a school program that provides special services for identified gifted students. In a pullout program, the taught material will be differentiated according to the level and pace of the gifted children. As a consequence, the children will be more involved at their level and will not have to wait a substantial part of the lesson for other children to understand what they have already mastered.

2. Social and emotional needs of gifted students

In some cases, gifted students' focus on intellectual growth means their social and/or emotional growth lags behind. For this reason, many gifted students are socially awkward. Because they spend so much time in their own heads, they do not pick up common social cues. Their differences from their age peers—as opposed to their intellectual peers—tend to isolate them.

This is especially true for highly gifted students. Their level of knowledge tends to make them appear to be trying to act superior, when all they want is to share their enthusiasm for what they have learned. Highly gifted students will learn to withdraw from sharing their thoughts, feelings, and interests with other students in a regular classroom. This is one reason self-contained gifted classes are best suited to meet these students' needs.

We all seek to find a place we feel we belong; we feel more at ease when we find our peer group. The isolated gifted student is no different from any other minority student who finds herself alone among those who are not like her. In the regular classroom these students can feel isolated and alone, estranged from their classmates.

---

[5] Peterson, Jean Sunde, "Myth 17: Gifted and Talented Individuals Do Not Have Unique Social and Emotional Needs." Gifted Child Quarterly, Volume 53 Number 4 Fall 2009 280-282 © 2009 National Association for Gifted Children.")

[6] Rogers, Karen B. *Re-forming Gifted Education: How Parents and Teachers Can Match the Program to the Child.* Scottsdale, Ariz: Great Potential Press, 2002.

The social and emotional deficiencies of highly gifted students can disappear when they are placed in self-contained gifted classes. I've seen them come into my class and relax for the first time; they blossom when they are placed with other students like themselves. Placing gifted students with their intellectual peers allows them to feel a sense of belonging.

3. Testing to identify gifted learners

The best kind of testing

Gifted and talented tests do not measure what kids know, but rather how they think and learn. **The best tests—those that use patterns and spatial relationships—yield the most valid IQ scores.** These tests are also the best to address language and cross-cultural issues. They are open-ended so there is no ceiling to limit how far children can go. And the best time to test is before they enter school. The downside to these tests is that they have to be individually administered, making them more costly than group tests.

Group tests like the Otis-Lennon (OLSAT) and Cognitive Abilities Test (CAT), on the other hand, are generally used because they are much more cost effective. They were developed to test large numbers of students more cheaply.

Why group testing misses some qualified students

Unfortunately, group tests like the CAT and the OLSAT, due to their reliance on reading skills, do not meet the needs of potentially gifted students with *special needs* that are the result of learning disabilities, language barriers, or cross-cultural limitations. Retesting with the same test will not address these students' needs. Rather, students with these issues need to be *individually tested.*

When I began teaching in the GATE program in Davis, students in the third grade, who were recommended by parents or teachers, took the Cognitive Abilities Test (CAT), with those having an IQ score of 130 and above admitted to the program. Eventually, *all* the third graders in the Davis Joint Unified School District were tested in the spring. Though this led to significant growth of the program, **the group testing still missed the gifted students whose giftedness didn't show up.**

The educational success of those students whose aptitudes and needs have been misunderstood depends upon GATE testing and programs. Therefore, **it is especially important for districts to be careful to select tests that are not racially or socio-economically biased.** Since all students in a district deserve access to GATE services, districts must carefully research which test(s) it will use to identify its gifted students—whether or not it has a self-contained program.

Some districts provide GATE services only if they get state funding for these programs. This is understandable in tight budget times, but districts should be encouraged to include them. One possible source to benefit GATE programs/services could be funding targeted for students who are racially, culturally, or socio-economically diverse.

Individually testing special needs students Is especially important

Alternative testing is important in order to identify children with learning disabilities, such as attention deficit disorder (ADD), attention deficit hyperactivity disorder (ADHD), and Asperger's/autism spectrum disorders, as well as language barriers, different ethnic backgrounds, or socio-economic issues. **Some may also be identified as gifted**; and it is precisely because of their "risk factors" that these students often fail to be identified by either their parents or teachers.

In the early years of the Davis program, in certain cases the district also provided individual testing by a school psychologist. As the Davis program grew, the district couldn't afford to provide individual testing, so it began to allow parents to have their children privately tested for the program.

If private GATE testing is not allowed, **districts must provide individual testing for some students.** Otherwise, many gifted students will not be identified. To rely only on tests that can be administered in large groups (such as the OLSAT) will mean the district is *discriminating against* a significant number of gifted students with learning disabilities, language difficulties, or socio-economic issues.

4. Teaching gifted students together

How this is done

Gifted students can be taught together in two ways: 1) in a self-contained classroom (where they spend the entire day together); or 2) in a pullout program (where they are in a regular classroom, but leave to be taught separately with other gifted students in some subjects). The main advantages to grouping them for instruction are that

- the gifted students do not have to compromise their aspirations or pace of learning to accommodate the lower-ability students.
- the teachers—not having to focus on the basic skills—can concentrate on higher-level thinking and research skills.

Teaching gifted students together offers them a more challenging environment, where it is more likely they will get a more positive attitude toward learning.

An added advantage of the pullout program is that these students have the opportunity to interact with both gifted children in the pullout program and with non-gifted children in their regular classroom. A pullout program gives gifted children a worthwhile experience of interacting with children who are like themselves. Together with their gifted peers, they do not have to feel "different" and may feel more freedom to be themselves.

Why gifted students are best served in self-contained GATE classes

Because gifted students are so quick to learn, teachers find that meeting their needs in a regular classroom setting can be extremely challenging—for two reasons:

1. **Most gifted students may need only two or three repetitions before learning is complete.**
   Such rapid learning is one of the main arguments for why gifted students languish in regular classrooms. Most non-gifted students, research has shown, need a repetition of about eight times to

retain learning. While the rest of the class receives sufficient repetitions of the lesson before they are ready to move on, gifted students must sit and wait.

2. **The teacher has time to explore more subjects more deeply.** This is because the self-classroom can cover the required curriculum much more rapidly. Students in gifted classes

- read many more content resources and literature books than there is time for in a regular classroom.
- write more in-depth papers and reports that expand their opportunities to learn.

Gifted students deserve guidance that meets their needs in the whole classroom setting. All students are best served when appropriate instruction meets their unique needs all day, every day, in real time.

I must admit that I feel strongly that when there are enough gifted students to form a class, the district should provide it.

5. Why some gifted students prefer not to be in a GATE class

A good number of gifted children are not initially enthusiastic about being in a self-contained GATE program. By the time this program begins, usually in the fourth grade, these students have learned to enjoy hiding their giftedness—they have already had four years of learning how to "game the system."

Though they may be gifted, that doesn't mean they are all eager to be challenged by their teachers. Sometimes when parents enroll their children in a self-contained GATE class, they literally drag them in kicking and screaming.

1. **Frankly, some of these kids enjoy not having to work hard.**

    They have spent their first four years "skating," taking it easy, and they want to continue to fly under the radar. They have their own interests, and they don't want more challenging school assignments to interfere with their carefully guarded free time.

2. **Many of these students like having the extra time to read.**

    Some gifted students read several years above grade level, and they have become used to finishing their assigned work quickly and spending the rest of their time doing what they like best—reading. Many of these students have specific interests they enjoy having time to pursue, while others plow through their assignments.

3. **Not all gifted children are self-motivated, high achieving, eager, and well behaved.**

    Contrary to the pervasive stereotype, some gifted children initially read below grade level, produce written work that is illegible or non-existent due to under-developed fine motor coordination, repeatedly fail to complete assignments, and/or argue against being expected to do more challenging work than others in the classroom.

I have known or taught such students. Having appropriately challenging expectations for the first time in four years of school can be a rude awakening. Nonetheless, I usually found that once they are grouped with their peers and given more challenging work, most of them engage eagerly and feel good about themselves and what they can accomplish. This happens when they are grouped with their intellectual peers and are appropriately challenged.

6. Yes, the gifted need nurturing also

We all must remember that a designation of "gifted" is simply *an indicator of potential*. In order for that potential to be realized, these students must be nurtured with programs designed to meet their unique needs, which include unique social and emotional needs.

Though some think being identified gifted is an advantage, any advantage to be gained by being gifted is realized only if these students are provided with appropriate educational programs—under the careful guidance of trained teachers. They should not be expected to do it on their own. Too often, left to teach themselves, these students are ill equipped for the task.

7. GATE programs can be controversial

In some districts, self-contained programs for GATE students are controversial. The reasons are varied, but they are usually based on misconceptions.

1. Some people perceive GATE students as "special" and, therefore, that they have a negative affect on students not in the program.

Identified GATE students are no more special than any other of a district's students, and "special programs" in a district does *not* equal "special students." Gifted students are simply different. Districts that recognize differences among their student populations—and which seek to address those differences with special programs—should be applauded for their efforts, not criticized. In fact, the variety of programs offered by a district is usually one measure of the high quality of its education.

One way to address this complaint is to provide enough differentiation within the regular classroom programs that students there are challenged to reach their greatest potential. It should never be assumed that students in regular classrooms cannot achieve at higher levels.

2. Many who oppose GATE refer to "achievement" or "acceleration" as the primary factors of comparison between programs.

These are critical misunderstandings. Many GATE students are not initially high-achievers, nor do they necessarily need acceleration. Like all students, they need curricular approaches and teaching strategies that target their unique needs, and placing these students in GATE classrooms makes it more likely their needs will be met. If these students are left in a regular classroom with teachers who haven't been trained to identify or meet their needs, they will very likely underperform and will not be helped to reach their potentials. Though many of these students can do very well in a regular classroom, they are *not challenged* there.

3. And some people prefer to rely on anecdotal evidence to make their judgments.

Perhaps they don't support GATE because of a personal experience. Or they learned of an isolated example: it's often much easier to believe someone's personal testimony, especially that of a trusted friend, than to try to understand complex data or a more "abstract" statistical reality. However, there is compelling evidence to the contrary. The fact is that quantitative scientific measures are almost always more accurate than personal perceptions and limited experiences. And study after study has shown that grouping gifted students for instruction is the best way to educate them.

Unless the needs of unique groups of students are met—*including* the needs of *gifted students*, districts are failing in their responsibility to address the needs of all students in their schools.

8. In the end, all students need the best education possible

Intellectually gifted students have educational needs that must be taken into account—just as we recognize the special needs of the physically and/or learning disabled students, English language learners, and of students struggling below grade level. District decisions for GATE must be based on *best educational policy* for meeting students' needs.

Therefore, districts must offer a choice of both neighborhood services for GATE students and self-contained classes. At the same time, districts must devote adequate resources and teacher training in differentiated instruction to assure that GATE students who remain in neighborhood schools are properly served.

Parents, too, need to be better educated about making the best choice for their students. If districts provide effective neighborhood programs, then more parents will choose that option rather than moving their children to a self-contained classroom simply because it is the only option for meeting their gifted child's needs. But they need the *choice* of programs, as do their children.

Summary

Meeting the needs of gifted students is not an easy task. These students' needs are as diverse as, or more diverse than, those of any other students. Gifted students' IQs can range from 130 to 180 and above. They can have learning disabilities such as attention deficit disorder (ADD), attention deficit hyperactivity disorder (ADHD), Asperger's/autistic spectrum disorders, language difficulties, ethnic differences, socio-economic risk factors, or may be performing below grade level. Because they are not presenting with typical gifted characteristics, these students are difficult to identify.

Research has shown that parents are the best source for initially identifying gifted students. Teachers, too, must be able to identify gifted students in their classrooms. School districts must be prepared to use group tests for all students, as well as individual tests for students with risk factors. And teachers, whether they are in regular classes or in self-contained gifted classes, need training in order to understand how to meet the diverse needs of gifted students.

The best place to meet the wide range of abilities and needs of gifted students is in a self-contained class. But these needs can be met in a *regular* classroom by *differentiating* to meet the needs of gifted students. Gifted students learn much more rapidly—and need deeper and wider experiences with the curriculum—than students who are not gifted. Once they are grouped with their intellectual peers and taught separately, they feel much more comfortable and can relax.

Although self-contained GATE programs can be controversial, once the specific needs of gifted students are well understood, it is usually clear that these programs are the most effective and best places to meet these students' intellectual needs as well as their social-emotional needs. Gifted students need and deserve to be taught in programs designed to meet their unique needs. Once they are placed with their peers their learning takes off and they are able to thrive.

For Parents

Parents are often the best resources for identifying gifted students, but they, too, must be educated about how to best address gifted students' learning needs. Information in this chapter will help parents to know how to be advocates on behalf of their gifted children.

CHAPTER 2

Transitional Challenges When Students Move from a Regular Classroom to a Self-Contained GATE Classroom

In the spring of 1991, I held a workshop at a conference of the California Association for the Gifted (CAG) called "Meet Me in September: Entry Experiences in a Gifted Class". It was about transition issues that arise when students first enter a self-contained gifted class. I included two parents in my presentation so they each could share their experiences from a parent's perspectives. The information in this chapter is from that workshop.

I had in mind the challenges fourth grade students face entering a self-contained gifted class for the first time because that is often the point at which GATE students are taught separately (and was in my district). But it would apply to any gifted child's education when the child has spent a year or more in a regular class and is then placed in a class of his intellectual peers.

Further, one of the first things I learned when teaching a GATE class is that the students aren't the only ones who can find the transition to a self-contained gifted class challenging—so can their parents. Therefore, in this chapter I will discuss the issues that face both the students and their parents, and how their teachers can meet the challenges.

1. Differences between a regular classroom and a GATE classroom

To do well teaching a class of gifted students, you must first understand that it isn't at all like teaching a class of regular students. To point out the wide variety of differences between the two, I use the following list of contrasting variables:

Differentiating variables as they apply to learning

grade-level – above-grade-level	same – different
slow-paced – fast-paced	concrete – abstract
simple – complex	linear – random
overview – in-depth	random – organized
short-term – long-term	received – explored
rigid – flexible	passive – active
certain – ambiguous	closed – open
information-based – analysis-based	conforming – non-conforming
isolated – integrated	teacher-directed – student-directed
limited – optional	dependent – independent
known – unknown	teacher-evaluated – self-evaluated
familiar – unfamiliar	

The first in the list for the gifted student is the most obvious: going from the grade level determined by age to a level of work that would ordinarily be required in a higher grade. The second variable is going from a relatively slow pace of learning to one that picks up considerably, and so on. Going into detail isn't necessary to show you the contrast between these variables that differentiate a gifted class from a regular class.

General elements of differentiation as they apply to gifted students

All of the variables mentioned above fall into one of the four elements of differentiation that teachers need to take into consideration in developing their course work, and it will be in these areas that the teachers will require more of their gifted students:

Content. Every area of the curriculum is adjusted by level, pace, complexity, and depth to meet the needs of the more capable students.

Concepts. The ideas, issues, themes are usually more advanced than they would be in a regular classroom. And because students are more capable of discerning what is important in issues and can perceive concepts faster, the class simply moves more quickly through the lessons.

Process. All students process their learning in the following ways: they read, research, write, organize, revise, think, create, speak, listen, observe, present. In a gifted class, however, the processes are done at more advanced levels.

Products. All work that is produced (presented in writing, orally, or artistically) is expected to be of a higher caliber. Of course not all gifted students are more capable in all three areas, however. For example, some can write much better papers but become too nervous when having to present the same ideas orally. But one can hope that the gifted student will recognize his weakness in oral presentations and be willing to work to improve. And, for example, some individuals (no matter how much they try) will never become artistically adept. But gifted students are often better able to discern subtle differences between classic paintings. With help and support from parents and teachers, students will learn to produce the higher level work that is expected of them.

2. Challenges facing STUDENTS entering a self-contained gifted class

Students who move from a regular classroom to a self-contained gifted classroom in fourth grade face a number of challenges. Having become used to being in a class where they are not challenged at their ability level *or* not having to work hard and easily floating at the top of the class are just two examples of how these students face new challenges. Below is a list of these and other ways gifted students are challenged when they enter a gifted class for the first time.

1. Acclimating to a GATE class

Some children love being in a self-contained gifted class, learning alongside kids like themselves for the first time. Others, however, resist having to do a higher level of work, and resisting being in this new environment makes acclimating a challenge for these students. The socio-dynamics of a gifted class are going to be quite different from what they were in a regular classroom. These are just a few of the students that teachers will have in the new class, students with fears the teachers will have to help them face and overcome.

For example, some students are happy they have always been at the top of the class and don't want to be where they can't be the best. Other students don't want to leave their good friends behind in their neighborhood school and worry about not having friends in the self-contained class. And then there are those who have never felt they fit in and don't expect to fit in here.

Some highly creative students are worried they will be constrained by new directions and expectations. And, importantly, there are always a few students who have been able to mask learning disabilities and who are now afraid that their weaknesses will show up for all to see. These are just a few of the students that teachers will have in the new class, students with fears the teachers will have to help them face and overcome.

Many of the students' concerns will solve themselves in time. For example, the students who always wanted to be on top may take up the challenge of remaining there; it will just take a considerable effort. In time they will make new friends in this class, though they can continue to have the old friends in their home neighborhoods. And those who have never fit in may find that they actually fit in here. It is up to the teacher in all of these cases to keep those early fears in mind and make sure the students *are* adjusting.

The students with learning disabilities, however, will probably be more of a challenge—but not one that can't be dealt with. It is important for those students (and their teachers) to recognize their weaknesses and to work on them—or to learn how to work around them. That is why close observation by the teacher is so important. Her help and encouragement at a time when the student is still young can have a huge positive effect on that student's ability to learn and adjust as he grows older.

2. Competing with intellectual peers

Competing with a class full of their intellectual peers is a major challenge for students entering a self-contained gifted class for the first time. In any classroom, students' ability levels will tend to define a normal distribution curve. Students in a gifted class are no different. Despite my emphasis on individual goals, on individual progress, and on individual evaluation, students may feel badly when they compare their accomplishments with those of a classmate. You can bet that each student has some idea about his or her ranking in the class. They will wonder, "Can I compete?" They may be plagued by self-doubt.

One of our roles as teachers is to help all students feel comfortable with their own—and each other's—strengths and weaknesses. Acknowledging weaknesses is as important as acknowledging strengths. All students need to feel they are valued and appreciated for their personal characteristics, as well as for their academic performance, whether that performance is higher or lower than a classmate. A big part of our job is to help our students confront and remedy weaknesses, not fear or try to hide them.

3. Being different

Is it a blessing or a curse? Am I really gifted? or Have I been misidentified? And what difference does it make?

Being different is inherent in being identified for placement in a differentiated gifted program. Some of these students have felt "different" for years; others have not. But placement in a self-contained gifted class highlights the fact that these children *are* different in some way. These children can be acutely sensitive about this. They need experiences that help them understand how they are different from—and how they are the same as—others.

Bringing gifted students into a self-contained class may provide them with their first opportunity to identify with other students who are like themselves. To see they are different from some students, but the same as others, is a relief. I've seen students come in to my classroom looking anxious; and then when they find others like themselves, they relax for the first time in their school day setting.

Students will explore how they feel about being different from some students and like others, and they will decide what they are going to do about it.

Incidentally, being in a self-contained gifted class can make some children feel different, rather than feel accepted. A child who does not identify with other members of the class may not benefit from a self-contained placement. I've had a few students who, after a year in the self-contained program, return to their neighborhood schools.

On the other hand, some gifted students settle in to a self-contained class as many of us settle into a pair of comfortable old shoes. To some kids it is a wonderful relief not to be at the top of the class. Many students appreciate the freedom of being lost in the crowd, of finding their places in the middle of the class.

4. Learning new social skills

It is a challenge for many of these students to learn the skills necessary for successful social interactions. Regardless of the typical diversity in academic performance, gifted fourth grade students are usually highly verbal. Children who have been able to dominate social situations can find it very frustrating to encounter a room full of similarly-inclined classmates.

On the other hand, some of these students are acutely withdrawn and need reassurance of being accepted before they come out of their shells. I've found that many of these students need—and appreciate—guidance in learning new social skills.

5. Confronting new threats to motivation

One of the most difficult adjustments a gifted student faces is the heightened academic challenge of the self-contained gifted class. The student moves from a class in which she often performs tasks quickly, easily and well, to a class in which tasks require greater time and effort, and products are evaluated by higher or different standards.

Students who enter a special program as late as the fourth grade may encounter an especially difficult adjustment if they have begun to equate their high achievement or ability with the ease and speed with which they complete assignments and with the high evaluations their work receives. This is one of the biggest challenges I faced as a fourth grade teacher at the entry level of a self-contained gifted program.

One of the most important things we can do for our gifted children is to provide them with opportunities to involve themselves in effortful quests as early in their schooling as possible. Otherwise, they associate being smart with being able to do school work quickly and easily; and when they eventually are unable to perform this way, they doubt their abilities. The earlier in their schooling that they understand that learning requires effort and is difficult, the better it is for their long-term success.

Yes, gifted students run a high risk of becoming conditioned to tying their motivation to ease, speed, and level of achievement. The "teacher pleaser," the "perfectionist," and the "fly-by-the-seat-of-his-pants" students who expect to maintain their positions at the top of the class with minimum effort face a dilemma unless they can hitch their motivational energy to a new star. **We must teach our students to focus on learning to learn, rather than on simply doing well.** I'm speaking here of an internal, rather than external locus of control.

One part of this challenge for me is to convince students how capable they are—to experience the satisfaction of completing a project they did not believe they could do. Testing their real potential may be a new experience for many gifted kids. But when their abilities are tested and they do well, they are able to feel a greater sense of accomplishment and a better, more realistic, sense of themselves as learners.

By fourth grade, some of these kids would rather not do anything than risk not doing it "right" or "perfectly." Helping students confront these kinds of threats to their motivation is a challenge my students hand to me every day. Putting out effort and time for uncertain rewards, or even frustration, can be a risky venture. A few students, even this early in their education, may have decided not to face this challenge.

6. Accepting new learning roles

Students in my class are expected to play a role in making decisions about their learning. I expect them to become self-directed, independent, and assertive. Students must learn to pace themselves and manage their time to complete long-term projects. Students are expected to work at a level that challenges and extends their abilities, not simply coast where they feel comfortable. A student who has done well on teacher-directed, convergent, product-oriented projects needs support and encouragement to become comfortable with divergent, process-oriented, self-directed activities.

It is our job to teach them how to make these transitions. This requires us to determine their individual levels in each subject and to push them to work above those levels. I create detailed assignment expectations and deadlines to help them learn to pace themselves. I provide them with different options to fulfill a single assignment so they can decide for themselves which option to take. And I give them performance rubrics so they have information about how to evaluate their work.

Before long, students realize they are more capable than they thought, and they enjoy becoming more autonomous in their learning.

7. Encountering a process-oriented curriculum

Students are expected to use their basic skills in reading, writing, and mathematics as means to productive ends, rather than as ends in themselves. Although knowledge and comprehension of content are essential, students are expected to work at the higher processing levels to apply, analyze, synthesize, and evaluate data. I model how this is done.

Encountering work that requires time and thought—and that involves an uncharted route to a variety of results—can be a challenge. Our role is to provide support and encouragement to both students and parents while they make the transition from largely information-based learning situations to a process-centered learning environment.

8. Meeting higher expectations for the quality and quantity of work— *especially* as it applies to writing

It is our job as teachers to challenge each student at his/her individual ability levels in all subjects, but this especially applies to how students express themselves clearly in their writing. Therefore, with my gifted students, I expect a great deal of quality writing. This becomes a major transitional issue when they come into a self-contained fourth grade gifted class. It is our job as their teachers to help guide them through their frustrations and anxieties.

I also require my fourth graders to use cursive handwriting instead of printing. The transition from printing to cursive used to be standard for third grade; but I always spend time at the beginning of the year reviewing these skills. To help them in this area, I provide writing-fluency drills for speed and accuracy. It is important to build their writing skills as early as possible.

And be aware that these higher expectations require a significant adjustment for many students *and* their parents. It is our job to help students understand how these expectations relate to their abilities and needs—and to what will be expected of them as the years progress.

9. Working at a faster pace, in greater depth, with more complexity, at a higher level

Teachers must push students to meet higher and higher standards as early in their schooling as possible. Students need to learn early that learning should require effort, so that they don't conclude that their high abilities mean that learning will always be easy.

So I push students to work at a faster pace, in greater depth, with more complexity, and at higher levels to master the processes of education. Most students soon learn that they enjoy being challenged in these ways. It helps them to gain confidence in themselves and to understand that *they* are responsible for their learning, not their teachers, not their parents, nor anyone else.

3. Challenges facing PARENTS of students entering a self-contained gifted class

1. Expectations vs. Realities—the kinds of reactions some parents have

1. First they may worry about whether placing their child in a gifted class is the right choice. And once the child is in the class, they stew about their decision to place their child in a special program.

    Consider this: Baring very unusual circumstances, the time to evaluate the correctness of the decision is at the end of the year—*after* your child has experienced being in a self-contained gifted class.

2. Some parents whose children have always performed with ease at the top of the class become very concerned when their child suddenly experiences frustrations and difficulties with what is expected of him.

    Consider this: This could well happen to their child when he goes off to college! It is better to have the experience of being challenged at this stage when parents and a caring teacher can guide the child.

3. Other parents realize that even though their child is progressing wonderfully, many other children are progressing faster or working at higher levels.

Consider this: It is unwise to compare your child to others. Talk with your teacher to get a better sense of how well your child is doing—and see what your child is learning from being with other gifted children.

4. And some parents may expect their poorly motivated child to become motivated once placed in a special program, but they do not see it happening quickly.

Consider this: This sometimes happens, but that doesn't necessarily mean the student shouldn't be in a GATE program. It will take time for some poorly-motivated students to become hooked into learning in this new setting. Again, discuss it with the teacher, and—if there is a parent-support group—bring the issue up with other parents.

2. What is my short-term role as a parent?

Quality Control—check your student's work to see that a quality effort has been applied. You usually know your child well enough to tell when he is cutting corners unnecessarily or simply whipping through an assignment to get it done—at a time when you know that giving it more thought would be beneficial. When the assignment calls for thoughtful work, ask questions of him in a way that makes him realize he needs to put in more effort.

Time Management—help your student to manage time so that all her work is completed when it is due. Help her break patterns of leaving things to the last minute—or of dawdling when doing assignments so that her time is used ineffectively. Keep the emphasis on what will help your child, not on his doing it only because you make him do it.

Enrichment—provide enrichment experiences for your student when possible. A student who is weak in science would benefit from a trip to a science museum or membership in a science-oriented activity. Students who don't like math might benefit from an after-school math enrichment program. A child who hates to write might become better at it if each evening he were asked to write one sentence about something he did that day that he enjoyed, perhaps keeping a "diary" so that he could look back after a while and see how his writing had improved, how he was able to write more easily. But all such enrichment activities need to be pleasant and not restricted only to areas where he needs help. Opening a child's mind to interesting new ideas or activities is always beneficial.

A Positive Attitude—maintain a positive attitude toward the new class.

Communication—keep communication lines open with your child's teacher.

3. What is my long-term role as a parent?

Awareness of their capabilities—learn about the capabilities of your children so that they, too, can realize what they are capable of doing. That can open up channels of communication with your children to their delight as well as yours. This is not to say that you should push them to do better, but you can do your part in helping them want to do so.

Acceptance of their strengths and weaknesses—you can always encourage their strengths, but in recognizing and accepting their weaknesses, you might also provide activities that strengthen those weak areas and perhaps help them to become interested in learning more. You never know when a weakness will become a strength.

Provide extra help in particular areas if they need it—be ready to help or arrange tutors when needed. This is one of the reasons you need to stay in touch with the teacher. He may well suggest where more help is needed.

Advocacy. Be a part of a parent group that can advocate on behalf of these students and this program. There will probably always be parents—and maybe even educators—who disapprove of having self-contained gifted classes. It is at such times that having parental support of such classes is extremely important. But even when there isn't a problem, parents learn from each other. Make sure such a group exists.

Needless to say, I feel most gifted students *should* be in a self-contained class. They need to be challenged, and that is the best setting for it. And their being together provides one of the main advantages of a self-contained class—the opportunity it creates for a parent support group.

Such a support group enables parents to discuss their concerns and learn from others. That is why, in the CAG workshop, I asked two parents to discuss these issues from a parent's perspective.

4. Ways TEACHERS of students entering a self-contained gifted class can deal with the challenges

Many of the challenges facing students become challenges for teachers as well. It is up to teachers to provide the transition from the regular classroom to the gifted classroom. In other words, readiness preparation must be a strong component of any entry-level gifted class. The later the level at which a student enters a self-contained gifted class, the more critical readiness steps become—and, I might add, the more difficult they are to achieve.

Before you can help them make the transition, however, you must **first find out the level of each child's skills.**

I have already spoken about the diversity that can be expected among a group of students placed in a self-contained gifted class. But before you can begin to build on students' independent learning skills, you need to find out each one's current skill levels.

In the following pages, I show some of the strategies I use both to assess and to develop students' learning needs—in **Literature and Language Arts** and in **Social Studies and Science**:

Literature and Language Arts

1. Begin with the familiar

I use the standard fourth grade reading textbook at the beginning of the year to provide a familiar common base for learning. In a large group setting, we discuss the level of written responses that I expect. Using oral sharing and applying point values to responses, students learn, for example, that they need to rephrase the question in the answer, and provide evidence (details) from the reading to support their conclusions. In these ways we are helping students with the readiness steps they need to reach in order to produce higher-level work.

This process emphasizes to students that it is the quality of their thinking and writing that is important. This may be the first time students learn that there is not just one correct answer, but that responses from different points of view are accepted.

2. Introduce the unfamiliar

For example, incorporate an independent reading component in the first week or two of class. Most students will be used to some independent reading as a part of their regular classroom programs. But, in my classroom, independent reading soon becomes a major component of the reading program.

From a classroom collection or reading list, require students to choose books they will read independently. Initially, students use a uniform-response format to provide written, oral, or visual responses. We set priorities and goals for these assignments.

Students then share with the rest of the class the variety of responses that come from the same assignment format. Then I provide resources for alternative response formats and objectives to teach students how to create individualized responses. I lead discussions to facilitate interactions between and among the students, rather than just between the students and me.

3. Teach the objectives of various response formats

I teach the elements of dramatic structure, explaining how characterization, setting, and plot development lead to the climax and resolution of a story. We spend a lot of time on descriptive writing. I provide examples of a variety of prepared response formats, such as the Junior Great Books Program's interpretive questions (p. 119). Then I teach the students how to design their own response activities to accomplish the same objectives.

I also think it is important to teach Bloom's Taxonomy of higher-level thinking skills (pp. 265-268) as ways to respond to literature—from knowledge and comprehension, to application, analysis, synthesis, and evaluation, and I provide incentives to encourage original responses to lesson objectives.

4. Integrate language mechanics skills and writing fluency

Teachers would do well to build language mechanics skills through whole-class, small-group, and independent activities. Increased demand for quality and quantity of written responses mean that skill-building activities must be integrated into daily lessons.

Timed writing drills can be used to develop writing fluency.

Use "write, revise, and rewrite" editing groups and other cooperative strategies to assist students in developing their written language skills. In this way students learn from each other, and they learn to trust each other with critiquing their work.

Social Studies and Science

1. Teach research skills

Use the standard grade-level social studies or science texts to teach note-taking and outlining skills. Teach students how to do research for topic selection—how to break down a topic into component sub-topics, gather information, organize information, draft, revise, and finalize presentation of information. Model and practice all of these activities using a common text.

Once students learn each of these elements in a group setting, most are ready to branch out on their own to choose individualized research topics.

These kinds of activities are aimed more at teaching mastery of learning techniques than on learning the content. The content is important, but it is secondary to learning the processes.

2. Assign a short-term independent research project

Provide independent practice of research skills using a high interest topic such as animals. Requiring students to stay within a specific animal family simplifies the format. For example, I ask my students to do a Mammal Report. Each child chooses the mammal she wants to research, but the whole class follows that same format of elements to be included in the report.

In the process, students learn the common characteristics of mammals while learning how to do all the basic elements of a research project. They get to express their individuality, their personal interests, within a task structured for a uniform purpose for the whole class. In this way they learn that individuality and conformity can operate simultaneously—the students have taken alternative pathways to a fixed end.

3. Integrate content with process

As I have explained, I use our literature work as the basis for developing writing skills; I use social studies or science as the basis for research skills; and I use both for developing critical thinking in large-group discussions.

Eventually the boundaries between these subject areas become blurred as we move to a more integrated treatment of the academic disciplines. We use content as a means to an end, but our primary goal is learning processes.

4. Restructure the use of time

Early in the year, although there are not rigid time blocks for different subject areas, there is a clearer sense of division. As time goes on, students manage their work in larger blocks of time. For example, different students may be working on math, literature, and research all at the same time. Some students prefer to work on math and writing in class, but take their reading home; others prefer to do math at home, while concentrating on research and writing in the classroom.

My teaching of directed lessons becomes more of an interruption of their use of class time for independent activities. Having students occupied with working independently frees me to provide support for students individually or in small groups.

Conclusion

It is not possible for me to provide you with more than an overview of the kinds of approaches I take 1) that help make the transition to encountering work that requires time and thought, and 2) that involve an un-prescribed route to a variety of results. Our role then at all levels, but especially at the point of entry, is to provide support and encouragement to both students and parents, while they make the transition from largely information-based learning situations to a process-based learning environment.

By the end of the year, if the transition has been a success, students will feel confident with their independent learning skills. They should be prepared to set goals, order priorities, manage time, pace themselves, make decisions, follow projects through to completion, and evaluate their products.

In helping students to take responsibility for their transactions with ideas, **we are helping them to become independent learners—the overall goal for these bright and capable students.** They will have gained a sense of power over their own learning and a sense of purpose for being in school. They will also have gained confidence and mastered many of the skills necessary in learning how to learn.

And when the students become independent learners—whether it be sooner or later, teachers always feel a true sense of accomplishment. That is when they know they chose the right profession. That is when they know all the extra effort was worthwhile.

Note: If you would like to know more about my school district's gifted program when I was teaching, see Appendix L: "An Overview of the Davis Joint Unified School District's Self-Contained Gifted Program in 1991" (p. 360-361). There will have been many changes in the program since then, but this kind of information may still be useful to teachers and parents.

Summary

Standard texts can be used effectively to produce the security of the familiar, at the same time that they facilitate a transition to a different way of doing things. Using the social studies text early in the year at a fast pace can provide an overview of the content for the year. That overview can later provide the basis for in-depth research in particular areas.

I use my California History text in this manner. After reading from the text, individually and together, to learn the basic content, I provide a standard format for students to follow for an in-depth research project on a particular period of California history.

Usually by December or January most students are ready to explore literature and research activities following their unique interests and needs.

By late February or early March, we begin an intensive story-writing project that is the major focus of class time for about five weeks. In late April we begin work on a Shakespeare play that the students perform the first week in June.

Compacting and individualizing the curriculum in some areas buys me time to devote to the book writing and Shakespeare projects later in the year.

CHAPTER 3

Differentiation: Addressing the Needs of Gifted and High Achieving Students in a Regular Classroom

Often a regular classroom will have one or more gifted students in the class, so their teachers need to know how to differentiate curriculum to meet their needs. The need for differentiation can also apply to students who are not gifted but who are high achieving, as well as for students who have other needs.

The reasons for gifted students being in a regular class are varied: some districts are not large enough to be able to provide separate classes for them; some parents don't want their children to leave their neighborhood schools; in some districts the schools with self-contained GATE classes may be too far away for some students to be able to attend; and some students may have not yet been identified as gifted. In these situations, gifted students may be well served in neighborhood schools as long as teachers are trained to meet their needs. Whatever the reason, they still need instruction at their level.

It is therefore important that *all* classroom teachers—including those who teach regular classes—know how to differentiate curriculum to meet the needs of gifted and high-achieving students. It is also important to note that these techniques are useful in working with *any* students whose abilities and needs fall outside the grade level range.

1. Differentiation—and why teacher training is essential

To address the needs of students outside the grade-level range, teachers can use **differentiation**—providing different curriculum and techniques than for the rest of the class. Differentiated curricula can be provided by using **individualized instruction** (providing a unique program for just one student); **cluster grouping** (grouping students with similar needs within the class and using a different curriculum and techniques); and **a pullout program** (pulling students out of their regular classroom to be taught by a specialist in GATE teaching). But all teachers must be trained in these techniques in order for this to work.

These are techniques I learned in teaching the self-contained GATE classes, and I have no doubt that all my students benefited. When I went back to teaching in my neighborhood school, I was able to put these practices to good use there as well. Had I not had the experience with GATE, however, I would not have known about these effective techniques.

There is no reason that regular classroom teachers cannot employ many of the same kinds of approaches GATE teachers employ. These are techniques that are useful for *any* classes with a broad range of students, but the key to successfully teaching such a class is teacher training. These approaches should be a part of every teacher-training program.

Especially for *gifted* students in a regular class, an advantage of the pullout program is that they have the opportunity to interact with both their gifted peers in the pullout program and non-gifted children in their regular classroom. A pullout program gives gifted children a worthwhile experience of interacting with children who are like themselves. Together with their gifted peers, they do not have to feel "different" and may feel more freedom to be themselves.

Every classroom has students with a wide range of needs and abilities. Differentiating instruction is not easy, but it is the best way to be sure that each child is taught using techniques designed to motivate and help her realize her highest potential. Every child deserves instruction that meets his individual needs. Supporting and stretching *all* students to achieve their best should be the standard for every teacher in the district.

2. Some problems with having gifted students in a regular class

Some people think that when high achieving students are placed in the regular classroom, they will perform as well as they would have if they were placed with other GATE students, but this is often not the case. Here are some of the reasons they might not do well:

Their needs may be squelched in favor of helping others. Instead of being encouraged to pursue their own learning, these students' needs are sacrificed for the needs of classmates. It is not the responsibility of GATE students to serve as tutors, role models, or in other ways imagined to benefit non-GATE students. Without educationally appropriate curriculum and teaching strategies, these students languish. They are left to find their own way, they are used to help other students—and it isn't right.

They may be resented. When kept in neighborhood classrooms, some high performing students are used to tutor or help their classmates, and they are not appreciated for their role as "teacher." Instead of being seen as normal peers, they start to be viewed as clearly smarter. Their relationship as peers is broken.

Bored, they may become disruptive, or simply tune out. Having to wait while other students learn can test some students beyond their ability to handle it. Just as it is not right to expect students needing Special Education services to be taught at rates that are standard in a regular classroom, it is not right to expect gifted students to wait for other students to learn.

They may hide their abilities in an effort to fit in. Some students feel uncomfortable about being so far ahead of kids in regular classrooms. Sometimes such students quietly pretend they are not so bright so they won't be seen as different. And without specialized training, regular classroom teachers have a difficult time providing the kind of accelerated or advanced curriculum these students need.

They can feel isolated and think they stand out as too different from their classmates. Sometimes these students isolate themselves on purpose so that they feel free to do what they most enjoy. Many times this means sitting with a book and reading when not required to do something else. You will frequently find these students reading during recesses instead of being out on the playground with their classmates. You can learn a lot about the student by looking at what she is reading. This can help you to provide appropriate lessons for these students. Pairing these students with appropriate buddies will help them to become integrated socially. This step can't be over-emphasized.

And a gifted student who prefers to be in a regular class where he believes he won't be challenged to do harder work may get his wish, i.e., he won't be challenged! Some gifted students realize they won't have to work as hard in a regular classroom, so they don't, and they don't let on that they could do better—or they take advantage of the teacher who doesn't have the time or energy to provide more challenges. They may be lazy or simply prefer a slower pace. Others just like to be at the top of the class without having to work hard. Still others like to finish their work quickly so they have time to read—a favorite activity of many gifted students, and these students don't want to give up this carefully guarded time. Whatever the reason, teachers need to keep a keen eye out for such students to make sure they are doing the level of work of which they are capable.

To avoid these kinds of problems, high-potential-ability students should have their learning needs nurtured *throughout* their education, not just when they demonstrate high academic ability.

3. Assessing the needs of academically-gifted students

The achievement tests students take each year will give grade-level indications for reading, writing, and math. Teachers should use this information to create differentiated lessons in each subject. This means that even though many lessons are presented to the whole class, the expectations for how students respond will be differentiated to address students' unique needs.

It is also important to note that many students who are identified as gifted qualify on just one of the two main parts of the tests—either reading or math—but not as a combination of both. As a result even these gifted students need differentiation in only one of the two areas. Only identified gifted students who test high on both reading and math need differentiation for both.

Reading and writing

Use the results of the achievement test to decide at what level students should be working. All students are best served when instruction is geared to their individual needs. This is as true for gifted and high achieving students as it is for students who are struggling below grade level.

In the chapter on Reading, I describe how I use Literature Discussion Groups that use literature books at each student's reading level. As I explain in that chapter, I begin these groups after I use the grade level textbook for several weeks, which enables me to get to know how students are doing on assignments given to the whole class before I begin the discussion groups.

I will also have completed several weeks of the daily descriptive writing paragraphs. These help me to see what kinds of help and what differentiations students need in order to be challenged at their ability levels.

Math

Use the results of the achievement test to decide at what level students should be working. If necessary, some students should be given work that is individualized to meet their unique needs. They can work at a higher place in the grade-level textbook, or be given a higher-grade-level book or supplementary resources. As I said above, it is as important for these students to be given ability-level work as it is for those who are working below grade level. Frequently, however, these students are neglected as long as they are doing well at grade level.

4. Recognizing the needs of students gifted in non-academic areas

It is also important to recognize that some students are gifted in one particular non-academic area that is not identified by tests. These students need nurturing as well. They are the students who excel in the arts: performing in drama, music (singing, dancing, playing an instrument), or the visual arts (drawing or painting). They are also students who are athletically gifted. All of these students should have these gifts nurtured.

The artistically gifted

In the earlier chapter about the arts, I discuss how to nurture students who are artistically gifted. In my classes (both regular and self-contained GATE) we did a Shakespeare play that gave students opportunities to develop and display their gifts for acting (though it doesn't necessarily have to be Shakespeare).

But productions don't need to be restricted to drama [plays]. Other teachers at my school who had musical talents (not my forte) presented musical productions so students with talents in dancing, singing, or playing musical instruments had opportunities to develop and share these talents. I strongly encourage all teachers to provide opportunities for their students to perform on stage.

It is easier to have drawing, painting, and sculpting art activities in your classes, but keep an eye out for the students who excel in these areas and provide them with opportunities to explore their gifts. For example, you could have them design the program for the play, paint the sets in an imaginative way, provide specific drawings in a science class to illustrate what you are teaching, or draw/paint a scene of a pioneer family in their covered wagon as they head west. Students gifted in these ways will appreciate having their talents sought out!

The athletically gifted

It should be easy to spot these students during the P.E. period. They will be well coordinated in all P.E. activities. They will be fast runners, accurate ball throwers, great kickers, etc. Meeting these students' needs may not be easy, but it will be helpful if you can try.

Enrichment activities outside of school

Most of the students in these categories will be taking specialized lessons or be on sports teams after school. But it wouldn't hurt for teachers to check with the parents of these students to be sure they are aware of their children's gifts, as some parents may take their children's special talents for granted and not be aware they need special support and nurturing.

5. Understanding intra- and inter-personal giftedness

Intra-personally-gifted students

Intra-personally-gifted students are adept at knowing and managing themselves. This is emotional intelligence: the ability to know, to understand, and to manage themselves. Their self-knowledge enables them to be aware of their strengths and weaknesses. Intrapersonal communication is a self-talk conversation.

Emotions, feelings, perceptions and attitudes within a person are called intrapersonal skills, such as self-confidence, self-esteem, patience, and the ability to be straightforward. They are more self-aware. These students can be more assertive, strong willed, and independent than their classmates. They may feel a greater sense of empathy and social responsibility than others. They are frequently more adaptable: they are flexible and good at problem solving. They are better at stress management: impulse control and stress tolerance. They are persistent and resilient in the face of challenges.

Inter-personally-gifted students

Inter-personally-gifted students are adept at relating to, understanding and interacting with, others. These students learn through interaction. They usually have many friends and have empathy for others; many have what we call street smarts. They learn easily through group activities.

6. More information about giftedness

Two books I have found especially useful in understanding the different areas of giftedness are *All Kinds of Minds,* by Melvin Levine (who describes visual-spatial, bodily-kinesthetic, musical, intra- and inter-personal, linguistic, and logical-mathematical intelligences); and *Multiple Intelligences,* by Howard Gardner. I recommend them to both teachers and parents.

You can find more information on giftedness in the bibliography on the next page.

Bibliography of Beginning Readings in the Area of Gifted/Talented Education

Alvino, James, et al. *Parent's Guide to Raising a Gifted Child*. Boston: Little, Brown and Co., 1985; and NY: Ballantine Books, 1985. (Includes wide variety of topics and information.)

Baskin, B. & Harris, K. *Books for Gifted Children*. NY: R.R. Bowker Co., 1980. (Listing of books for gifted children to read.)

Delisle, James R. *Gifted Children Speak Out*. NY: Walker and Co., 1984. (Candid comments about growing up gifted from gifted students in U.S..)

Ehrlich, V. *Gifted Children: A Guide for Parents and Teachers*.

Englewood Cliffs, NJ: *Prentice Hall*, 1982. (Practical suggestions.)

Feldhusen, John. *Toward Excellence in Gifted Education*. Denver: Love Publishing Co., 1985. (Issues concerning gifted in schools.)

Galbraith, Judy. *The Gifted Kids' Survival Guide (For Ages 10 and Under)*. Minneapolis: Free Spirit Publishing Co., 1984.

Galbraith, Judy & Delise, James. *The Gifted Kids' Survival Guide II*.

Kaufman, Kelice. *Your Gifted Child and You*. Reston, VA: Council for Exceptional Children, 1976. (Suggestions for developing creativity.)

Kerr, Barbara. *Smart Girls, Gifted Women*. Columbus, Ohio: Ohio Psychology Publishing Co., 1985. (Understanding and guidance for gifted females; includes brief biographies of eminent women.)

Lewis, David. *How to Be a Gifted Parent—a Practical Guide to Encouraging Young Children to Develop a Constructive and successful Approach to Their Own Abilities and Skills*. NY: Norton, 1981.

Perino, Sheila and Joseph. *Parenting the Gifted: Developing the Promise*. NY: R.R. Bowker Co., 1981. (Characteristics; supportive strategies.)

Saunders, Jacqulyn. *Bringing Out the Best*. Minneapolis: Free Spirit, 1986. (Information and topics dealing with young gifted children.)

Schmitz, C. and Galbraith, J. *Managing the Social and Emotional Needs of the Gifted: A Teacher's Survival Guide*. Minneapolis: Free Spirit, 1985. (Useful for parents to cooperate with school situations.)

Stone, Nancy Alvarado. *Gifted Is Not a Dirty Word*. Irvine, CA. Technicom, 1989. (Practical balanced advice from a parent/psychologist/ Mensa coordinator.)

Takacs, Carol A. *Enjoy Your Gifted Child*. Syracuse, NY: Syracuse Univ. Press. 1986. (Insight into gifted as it applies to parents and adults who have contact with the gifted child.)

Vail, Patricia L. *The World of the Gifted Child*. Syracuse, NY: Walker and Co., 1976; NY: Penguin, 1980. (Parenting; anecdotes; activities.)

Webb, J., Meckstroth, E., and Tolan, S. *Guiding the Gifted Child: A Practical Source for Parents and Teachers*. Columbus, Ohio: Ohio Psychology Publishing Company, 1982. (Focuses on the psychological aspects of gifted—a must for anyone concerned with gifted youth.)

Summary

Gifted or high achieving students in a regular classroom need differentiated approaches to meet their needs. For this reason it is essential that regular classroom teachers be trained in differentiating curriculum for these students. Regular classroom teachers should create lessons that meet all the various kinds of giftedness of students in their classes, as well as for students who are not identified as gifted. Much of what I discuss throughout this book address differentiating for all students in your class.

For Parents

Whether or not your children are identified as gifted, many of them need differentiated approaches to meet their needs in different areas of the curriculum. And even if your children are not gifted or high achievers in academic areas of the curriculum, they may be gifted in non-academic areas. So parents should be on the lookout for *all* kinds of giftedness in their children. If their needs aren't being met in the classroom, parents should try to arrange for their children to take enrichment programs after school if they possibly can.

Final Thoughts

From the beginning, *The Conscious Teacher* has been the story of my personal journey. I believe that's the way all teachers should approach their work. Your teaching journey should be uniquely yours as you reveal yourself to your students. And you must create your classroom environment based on what is important to you, what works best for you.

If you think you are there to "play the role" of teacher, you won't do well. The students need *you*. Being an effective teacher requires you to know yourself, to be truly conscious as you engage with your students.

In *The Conscious Teacher* I have shared what I did that motivated students and enabled me to know they were learning, and I hope that you will find some of my ideas useful. I believe my ideas will be especially helpful to new teachers who are just learning how to teach, but I also think experienced teachers may find new ideas here as well.

Besides giving you the ideas that worked for me, however, I hope my story will give you the confidence to create a teaching style that is uniquely personal to your own story. I believe this is the kind of relationship with students that results in truly effective teaching.

As in all endeavors, you get back in accordance with what you put in. Good teachers know that teaching requires a great deal of hard work, but that it can be an incredibly rewarding career.

It is not for everyone, however. Remember the phrase from George Bernard Shaw's *Man and Superman*: "Those who can, do; those who can't, teach." Meant to disparage teachers, this is a ridiculous statement. But some people think that way: perhaps they haven't succeeded in other endeavors, so they figure teaching elementary school children will be an easy alternative.

On the contrary, teaching is not for the faint of heart or the frail of mind. Teaching requires an incredible amount of energy, focus, and self-discipline—finely tuned attention to an infinite number of variables as well as the big picture. When done well, it is socially, emotionally, and intellectually demanding—and *highly* satisfying.

Anyone who might consider going into teaching can learn from this book how much thought—and self-revelation—is required to be a good teacher. While it is my hope that the ideas I share here will help those teachers dedicated to making it their life's work, I also hope that this book will caution those thinking of becoming teachers who underestimate the profession's demands. After reading this, they may reconsider wanting a career in teaching.

There are many rewards for teachers. Most gratifying for me is getting to know 30 or so individual students each year—learning about not only where each is academically so as to help them all advance, but also what each needs to feel good about himself and to get along better with classmates.

It is extremely challenging to figure out how to identify such a wide variety of needs during our year together. But each time I succeed in helping a student, whether by remediating a weakness or by finding ways to challenge students who are already advanced, I feel a real sense of accomplishment.

Interacting with students on a personal, individual level was what satisfied me most and brought the best results in students' learning. Using my sense of humor helped make it playful and fun both for my students and for me.

I enjoy the challenges presented each day. I am always trying to think of ways to encourage and excite students to learn. I revel in the fact that teaching is not routine, that each day is different, and that—with work—I can make a real difference in students' lives.

I also love learning something new right along with my students. Their questions challenge me to research for answers; their research papers present me with new information. My greatest reward, however, is watching each student grow and advance. It is always exciting to watch them as they accumulate knowledge, learn new skills, and gain confidence. And I feel deep pleasure in helping them to learn more about themselves, and to learn what personal characteristics, talents, and interests make each of them unique.

How well the students do later will depend greatly on what they have learned in the lower grades, particularly in the intermediate grades. When they get a strong foundation, they will be much more capable in the upper grades. It is, therefore, up to us as teachers to do our utmost to be creative, to work hard, and to see that every single student benefits from his and her year in our care. For me it has been worth every moment.

Appendices

How to Get the Job You Want: Consider Substitute Teaching

"THE BICENTENNIAL SUBSTITUTE"

Call

Debbie Taggart

756-0511

- I'll bring all my own activities for just one day or for several days.

- Or, I'll follow your plans and just fill in with my own materials where you want them.

- Individual and group activities for primary & intermediate grades.

- Focus will be on Bicentennial theme and can include:

        Bicentennial Slide Show:
                Boston   Philadelphia
                Lexington   Washington, D.C.
                Concord
        Dramatics
        Creative Writing & Language Arts Activities
        Literature
        Math
        Science Demonstrations
        Arts & Crafts

Experience:

- Classroom teacher in first, third, & fourth grades in Calif. 9/67-6/68, 9/68-6/69, 9/70-6/71.

- Teacher of Mexican American & Black children, grades 1-6 at Guadalupe Catholic School, Texas, 11/71-1/72.

- MGM Coordinator at WDI, 1/74-5/74.

- Took "Project Create" class for substitutes, fall 1974.

- Substitute teacher 10/74-present, including fifth grade long-term position at Pioneer 10/75-12/75.

- Summer School teacher first, second, third grades at WDI, Summer 1975

Get to Know Each Other Right Away

YOUR NAME _____

MAKING NEW FRIENDS

Try to find a classmate who fits each of these descriptions, then ask that person to sign on the line. Even if you don't fill all the lines, see how many different names you can get—and how many new friends you can meet.

Find someone who...

1. is taller than you _____
2. is left-handed _____
3. walks to school _____
4. has curly hair _____
5. has no sisters or brothers _____
6. has initials that spell a word _____
7. was born in your town _____
8. is new to your school _____
9. went camping this summer _____
10. is the oldest in the family _____
11. has an unusual pet _____
12. collects stamps _____
13. has blue eyes _____
14. was in your class last year _____
15. is on a sports team _____
16. has been to Disney World _____
17. has an eight-letter name _____
18. collects coins _____
19. has had a broken arm _____

20. has freckles _____
21. has a birthday this month _____
22. has traveled to five states _____
23. has long hair _____
24. was born in another country _____
25. lives in an apartment _____
26. wears glasses _____
27. takes music lessons _____
28. can whistle _____
29. just moved to a new home _____
30. has seen two oceans _____
31. is the youngest in the family _____
32. rides a bus to school _____
33. has been a hospital patient _____
34. loves to read _____
35. has red hair _____
36. has a tooth missing _____
37. has eaten a strange food _____
38. hasn't talked with you before _____

About Me

1. My name is _____ .

2. My birthday is _____ I am _____ years old.

3. My favorite subjects in school: _____
    _____

4. My hardest subjects in school are _____
    _____

5. My hobbies are _____
    _____

6. Describe a special talent or skill you have. What are you doing
    (have you done) to develop it? _____
    _____

7. What characteristic(s) is(are) most important to you in a friend?
    _____

8. I feel good when _____

9. I worry when _____

10. I like to _____

11. I don't like to _____

12. Tell one of your hopes about being in this class.
    _____

13. Tell one of your worries about being in this class.
    _____

14. On the back of this page list three dreams you have for yourself.

Establish Your Routines from Day 1

Assignments for August 31 – Sept. 4   1998-99

Monday 31	Tuesday 1	Wednesday 2	Thursday 3	Friday 4
Welcome to 6th grade! Room 20 •Remember red "daily folder." Return all notices, forms & book contract tomorrow. Get parent signature.	Literature: Bridge to Terabithia Chaps. 1-3 →Return Notices MAD - Read, outline, take notes; & prepare to give oral overview & assigned chapters with 2 other classmates next week. Assigned Chap. Math - Review Math Concept + skills. Rounding review p. 64 addition review p. 34	Terabithia Chaps. 4-6	Chaps. 7-9 →	Chaps. 10 - end.
			Math Concept + skills. Complete(+) 3 digit mult. p. 904 (odd only)	12" tissue table chart on a day. "Math Concept Review" sheet due "Review Test in class"
		School Supplies!		
Mark Your Calendar: "Back to School Night" in Rm. 20 Mon. Sept. 14 from 8-9 pm.				

Parent Signature _____

- Your child will receive an assignment schedule each week. The red folder should go back & forth between school & home every day. It will hold all school notices and assignment that are complete or need to be completed. Your signature on any "completed" assignment will appear on your child's points. Debtorah Nichols Pa u/o5

2wkcal.doc

Assignments for Sept. 8-11

Monday	Tuesday	Wednesday	Thursday	Friday
Labor Day Holiday	7 Literature Reading MAD overview presentation	8 (20 pgs per day minimum or 1 literature log per week) MAD chap 1 Reflection check	9 MAD chap 1 outline due	10	11
	Math - Fractions Review Times Table	Spotlight on Literature "Last Summer with Maizon" Practice (2.5/day)	worksheet →	worksheet →	1,2 outline due
	Story Grammar Practice Spelling	p. 2 → p. 1 → p. 1,2 →	p. 3 → p. 3 → pp. 3,5,6 →	Art Class p. 7 → p. 5 p. 7 → p. 5,7 pp. 2,4 → p. 5,7
	14 Rm. 20 "Back to School Night" 7:00-8:00 Science Rm. 12 8:00-9:00 Classroom Rm. 20 # Please come to learn about your child's classroom program.			Some students are doing articles on the Bone Estraño column which are due 9/11.

2x4tcal.doc   due 8/9/98

_____

Parent signature

212

SSR Bookmarks

Name:		Name:		Name:	
Title:		Title:		Title:	
Author:		Author:		Author:	
No. Pages:		No. Pages:		No. Pages:	
Date:	Pages Read:	Date:	Pages Read:	Date:	Pages Read:

APPENDIX D

Create a Plan for
Parent-Student-Teacher Teams

Back to School Night
Tuesday, September 19, 1989
Agenda

I.   Welcome & Introduction
  A.   Education
  B.   Teaching

II. Weekly Schedule and Classroom Organization
  A.   Weekly Calendar
  B.   Assignment Notebooks

III. Curriculum
  A.   New State Adopted Texts
  B.   Other Subjects: Science/Health – Tisa Owen
       Music/Recorder – Alice Alford
  C.   A Differentiated Curriculum: Integration
  D.   Transition

IV. Evaluation: Learning/Grades Paradox
  A.   Learning Loop: Set Goals
                        Provide Instruction
                        Present Challenges
                        Offer Opportunities
                        Evaluate
                        Repeat
  B.   Grading: What is the standard?
  C.   Class Profile: A Spectrum of Diversity

V.   Questions & Discussion

VI. Other Announcements
  From Debbie:
           Parent Inventory
           Student Goals
           Books about gifted education
           Parent help in classroom

VII. Closing

Parent Information Packet
(Please read before "Back to School Night." Bring this with you on Mon. Sept. 13.)

Dear Parents: Welcome to 6th grade and the 1999-2000 school year!

Dates to Remember:
Monday, Sept. 13 from 8:00 to 9:00 p.m. "Back to School Night" in Room 20. The Science presentation for 6th grade parents is from 7:00 to 8:00 pm in the Science Lab, Room 12.
November 1-5: Parent-Teacher-Child Conferences. Please return pink request form and Student Information Sheet. Conference appointment requests will be scheduled on a first come first served basis. Don't forget to consider your child's after school schedule. **Students must attend the conference.**
December 6-10: Walker Creek - Outdoor Education Program. (See letter from Mark Cary.)

Home/School Communication: Each student has been given a "Daily Folder" (red/orange). All weekly classroom assignment calendars & Patwin newsletters; other parent information forms; and separate homework papers are placed here. You should see this folder and its contents daily. Establish a regular routine for reviewing, signing, and replacing papers in this folder. Any notes from you can be sent to me by way of this folder. These folders are kept on top of students' desks all day every day.
Phone Messages for DNP: You can leave messages on my classroom voice mail by calling 757-5383, ext. 120. I do not have time during the school day to pick up messages. I will try to get back to you as quickly as possible, but sometimes it is a day or two before I have a chance to return calls. When I have meetings immediately after school I don't even have a chance to pick up messages. (If you want to leave a message for your child do not leave it on my voice mail, please call the office with the message.) I prefer to limit phone calls at home in the evening, but if you have an urgent issue don't hesitate to call me at 756-7797. If I'm not available you can leave a message on the machine in my mailbox.

Homework & Weekly Assignment Calendars: All homework is an extension of work that we do in class. Most homework is due the next day, and is indicated on the assignment calendar on the day it is due. Assignment calendars should go home the first day of the week and are due the next day with a parent signature. Occasionally students add items to the assignment calendar after it is published. I return signed assignment calendars to students on the second day of each week so calendars can be posted at home, or be kept in the daily folders. An assignment calendar is posted on the classroom whiteboard.

Homework is practice for lessons we have done in class, or an extension of an ongoing lesson or skill. We have discussed the work, in many cases we do several examples together that students should copy, everyone has an opportunity to ask me or classmates for help or clarification, and some class time is given for independent work on the assignment. At the end of each day we review what is due the next day, and what materials must be packed in backpacks to complete the work. Therefore, by the time students get home with an assignment they should need little or no assistance.

Students should expect to spend about 1 hour on homework Monday through Thursday, depending on a student's use of class time, work quality, and skill level. In addition to homework, students are expected to spend a minimum of 20-30 minutes each day reading a literature book.
(Please refer to the articles I have provided about "homework.")

Homework Problems:

- Child is spending more than an hour or less than one hour. Please send a note telling me what is happening.
- Child doesn't bring home necessary materials. This should never happen, but if it does it means the child is not paying attention at the end of the day. If necessary, I will sign him/her out of the classroom each day checking to see that all materials are packed before he/she goes home. This, of course, is a last resort, since sixth grade students should take this responsibility themselves.
- Child doesn't complete homework. I expect students to spend one hour of scheduled homework time. If the student is really working for one hour, but can't complete assignments, send me a note. Usually this means that students have not listened during class, didn't ask questions to get help, or did not use their time effectively. I need to know what is happening at home in order to address this issue. Busy home schedules, visitors from out of town, and a variety of other circumstances are usually not sufficient to excuse incomplete homework.
- Child completes work, but leaves it at home. (See DNP's Backpack Rule below.) Since we correct work in class each day, work that is left at home loses its value. Late work is not corrected. Late work receives a zero score and is averaged with other grades for the subject.
- Work is missed due to illness absence. If students are able to complete work without the benefit of the classroom lessons, that is great. But in many cases it will be impossible for students to make up missed work. If there is essential work I will give extra time for it to be completed.

DNP's Backpack Rule: All school materials and your child's backpack should never be separated. The backpack follows materials to wherever homework is done, and is repacked before homework time is over. Then student should put the packed backpack by the door from which he/she leaves for school.

Student Progress Reports: Parents are expected to check student work regularly in order to be aware of progress and/or need for additional help or support. This is the best way for you to have a complete, accurate, and timely picture of your child's academic progress. On the first day of each week you should see and sign the assignment calendar. The next day you may keep the calendar at home for reference, or it can stay in your child's daily folder. Since homework is not due until the next day, you should ask your child to share his/her work with you before it is due so that you can monitor progress. This allows you to check your child's work against the assignment calendar, so that you will know right away whether or not work is being completed. This is especially important if your child has had difficulty in the past being responsible for completing assignments.

Students will have three spiral notebooks for regular assignments in language arts, social studies, and math. These notebooks will provide a cumulative record of students' work. Students are responsible for keeping each notebook organized. Assignments are labeled (subject, title, page number, etc.), dated, corrected with red pen or pencil ('C' for correct, 'X' for incorrect, and/or comments), and scored. Even if you don't see your child's work every day, the cumulative record of the spiral notebook will give you a clear picture of your child's performance. I evaluate students' notebooks periodically. A complete and carefully maintained notebook is an important part of both achievement and effort grades on the report card.

Students also complete assignments and take tests that are not kept in the spiral notebooks. When these assignments are corrected and returned to students they should be placed in pocket folders that I have provided for each subject: yellow - language arts; blue - social studies; red - math. This organizational system also allows you to see your child's work. Please do not remove completed and corrected work from folders. From time to time we will clear out corrected work and place it in a portfolio in the classroom. At the end of each grading period work in portfolios will be reviewed as part of the report card and parent-teacher-student conference evaluation process.

Evaluation and Grading: Students are actively involved in evaluation processes both with their own and other students' work. A variety of evaluation systems are used. Assignments are:
1. Recorded to indicate completion.
2. Holistically graded with a +, /+, /, /-, or - evaluation (/ stands for a check mark). These markings are roughly equivalent to A, B, C, D, or F grades.
3. Corrected with written comments.
4. Given letter grades and/or percentage scores.
Grades in Language Arts, Math, and Social Studies are based on:
- completion of regular assignments,
- oral participation, and
- achievement level on tests and projects.
(These three elements are weighted approximately equally.)
Grades in Computer Lab, Art, Handwriting, and P.E. are based on participation and effort.

Student Behavior Expectations: Students are expected to be responsible and respectful, and to contribute to a classroom environment that is peaceful and productive. Students are expected to cooperate and participate actively in all class activities. That means they will listen, speak, work and learn together with their classmates and teachers. Students will be positively recognized for appropriate behavior. It is expected that each student will feel rewarded by his/her efforts to achieve behavioral and academic goals.

Students who are unable to follow behavior expectations will be reminded of the expectations and will be asked to take a "time-out" at the classroom "Counseling Center." Parents will be notified through a "Student Bulletin" if difficulties persist.

Please write a note or call before a <u>concern</u> becomes a <u>crisis</u>! I prefer to communicate through notes, but you may leave messages on the classroom voice mail as well. If you want to conference with me, please make an appointment in advance so that I can plan accordingly. Please keep in mind that I use my time in the classroom before and after the school day to plan, review student work, set up materials, etc. I count on having this time for my daily planning and preparation.

I look forward to meeting you Monday night!

Deborah Nichols Poulos

++

"Back to School Night" Parent Information Response: Student's Name _____

_____ I have read and intend to support the homework and behavior management plan for my child this year.

_____ I have some questions/concerns about the stated plans for my child. Explain concerns/questions on an attached page.

Parent signature: _____   99btsn.doc

218

Back To School Night Questionnaire

Child's Name:_____

Parent Name(s):_____

1. What particular goals would you like to see your child work toward this year?

2. What interests or hobbies does your child enjoy outside school?

3. Is there anything you can tell me about your child that would help me to know and/or get along more easily with him/her?

Please fill this out and return it to me at Back To School Night or send it to school with your child.   Thanks!

Patwin School
Fifth Grade, Room 20
Nichols Poulos
Back-to-School Night

STUDENT GOALS

_____
Student's Name

1. List three goals you have for your child this year. Consider academic, social, and emotional issues.

A.

B.

C.

2. List words or phrases describing your child which may help me to better understand her/his needs.

3. List interests or hobbies that your child pursues out of school?

4. Would you be willing to share a talent, hobby, profession, slides/pictures from a trip, etc. with our class? Would you be willing to arrange for someone to give a talk or demonstration to our class?

5. Would you be willing to help in the classroom? Art, computers, literature, social studies, math, music? At what time(s) and how frequently would you be available?

1996-1997 Weekly Schedule
Sixth Grade - Room 20
Deborah Nichols Poulos

Time	Monday	Tuesday	Wednesday	Thursday	Friday
8:30 8:50	Opening/ DIRT	Opening	Opening/News DIRT	Opening/News DIRT	Opening/News DIRT
8:50	Core Program	**LIBRARY SKILLS/ RESEARCH** 8:35 - 9:10	Core Program	Core Program	Core Program
10:05			SCIENCE		
10:15					
10:30					
10:45					
10:45 11:00	RECESS	RECESS	RECESS	RECESS	RECESS
11:00 11:15	Core Program	SCIENCE	Core Program	COMPUTER LAB	SCIENCE
11:30					
11:30 11:40					
11:40 12:00					
12:00 12:20	DIRT/ Story Time	DIRT/ Story Time	DIRT/ Story Time	DIRT/ Story Time	DIRT/ Story Time
12:20 1:05	LUNCH	LUNCH	LUNCH	LUNCH	LUNCH
1:05 1:30 1:55	6th MATH	6th MATH	6th MATH Dismissal	6th MATH	6th MATH
1:55 2:05	RECESS	RECESS		RECESS	RECESS
2:05 2:35	P.E. ROTATION	P.E. ROTATION		P.E. ROTATION	Class P.E. Option
2:35 3:05	SECOND LANGUAGE	SECOND LANGUAGE		SECOND LANGUAGE	SECOND LANGUAGE
3:05	Clean-up & DISMISSAL	Clean-up & DISMISSAL		Clean-up & DISMISSAL	Clean-up & DISMISSAL

"Core Program" refers to Literature, Language Arts, Writing, Social Studies, Art & Music Appreciation. The length and frequency of lessons in these subjects will vary. Whenever possible core subjects will be integrated.

Note:
BOLDFACE CAPS - fixed schedule periods
Lowercase - flexible schedule periods

96daily6.doc

Back-to-School Night
Patwin School
Fifth Grade, Room 20
September 16, 1992

Dear Parents:

My goal is to create and maintain a classroom environment that supports each child's social, emotional, and academic development. The study of United States history and geography is a focal point of the fifth grade year. Students will read literature and create written work related to this focus. The curriculum includes math, science, physical education, art, and music. Your support at home will enhance your child's success in the classroom. I hope the following will be helpful.

School/Home Communication - Weekly notices and bulletins go home on Mondays. A routine for receiving and returning notices is recommended. I will use students' assignment notebooks when I need to send an individual note home.

Assignment Notebooks - I have provided each student with a "steno" notebook in which assignments are recorded daily. The assignment notebook is intended to help students to be accountable for their work. Checking your child's notebook at least once each week will help reinforce the importance of keeping a neat and accurate record of assignments. I hope the notebook will assist you in monitoring your child's assignments.

Homework - This year I am trying a new system for math lessons and assignments. Your child will have a homework assignment from the "Student Resource Book" four days a week. These assignments will be corrected in class the following day, and should be kept in order in a math spiral notebook. Other homework will be work that was not completed in class. From time to time students will have homework associated with special projects.

Most assignments are due the day after they are given. Reviewing assignments with your child at least once or twice a week will help reinforce conscientious work habits. Setting aside a special time when your child shares with you his/her activities, concerns, accomplishments, and challenges is very important. Comment on your child's improvement, effort, thoughtful responses, lively details, etc. Keeping a positive focus will help motivate your child to look forward to these weekly reviews of his/her work.

Study Time - Your child needs to have a quiet space where he/she can work on assignments at home. Students should spend about 30 minutes per day on homework. Let me know if your child is spending too much time on homework.

When assigned homework takes less than 30 minutes I hope students will use the rest of their time to review work, practice a skill, read, etc.

Student Behavior - My management style relies primarily upon developing a personal relationship with each student. I expect students to behave and conduct themselves in ways that contribute to the overall environment of the classroom. I recognize and appreciate students' efforts to develop and use good judgment in behaving appropriately. Occasionally I will ask a student to speak with me during recess or after school to discuss his/her behavior. If there is a persistent problem, I will call you or write a note so that you can participate in working out a solution.

Student Assessment - I hope to maintain student portfolios of work in math, literature/language arts, and social studies. Every three to four weeks students will review their files and select examples of their best and worst work. Portfolios should assist us in setting and reviewing goals. At conference time the portfolios will be used to display and assess student progress.

I am looking forward to a great year with your children. Please feel free to contact me any time you have questions or concerns. The best way to communicate with me is through notes. It is sometimes difficult to make or receive telephone calls at school, and I try to maintain my time at home in the evening for my family. However, should you have a concern that requires an immediate response, please do not hesitate to call me at 756-7797.

Sincerely,

Deborah Nichols Poulos

****

Parent Letter Survey

Did you find this letter helpful? _____

I would appreciate any comments that you may wish to make concerning this letter or the program it outlines.

Comments:

_____
Name

Back-to-School Night Information Packet
September 16, 1997

Dear Parents:

Sly Park - 6th grade Outdoor Education Program - October 13-17. First installment checks or scholarship requests were due Fri., Sept. 5. It would be very helpful if we could get a few parents with pick-up trucks to transport luggage, and a few cars to take overflow passengers from the bus. If you can drive up on Monday, and/or back on Friday, please let me know. A note rescheduling the parent meeting night to Tues., Sept. 23, at 7:00 pm, was sent home last Thursday.

Fall Conference Appointment Schedule - Parent-Teacher-Child Conferences will be held November 3-7. Conference appointment request forms are available tonight. If you want to request a specific time, please indicate three preferred days/times, if possible, and any days/times you are unavailable. Don't forget to consider your child's after school schedule as well. Students are required to attend the conference.

The Sixth Grade Program - The parent letter in the packet sent home on the first day of school gave an overview of the sixth grade curriculum.

Morning Program

Social Studies - Topics to be studied include: Early Man, Early Middle Eastern Civilizations (Ancient Egypt & Mesopotamia), Early Asian Civilizations (Ancient India & Ancient China), Foundations of Western Civilization (Ancient Israelites, Ancient and Classical Greece), Rome (The Rise, The Empire, Christianity, The Fall), and Geography. Students will learn through reading in the text, related literature titles, and research sources; as well as through projects and audio-visual materials.

Literature - Students will choose and be assigned to read various novels throughout the year. Students will read from the literature text book and complete related vocabulary, comprehension, and grammar/usage exercises. Students will read literature titles related to the social studies topics above. I hope to find six parents who will lead small literature discussion groups beginning in November. Let me know when you are available. Sign-up tonight.

DIRT (Daily Independent Reading Time) - Students have at least 20 to 30 minutes of DIRT each day.

Writing - Students will practice and develop their writing skills across the academic subjects. At first we will focus on the skills necessary to pass the 6th grade writing competency test. For this test students must write a two paragraph essay with clear topic sentences, topic development with at least three detail/supporting sentences, and clear concluding sentences. Correct spelling, mechanics, grammar, and usage are required to pass this writing competency test.

In writer's workshop, students will draft, edit, rewrite, and publish. We will focus on clear expression and organization, as well as vivid and lively description. We will work on these goals through both creative and research/report writing.

Computer - Students began keyboarding skills practice last week. If you have a computer at home please insist that your child practice correct posture and keyboarding. Students must master keyboarding to facilitate longer writing projects. After a review of keyboarding, one hour per week will be spent on word processing to practice writing skills. Word processing is an integral part of the development of your child's writing skills. Other computer programs will be used as they relate to the sixth grade program goals.

Library Skills - Students have a lesson each Thurs., 9:20-9:55 a.m., with Librarian Wendy Chason. After the lesson students have time to select books and locate research resources.

Science - Students attend science classes Mon. & Thurs., 10:52-11:52 a.m. and Weds., 10:35-12:15, taught by Mrs. Rachel Milbrodt. The Science Lab is in Room 12.

Drama, Art, Music - The dramatic arts, visual arts, and oral presentations will be integrated with the academic subjects. If you are interested in helping with art activities let me know, will incorporate music into her lessons on Tuesdays. Instrumental music lessons are available through the district's program.

Afternoon Program

Math - The math period is from 1:05 to 2:05 p.m. M, T, Th, F, and 1:05 to 1:30 p.m. on Weds. Our math program began last Mon., Sept. 8th. Sixth graders are expected to have mastered their basic addition, subtraction, multiplication, and division facts. Any drill your child needs on these facts should be done at home. Homework will be assigned regularly and will be corrected by students in class the next day. Homework will review and reinforce classroom lessons. If your child is unable to complete the assigned homework in a reasonable period of time, please modify the number of problems worked and attach a note.

MathLand adopted materials, as well as other materials, will be used to meet grade level expectations. Lessons focus on concept development, problem solving, and computation skills.

Physical Education - Students will participate in a P.E. rotation program. Students from all the classes will be mixed together for a several week rotation through playground games, basketball, and volleyball. P.E. is M, T, Th from 2:15 - 2:40 pm. We may add an additional class P.E. period on Fridays.

Storytime & Preparation for Dismissal - Read aloud, and review assignments and materials to take home.

Homework Plan and Assignment Notebooks

Students are expected to spend about one hour on homework and to read for 30 minutes at home each day. Assignments are usually made at the beginning of the week. I have provided each student with a red "Homework" folder. You should see this folder with work inside every day. Unless otherwise specified, work assigned one day is due the next day. Time is available to work on assignments in class. The time a student spends completing work at home will depend upon how well he/she uses class time, his/her skill level, and the quality of work she/he produces. Please let me know if your child is spending too much or too little time on homework.

Each student should have a notebook for recording assignments and for messages between home and school. All assignments must be recorded weekly/daily and checked off when completed. I encourage parents to set up a routine for checking and signing the assignment notebook each week. Students are responsible for sharing completed assignments with parents. Parents are expected to check student work regularly in order to be aware of progress and/or need for additional help or support.

Late or Incomplete Assignments - Students are expected to complete all assignments on time, and to have all necessary materials in class each day. If an assignment was completed, but left at home, it is counted as an incomplete assignment. If incomplete work is turned in the next day, and if it is satisfactorily completed, it will receive a 'C' grade. If incomplete work is not turned in after one day it receives an 'F' grade.

Parents should be aware of assignments so they can help support their students. Most students will need extra support during the next few weeks to help establish these routines. If your child has special needs, or has had difficulty with incomplete work, it is especially important that you stay directly involved in supporting and reviewing his/her work.

Classroom Management Plan
(Behavior Expectations)

Students are expected to be responsible and respectful, and to contribute to a classroom environment that is peaceful and productive. Students are expected to be cooperative and active participants in all class activities. That means they will actively engage in listening, speaking, working and learning together with their classmates and teachers.

Students will be positively recognized for appropriate behavior. It is expected that each student will feel rewarded by his/her efforts to achieve behavioral and academic goals.

Students who are unable to follow these behavior expectations will be reminded of the expectations, be asked to take a "time-out" outside the classroom until he/she feels he can successfully follow the behavior expectations, and/or be asked to attend the "Lunch Club." If difficulties persist, parents will be asked to assist their child and the teacher in developing a plan to help establish successful classroom behavior. If necessary the school principal will be involved in these discussions.

The Lunch Club - Last year I discovered that "The Lunch Club" was a useful tool to assist students in taking responsibility for assignments and behavior expectations. One day a week I ask students needing this assistance to stay in the classroom during the lunch recess. They eat their lunch in the classroom, then work on class assignments or silent sustained reading. I excuse them before the end of the period to take a break before the next class period begins. For some students this is not sufficient time to complete incomplete work.

Evaluation and Grading

Students will be actively involved in evaluation processes both with their own and other students' work. The following evaluation methods will be used either separately or in combinations depending upon the kind of work being evaluated. Assignments will:

1. Be recorded to indicate completion.
2. Be holistically graded and will receive a +, /+, /, /-, or - evaluation (/ stands for a check mark). These markings are roughly equivalent to A, B, C, D, or F grades.
3. Be corrected and evaluative comments will be made.
4. Receive letter grades and/or percentage scores.

Working With Your Student At Home

Reading: If fluent reading at grade level has not been reached by your child, read aloud to him/her, or ask your child to read with you. It is important that your child sit next to you so that he/she can look at the words as you read them following along as your finger points out where you are. Stop periodically to discuss the vocabulary and the meaning of the story. Relate the story to other stories or to personal experiences. Reading should be a pleasurable experience. Be sure your child has at least 30 minutes of reading time at home every day.

Writing: When students are asked to go through a multiple draft writing process, it would be very helpful to your student and to me if you would correct your own child's drafts. Use a contrast color pen or pencil and write corrections directly on student's work. Look for spelling, punctuation, capitalization, grammar, usage, complete sentences, paragraph divisions, as well as check to see that the ideas are clearly presented and well organized. Students should not have to look up correct spelling in the dictionary, etc. This will only frustrate them, slow them down, and discourage them from writing. Seeing corrections made on their own work, and redrafting, helps to reinforce direct lessons focused on the conventions of correct writing. Students should be encouraged to proofread frequently during and after writing, but proofreading only goes so far. Students have to learn what is correct through the writing process and instruction in conventions over time. Our goal is that eventually they will have all the knowledge and skills to correct their own writing. For now, they need a lot of help from us to see their mistakes. The best feedback students can receive on their writing is immediate. You can make a big difference in providing this type of help to your child.

Math: Don't be shy about helping your child with math. Even if you show your child a different way to solve a problem than he/she already knows or has been taught, it only adds to your child's repertoire of math knowledge to learn another technique. Share your technique. Work a specific example. Set up a similar example for your child to try with your help. Work on the technique until your child can complete an example alone. Then give two or three more problems to practice and reinforce the technique. Mathematical reasoning and problem solving should not be mystifying or threatening. If you don't know how to solve a problem that your child asks you about, say so. Developing a positive attitude about math learning is essential to all students. Parents are very important in providing positive support for learning successful math skills. Perseverance, practice, logical reasoning skills, and clear instruction are necessary to achieve math competence. If your child comes home with a math assignment that neither you nor your child are able to complete, substitute an alternate assignment that you can help your child complete, and send a note to school asking for more support and help from the teacher.

Long Term Projects and Reports: When your child is assigned long term work, it is important that you help her/him to schedule time over the term of the project to complete its parts. All long term projects need to be broken down into smaller manageable parts. Sixth graders need help to manage their time to complete this work.

Please write a note or call before a <u>concern</u> becomes a <u>crisis</u>! With only three phone lines available to all the staff at Patwin, making or returning phone calls is a real challenge. For this reason I prefer to communicate through notes. Please make an appointment in advance if you want to conference with me before or after school. If you have not already done so, please let me know where I can reach you by phone between 3:05 and 5:00 p.m. If you must reach me at home, please call between 6:00 and 7:00 pm., at 756-7797, fax 753-5333. I hope to have my own email account soon. Anita's home number is 758-4373. We both have message machines.

Deborah Nichols Poulos - I received my undergraduate degree in English and my teaching credential from UC Davis. I have completed over 110 units of post-graduate coursework, including work for a master's degree in gifted and talented education from CSU Sacramento. I have taught in Davis since 1978 at WDE, WDI, Valley Oak, and Patwin, including seven years teaching 4th grade in the Special Abilities Program. Besides teaching my interests include house design and construction, reading, writing, and traveling. I designed and was the general contractor for construction of my home in Village Homes sixteen years ago. My husband and I did the same thing in building our current home in North Davis eleven years ago. Two years ago I was fortunate to receive a half year sabbatical leave from the school district that allowed me to visit ancient sites and archaeological museums in Italy, Greece, and Turkey. I am still working on organizing and incorporating the information and materials from this trip into my sixth grade ancient civilizations curriculum.

My husband John, a law professor at UCD, and I have four grown children: Kelly, Matt, Alekka, and John; and three grandchildren. Kelly is completing her degree in environmental studies at UC Santa Cruz fall quarter. Matt, who completed a master's degree in French Literature two years ago, works in Governor Wilson's press office. Alekka practices law in Davis with her mother. She and her husband, Michael Fullerton, are the parents of four-year-old Elsie and eighteen month old Graham. John practices law in San Francisco. John and his wife, Michele Granger, the gold medal game pitcher on the first U.S. Women's Softball Olympic Team, are the parents of seven month old Kady.

Anita Nyland - I received my undergraduate degree in Political Science and Economics and my teaching credential from UC Davis. I have taught grades 3-6 in the Pierce School District, north of Davis, and in New York City. I taught recorder in the 4th grade elementary music program for the DJUSD for three years, and have substituted at all elementary grades.

My husband Tom is a professor of veterinary radiology at the UCD Vet Med School. Our two children are Janice, 16, and Mike, 22. Mike, an avid golfer, is a senior at UCD. Janice, an avid tennis player, is a senior at Davis High. I also play tennis, and am part owner in a cattle and sheep ranch in Calaveras County.

Thank you for coming!

Deborah Nichols Poulos and Anita Nyland

++

"Back to School Night" Parent Information Response: Student's Name _____

_____ I have read and intend to support the homework and behavior management plan for my child this year.

_____ I have some questions/concerns about the stated plans for my child. Explain concerns/questions on an attached page.

Parent signature: _____   97btosch.doc

Back-to-School Night Information Packet - "Math"

September 14, 1998

Jear Parents:

Since your child is coming to my class for math, I want to give you some information about my expectations. I have included a few excerpts from my "Back to School Night" letter. Feel free to stop by Room 20 to introduce yourself sometime when you are at Patwin.

Math - Students took a math placement test week before last, and scores from last spring's SAT-9 tests were reviewed, to determine beginning math groups which began Mon., Sept. 8th.. Math placements will remain flexible to meet each student's needs. A single subject spiral notebook will be used for daily assignments. A variety of materials and teaching strategies will be used to meet grade level expectations. Lessons focus on concept development, problem solving, and computation skills. Daily homework will be corrected by students in class the next day. Homework reviews and reinforces classroom lessons. If your child is unable to complete the assigned homework, please modify the number of problems worked and attach a note. A calculator will be checked out to each student this week. Students are responsible for returning calculators at the end of the year. Please assist your child at home if he/she has not mastered basic addition, subtraction, multiplication, and division facts.

Homework Plan and Assignment Calendar - Each student has a blue math folder. You should see this folder and/or the math spiral notebook with work inside every day. **Parents are expected to check student work regularly in order to be aware of progress and/or need for additional help or support.** A parent signature on a completed assignment is worth 5 points. Unless otherwise specified, work assigned one day is due 'he next day. Time is available to work on assignments in class. Time spent completing work at home depends upon a student's use of class time, his/her skill level, and work quality. Please send a note if your child is spending too much or too little time on homework.

Establish a routine for completing homework each day, and for sharing completed work before it is turned in. Even when work is completed in class it should be taken home to be shared with parents before it is turned in. Regular parent review of class assignments is the best way for you to have a complete, accurate, and timely picture of your child's academic strengths and weaknesses. Your involvement is essential to your child's success in school.

Classroom Management Plan (Behavior Expectations) - Students are expected to be responsible and respectful, and to contribute to a classroom environment that is peaceful and productive. Students are expected to cooperate and participate actively in all class activities. That means they will listen, speak, work and learn together with their classmates and teachers. Students will be positively recognized for appropriate behavior. It is expected that each student will feel rewarded by his/her efforts to achieve behavioral and academic goals.

Students who are unable to follow behavior expectations will be reminded of the expectations and will be asked to take a "time-out" at the classroom "Counseling Center." Parents will be notified through a "Student Bulletin" if difficulties persist.

Evaluation and Grading - Students are actively involved in evaluation processes both with their own and other students' work. A variety of evaluation systems are used. Assignments are:
1. Recorded to indicate completion.
2. Holistically graded with a +, /+, /, /-, or - evaluation (/ stands for a check mark). These markings are roughly equivalent to A, B, C, D, or F grades.
3. Corrected with written comments.

4. Given letter grades and/or percentage scores.

Late or Incomplete Assignments - Students are expected to complete all assignments on time, and to have all necessary materials in class each day. A satisfactorily completed assignment turned in a day late will receive a 'C' grade. Work turned in after one day receives 'no credit,' equivalent to an 'F' grade. This policy is intended to address chronic late and incomplete work. Modifications are made for absences and extenuating circumstances on an individual basis. If your child has special needs, or has had difficulty with incomplete work, it is especially important that you stay directly involved in supporting and reviewing his/her work.

Working With Your Student At Home

Math: (See attached "Homework" articles.) Don't be shy about helping your child with math. Even if you show your child a different way to solve a problem than he/she already knows or has been taught, it only adds to your child's repertoire of math knowledge to learn another technique. Share your technique. Work a specific example. Set up a similar example for your child to try with your help. Work on the technique until your child can complete an example alone. Then give two or three more problems to practice and reinforce the technique. Mathematical reasoning and problem solving should not be mystifying or threatening. If you don't know how to solve a problem that your child asks you about, say so. Developing a positive attitude about math learning is essential to all students. Parents are very important in providing positive support for learning successful math skills. Perseverance, practice, logical reasoning skills, and clear instruction are necessary to achieve math competence. If your child comes home with a math assignment that is confusing to him/her or you, substitute an alternate assignment that you can help your child complete, and send a note to school asking for more support and help from me.

Please write a note or call before a <u>concern</u> becomes a <u>crisis</u>! I prefer to communicate through notes, but you may leave messages on the classroom voice mail as well. If you want to conference with me, please make an appointment in advance so that I can plan accordingly. Please keep in mind that I use my time in the classroom before and after the school day to plan, review student work, set up materials, etc. I count on having this time for my daily planning and preparation.

I'm happy that your child is in my math class.

Deborah Nichols Poulos

++

"Back to School Night" Parent Information Response: **Student's Name** _____

_____ I have read and intend to support the homework and behavior management plan for my child this year.

_____ I have some questions/concerns about the stated plans for my child. Explain concerns/questions on an attached page.

Parent signature: _____   btsnmath.doc

Sixth Grade Curriculum

Literature/Language Arts - The district's new language arts program includes a student text and a vocabulary & comprehension "Practice Book," and a "Grammar Book." These non-consumable workbooks must be returned in good condition at the end of the year. We will also use the new Spelling text. Assignments will be kept in single subject spiral notebooks.

SSR(Silent Sustained Reading) - Students have at least 20 to 30 minutes of SSR each day, and are required to read a minimum of 20 pages in a selected literature book during this time in class and at home. Students will choose and be assigned to read many novels this year, including titles related to the social studies topics. **Literature Discussion Groups:** I hope to find six parents who will lead small literature discussion groups every two weeks beginning in November. Sign-up at Back to School Night or send a note.

Writing - Students will practice and develop their writing skills through creative, essay, and research/report writing. Students will draft, edit, rewrite, and publish their writing. We will focus on clear expression, description, and organization. Sixth graders are expected to pass a writing competency test. Students must write a two paragraph essay with clear topic sentences, topic development with at least three detail/supporting sentences, and clear concluding sentences. Correct spelling, mechanics, grammar, and usage are required.

Social Studies - Topics include: Early Humans, Early Middle Eastern Civilizations (Ancient Egypt & Mesopotamia), Early Asian Civilizations (Ancient India & Ancient China), Foundations of Western Civilization (Ancient Israelites, Ancient and Classical Greece), Rome (The Rise, The Empire, Christianity, The Fall), and Geography. I am a "field test" teacher for two new social studies texts under consideration by the district for adoption. Part way through the field test process we will exchange one of the programs for another. For this reason the class has the opportunity to use brand new materials. I am excited about this opportunity. I have all the current <u>Messages of Ancient Days</u> (<u>MAD</u>) texts in the classroom. Students are welcome to check out a copy and keep these at home as a supplementary or enrichment resource for the 6th grade program. I expect to read the text out loud in class in order to give all students access to vocabulary and concepts. Parents are encouraged to reinforce the reading at home through rereading and discussion. This rich and exciting curriculum is demanding. We will complete several long term projects during the year.

Math - Students' math placement tests taken at the end of 5th grade and scores from last spring's SAT-9 tests will be reviewed to determine beginning math groups. We expect to regroup among the three classrooms for math. I will teach math to all the students in this classroom who are placed in the medium to high group. Mr. Davenport will do the same. These groups will work on sixth grade math skills and concepts. Mrs. Bowen & Mrs. Nahal will work with a smaller group of students (about 20) who are not ready for grade level math work. As soon as possible a math aide will be hired to work with this group. The two grade level and above classes will have about 35 students each. A single subject spiral notebook will be used for daily assignments. A variety of materials and teaching strategies will be used to meet grade level expectations and individual student needs. Lessons focus on concept development, problem solving, and computation skills. Daily homework will be corrected by students in class the next day.

Homework reviews and reinforces classroom lessons. If your child is unable to complete the assigned homework, please modify the number of problems worked and attach a note. A calculator has been checked out to each student. Students are responsible for returning calculators at the end of the year. We will spend about three weeks with math review before determining our math groups. Please assist your child at home if he/she has not mastered basic addition, subtraction, multiplication, and division facts.

Computer Lab - Students will be scheduled into the lab for keyboarding practice soon. If you have a computer at home please reinforce correct posture and keyboarding. Students are expected to master correct computer keyboarding to facilitate longer writing projects. Word processing, an integral part of the writing program, will be the focus of our time in the lab. Other computer programs will be used as they relate to the sixth grade program goals.

Students who have computers available at home are encouraged to use them. However, intention to use a computer at home does not excuse students from using class time to begin hand writing assigned work. Any long term projects done on home computers are expected to be submitted in draft form and revised well in advance of final due dates. Last minute computer glitches are not accepted as excuses.

Library Skills - Students have a lesson each Thurs., 9:15-9:55 a.m., with Librarian Wendy Chason. After the
lesson students have time to select books and locate research resources.

Science - Students attend science classes Mon. & Thurs., 10:50-11:50 a.m. and Weds., 9:55-10:35, taught by Mrs. Rachel Milbrodt. The Science Lab is in Room 12.

Drama, Art, Music - Dramatic arts, visual arts, and oral presentations will be integrated with the academic subjects. If you are interested in helping with art activities let me know. Classroom music is limited to occasional music appreciation and/or attendance at the Patwin chorus. Instrumental music lessons are available through the district's program.

Physical Education - Students will participate in a 25-30 min. P.E. program four days per week. The goals of our program are fun, participation, fitness, and cooperation. If your child is unable to participate fully in P.E. please send a note. Due to recent physical limitations I hope to recruit several parents who can come in regularly, or from time to time, to assist with P.E. (See DNP's health.)

Dear Parents,   September 7, 1994

Welcome to the 1994-95 school year! We are a combination class with eleven fifth graders and nineteen sixth graders. Parents usually have more questions when their children are assigned to combination classes, and I want to use this letter to answer some of yours. Our **"Back to School Night"** program on **Tuesday, September 21st** will provide a fuller opportunity for us to discuss this years' program.

Last years' fourth and fifth grade teachers worked together to select students for placement in this class and in the other 5/6 combo taught by Ms. Elinor Olsen. We selected students who will benefit from and be successful in a combined class. A combination class presents both challenges and opportunities that are not present in a straight grade class.

Ms. Olsen and I are looking forward to working together to plan and coordinate activities for our students. She has taught fifth and sixth grades for the last five years at WDI, and before then she and I taught together at Valley Oak in the district's self-contained gifted program. I have taught 6th grade, 5th grade, and two 4/5 combo classes (one as a part of the Special Abilities Program).

Social: We have placed students within groupings that include friends. We will build a single classroom community, and we will regroup in some subjects so that students have opportunities to get together with classmates at the same grade level in other classrooms. An example of this will be in Physical Education. All Patwin's sixth graders will have P.E. three times a week together, and the fifth graders will be grouped together from Mrs. Allen's, Ms. Olsen's, and my class for that same program.

Academic: Students will go to the science class for their appropriate grade level. Literature and language arts will be taught within our classroom. Social studies will be split so that each grade gets its appropriate curriculum: for fifth graders that is U.S. History and geography from the time of the first inhabitants of North America to 1850, and for the sixth graders that is the study of ancient civilizations to the rise of Christianity. This will require some creative combining! We will begin together with a study of geography. After laying the groundwork for studying people, places, culture, society, and the past, we will begin to focus on the separate grade level curriculua. During the first few weeks I will be assessing the students' math abilities. Students will work collaboratively and alone on a variety of problem solving activities, and they will complete some computational review work. Once I know where the students are, I will be ready to plan our strategy for managing math. We will discuss that at "Back to School Night."

I hope this information is helpful to you. I am looking forward to getting to know your children and you, and to working together to make the year both academically and socially rewarding. **Please complete the attached information form** on your child and **return it to me tomorrow morning.**

Sincerely,

Debbie

Deborah Nichols Poulos   56sept1.doc

September 6, 1996

Dear Parents,

Welcome to 6th grade and the 1996-97 school year! The "Back to School Night" program for 6th grade parents will be **Monday, Sept 16 from 8:00 to 9:00 pm** in the classroom, Room 20. The Science presentation for 6th grade parents is from 7:00 to 8:00 pm in the Science Lab, Room 12. I hope you will come to hear important information about the year, meet other parents, and ask questions. I look forward to meeting you.

Sly Park - 6th grade Outdoor Education Program - All three Patwin sixth grade classes will go to Sly Park, near Pollock Pines, the week of October 7-11. Information packets will be given to parents at Back to School Night, and a special parent meeting will be announced in the weekly Patwin Newsletter. Letters about the cost of the program went home Weds. with the foreign language placement letters. The **first payment** of all ($133), half ($62.50), or one quarter of the cost was **due Fri., Sept. 6.**

Math Placement - Students will take a math placement test next week to determine their beginning math groups. Initial placements will be changed as needed depending upon students' needs. The math period will be M, T, TH, F from 1:05 -1:55 pm, and W from 1:05 - 1:30 pm.

Second Language Classes - Second language classes begin next week, and will meet on M, T, Th, F from 2:35 - 3:05 pm. Students will take French or Spanish. This schedule will mean that students may not be dismissed to go home until 3:10 pm.

Physical Education - All 6th grades will participate in a P.E. rotation program. Students from all classes will be mixed together for a five to six week rotation through three sports/games. P.E. will be M, T, Th from 2:05 - 2:30 pm.

Social Studies - Our first unit is the introductory chapters from the textbook, <u>Messages from Ancient Days</u> (<u>MAD</u>). We will learn about the work of historians and archaeologists, and we will study the beginnings of civilization in the Mediterranean region. Our curriculum includes the ancient civilizations of Mesopotamia, Egypt, Greece, Rome, Israel, India, and China. We also study Early Man. I have just returned from a four and a half month sabbatical study trip through Italy, Greece, and Turkey visiting archaeological sites and museums. I am looking forward to sharing what I have learned, my 20 hours of video tape, and all the books and slides I have collected.

Literature - I will be using the spring Gates-McGinitie Reading Test results to assess students' reading levels. We are beginning our literature study using the Houghton-Mifflin text and workbooks. After I have 6 parent volunteers I will set up the small literature discussion group program to begin in early November. Students are expected to spend at least 30 minutes a day reading literature at home. Time is set aside for silent sustained reading in class, as well.

Writing - Improving writing proficiency is a big part of the 6th grade program. Two short writing assignments will be due each week for the next eight weeks. Each assignment will require an edited rough draft attached to a polished draft. It is expected that with help from a classmate, friend, or parent, the student will present a polished draft that has been corrected for spelling, writing mechanics, grammar and usage. Once this basic proficiency is reached we will work on the stylistic elements of writing.

Students are required to write a five sentence paragraph about a topic of their choice. Self selection of topics requires students to discover and write about topics of interest to them. We will spend 25 minutes of class time each day in Writers' Workshop. Time will be required at home to make corrections on rough drafts. If you will not be able to provide spelling, mechanics, grammar and usage corrections on your child's work (one paragraph) twice a week, please let me know right away. If a few parents can help other students with this kind of correcting work in the classroom or at home, please let me know. Later this fall students will research, take notes, draft, revise, edit, and redraft on the way to longer polished writing products.

Homework and Assignment Notebooks - Students should expect to spend about one hour each day to complete class assignments. This is in addition to the 30 minutes of literature reading. Work assigned one day is usually due the next day. Time is available to work on assignments in class. The time a student spends completing work at home will depend upon how well he/she uses class time, his/her skill level, and the quality of work he/she produces. Please let me know if your child is spending more or less time on homework. Ask your child to bring home work completed in class.

I would like each child to use an assignment notebook to record all assigned work each day. Steno type notebooks work well for this purpose. I hope most students can get their own steno notebooks, but I have several available in case your child needs one.

Late or Incomplete Assignments - Students are expected to complete all assignments on time, and to have all necessary materials in class each day. If an assignment was completed, but left at home, it is counted as an incomplete assignment. When late work is turned in it is checked off as complete, but it is not graded. If family circumstances prevent a student from completing an assignment on time, please send me a note so that I can determine whether credit for the work can be given. Chronically late and incomplete work will result in a failing grade for the class.

Adapting Assignments to Meet the Special Needs of Students - The sixth grade curriculum is a demanding high level curriculum. Students whose reading, writing, or math skills are below grade level will not be able to complete regular assignments at the expected level. The time to negotiate changes in expectations is before students, and parents, reach the frustration level. I am working with the Resource Specialist and the Reading Specialist to adapt assignments for students identified for these programs. If your child is working at the frustration level at home, please let me know immediately.

Homework Routines - Most students will need some extra support from you during the next few weeks to help establish homework routines. If your child has had difficulty completing assignments in the past you should require your child to show you all of his/her work before it is turned in. This will support him/her in getting off to a good start this year.

Please write a note or call before a concern **becomes a** crisis! It is next to impossible to get to a free telephone during the day at school, so I prefer to communicate through notes. If you need to reach me by phone at home my number is 756-7797. I am usually home from school by 5:30 pm, and don't mind receiving calls until 6:30. We eat late and go to bed early, so I would appreciate any calls before 7:00 pm.

Literature Volunteers Needed! We have had two years of a very successful literature reading/discussion group program. The average increase in reading skills for each of the two years has been 1.6 years. Some students have made three or four years of growth. I will talk about this at Back to School Night. One morning per week for 30 minutes from 8:40 to 9:10 am is when I need discussion leaders. Let me know what days and times you could be available.

See you at Back to School Night!   Deborah Nichols Poulos

SCRIP - First SCRIP order due Thurs., Sept. 12.

September 20, 1999   **Math Information Letter**

Dear Parent,

Today was the first day of our 6th grade regrouped math classes. Your child has been assigned to my math group. For about the next four weeks we will be working from an algebra program called "Hands on Equations" (HoE). Today I introduced the program, modeled how I want students to show their work and check their solutions.

I expect students to keep an orderly notebook with their name, the date, page or lesson number on every page (back to back). Students will correct their own work in class each day with a red pen or pencil using 'C' for correct & 'X' for incorrect. Additional work and notes added to assignments during correcting should be shown in red. No pages of completed work should be removed from the notebook.

All math assignments will be kept in a single subject spiral notebook. I bought red spiral notebooks for the students, but I may not have enough. (Some students will use an alternate color notebook that they have provided themselves.) I have also provided a red pocket folder in which students should keep this "HoE" packet, as well as any other packets I provide during the year. Students are expected to keep these packets protected in the folders and return them in reasonably good condition (all pages intact) at the end of the unit. Any other supplementary math worksheets should be kept in these math folders, as well. When corrected work and tests are returned, students should store them in these folders until I ask them to move work to the classroom portfolios. This will give you time to see worksheets and test results before they are stored in the classroom. I plan to move work from the folders to the classroom portfolios at the end of each unit. There will be periodic tests during a unit and a final unit test.

You should expect your child to come home with one or more example problems completed, plus additional work completed during class work period. Our math periods usually begin by correcting the previous day's assignment. Work that is incomplete or left at home does not receive credit, and is of little value to the student's math learning process. (Incomplete and missing work will negatively affect students' achievement and effort grades on the report card at the end of the grading period.) After correcting we spend a little time going over questions about trouble problems from the previous day's lesson. This is an important lesson period even for students who did not miss any problems, for different ways of looking at problems and other instructional information is a part of this "debriefing." Then the lesson for the next day is presented. We have questions and lots of discussion. I model problems which students are expected to copy into their notebooks, students model problems, etc. At the end of the lesson students get from 10 to 20 minutes to work on the assignment for the next day in class. This gives me a chance to give individual help to students who need it, and let me know they need it. This also gives students a chance to work together. By the end of the math period, if anyone still doesn't understand what to do, they can meet with me during recess or after school. Students may exchange phone numbers with classmates to discuss work over the phone at home. Assignments are considered to be learning experiences. I do not give achievement grades on the number of correct or incorrect answers on daily practice.

I prefer for you to communicate immediate issues through notes. I frequently can't answer phone messages until the next day. But if you want to reach me by phone the number is 757-5383, ext. 120.

Thanks,

Debbie

Deborah Nichols Poulos

October 21, 1996

Dear Parent,

Beginning this week a math aide will be working with your child two math periods per week. The aide, Jo Cowen, will work with a small group of students who have not yet mastered the basic math skills and concepts required to proceed with the regular 6th grade math program.

The math program for these students will focus on mastering the following skills:
Place Value Skills - Reading and writing large numbers, rounding to different places, and comparing & ordering numbers to the billions place and the thousandths place.
    Using (>) - "greater than" and (<) - "less than" symbols.
Adding/Subtracting Skills - Knowing basic facts from 0 to 20 with speed and accuracy.
Addition Skills - Adding multi-digit numbers with regrouping and correct decimal alignment.
Subtraction Skills - Subtracting multi-digit numbers with regrouping and correct decimal alignment.
Multiplication Skills - Knowing times table facts to 12 X 12 with speed and accuracy. Multiplying 2-digit numbers.
Division Skills - Knowing division facts to 144 divided by 12 with speed and accuracy. Dividing 2 & 3-digit numbers by 1 & 2-digit numbers, with and without remainders and decimals.
Basic Concepts - Understanding the relationships between the functions of addition, subtraction, multiplication, & division. Solving simple word problems in which basic operations must be selected.
Vocabulary - Knowing the meaning of: sum, difference, factor, product, dividend, divisor, quotient, etc.

**All of these skills are required before students can be successful
with the regular sixth grade math program.**

The 6th grade math program builds on these skills to teach the following skills:
Fractions Skills - Adding, subtracting, multiplying & dividing fractions. Understanding equivalent fractions, simplifying fractions, converting improper fractions to mixed numbers and vice versa, converting to common denominators.
Multiplication Skills - Understanding multiples, factors, and prime factors; and prime and composite numbers. Understanding exponents and squares, and the basic properties of muliplication (associative, commutative, and distributive).
Fractions/Ratios & Decimals/Percent Skills - Understanding the relationships between these. Finding equivalencies and calculating values.
Geometry Skills - Knowing geometric vocabulary for points & lines, and plane & solid figures. Finding perimeter & circumference; area of rectangles, triangles, & circles; and using "pi." Finding surface area & volume.
Data Collection & Analysis Skills - Recording, interpreting, graphing different kinds of information on line, bar, and circle graphs.
Probability - Understanding and using probability.
Integers - Coordinate graphing; and adding, subtracting, & multiplying positive and negative numbers.

Any additional time you can spend with your child at home will help speed up his/her progress to be ready for the 6th grade math program. An important part of your child's success will be setting dated goals and setting aside regular homework time for drill exercises and problem solving practice. Thank you.

Sincerely,

Curriculum Information Letter to Parents
October 5

Dear Parents,

We have just completed five busy weeks of school. We have finished our unit on <u>The Mixed-Up Files of Mrs. Basil E. Frankweiler</u>, artist research and presentations, a unit on immigrants, and math units on geoboard geometry and chapter one in the text. As a culmination of our literature unit students prepared and presented scenes from every chapter of the story, and completed a vocabulary, comprehension, critical thinking, and personal response test.

Literature/Language Arts - For the next several weeks we will use the literature text and support workbooks as the basis for our literature and language arts work. Those students who need additional challenges will be participating in supplementary literature reading and writing activities. Students needing additional support in reading and writing skills will be concentrating their efforts on the text and related exercises.

Math - For the last two weeks we have been working to establish a process that will allow for individual progress in math. I am incorporating a lot of manipulative and visual materials in the math program. The text publishers provide extensive diagnostic materials that I am using in designing our use of the text. After taking a pretest students receive practice assignments that are directly related to the problems missed. After completing and correcting assignments students may take the pretest again, or go on to the posttest. Similarly, the missed items on the posttest will result in another assignment designed to reteach and provide practice in areas of weakness.

Since students will be working on assignments which target their individual areas of need, rather than on uniform assignments for the whole class. It is my hope that **motivation** and **learning** will be optimized for each student. The downside of this type of program is not being able to monitor students' work on a daily basis. **For this reason it will be very important for you to check on your child's progress frequently**. Dated and labeled (page and problem numbers) pages in the math spiral notebooks should provide clear evidence of your child's daily progress, and the "Math Progress Log" should provide a summary of daily work completed. Since problems will vary in difficulty and amount of time needed to solve, it is impossible for me to state an exact number of problems which should be completed each day. I can say that **ten (10) problems is a daily minimum**, but two or three times that number may be appropriate in some cases.

Our math period is 50 minutes long. Each day students will receive a 15-20 minute group lesson, and will have at least 20-30 minutes of independent work time. I am establishing **Wednesday as our "test day"** so that testing can occur in a quiet, controlled, environment. There is no requirement that students demonstrate mastery on one chapter before going on to the next chapter. It will usually take less than a day to create the individualized assignment list after completion of a pre or posttest. But students should never be "waiting" for the results of the test without proceeding to work on practice problems from the text.

With a few more weeks of experience with this process I hope students will feel comfortable and confident. So far everyone seems enthusiastic, but some are still a little shaky about the mechanics and some are having trouble being accountable. That's why I have provided this rather lengthy description of the process for you. **Please let me know if you have any questions or concerns about how to assist your child in being successful.**

"A Time For Sharing" – Two weeks ago I passed out bright pink forms with the heading "A Time For Sharing." The purpose of these forms is to remind and encourage your child to share class work at home. There are lines on which to indicate you child's name, the date, the subject of an assignment shared, your comments, and your signature. These are accessible to students at all times. I would like to get at least one per week.

Reminder - Please return the bright gold "Student Goals" sheets that I distributed at "Back to School Night."

Return Response - Please sign and return the tear-off below so that I know you received this letter. Thanks,

Debbie

_____

_____

Parent Letter #1

_____ Student's name

_____ Parent Signature

Comments:_____

Homework Policy Plan
Valley Oak School
Fourth Grade – Special Abilities Class

Dear Parents,

Homework will consist primarily of completing regularly scheduled class assignments. You can expect almost daily assignments in math, reading, and writing. Children may have homework in these subjects depending upon how well they use their class work time and how quickly they work. Children will have homework on a less regular basis in other subject areas in order to complete class assignments or projects.

Usually a child will not need to spend more than 30 minutes or so completing class assignments at home. If your child is spending more than this amount of time to complete assignments on a regular basis, please let me know.

Each child will keep an assignment notebook for recording daily assignments. Please ask your child to show you this assignment notebook and the completed assignments from time to time. This will provide a means for you to keep informed of your child's daily work, and will help your child to understand the value of the assignment notebook. Please add an encouraging note to your child about the work he/she is doing.

You may use your child's assignment notebook for messages you wish to communicate to me. This notebook can provide a convenient place for you to note reasons for absences or times your child will need to leave the class for doctor/dentist appointments. I will use your child's assignment notebook for notes to you as well.

In the event that your child has repeated difficulty completing assignments on time, I will use the **assignment notebook** to let you know **what work needs to be completed**.

Assignment Notebook Responsibilities:

Student: • Record all assignments in an orderly fashion.
• Complete all assignments as directed.
• Periodically review assignment notebook & assignments with parents.

Parents: • Periodically review assignment notebook & assignments with your child.
• Write a note from time to time (once a week or so) to your child about his/her progress.
• Check for notes from Debbie about incomplete assignments.

Teacher: • Assignments will be written on chalkboard each day.
• Assignments will be monitored for completion.
• Incomplete assignments will be noted in students' assignment notebooks.

It is of critical importance that children keep up with their assignments on a daily basis. I greatly appreciate your support and assistance in helping you child to be a responsible student. Please sign and return the slip below indicating that you have read and intend to support this homework policy plan. Thank you.

I look forward to a very successful 1989-90 school year.

Sincerely,
Deborah Nichols Poulos

_____

_____

I have read and intend to support the homework policy plan for

_____'s class.

Parent Signature: _____

HOMEWORK PLAN

Homework will consist primarily of completing regularly scheduled class assignments. From time to time specific "homework only" assignments will be made. Your child should use his or her "assignment notebook" in which to record all assignments. Your child should get in the habit of taking this notebook back and forth between school and home each day so that you have a regular means of keeping track of your child's assignments.

At the end of each week a "Congratulations" note will be sent home with each child who has completed all of the week's assignments on time. A "Late or Incomplete Assignment" note listing any assignments not completed by Friday will also be sent home at the end of each week. Both notes must be signed by a parent and returned on the first day of the next week.

All assignments are expected to be ready to be corrected or turned in when they are due. If incomplete or late assignments are turned in by the end of the week during which they were due or the first day of the next week credit will be given. However, late or incomplete work may not be evaluated. If a student receives three "Late or Incomplete Assignment" notes a student-parent-teacher conference will be scheduled. Students who consistently complete all of their assignments on time will receive recognition for their efforts.

It is of critical importance that children keep up with their assignments on a daily basis. It is in consideration of your interest in being kept informed of your child's assignments and work that this system was devised. This system is more workable than requiring children to stay after school to complete their work, since after school schedules are busy and transportation arrangements are frequently complicated.

We hope that we can all work together to make the system an effective one. Each of us has an important role to play.

1. Completing and returning assignments is the child's responsibility.
2. Signing and returning notices is the parent's responsibility.
3. Preparing and sending home notices is the teacher's responsibility.

DEBORAH NICHOLS POULOS

Dear Parent,   November 5, 1999

During the first grading period your child demonstrated consistently above average or outstanding reading and language arts skills. For this reason I have proposed a modified approach to our regular spelling, grammar, and Spotlight reading & practice book lessons. I have met with your child to explain the system. Students in this group will have the opportunity to work more independently, with partners, and to use more of the language arts/reading period for social studies related reading, research, and writing. Opportunities for more independence, however, brings risks. Students will must keep in touch with me if they need additional support and assistance. They will also need monitoring from you.

These students will continue to take the lesson tests at the end of each week in spelling, grammar, and the reading text book assignments. Your child will continue to receive the weekly assignment calendar that will show the standard lesson schedule, but will modify according to the directions that follow.

In the case of grammar lessons, instead of completing all items on pages 32, 33, & 34 for Tues., Weds., & Thurs., students will meet in their partner groups on Monday to discuss and learn the lesson concept for the entire week. Then they will work together to complete the first three items of practice from each page. (That is, p. 32, items 1-3; p. 33, items 1-3, and p. 34, items 1-3.) On Tuesday morning all these students will meet with me to correct their work and to be sure they understand how to apply the week's lesson concepts. On Tues. they will decide on a writing topic that demonstrates application of the grammar lesson concepts. As a "rule of thumb" the paper should be about three paragraphs long. The paper will be due each Thurs. and will be shared in the partner groups, either reading aloud or passing papers to be read silently. This written work will be evaluated by me. This work and the test would complete students' grammar responsibilities for the week,

For Spelling, there is slightly more variation in the students' needs. Some students are being excused from writing the spelling lesson words many times. Some students need to continue to write the words several times to maintain their strong performance on tests. I am allowing students to judge this for themselves and to adjust, if necessary, after seeing test results. Despite these variations, the minimum spelling lesson all these students are responsible for are: "word sort," "build vocabulary," "word study," "proofreading" (corrections only, entire paragraph does not need to be copied), and "use the dictionary." These will be corrected according to the schedule in the weekly calendar.

When a Spotlight story is assigned these students will be expected to read it on their own. Sometimes this will mean the story will have to be read at home. This group of students will usually be excused from the Practice Book exercises, except for the first page (vocabulary lesson). They will take the vocabulary/comprehension test on the story at the end of the week.

Please sign and return the slip below if you agree to these modifications. Please feel free to note any comments or questions. Thanks, Debbie

++
Return to DNP by Monday, Nov. 8th.

My child, _____, has my permission to participate in the modified Spelling, Grammar, and Spotlight reading and Practice book assignments. I understand that I will need to continue to monitor my child's work to see that it is regularly completed.

Parent signature: _____

October 21, 1996

Dear Parents,

Parent-Student-Teacher Conferences are scheduled for the week of November 4-8. Remember that students are expected to be a part of this conference. We will summarize student progress and set future goals. I look forward to meeting with you and your child for this important educational program review meeting. Please come to the courtyard side of the classroom and knock on the door to let me know you are here. Please call the school office if you need to cancel your appointment.

The following schedule represents my best effort to accommodate parent requests. I was not able to accommodate everyone's preferred time. I know that your child's academic success is one of your top priorities, and I hope you will be able to set aside this time to review your child's progress. Appointments are for 25 minutes.

(Names shown in **bold type** indicate confirmed conference times requested at Back-to-School-Night or with the appointment request form. If your appointment is not already confirmed, please return the attached response form.)

Mon., Nov. 4	Tues., Nov. 5	Weds., Nov. 6	Thurs., Nov. 7	Fri., Nov. 8
3:35-4:00 p.m. **B. Lee**	8:05-8:30 a.m. **R. Al-Zaben**		8:05-8:30 a.m. **I. MacKenzie**	8:05-8:30 a.m. **A. O'Brien**
4:00 Mike Lopez	1:40-2:05 p.m. **Keith K.**	1:40 D. Bedard	1:40 **A. Letro**	1:40 **J. Velinsky**
4:25 **A. Kaseman**	2:05 M. Rikimaru	2:05 T. Torres	2:05 J. Denton	2:05 D. Goode
4:50 **S. Phillips**	2:30 T. Hattori	2:30 L. Sitts	2:30 E. Moore	
5:15 **B. Wilhelm**	2:55 N. DeRonde	2:55 Nicole Lopez	2:55 T. Johns	
5:40 **A. Kluk**	3:20 F. Beegle	3:20 D. Haff	3:20 **H. Schindel**	
6:05 **M. Chandler**		3:45 N. Driemeyer		
		4:10 **D. Lew**		

Before you request a change in your assigned appointment, please understand the complexity of the conference week schedule. Some of these appointments have been coordinated with other teachers for the convenience of parents with more than one child at this school. Also, keep in mind that I will be holding 29 conferences during the week, in addition to performing my regular teaching and program planning responsibilities. I must reserve a block of time each day to accomplish this work.

Thank you for cooperation.

Sincerely,

Deborah Nichols Poulos

Last week the students took the Gates-McGinitie Reading test for vocabulary and comprehension. I will share the results of this test with you at the conferences. The special reading program is still being set up. I will be suggesting that a few students get some additional reading support through small group "pull out" or "push in" programs. If your child participated in special reading last year, and you have specific comments or suggestions, please write me a note so that I can take your views into consideration.

I am still in search of good field trips for the year. I haven't received any suggestions. Please let me know if you have an idea. I will be working on field trip plans during the next two weeks. I would like to go on a trip or two before the winter break.

Miss Stolp has planned some interesting lessons for the class and she is excited about her two week solo. I hope you had a chance to read about her plans in the note she sent home last Thursday. Although I won't be in the classroom during this time, I will be on campus and will be meeting with Lori each day.

Debbie

Classroom Volunteer Survey

Name _____

Please mark any of the following that apply:

____ I am interested in attending a Classroom Volunteer Training Workshop.
____ I could attend a workshop during the school day.
____ I am available to work in the classroom on a weekly basis.
____ I am available to work in the classroom on an occasional basis.
____ I prefer to work directly with students.
____ I prefer to do paperwork, eg. correcting papers, preparing materials, etc.
____ I will do whatever is needed.
____ I am especially interested in doing _____.

Other comments:

I will send a follow-up note with a specific workshop date to those of you who return this survey.

Some possible times are: Monday, Nov. 2, 2:10-3:05 pm.
Wednesday, Oct. 28, 8:30-9:30 am. or Nov. 4
Wednesday, Oct. 28, 12:30-1:30 pm. or Nov. 4

(Cross out or circle times that are either impossible or possible for you.)

Thank you for your willingness to help!

Updated Reminder Letter to Parents
January 7th

Dear Parents,

Now that we are back from vacation, I thought this would be a good time for me to give you some "New Year's" information. We are already off to a great start in the classroom!

Classroom Supplies: At the beginning of the year I requested that each child provide supplies. The following is an update of that list: 3 pocket folders, 3 standard size (single subject) spiral notebooks, 8 felt tip marketing pens (optional), a standard size three ring binder, and a small "steno-pad" assignment notebook. There should be one spiral notebook each for math, literature, and social studies or research projects. Assignments should be done sequentially and kept in the notebook. For this reason notebooks must be in the class every day.

The pocket folders are for other kinds of work, and for short and long term storage of separate papers.

The binder is for organization and storage of the California Weekly Explorer publications, as well as for long term reference information.

The small assignment notebook is for recording assignments and due dates. You may want to use these for messages to me, and I can use them to send messages to you.

I cannot over-emphasize the importance of these items as organizational tools. Our in-depth and long-term projects necessitate comprehensive storage devices. Most children use backpacks for transporting their work between home and school. I encourage you to regularly help your child clean out his/her backpack and to keep materials organized. A routine check of work in each of the three notebooks should allow you to keep track of your child's progress. You should be able to find daily assignments in both the math and literature notebooks. I expect all assignments to be dated, clearly labeled, and neatly written and organized. If the work you see doesn't meet your expectations, please make your standards clear to your child. I do the same.

Complete/Incomplete Assignments: As you know from our conferences and parent meetings, we have had a serious problem with incomplete assignments. Even though sufficient classroom time is provided for most assignments, several students are regularly choosing not to use their class time to complete assigned work, nor are they completing assignments at home. I have found this situation to be quite burdensome. Trying to move forward, follow up, and account for large numbers of incomplete assignments slows the progress of the entire class, and encroaches on the time that would ordinarily be used for enrichment activities. It can place a dark cloud on a smooth functioning of our classroom routines. Additionally, students who are not using their class time to complete assigned work are more likely to disrupt the work of others. I have tried to improve the situation through a variety of "carrot and stick" techniques, as well as through parent and student conferences. Unfortunately, neither incentives nor restrictions have had the desired effect. Extraordinary attention to these kinds of details puts a further drag on the overall classroom operation.

Over the vacation I did a great deal of thinking about this situation. When all is said and done, I believe each of you is in the best position to deal with your child's work and study habits. No one system that I can devise will work for all kids, and may, in fact, run counter to family values, priorities, and schedules. If you have a reliable means of checking up on your child's work, you should be able to design individualized plans that suit your family and your child. I realize that this puts a burden on you to check your child's assignment notebook, check folders and notebooks for evidence of appropriate work, and to set expectations for your child. I feel that my primary time and effort must be devoted to providing the educational program and giving feedback to students on their work. This approach will free me to spend more of my time and energy in those endeavors.

Therefore, I will not be keeping children in the classroom during recess or after school to complete their work. Some classroom activities will be available only to students whose work is complete. In this way I hope to encourage and reward students who are completing required work.

Conferences: If you want to talk with me about your child, I would appreciate it if you would pre-arrange a time for that type of meeting. It is easiest for me to hold conferences when they do not occur on a "drop in" basis. I hope I do not sound stingy with my time, but all of my non student contact time before school, during recesses, prep time, and after school are the only times that I usually get to plan prepare materials and lessons and give feedback on student work. When the kids are in the classroom I am focused only on them.

Parent Meetings: The two informal parent meetings we have had this year have been helpful to me. I am available for an evening meeting every month. I encourage you to take advantage of this opportunity to talk with me and the parents of other students in the class. The "parent grapevine" is a fairly good tool for keeping track of what's going on in class.

Teacher Bulletins: I will try to do a better job of sending home informational bulletins, such as this one. I will try to send a note home every two weeks. You can look for the next one about Thursday, January 24th.

Current Bulletin: We are reading *The Door In The Wall*, and are doing a variety of literature and language arts activities with this story, which is set in thirteenth century England. This unit will last about two weeks. Spelling activities are incorporated into the *Door in the Wall* unit. We are working on parts of speech, vocabulary development, and literary analysis. In math we are doing a whole class unit on Multiples. This unit is activity and problem solving oriented. So far, so good. During this unit I do not expect textbook math work. The Multiples unit has occasional homework activities, but you may want to encourage your child to continue to practice textbook problems at home. We will spend about three weeks on this unit. A schedule for California History Project oral presentations went home before vacation. A copy is posted in the classroom. If you don't know when your child's presentation is scheduled, ask your child to copy his/her date from the chalkboard.

Thank you for all your help and support. You help and support me in many ways. I appreciate all of your efforts on behalf of your children, the class, and me.

Sincerely,
Debbie

Dear Parent,   February 23, 1999

This letter details some of the specific work that has been included in the second trimester grading period.

Reading/Literature: Students have 20-30 minutes of SSR time in class each day, and are expected to read as long at home, for a minimum of 20-30 pages per day. During our study of Ancient Egypt, beginning in early November and ending in mid-January, students read The Golden Goblet and Pyramid, as well as other titles related to their research. If not reading for research, students read free choice literature selections. Beginning in late January we started our parent led literature discussion groups. Students have weekly reading requirements (due Fri.), as well as a lit. notebook in which they write 10 interesting vocabulary words and ask two thought provoking questions from the story. Students also read an assigned story from the literature text and take a 10 question vocabulary and comprehension test each week. Some students complete vocab/comp exercises from the Practice workbook, as well. A high priority is placed on reading, and students are expected to fulfill the 100 to 150 page per week requirement. Grades for this period are based on completion of assignments, performance on tests, participation in class discussions; and demonstration of sustained silent reading during class SSR periods.

Language Arts (LA): Students have completed lessons from their (GR) Grammar Practice Books (pages 31-90) in their LA spiral notebooks. Weekly unit tests assess students' level of accomplishment. Students have completed (SP) Spelling Lessons 9-21. SP lessons focus on lists of 20 words grouped according to a common spelling feature, as well as three review and two challenge words. Students complete (in cursive) two pretest lists, a word sort; build vocabulary and word study; proofread; and dictionary and test yourself practices in their LA spiral notebooks; and take a final test each week. Students correct their own GR and SP lessons. Students completed regular writing assignments during our Egypt research. Recently we've focused on writing a five paragraph essay, the district's new 6th grade writing expectation, and we have completed our winter writing sample practice test. Grades are based on maintaining a complete, neat, well organized LA notebook, performance on weekly tests, overall quality of all written work, and oral participation in lessons.

Math: Students in my math group have completed units on integers and graphing; fractions review; and ratio, decimals, proportions, and percent, including rounding review. Several students pursued a geometry independent study unit. Within the focused units we continually review math computational and problem solving skills. Students are expected to maintain their daily practice lessons in their math spiral notebooks which they correct themselves in class. Weekly quizzes and other diagnostic tools assess progress, and unit tests assess achievement at the end of each unit. Grades are based on maintaining a complete, neat, well organized math notebook; completion of worksheets and quizzes; performance on unit tests; and oral participation in lessons.

Social Studies (SS): Our major social studies work during this grading period focused on our Ancient Egypt research and report. Last month students researched, wrote, and presented readers theater presentations from the Ancient Israel chapter of the Ancient Worlds textbook. Recently students have worked on writing subtopic paragraphs in preparation for writing a five paragraph essay on a topic from one of three chapters in the textbook -- Ancient India, China, or the Americas. This work has focused on helping students to construct topic sentences, three supporting detail sentences, and concluding sentences; as well as introduction and conclusion paragraphs. Grades are based on the Egypt report, the readers theater presentation, and participation in social studies lessons.

I hope this information helps you to review your child's work and understand the criteria by which his/her work was assessed for this grading period. I look forward to meeting with you and your child to discuss performance during this grading period, and to set goals for the last grading period.
Sincerely,   Deborah Nichols Poulos   99fgrade.doc

Spring Parent-Student-Teacher Conference Letter
February 26, 1999

Dear Parents,

I am looking forward to meeting with you and your child at our conference during the week of March 8-12. Your child's second trimester report card is attached to this letter. Please bring this report card with you to the conference. At this time I do not yet have students' science grades, nor the math grades for students who go to Room 22. If necessary, I will fill in these grades at our conference appointment. Below, I explain the basis for this trimester's grades.

Weekly Assignment Calendars:
As you know students receive a weekly assignment calendar on the first day of each week, and parent signatures are due the next day. If students show me a parent signature later in the week I check that off as well. The assignment calendars are especially important because they provide you with the information you need to accurately monitor your child's work at home. Twelve assignment calendars were included in this grading period. The following summarizes my assignment calendar records.

_____ Number of assignment calendars returned on due date with parent signature.
_____ Total number of assignment calendars returned with parent signature.

Personal Responsibility: This section is self-explanatory.

Reading/Literature: Achievement is based on Spotlight on Literacy reading, daily assignments, and tests; and required literature reading, accompanying written assignments, and tests. Effort is based on maintaining a complete and orderly notebook of daily assignments, oral participation, and productive use of the sustained silent reading period. (Students who do not go to RSP have a minimum of 2 hrs. 30 mins. of class time for SSR each week. Students who go to RSP must make time for silent reading at home.)

Language Arts: Achievement is based on Spotlight on Literacy daily grammar assignments and tests; Scholastic Spelling daily assignments and tests; various other writing assignments; oral participation; and the quality of written work in all subject areas of the curriculum. Effort is based on maintaining complete and orderly grammar and spelling notebooks of daily assignments, oral participation, productive use of class time, and overall quality of written work.

Mathematics: Achievement is based on daily assignments, participation in daily math lessons, and performance on tests. Effort is based on maintaining a complete and orderly math notebook of daily assignments, class participation, and productive use of class time.

Social Studies: Achievement is based on daily assignments, oral participation, tests, and special projects. Effort is based on maintaining a complete and orderly MAD (Message of Ancient Days) notebook, oral participation, productive use of class time, and overall quality of work. Since the Egypt Journal Project took the place of Spotlight and Spelling lessons for five and a half weeks of this grading period, I had expected to average these grades with Reading/Literature and Language Arts. However, I decided not to do this.

Computer, P.E., and Art grades are based on my assessment of student's effort during these activities.

I hope this helps you to understand your child's report card and to prepare for our conference.
Sincerely,

Debbie

Working With Your Student At Home
(See DNP's "Homework" articles, too.)

Reading: If fluent reading at grade level has not been reached by your child, read aloud to him/her, or ask your child to read with you. It is important that your child sit next to you so that he/she can look at the words as you read them, following along as your finger points out where you are. Stop periodically to discuss the vocabulary and the meaning of the story. Relate the story to other stories or to personal experiences. Reading should be a pleasurable experience. Be sure your child has at least 20-30 minutes of literature reading time at home every day.

Writing: When students are asked to go through a multiple draft writing process, it would be very helpful to your student and to me if you would correct your own child's drafts. Use a contrast color pen or pencil and write corrections directly on student's work. Look for spelling, punctuation, capitalization, grammar, usage, complete sentences, paragraph divisions, as well as check to see that the ideas are clearly presented and well organized. Seeing corrections made on their own work, and redrafting, helps to reinforce direct lessons focused on the conventions of correct writing. Students should be encouraged to proofread frequently during and after writing, but proofreading only goes so far. Students have to learn what is correct through the writing process and instruction in conventions over time. Our goal is that eventually they will have all the knowledge and skills to correct their own writing. For now, they need a lot of help from us to see their mistakes. The best feedback students can receive on their writing is immediate. You can make a big difference in providing this type of help to your child.

Math: Don't be shy about helping your child with math. Even if you show your child a different way to solve a problem than he/she already knows or has been taught, it only adds to your child's repertoire of math knowledge to learn another technique. Share your technique. Work a specific example. Set up a similar example for your child to try with your help. Work on the technique until your child can complete an example alone. Then give two or three more problems to practice and reinforce the technique.

     Mathematical reasoning and problem solving should not be mystifying or threatening. If you don't know how to solve a problem that your child asks you about, say so. Developing a positive attitude about math learning is essential to all students. Parents are very important in providing positive support for learning successful math skills. Perseverance, practice, logical reasoning skills, and clear instruction are necessary to achieve math competence. If your child comes home with a math assignment that is confusing to him/her or you, substitute an alternate assignment that you can help your child complete, and send a note to school asking for more support and help from me.

Long Term Projects and Reports: When your child is assigned long term work, it is important that you help her/him to schedule time over the term of the project to complete its parts. All long term projects need to be broken down into smaller manageable parts. Sixth graders need help to manage their time to complete this work. We work on this all year.

CLASSROOM MANAGEMENT PLAN

Valley Oak School's handbook asserts that each student has the right to be safe, to be happy, to learn, to be his/herself, and to hear and be heard. Students are expected to

1. be cooperative and compassionate participants in classroom activities;
2. be active listeners, workers, learners;
3. be responsible for completing assignments on time.

The following consequences will occur if students do not behave appropriately:

1. Student will receive an informal verbal warning.
2. Student's name will be entered in a dated log.
3. Student will conference with teacher.
4. Student's behavior will be communicated to parent through a note or by phone.
5. Students exhibiting "extreme" behavior will be referred to the principal.

Students will be positively recognized for appropriate behavior through praise, personal notes, etc. It is expected that each student will feel rewarded by achievement of her/his personal and educational goals.

EVALUATION PLAN

Students will be actively involved in the evaluation processes with both their own and other students' work. The following evaluation methods will be used either separately or in various combinations, depending upon the kind of work being evaluated:

1. Some assignments will not be graded.
2. Some assignments will receive a simple +, /, or – evaluation notation.
3. Some assignments will be corrected, and evaluative comments will be made.
4. Some assignments will be graded with numerical or percentage scores.
5. Some assignments will receive letter grades.

50 WAYS TO VOLUNTEER IN THE CLASSROOM

1. Be a PTA Room Parent.
2. Be a class book club account (about one hour per month).
3. Sponsor a magazine for the class.
4. Be a class computer volunteer.
5. Volunteer to help a new student learn English.
6. Volunteer regularly in class to help in other ways.
7. Send clean, empty 28 oz. peanut butter jars to class for use in math.
8. Teach the class about your native country and/or culture.
9. Share your career or interest with the class.
10. Share a holiday or seasonal activity with the class.
11. Drive on field trips.
12. Walk or ride bikes with the class on short field trips.
13. Bake items for the class cupcake sale.
14. Help the children sell items at the class cupcake sale at lunch or after school.
15. Help out with a class project from time to time.
16. Help the teacher with typing or word processing.
17. Suggest and/or help plan a pertinent class activity.
18. Take and develop pictures or slides of any class or school activity and share them or donate them to the class.
19. Volunteer some time each week in the school library.
20. Donate appropriate materials for use in our classroom program at any time during the school year.
21. Correct spelling.
22. Correct math - daily math.
23. Read aloud - listen to children read aloud.
24. Monitor a specific child.
25. Sponsor a trip to the Science Center.
26. Oversee a reading group.

27. Administer an oral reading test.

28. Correct Gates-MacGinitie tests.

29. Record programs.

30. Donate Kleenex and Band-Aids.

31. Send in videos that augment lessons.

32. Donate blank videotape.

33. Use the video equipment or teach others to use it.

34. Help students catch up on work.

35. Plan to be consistent.

36. Help with cursive writing.

37. Plan a cooking event.

38. Take down bulletin boards.

39. Housekeeping - sink area/dust books

40. Simple sewing

41. Filing

42. Help before school with the student store.

43. Oversee noontime games.

44. Assist with music program.

45. Lead a Great Books discussion.

46. Make phone calls to others.

47. Organize field trips.

48. Organize a class potluck.

49. Help supervise Book Buddy activities.

50. Your idea _____

APPENDIX E

Report Cards and Conferences

Student Self-Evaluation

Name _____ Date _____

Classroom Behavior	Usually	Sometimes	Rarely
I follow school/playground rules.			
I follow classroom rules.			
I am considerate and work well with others.			
I respect other students and myself.			
I listen and follow directions.			
I am quiet during work time.			
I use class time productively.			
I complete assignments on time			
I seek help when I need it.			
I move carefully within the classroom.			
I take care of our room and respect other people's property.			

I do my best work in _____.

My favorite subject/activity is _____.

I need to improve _____.

Write a sentence about a specific goal for each area of school evaluation.

Social Development _____

_____

Work/Study Habits _____

_____

Academic Achievement _____

_____

March 4, 1997

Dear Parents,

Attached is your third trimester parent-teacher conference appointment. Conferences have been scheduled for the week of March 17-21, from 1:40 to 3:20 p.m. Please return the response portion of the page by Friday, March 7.

If you are unable to come to Patwin to meet with me at the indicated time, you can request a telephone conference. I will call you for the telephone conference at the scheduled time, so please indicate the phone number where I can reach you then.

I have set aside four alternate conference times for Fri., March 14, at 2:15, 2:35, 2:55, and 3:15 p.m. I will fill requests for these times on a first come first served basis by March 7.

Please let me know if you don't feel that a conference is necessary.

Your child's report card will be sent home a few days before the scheduled conference so that you both may discuss progress. This time I am leaving it up to you to decide whether or not to bring your child to the conference.

On Thursday, March 20, from 9:45 to 10:45 a.m., Dennis Bonnar Emerson Junior High Counselor, will be in Room 20 to discuss the junior high program. Program planners will be sent home that day. Please feel free to attend this meeting. Other junior high meetings for parents will be held later in the spring and summer.

I am looking forward to meeting with you and your child.

Sincerely,

Deborah Nichols Poulos

Spring Parent-Student-Teacher Conference

March 9-13, 1998

Dear Parents,

Last Thursday your child brought home a report card and a portfolio of work (about an inch and a half to two inches thick, if complete) for this trimester. Students are responsible for maintaining a complete portfolio of their work for each grading period. Students are encouraged to regularly review their work with you. Your child was expected to review and discuss this grading period's work with you prior to this conference. We hope you have had an opportunity to discuss strengths and weaknesses, to comment on progress, and to help your child identify future goals.

Attached to this note are a few work samples from last week. If your child completed and turned in all of the assignments, the following work will be attached:

Literature/Language Arts:
- Spelling Unit 17: Cursive handwriting practice of the spelling words and the worksheets for Practice A, B, C (including a paragraph), and test.
- Writing/Literature: The Cay - Students were asked to write a paragraph to describe the relationship between Philip and Timothy, and to discuss how and why their relationship changed as the story evolved. Students wrote a first draft and a revised draft. The Rainbow People - Students were asked to write a paragraph telling me about something that interested them from this book. They were asked to include details, examples, and explanations.

Note: Each student is assigned between 20-30 pages of literature reading each day. Thirty minutes of SSR (silent sustained reading) time is provided in class, and students are expected to read another 30 minutes at home each day.

Social Studies:
- Labeled map of China, showing topographical regions in colored pencil.
- MAD textbook outlines
- Unit test for Chapter 9: China

Note: Students are provided with the questions in advance for Part II of the test. They are expected to prepare written responses to these questions to use during the test. They may also use their outlines, key terms, and other notes. For the last several tests they have used their texts as well.

Math:
- an in-class quiz on fractions
- a unit post test on Integers
- a pretest on Ratio, Proportion, and Percent

Note: Students have math homework four days a week. Their grade is based on complete homework, class participation, and test performance.

Thank you for the opportunity to meet with you and your child.

Sincerely,

Debbie

Deborah Nichols Poulos

Progress Report
January 28, 1994

Name _____

Work and Study Habits:
_____Works productively & follows directions.
_____Needs reminders to work productively & to follow directions.
_____Needs frequent reminders to work productively & follow directions.

Literature:
_____Reads during Silent Sustained Reading (SSR).
_____Usually has a book to read.
_____Has difficulty staying focused during SSR.
_____Needs frequent reminders to have a book and read during SSR.
_____Assignments are: detailed   lack detail
                      carefully completed   not carefully completed
                      incomplete

Spelling Final Tests: _____ % average   Spelling Sentences: _____

Descriptive Writing: _____ regularly writes more than required
                     _____ regularly meets requirement
                     _____ sometimes meets requirement
                     _____ does not meet requirement

Language Mechanics: _____ Excellent
                    _____ Above average
                    _____ Satisfactory
                    _____ Needs Improvement

Cursive Handwriting Skills: _____ Has mastered cursive writing.
                            _____ Nearing mastery of cursive writing.
                            _____ Needs more practice on cursive writing.

Fractions Unit: _____ % Pre-test 11/3/93   _____ % Post-test 1/18/94
                _____ Strong understanding of fraction skills and concepts.
                _____ Basic understanding of fraction skills and concepts.
                _____ Difficulty with basic operations.
                _____ Difficulty with basic fraction skills & concepts.
                _____ Difficulty with advanced fraction skills & concepts.

Complete Homework: _____ Excellent _____ Satisfactory _____ Needs Improvement

Letter to Parents about Fall Progress Reports

Dear Parents,

As you know from the "Patwin Weekly Notice," teachers at Patwin hope to use student evaluation practices that are consistent with current research on student learning and assessment. Students need to receive feedback that will help them to achieve steady progress toward specific learning goals. Whether a student is working below grade level, on grade level, or above grade level, each student needs to feel that effort is both required and rewarded. Parents need to know how their child's progress compares to the normal range of students at the same grade level, and how they can assist their child in meeting his/her learning goals.

I believe that traditional letter grades at the elementary level are counterproductive to the above-described purpose of student assessment. Using a normal curve and letter grades requires that some students are at the top and some students are at the bottom. Applying letter grades to these positions on the normal curve is rewarding to some students and punishing to others. These letter grades can give students a false message that they have either "made it" or "failed" to make the grade. Just as low grades can be defeating for students, high grades can lead students to believe that they don't need to continue to challenge their abilities and to progress. We have seen the "low students" who give up in defeat, and the "high students" who coast. It is my hope that every student in the class can feel success in his/her achievements. Success breeds the confidence students need to encounter and ultimately master future learning challenges.

It is with these ideas in mind that I approach this fall's progress reports. I will be using one of the district's standard report card forms, but I will be using it in a manner that I think is more consistent with the above-described perspective. Rather than using A, B, C, D, F, the usual achievement code for fifth and sixth grade students, I will be using a +, / +, /, and NI (needs improvement) code. I will use the standard E, S, N, Effort code.

Let me know if you have questions or comments about this assessment practice. I hope that you will find that this system meets the needs of both you and your child.

Sincerely,
Deborah Nichols Poulos

Mathematics Third Trimester Grade Report   June 12, 2000

Dear Parents,

This trimester students have completed units on:
- ratios, decimals, proportions, percents
- geometry
- measurement, including perimeter/circumference, area of polygons and circles, surface area and volume
- data display, analysis, and statistics
- probability of independent and dependent events

Throughout these units we continued to review math computational and problem solving skills. Students participated in a variety of classroom activities. Students completed daily practice lessons from worksheets or the textbook in their math spiral notebooks. These assignments were corrected by students in class and periodically turned in. Frequent quizzes and other diagnostic tools were used to assess progress, and unit tests were used to assess achievement at the end of each unit.

Grades are based on participation in lessons; maintenance of a complete, neat, well organized math notebook; completion of homework and quizzes; and achievement on unit tests. Effort is based on being prepared for and participating in class, completing assignments, and using class time productively.

Name: _____

Homework Average:	**Quiz Average:**	**Unit Test Average:**	**Final Test:**
90 - 100% _____	90 - 100% _____	90 - 100% _____	90 - 100% _____
80 - 89% _____	80 - 89% _____	80 - 89% _____	80 - 89% _____
70 - 79% _____	70 - 79% _____	70 - 79% _____	70 - 79% _____
60 - 69% _____	60 - 69% _____	60 - 69% _____	60 - 69% _____
below 60% _____	below 60% _____	below 60% _____	below 60% _____

Math Grade for Third Trimester: Achievement _____   Effort _____

Sincerely,

Deborah Nichols Poulos

Fifth Grade Parent Feedback Form

Dear Fifth Grade Parent:

The fifth grade teachers would like to have your comments on the following topics. Please comment as fully as possible on each topic.

1. What has been your child's response to the homework this year?

2. What has been your child's response to the fifth grade curriculum?

3. What has been your child's response to social interactions with his/her peers, both in and out of the classroom?

4. What has been your response to communication between school and home so far this year?

5. What has been your response to the alternative student evaluation that the fifth grades are trying this year?

    ____ I prefer effort grades (E, S, N) and narrative information about achievement.

    ____ I prefer the traditional graded (A, B, C, D, F) report card.

6. Other Comments -

APPENDIX F

Reading

Tools for Sounding Out Words[1]

Vowels and Consonants

The English **vowels** are **a e i o u.**[2] Vowels can be long, short, or silent:

Long vowels: (they sound like their names)
A long vowel sound is marked with a flat line over the vowel: **ā ē ī ō ū**
A common arrangement for the long vowel sound is consonant-vowel-consonant-silent e (**CVCe**):
hāte Pēte bīte tōte cūte   (With no **e**'s on the end: hăt pĕt bĭt tŏt cŭt)

Short vowels:
A short vowel sound is marked with a cupped mark over the vowel: **ă ĕ ĭ ŏ ŭ**
A common occurrence for the short vowel sound is **CVC** (consonant-vowel-consonant):
căt bĕt hĭt cŏt gŭt

Consonants are all the other letters of the alphabet: **b c d f g h j k l m n p q r s t v w x y z**

Syllables

As students progress to learning longer words, you will teach them how to break words into syllables so that they can use this as a help to sound out new words.

Vowel Digraphs

A vowel digraph is two vowels together that make one sound. Examples are the following:

ai—ā as in **main, aide**
ay—ā as in **play, slay**
aw— as in **paw, law, saw**
ea—ĕ as in **head, lead**
ea—ē as in **read, lead**
ough—ŭ as in **tough**
ough—ō as in **though**

ough— as in **thought**
ee—ē as in **feet, beep**
ie—ē as in **chief, thief**
igh—ī as in **light, high**
oi— ōē as in **coin, avoid**
oa—ō as in **boat, coast**

oo— as in **book, hook**
oo— as in **moon, boot**
oy—ōē as in **boy, toy**
ow—ō as in **tow, slow**
ow— as in **cow, town**
You will notice several instances where **y** and **w** act like vowels.

Consonant Digraphs

A consonant digraph is two consonants together that make one sound, like the following:

ch—as in **church, chimney**
kn—as in **know, knot, knave**
ph—as in **phone, phantom**
sh—as in **shine, show**

ck—as in **check**
gh—as in **rough**
gh—as in **ghost**
ng—as in **song**

th—as in **throw, with, thing**
th—as in **this, that, though**
wh—as in **when, where**
wr—as in **write, wring**

Consonant Blends

Consonant Blends are two consonants that are blended together, as shown in the following:

bl—as in **blue**
br—as in **brown**
cl—as in **clean**
cr—as in **cream**
dr—as in **dream**

fl—as in **float**
fr—as in **free**
gl—as in **glass**
gr—as in **green**
pl—as in **please**

pr—as in **prize**
qu—as in **queen**
sc—as in **screen**
sk—as in **skill**
sl—as in **slam**

sn—as in **snake**
sp—as in **spell**
st—as in **stay**
sw—as in **swift**
tr—as in **train**

[1] Make classroom posters to show all of this information. The students may want to add to them.

[2] If you are asked, two letters that are usually consonants can be used as vowels when they have the *sound* of a vowel.

Y can sometimes sound like an **i** (as in cry, type, crypt, Egypt). :

W, when it follows an **o** (as in **low** or **crow**) takes on the sound of the **o** (or is simply silent).
But unless a student brings up the subject, I wouldn't mention this until they first have a basic understanding of **a e i o u.**

Child's Name _____ Date _____

Book Title _____

Parent Helper _____

Please listen to the child read for about 10 minutes. You may also read to the child if he/she is having difficulty. Then ask some of these questions:

"Tell me about what you (I) just read."
"Who is your favorite character in this story? Why?"
"Why do you think the book (story) is called _____ ?"
"What do you think will happen next in the story? Why?"

Please write a few comments about the child's reading:

fluency

types of errors

strategies he/she uses with errors

comprehension

attitude or comfort level

anything else you notice

About Reading and the Development of Strong Reading Skills at the Intermediate Level:

Students are required to always have a literature book to read during classroom SSR time and for their reading time at home. I have many books available in the classroom, and the Patwin and Yolo County libraries have many more choices.

Reading Levels: It is essential for strong reading development that students select books that are at the appropriate level for them to read. This means that books should neither be too difficult, nor too easy. I suggest the "Five Finger Rule" to aid in book selection.

"The Five Finger Rule"
1. Open the book you are considering to a full page of text.
2. Read the entire page.
3. Put down one finger for every word you come to that you do not know and cannot figure out, either by sounding out or using context clues for meaning.
4.   If you have put down five fingers by the time you have read the entire page then the book is probably too hard for you.
        If you have put down no fingers by the time you have read the entire page then the book is probably too easy for you.
5. In either case you should select another book, and start the process again.

This book choosing technique is especially important for students whose reading skills are below grade level. Students reading below grade level sometimes have a hard time choosing books that they feel "look too easy." They need a lot of support in selecting books that are good for them, and that will support growth in their reading skills. Choosing books that are too difficult can interfere with a child's reading development and take the joy out of reading. Lastly, students must read regularly in order to improve their skills.

The following list of books integrate with the sixth grade social studies topics and are required reading this year. I have class sets available.
Seth of the Lion People & Maroo of the Winter Caves (Early Humans)
The Golden Goblet (Egypt)
Seasons of Splendour: Tales, Myths and Legends of India (India)
The Rainbow People (China)
The Bronze Bow (Israel)
The Eagle of the Ninth (Roman)

Grade level readers should be able to read these books independently at the rate of 20 to 30 pages per day. If a student's reading skills do not allow him/her to successfully meet this expectation modifications will need to be made. Students may request the book in advance so they can take more time, or a parent may read the story to, or with, the student. If your child has special needs with regard to reading level or rate, please help him/her to make these arrangements.

Background of Bloom's Taxonomy

In the early 1950s, Benjamin Bloom set about to develop a framework for categorizing educational goals, collaborating with Max Englehart, Edward Furst, Walter Hill, and David Krathwohl. Then, in 1956, he published *Taxonomy of Educational Objectives*. This became known as Bloom's Taxonomy—a set of hierarchical models used to classify educational learning objectives into levels of complexity and specificity. The lists cover the learning objectives in cognitive, affective and sensory domains.

The framework (of the kinds of techniques or "goals" he felt students should learn) consists of six major categories: Knowledge, Comprehension, Application, Analysis, Synthesis, and Evaluation. The sub-categories under the first category, Knowledge, were presented as "skills and abilities," with the understanding that knowledge was the necessary precondition for putting these skills and abilities into practice.

While each category contains subcategories (all lying along a continuum from simple to complex and concrete to abstract), the taxonomy is popularly remembered according to the six main categories.

The authors' brief explanations of these main categories, listed in the text, are from the appendix of *Taxonomy of Educational Objectives*. The 1984 edition of *Handbook One* is available in the Center for Teaching (CFT) Library in Calhoun 116. See its ACORN record for call number and availability.

While many explanations of Bloom's Taxonomy and examples of its applications are readily available on the Internet (e.g., is *The Best Resources for Helping Teachers Use Bloom's Taxonomy in the Classroom*), the guide to Bloom's Taxonomy in the 1984 edition of *Handbook One* is particularly useful because it contains links to dozens of other web sites.

Following are three different documents explaining Blooms Taxonomy.

Bloom's Taxonomy

Bloom's taxonomy is a set of hierarchical models used to classify educational learning objectives into levels of complexity and specificity. The three lists cover the learning objectives in cognitive, affective and sensory domains.

If you have any doubts about how to use Bloom's taxonomy, there is considerable help on the internet for suggestions in how to use it. An example is *The Best Resources for Helping Teachers Use Bloom's Taxonomy in the Classroom.*

Bloom's Taxonomy
Action words for inquiries

Knowledge—The student recalls and recognizes information.

Define	Narrate	Relate
Label	List	Name
Report	Recall	Tell
Repeat	Memorize	Locate
Record		

Comprehension—The student changes information into a different symbolic form of language.

Identify	Restate	Express
Explain	Discuss	Review
Describe	Recognize	Report

Application—The student solves a problem using the knowledge and appropriate generalizations.

Demonstrate	Interview	Illustrate
Dramatize	Schedule	Translate
Practice	Apply	Interpret
Operate		

Analyze—The student separates information into component parts.

Debate	Question	Criticize
Distinguish	Inventory	Solve
Diagram	Differentiate	Experiment
Compare		

Synthesis—The student solves a problem by putting information together that requires original creative thinking.

Compose	Arrange	Assemble
Design	Plan	Prepare
Catalog	Formulate	Construct
Propose	Organize	Classify

Evaluation—The student makes qualitative and quantitative judgments according to set standards.

Select	Predict	Assess
Measure	Rate	Estimate
Judge	Choose	Evaluate
Value		

"Bloom's Taxonomy"

I. *Knowledge* (recall of information)

  A. Knowledge of specifics (isolated bits of information)

    1. Knowledge of terminology

    2. Knowledge of specific facts (dates, events, persons, places, etc.)

  B. Knowledge of ways and means of dealing with specifics (passive awareness of how to organize, study, judge, etc.)

    1. Knowledge of conventions (awareness of characteristic ways of treating and presenting ideas and phenomena—correct form and usage in speech and writing)

    2. Knowledge of trends and sequences (awareness of the processes, directions, and movements of phenomena with respect to time)

    3. Knowledge of classification and categories (awareness of fundamental classes, sets, or divisions for a given area)

    4. Knowledge of criteria (awareness of existing criteria by which judgments are made)

    5. Knowledge of methodology (awareness of the skills of inquiry)

  C. Knowledge of the universals and abstractions in a field (awareness of major sciences and patterns by which phenomena and ideas are organized)

    1. Knowledge of principles and generalizations (awareness of the abstractions which summarize observations of phenomena)

    2. Knowledge of theories and structure (awareness of the body of principles and generalizations and their understanding information)

II. *Comprehension* (lowest level of understanding information)

  A. Translation (ability to alter the form of communication without changing the original idea—paraphrasing, putting verbal material into symbolic statements, etc.)

  B. Interpretation (ability to reorder, rearrange, or provide a new view of original material—explaining, summarizing)

  C. Extrapolation (ability to go beyond the original data and determine implications, consequences, effects, etc.)

III. *Application* (ability to use abstractions—general ideas, rules of procedure, etc.—in specific and concrete situations)

IV. *Analysis* (ability to separate a communication into its parts in order to see its organization, effects, basis, and arrangement)

V. *Synthesis* (ability to arrange and combine parts, pieces, or elements into a pattern or structure not clearly there before)

  A. Production of a unique communication (ability to convey ideas, feelings, and or experiences to others)

  B. Production of a plan or proposed set of operations (ability to develop a plan of operations which satisfies the requirements of the task)

  C. Derivation of a set of abstract relations (ability to develop or deduce a set of abstract relations to explain specific data)

VI. *Evaluation* (ability to make judgments using criteria

  A. Judgments in terms of internal evidence (ability to evaluate a communication using logical accuracy, consistency, and other internal criteria)

  B. Judgments in terms of external criteria (ability to evaluate a communication using selected or remembered criteria)

BLOOM'S TAXONOMY

The building blocks of knowledge
Extending student's thinking

EVALUATION: Judging the information,
student assesses, rates, values, selects
"if our population continues to grow,
what will the U.S. be like in 2000?"

SYNTHESIS: Doing something new & different with information. Student hypo-
thesizes, abstracts, creates, designs.

ANALYSIS: Examining specific parts of the
information. Student classifies, cate-
gorizes, compares, analyses, makes cause
& effect relationships. "Compare the results of the first experiment with results
of the second."

APPLICATION: Using the information. Student
constructs, interviews, applies, lists.

COMPREHENSION: Understanding the information,
student demonstrates, explains, describes, interprets,
summarizes.

RECALL: Learning the information. Remembering knowledge.
Student recalls, recites, lists, labels, names, repeats.

Class Discussion/Participation Rubric

4. **Preparation** - Student is thoroughly prepared. All reading and assignments are complete, and materials are in class.

    Attentiveness - Student listens attentively to speaker.

    Participation - Student participates actively, both responding to questions and initiating ideas.

    Contribution Level - Student makes connections with, and expands upon, ideas expressed by others and presents evidence to support ideas, citing from text when appropriate. Student may make insightful comments on the topic and may discuss alternative perspectives.

    Speaking Skills - Student projects voice and speaks with clarity of expression.

    Respect - Student shows respect for the views of others.

---

3   **Preparation** - Student is prepared. All reading and assignments are complete, and materials are in class.

    Attentiveness - Student listens attentively to speaker.

    Participation - Student willingly participates when called upon. Student may initiate.

    Contribution Level - Student responses are reasonable and reflect accurate comprehension. (Student may demonstrate some characteristics of a '4' Contribution Level.)

    Speaking Skills - Student speaks clearly and audibly.

    Respect - Student shows respect for the views of others.

---

2   **Preparation** - Student is somewhat prepared. Reading and/or assignments are partially complete, and materials may not be in class.

    Attentiveness - Student is intermittantly attentive.

    Participation - Student participates passively, contributing only when called upon.

    Contribution Level - Student responses may or may not be reasonable or accurate.

    Speaking Skills - Student may or may not speak clearly.

    Respect - Student shows tolerance for the views of others.

---

1   **Preparation** - Student is unprepared. Reading and/or assignments are incomplete, and/or materials are not in class.

    Attentiveness - Student is inattentive and distracts from discussion.

    Participation - Student responds minimally when called upon.

    Contribution Level - Student responses may or may not relate to the topic.

    Speaking Skills - Student may or may not speak clearly.

    Respect - Student shows intolerance and/or disrespect for the views of others.

Thinking about my Reading

Fiction Books   *Level I*
Author
1 What do you know about the author?
2 What is the author trying to tell you in your book?
3 What did the author have to know about to write this book?
4 What sorts of things does your author like or dislike? (people, places, behaviour, feelings)

Characters (people, animals, toys . . .)
1 Who are the main characters in your story?
2 Do you like them? Tell me why.
3 Do you dislike them? Tell me why.
4 Choose one character. Why is this character important in the story?
5 Do you know anyone like the characters?
6 Do any of the characters change?
7 Do any characters do things that you think are good?
8 Do any characters do things that you think are wrong?

The Story
Plot
1 Tell me the main things that happened in your story.
2 Were you able to guess what was going to happen at the end?
3 Can you think of another way your story might have ended?
4 What do you think was the best part of the story? Why?

Setting
1 Where does the story take place?
2 Tell me what the place was like.
3 Have you ever been to a place like this?
4 Did the story take place a long time ago?
5 Is it about the future?
6 Is it happening now?

Mood
1 How did you feel while reading the book?
2 Why did you feel that way?
3 What was the funniest part?
4 What was the saddest part?
5 What was the most exciting thing that happened or the strangest thing that happened?
6 What do you remember most about the story?

Style
1 What special words does the author use to help you?
   • hear things in the story?
   • see things in the story?
2 Tell me about any pictures the author has left in your mind.
3 What do you like about the way the author has written the story?

Thinking about my Reading

Fiction Books   *Level II*

Author

1 What do you know about the author?
2 Why do you think the author wrote the book?
3 What is the author trying to tell us?
4 What do we learn about the personality or the interests of the author?
5 What did the author have to know to write the book?

Characters

(The questions below assume that the main characters are people, but they are rele·
even when the main characters are animals, toys or whatever.)

1 Who are the main characters?
2 What kind of people are they?
3 Do you like/dislike them? Why?
4 Why are they important in the story?
5 Why did they behave as they did?
6 Do you know anyone like them?
7 How do they change throughout the story?
8 How are the characters different/alike?
9 Are people really like these characters?
10 Was the behaviour of a particular character right or wrong?

The Story
Plot:
1 What happened in the story? What was the sequence of events?
2 What might have happened if a certain action had not taken place?
3 Were you able to predict the ending?
4 What other way might the story have ended?
5 Under a heading (such as People, Animals, Places, Things) list important words.
6 Which chapter do you think is the most important to the story? Why?

Setting:
1 Where did the story take place?
2 What was the place like?
3 Could there be a place like this? Do you know of a place like this?
4 When did the story take place? (past, present, future)
5 Which part of the story best describes the setting?
6 How does the writer create the atmosphere for the setting?
7 Are there any particular words that create this atmosphere?

Mood:
1 How did you feel while reading the book? Why did you feel that way?
2 What was the saddest/funniest incident?
3 What was the most exciting/unusual/mysterious incident?
4 How did the author make you feel the way you did?
5 What do you remember most about the story?
6 Does the mood of the story change? How?

Style:
1 How did the author describe the characters?
2 Were there any unusual ways of saying things?
3 Does the author give you enough information?
4 How does the author keep you interested?
5 What special words does the author use to help you hear, see, smell, taste or feel things?
6 What pictures has the author's writing left in your mind?
7 What strengths does the author have? What do you like about his/her style?

Thinking about my Reading

Informational Books *Level II*

Content:
1 What is the book about?
2 Was the information presented clearly?
3 Did the title mislead you? (Did you expect to discover information that wasn't there?)
4 Did the content of the book give you enough information? If not, what else do you need to know? Will you need to go to other books?

Accuracy:
1 Who is the author? Is the author well qualified to write about this topic? (Check book jacket; title page; introduction; foreword; other books.)
2 Does the book provide up-to-date information? (Check publishing date. Are there any revised editions? Are there more recent books about the same topic?)
3 Does the author let you know when he/she is stating a fact or expressing an opinion? (Look for key words such as 'I think . . .' or 'Scientists believe . . .' or 'As far as we know . . .' or 'Perhaps . . .')

Style
1 Is the author's style clear and direct?
2 Was information well organized?
3 Is the information told straight to you or is it given in story form?
4 Does the book make you want to learn more about your topic?

Illustrations:
1 Were illustrations used?
2 Did the author use diagrams, photographs, maps, charts, graphs, tables?
3 If so, did these help you to understand the text better? If labels and captions were used, did they help?

Organization:
1 Did you use the Table of Contents or the Index?
2 Did they help you to find information quickly?
3 Did headings and sub-headings help you to 'see' what was in the book?

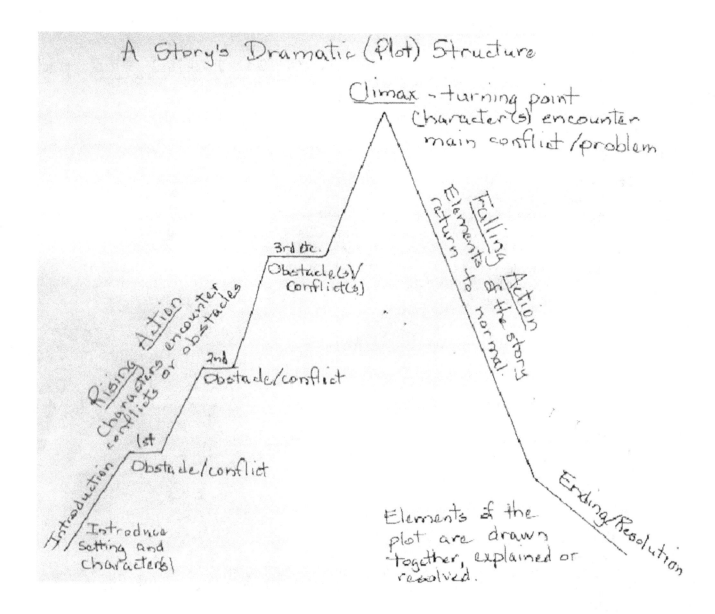

A Story's Dramatic (Plot) Structure

Climax – turning point
(character(s) encounter
main conflict/problem

Rising Action
Characters encounter
conflicts or obstacles

3rd etc.
Obstacle(s)/
Conflict(s)

2nd
Obstacle/conflict

Falling Action
Elements of the story
return to normal.

1st
Obstacle/conflict

Introduction

Introduce
setting and
character(s)

Elements of the
plot are drawn
together, explained or
resolved.

Ending/Resolution

Guidelines for Literature Discussion Leaders

Dear Literature Discussion Leader,

Thank you for leading a literature discussion group. Your main mission in working with the students is to help them learn to think creatively as they read. And to be an effective leader, you need to do everything yourself that you ask the students to do. This way you will better understand how the students are learning.

In my class there are four or five groups, each working independently on different books. To make working with the students easier, I group students by reading ability and assign books that are at their level. Sometimes a book will be read in a week. Other times it will take two or three weeks to complete. When one book is finished another should be selected and scheduled.

Discussions in our literature groups are modeled after the seven types of interpretive questions in the *Junior Great Books Program* below. (Please take a look so you know what I am talking about.) This technique is called "shared inquiry," and it focuses on questions that seek to explore literature. The piece of literature itself is the source for questions and answers. Therefore, **early on the students should understand that when they share an answer to a question under discussion, they must cite evidence from the text to illustrate and support their interpretation.**

To make this process easier, the students should read each selection with a notebook and pencil in hand so that, as they read, they can jot down their questions, thoughts, and feelings about the author's words. This will help to stimulate their thinking and to find the passages they need when they create and answer questions.

Writing and discussing questions are skills that require practice. Your skill and the students' skills will grow over time as you share in these discussions. Though at first the questioning models will seem foreign and artificial, with time everyone's ability to ask and discuss questions will become more and more rewarding.

The key is to focus on *truly* interesting questions—ones that engage the students' curiosity. Be sure to emphasize to them not to create a question just because it fits the model; most important is that the question interest them. And if the students *think* they already know the answer to a question, it is usually not very rewarding to spend time discussing it. Therefore, tell them to ask only questions they are truly curious about.

That means that when a question doesn't grab them, drop it, and go on to another question. Sometimes one question can hold the students' interest for the whole discussion period. At other times, they may go through a number of questions without finding any that capture their interest.

Emphasize that when students interpret something they read, they should not worry about getting it "wrong." Their interpretation is simply what they thought, how they responded. (Of course they should be able to show how they arrived at their interpretation—and they might then discover how they could have interpreted it better.) Then as others discuss how *they* were affected, the rest of the students may achieve new insight from the author's words. That is how people grow through reading.

Your general guidelines are on the next page. And remember, just like anything else, practice leads to improvement in both leading and participating in these discussions.

Good reading, and good luck. I hope you enjoy your participation with the students. I greatly appreciate your help.

Debbie

(over)

Seven Types of Interpretive Questions
(from the Junior Great Books Program)

1. **Meaning.** "What did the author mean when he/she said _____?"
2. **Use of language.** "Why did the author say _____ instead of _____?"
3. **Character Traits or Motives for Actions.**
   "Why did _____ act in a particular way…?"
   "Why did the author give _____ a particular characteristic?"
4. **Purpose.** "What was the author's purpose in choosing _____?"
   "Why was a particular passage included in the story?"
5. **Connections.** These questions should ask about relationships and connections between elements of the story.
6. **Sequence of Events.** These questions should ask about the significance of a particular sequence or the reason for a particular sequence.
7. **Overall problem of meaning.** This would be a suggested interpretation of the overall meaning of the story. What message did the author want to impart?

General Guidelines for Discussion Leaders

As a group leader you are responsible for the following:

- reading the same literature selection as the students in your group,
- preparing to lead, and leading, the discussion,
- keeping brief records on student participation.

Assignments:

1. **Select a book.** I will select the first book and give you a list of 8–10 books appropriate for your group, the members of which are at *roughly the same reading level.* You will then guide the students as they select the other books they will read with you—all from this list.

2. **Calculate a reading rate to establish a reading schedule.**
   - ask your students to read silently to themselves for five minutes;
   - have each student count the number of pages he/she has read and tell you;
   - calculate the average of everyone's rate (which should be comfortable for all the students).
   - using their average reading time, determine how many pages, or chapters, they must read before each meeting of the group. Set the assignment so it stops at the end of a chapter.
   - tell the students to read the book for a minimum of 30 minutes per day, seven days a week—during SSR (Silent Sustained Reading) time in the classroom and at home.

3. **Have the students keep a notebook and write questions.** From the time the students start reading the book, they should create interpretive questions (see top of page), progressing from #1 to #7 as they seem ready. At first they should concentrate on writing only #1 (Meaning) or #2 (Use of Language) questions. As you progress in your discussions, they should add questions #3 and #4 to their repertoire. It usually takes a while before students can write #5, #6, and—especially—#7. You will have to take more time to help them as the questions become more difficult.

Response to Literature Checklist

	often	occasionally	rarely
I. Enjoyment/Involvement			
• Is aware of a variety of reading materials and can select those s/he enjoys reading.	___	___	___
• Enjoys looking at pictures in picture story books.	___	___	___
• Responds with emotion to text: laughs, cries, smiles.	___	___	___
• Can get "lost" in a book.	___	___	___
• Chooses to read during free time.	___	___	___
• Wants to go on reading when time is up.	___	___	___
• Shares reading experiences with classmates.	___	___	___
• Has books on hand to read.	___	___	___
• Chooses books in different genres.	___	___	___
II. Making Personal Connections			
• Seeks meaning in both pictures and the text in picture story books.	___	___	___
• Can identify the work of authors that s/he enjoys.	___	___	___
• Sees literature as a way of knowing about the world.	___	___	___
• Draws on personal experiences in constructing meaning.	___	___	___
• Draws on earlier reading experiences in making meaning from a text.	___	___	___
III. Interpretation/Making Meaning			
• Gets beyond "I like" in talking about story.	___	___	___
• Makes comparisons between the works of individual authors and compares the work of different authors.	___	___	___
• Appreciates the value of pictures in picture story books and uses them to interpret story meaning.	___	___	___
• Asks questions and seeks out the help of others to clarify meaning.	___	___	___
• Makes reasonable predictions about what will happen in story.	___	___	___

Responding to Errors in Reading

Based on the way most of us were taught to read, we have told the child to "sound it out" when he comes to an unknown word. While phonics is an important part of reading, reading for meaning is the primary goal. To produce independent readers who monitor and correct themselves as they read, the following prompts are recommended _before_ saying "sound it out".

Give the child wait time of 5 to 10 seconds. See what she attempt to do to help herself.

"What would make sense there?"

"What do you think that word could be?"

"Use the picture to help you figure out what it could be."

"Go back to the beginning and try that again."

"Skip over it and read to the end of the sentence (or paragraph). Now what do you think it is?"

"Put in a word that would make sense there."

"You read that word before on another page. See if you can find it."

"Look at how that word begins. Start it out and keep reading."

"Tell the child the word.

Most important, focus on what the child is doing well and attempting to do. When the child is having difficulty and trying to work out the trouble spots, comments such as the following are suggested:

"Good for you. I like the way you tried to work that out."
"That was a good try. Yes, that word would make sense there."
"I like the way you looked at the picture to help yourself."
"I like the way you went back to the beginning of the sentence and tried that again.
"That's what good readers do."
"You are becoming a good reader. I'm proud of you."
from Reggie Routman Invitations. Heinemann Publishing (1991)

STUDENT BOOK REVIEW

AUTHOR _____
       (Last Name First)

TITLE_____

ILLUSTRATOR _____ **PUBLISHER** _____

Number of Pages _____ Reading or Age Level (if indicated) _____

Non-Fiction _____ Fiction _____ (Genre: Realistic, Historical, Humor, Fantasy,
                             Mystery, Science Fiction, Adventure, Classic, or
                             Other: _____)

Theme/Plot: _____

_____

_____

A character and explain his/her role in the story: _____

_____

_____

Retell an interesting part of the story: _____

_____

_____

Would you recommend the book to someone else? _____ Yes _____ No   Explain why:

_____

_____

(Add a piece of binder paper to write one paragraph for each response.)

Literature
& Weekly Writing II
"The Dragon Doctor"
Assignment given Monday, Oct. 23

Literature Due Dates:
Read Story: The Dragon Doctor, pp. 11-19 - Mon., Oct. 23.
Comprehension: Blue Book pp. 1 - Weds., Oct. 25.
Vocabulary: White Book p. 1 & blue worksheet - Thurs., Oct. 26.

Spelling Test on Vocabulary & Frequency Words - Fri., Oct. 27.

Writing Assignment (Blue Book p. 3) Due Dates
    Brainstorming and First Rough Draft - Tues., Oct. 24
    Polished Rough Draft - Thurs., Oct. 26
    Final Draft and Artwork - Mon., Oct. 29

Assignment: Completion of BB p. 3 will serve as the brainstorming for this assignment. Page 3 explains the writing assignment. Dialogue should be one page long. On another sheet of paper, write a dialogue between you and the animal that came to see you. Use your notes from p. 3. When you proofread your story, be sure you've used quotation marks correctly so there will be no mistake as to who is speaking. Use our list for words instead of "said."
    Artwork: Create an illustration of the animal. Use white 9 X 12 drawing paper provided.

Evaluation
Standard Criteria: (For all essays, stories, and research writing.)
    1. Neatly written in cursive or word processed.
    2. Correct spelling, grammar, and usage.
    3. Complete sentences, with varied beginnings.
    4. Paragraphs are developed from topic to supporting sentences.
Special Criteria:
    1. Use vivid verbs, adjectives, and adverbs.
    2. Use similes and metaphors whenever possible.

Use your **Writer's Handbook** for help.

Do your best and have fun!!!!!

The Egypt Game   Name _____
by Zilpha Keatley Snyder   Date _____
file: egyptg.doc

Answer these questions in complete sentences. Use a separate piece of paper if necessary.

1) Explain how the Professor stumbled upon the Egypt Game?

2) Name and describe the two main characters in the story.

3. Describe the paper-families game.

4. Give details about the two different reasons that each girl worried about the beginning of school.

5) What changed April's attitude about Elizabeth joining the Egypt game?

6. Give at least two specific examples that show April's relationship with her grandmother was improving?

7) Explain what this story has to do with Halloween. Be as specific and detailed as possible.

8. What was the story line of Aida?

9) Who was Marshall? Why do you think Security is an appropriate name for his octopus?

10) Why did Marshall become a hero to the neighborhood?

11. Why had the Professor begun to watch the Egypt game? How had his store changed by the end of the story?

12) Explain, in detail, why you did, or did not, like this story.

The Golden Goblet, Eloise Jarvis McGraw

Chapters 1-4:
1. What did Ranofer's future look like before his father died? What does it look like now?

2. Why does Ranofer discourage the affection and interest of Rekh the goldsmith and Heqet the apprentice?

3. Why does Ranofer decide he must confide in Heqet about the wineskins?

4. Do you think Ranofer is right to take the wineskin from Ibni the second day Ibni offers it to him?

5. What do you think will happen to Ranofer if Rekh discovers Ibni is indeed stealing the gold?

Chapters 5-8:
1. The Ancient tells Ranofer, "You have wisdom as well as youth. A most unusual combination." Do you agree with the Ancient that young people are seldom wise?

2. Why does Ranofer become uneasy when Gebu tells Wenamon, "There are far bigger birds in the air than Rekh the goldsmith ...?"

3. Why does it seem inevitable that Gebu will no longer send Ranofer to Rekh's after Ibni is fired from his job there?

5. Why is it so surprising that Gebu makes several trips out in the middle of the night?

5. Why does Ranofer angrily refuse Heqet's offer to share his lunch?

Chapters 9-11:
1. Why did Ranofer refuse to tell Gebu of his visit to Zau?

2. Do you agree with Ranofer's opinion of himself as a coward for being afraid to follow Gebu out late at night?

3. Why do you think Gebu was so angry with Ranofer for asking him about the floor plans for one of the tombs?

4. Why is Ranofer so horrified when he learns that Gebu has robbed a tomb?

5. Ranofer thinks that finding the goblet is the most important thing that ever happened. He believes that the goblet will set him free. Do you believe that Ranofer has reason to be hopeful?

Chapters 12-16:
1. Why does Ranofer follow Gebu and Wenamon to the Valley of the Tombs of the Kings?

2. Why do Heqet and the Ancient decide to go after Ranofer in the Valley of the Tombs?

3. While Ranofer is in the tomb, his fear becomes replaced with fury. What causes this change of feelings?

4. Why do the courtiers in the queen's chamber laugh and Queen Tiy's eyes glisten with tears when Ranofer tells her that what he wishes for most is a donkey?

5. How has Ranofer changed since we met him at the beginning of the book?   goldgobt.doc

Journey to Topaz   Name _____
Ch. 1

                              in
You have several challenges this chapter.
                             ^

1. Make a list of the characters and phrases that help describe them.. I
found over ten different characters and 2-4 describing phrases for each.

2. Describe the setting of the chapter. Some of you have actually been
there.

3. List the major emotions of the chapter and support them with phrases.

4. Make a **graph** of your choice to show an emotion(s) of the chapter. I
expect these to be quite varied and there no special form needed.

                                              and give supporting phrases
for each chapter we list the feelings, and generally
write a paragraph

The Bronze Bow by Elizabeth George Speare

Characterization:

Jesus: In this book Jesus is an important preacher and has the ability to heal the sick. He attracts crowds of thousands of people. Jesus talks of how the kingdom of God is not far away and how God loves everyone. Although Jesus is not one of the main characters in this book, I chose to discuss him because he has a big role in Daniel's decision to turn from violence. He helps Daniel realize that you don't always need to fight with a sword, sometimes the best thing [weapon] to fight a battle is love. Jesus was important to this story in guiding Daniel away from violence. I picked this character because of how much he helped Daniel and others see that violence isn't the only way to fight the Romans.

Good details

Daniel: In this book Daniel is a stubborn character who wants to avenge his father's death. He wants to kill Romans and drive Romans from his land. He joins a band of Zealots who are organizing a revolt against the Romans. He has close friendships with Joel and Thracia, and the trio try to avenge Daniel's father. I picked this character because he is the main character in this book and he is important in helping his friends' decisions to join the Zealots. His anger is important to the book. Something happens in just about every chapter because of his anger, then finally when he stops being angry and welcomes a Roman into his house it's a big relief.

well expressed

Joel: In this book, Joel is a Jew who is destined to become a rabbi until he befriends the wild Daniel. Joel is a dedicated student and also is very close to his sister Thacia.

Joel joins Daniel and the Zealots to revolt against the Romans. His role in the Zealot's band is as a spy for Rosh, the leader. He was important to the other characters because he stuck to Daniel and Thacia as friend and brother through thick and thin. I *good* chose him because he was such an important friend to Daniel throughout the book.

Thacia: ~~In this story~~ Thacia was a young girl with a big heart. Thacia is very brave and survives through a lot of conflict with the Romans. Although she is a girl, she joins in with her brother, Joel, and his friend, Daniel, in fighting the Romans. She is very important to Daniel in making him see past his hurt and anger. Thacia is important to the story in her role of taking care of her brother and Daniel. She also befriends Daniel's timid sister Leah. I picked Thacia because how loving and free of hate she *well stated* was in spite of what the Romans were doing around her. She was important to the story by making the story more real and she ~~made~~ helped keep the book from always focusing on violence.

Setting:

This book was set in Palestine around the years 20-30 AD. The main event that happened was the Jewish uprising against Roman rule. The Galileans, the people who lived near the sea, were a proud people unwilling to submit to Roman rule. Major historic events taking place at this time in addition to the Roman rule of the ancient Jewish state was the beginning of Christianity. Christ was alive, grown and preaching to thousands his message of love and peace and eternal life. One specific site ~~that~~ *in which* part of the story took place was the mountain where Rosh and his band lived. The mountain in Palestine overlooked the town of Ketzah, as well as the path from Ketzah to the mountain top. The path is crowded with rocks and boulders and is rough. The *great details* mountain contains caves where the band lives and is very desolate. Life for the outlaws is difficult. The mountain has wolves, jackals, panthers that Rosh's men hunt for food. At the very top of the mountain is a patch of green grass with pink flax *Terrific descriptive details.*

blossoms in the spring, but it is wild, not terraced and planted with olive trees like the

village. This mountain is where Daniel found Rosh's band after running away from his

life as a blacksmith apprentice in Ketzah.

Plot/Climax/Resolution:

This book is about a young man named Daniel. Daniel is very angry at the Romans

who rule his land and will do anything to kill them or end their rule. He fled his life as

an abused apprentice, ending up being rescued by Rosh. Rosh leads a band of

Zealots who plan a revolt against Roman rule. Daniel adopts their beliefs and way of

life. The high point of this story is when Daniel organizes his own battle against the

Romans. When he attacks, he and the other members of his band are seriously

injured. The turning point of this story occurs when Daniel talks to Jesus and decides

he wants to give up violence and become a Christian. He is not able to transition from *insightful observation*

the world of outlaws and violence easily, however. The point at which the major

question of the story is resolved comes when Daniel finally realizes that violence isn't

the best way to fight his enemy. He realized that hatred of the Romans wouldn't help

cure his sister or make him a hopeful man. He decided to follow Jesus and

immediately felt strong and sure and peaceful. His sister Leah was saved from fever *Terrific summary of the main themes.*

and Daniel was able to welcome a Roman soldier into his home.

An episode:

The episode that was most meaningful for me was the part when Daniel went to Jesus

for advice. While Daniel visits Jesus, he wonders what the preacher means by "the

kingdom is at hand." He goes to the house where Jesus is staying and asks him why

he does not join the attack against the Romans. Jesus replies that violence isn't the

only way, Daniel must give up his hate to truly know God and join God's kingdom.

Daniel leaves still confused but Jesus seems to know that Daniel's vow to live and die for God's victory is not a vow of hate. This episode is important for the overall plot by connecting Jesus' life and Daniel's life. Daniel behaves in a cruel manner toward his sister after this and instantly realizes the importance of love and kindness. Daniel learns to see the world differently and worries about Jesus' safety.

A+

Excellent, well written thoughtful paper!

2. who, img. to plot, rela. w/ each other
setting
episode
main idea climax, resolution
personal response.

March 20, 1998
DNP/ Nyland

THE BRONZE BOW

Characterizations:

Daniel: Daniel is the main character of this story. We see the story through his eyes. He has a relationship with all the other characters in the book. Daniel had many choices to make during the story. He had to decide whether to stay with Rosh or stay in the village and care for his sister and his grandmother before she died. Another choice involved whether he would follow the outlaw ways and beliefs of Rosh or the less violent beliefs of Jesus.

His relationship with Thacia begins as wary strangers who become good and trusting friends. Thacia wants to be better friends, perhaps even get married, but Daniel feels he is not worthy of her and says he has to be ready to fight the Romans.

His relationship with Jesus grows from Daniel not believing Jesus was giving the people the right message about dealing with the Romans to believing Jesus's message of love. After Jesus healed Daniel's sister, Leah, Daniel felt the truth of what Jesus had been trying to tell him.

His relationship with Samson goes from using him to get a higher place in his group to being like a father to him and Samson being like a baby. He later owes Samson his life after an ill-fated rescue mission.

Thacia: Thacia is the sister of Daniel's good friend Joel and a strong, kind hearted girl. She helped the relationship between Daniel and Joel survive hardships. She becomes attached to Daniel and his sister Leah. Daniel comes to rely on her to help him with Leah. She doesn't have a direct relationship with Samson, but she hears about him from Daniel and knows that he saved Daniel's life. Thacia knows Jesus as the rabbi who speaks at the waterfront and at Simon's home. She goes with her brother Joel to hear Jesus's message. I chose to write about Thacia because she had a nice relationship with Daniel and I think her relationship with him and Leah are important to the story.

Jesus: While Daniel appears to us as the main character, the story of how Jesus introduced his message to the Jews is one of the main themes. The focus or purpose of the book is to show how the message of Jesus began to spread through the Jewish community and how he was both admired and hated.

Jesus meets Daniel several times in the book and is as a teacher to him. He tries to comfort Daniel and teach him the power of love vs. hate. He also saves Daniel's sister Leah from a fever.

Jesus has no known relationship with Samson. He knows Thacia as one of his followers and comes with her when she asks him to go to Leah when she is dying.

Samson: Samson was a huge black slave that was "rescued" by Rosh and his gang. Daniel took on the responsibility of Samson's care and he removed the chains on Samson. Samson became a loyal friend. He protected Daniel as Daniel made sure Samson was fed and not harassed by the gang. Samson didn't have a direct relationship with either Thacia or Jesus. Samson is important because he saves Daniel and Joel.

Setting:

The story takes place in a village near Jerusalem in Galilee, the town of Capernaum, about three miles away, and the mountains above the village. The time is approximately 20-30 AD when Jesus is said to have lived. Daniel's village is small, dusty, and poor. The people are farmers and shopkeepers. The homes are made of clay and are small and poorly furnished. Capernaum is a larger city and had areas of poverty and wealth.

Plot, climax, resolution:

The plot is the story of a youth living in the times of the Roman rule over the Jews of Galilee. He is filled with hate and the desire for vengeance after seeing his parents killed by the Romans. He is rescued by an outlaw leader and lives with the gang of would be freedom fighters in the mountains above his home village for several years. He then meets Joel and Thacia, teenagers from his village and starts thinking about his home. He visits his grandmother and sister and realizes how hard their life has been since he left, but he still wants to live in the mountains with the man he considers the only hope for his people. He believes Rosh will be the great leader who will rally the Jews to fight and win against the Romans.

Daniel's grandmother dies, he feels compelled to go live with his sister who is unable to care for herself. She is so shy she has never been outside or spoken to a stranger. He resents this duty but he is fortunate that his friend Simon gives him a house for them to live in and the blacksmith shop where he can work and earn a living.

He goes with Simon to meet the strange new rabbi that Simon wants to follow, Jesus. He is disappointed that Jesus doesn't try to get the Jews to fight the Romans.

Rosh sends Daniel to recruit Joel for the band of his followers. He finds the luxury they live in surprising and feels out of place. Joel, Daniel and Thacia promise to always fight for the freedom of their people and pray for the strength to bend a "bow of bronze". Daniel is hurt by a Roman legionnaire and Joel and Thacia take care of him in secret until he is ready to return home.

Daniel sees Jesus speak a few times during the story and we start understanding his desire to follow the man, but his confusion over the message.

Daniel forms a group of young followers in his village with help from Joel and some of his friends from the city. They think they will one day join Rosh in the fight against the Romans. Joel is asked to get some important information for Rosh, but it turns out to just help Rosh rob from the wealthy Jews in the area that are friendly with the Romans. Daniel starts having doubts about the goals and sincerity of Rosh. Joel is arrested and is to be transferred to a Roman jail or some other horrible place.

Climax:

Daniel and his band of young boys realize that they need to rescue Joel. Rosh will not help them. They plan a daring rescue as Joel is being transferred, but the Romans far outnumber them and are much more skilled in fighting. They are saved by Samson who has been following his favorite young friend, Daniel. Joel is rescued, but one of the boys is killed, and Daniel is hurt. Samson is mortally wounded and captured by the Romans.

Resolution:

After the rescue of Joel, the band slowly regathers its courage and weapons. It was a frightening and humbling experience for them. They realized how difficult it would be to fight the Romans. Daniel goes back to the blacksmith shop and Leah. He tells Thacia he can't be married to her now because of his cause. Leah has been having talks with a young Roman legionary when Daniel is gone. When Daniel finds out he is furious and outraged. His anger sets Leah back to her mental state earlier in the story where she just sits and won't eat. Then Leah becomes very ill. He realizes she is dying from a fever and sends a message to Thacia to come, since she is Leah's only friend that except for the hated Roman. Thacia comes, bringing Jesus with her. Jesus saves Leah and Daniel realizes in that moment the truth and importance of Jesus's message of love. He pushes the hate out of his heart and goes to the young Roman and asks him to come and speak to Leah. He has been able to replace his desire for vengeance with love.

An Episode:

One specific episode that introduces us to Jesus and his followers begins with Daniel going to Capernaum to find his friend Simon. His friend Simon is with Jesus at the home of another Simon where the yard is filled with poor and sick people hoping for Jesus to help them. Inside the house, the women have cooked platters full of fish and bread. The close followers of Jesus eat only a little, surprising the young, hungry Daniel who would like to have more. But then he sees that the food is being saved for the mass of hungry people outside and he realizes how thoughtful these people are. Simon tells Daniel that he is going to stay with Jesus. The importance of the episode is that it helps us know more about Jesus and his followers and the message that Daniel is hearing and seeing.

DEBORAH NICHOLS POULOS

The Bronze Bow
By Elizabeth George Speare
3/2/99 DNP

Characterization:

Daniel: Daniel was the leading character in the story. He was an 18 year old Galilean. He was a patriot who hated Roman rule of his homeland Palestine. He was very kind to his sister Leah. He worked as a blacksmith. He was a member of Rosh's fighting force located in the mountains. He was a good friend to Joel. I chose Daniel to tell about because he was an interesting character.

Rosh: Rosh was a very important character in the story. He was the leader of the rebel fighting force. He was thought to be a hero to some and a robber to others. He organized the "freedom fighters." Rosh recruited Joel to be part of his group by spying in the city of Capernaum. Daniel was part of his fighting force also. I chose Rosh to tell about because he played an important role.

Joel: Joel was the son of a scribe. He was well educated. He hated the Roman rule almost as much as Daniel did. His father was wealthy. At the beginning of the story he lived in Ketzah. Later in the story he moved to Capernaum. His trade was sandal making. He was studying to be a rabbi. He was very good at spying. I chose Joel to tell about because he did the spying.

Leah: Leah was the Daniel's younger sister. While Daniel was living in the mountains, her grandmother cared for Leah. Leah was believed to be possessed by demons. She was afraid to go outside and she was afraid of people. When she was a little girl, she escaped from the house, and saw her father and uncle hanging crucified in the village. After that incident, she started behaving like she was possessed. Before the incident she was normal little girl. I chose Leah to tell about because she was the character who helped Daniel cook and do the gardening.

Setting: The time in history that the story took place was approximately 32 A.D. The story took place in the village of Ketzah, the city of Capernaum, and the mountains, all of which were located in Palestine. It was the time of Roman occupation of Palestine. The Roman emperor was Tiberius. Jesus was an adult and was teaching his beliefs and was performing miracles.

The village of Ketzah was home to Daniel, Leah, Joel, Malthace and grandmother. Jewish people lived in the village. The village was located at the base of the mountain that Rosh and his band of fighters lived. The village was small and the people were poor. The streets were narrow and dirty. The door yards were shabby and cluttered. The houses were made out of mud and had thatched roofs. The houses had dirt floors. In the floor, was a scooped out area that held the fire. The people slept on mats on the floor and they also managed to sleep on the roof. The rooftops were flat. The village was named for a plant that grew there. In the village square there was a water well.

Plot/Climax/Resolution: The plot of this story focused on events that would lead to a Jewish uprising against the Romans. A second plot involved the relationship of Leah and Daniel and how her illness affected their relationship. The plot reached its climax following many robberies done by Rosh and his band. They stole money and other items that belonged to the wealthy people who lived in Capernaum and the struggling farmers who lived out side of town. Daniel went into the mountains to warn Rosh of the increasing anger of the townspeople toward Rosh and his band. He also told Rosh about the arrest of Joel. Daniel expected Rosh to lead his band against the Romans. Rosh just laughed at him and sent him on his way. Daniel organized his own band and ambushed the legion that was taking Joel and other prisoners out of Capernaum. They were able to rescue Joel but lost Nathan in the fighting. If it hadn't been for Samson helping out, they wouldn't have been as successful as they had been. They realized that there just weren't enough of them to beat the Romans. They stopped meeting and stayed out of the way of the Romans. The story came to a close when Jesus came to visit Daniel and Leah. Leah was very sick and was near death. Jesus cured her and brought peace to Daniel.

An episode: Leah's moving to Capernaum from Ketzah. Because Leah was so afraid of leaving the house, Daniel had to find a way of moving her without her being able to see the out side and people in the road. It was important to move to Capernaum because that is where Simon's black smith shop was. Simon offered his house and shop to Daniel while he was away following Jesus. Daniel had to move Leah because grandmother had died and there was no one to take care of Leah. His neighbor, a carpenter suggested that Daniel use a litter to move Leah. A litter was a vehicle that was carried by four men. The riding space was enclosed so that once they got Leah inside she wouldn't have to worry about seeing anybody or to worry about being seen. Daniel convinced Leah that princesses used the litter when they traveled. The neighbor found four men to carry the litter. They all hid until Leah was safely inside. Daniel carried Leah from the house to the litter. This episode is important to the plot because it helped Daniel see that there still was a sense of helping and support in the Jewish community even though the Romans were in control.

Joanna #7
3/1/99
A+

The Bronze Bow
by Elizabeth George Speare

Daniel is the main character in The Bronze Bow. At the beginning of the story he is living in a cave in the mountains with a band of rebels, led by a man named Rosh. Daniel had been apprenticed to a blacksmith who was very mean. So Daniel ran away to the mountains where he was found by Rosh. He lived with Rosh and his band for five years until he goes back to the village. After he goes back to the village, because of his grandmother's death, his friend Simon, who is a blacksmith and a Zealot (or rebel against the Romans) decides to follow Jesus so he gives Daniel his blacksmith shop. Daniel and his sister Leah move into Simon's house, which is joined with the blacksmith shop. Many times Daniel goes into a nearby town to hear Jesus speak. He is torn between his hate of the Romans and his admiration for Jesus, who doesn't lead any rebellions.

great details

] run on

who speaks of love + peace brotherhood of man etc.

Rosh is the leader of a band of rebels that one day hope to defeat the Romans that are occupying Israel. His band steals from villagers and travelers, but always says that soon their army will be big enough to defeat the Roman army, if only they get more recruits. He seems to think that Daniel and everyone else are just tools in the process and he doesn't care about their feelings or think of them as people.

good (how/when is this most vividly revealed to Daniel?)

Jesus was a very important character in the story. He was a healer, a teacher and a bringer of hope. When he touched someone who was sick or in pain, the person got better. One of the many people he helped was Leah, His followers thought that he was the messiah. I think that he really helped Daniel. Daniel thought that the only way to defeat the Romans was to fight them. After talking to Jesus he realized that he didn't have to fight, even though he had made a vow to do so.

what did he realize? decide?

Leah was Daniel's sister. After her parents died, she never left the house. Everyone thought she was possessed by demons. When she and Daniel moved into Simon's house she started acting like a person again. She went outside in the garden, she cooked and took care of the house and began talking again. She also started talking to a Roman soldier over the garden wall. But one day Daniel started yelling at her about the soldier and she withdrew into herself again. And she didn't come out of it. Daniel went to get Jesus but he wasn't at his house. Daniel thought that Leah was dying. He sent a message to his friend Thacia, who then found Jesus and brought him to Leah. Leah was healed by Jesus.

great detailed description

The settings are a cave in the mountains, the village where Daniel's family lives (I don't know what it's called), a city called Capernaum and the area around Jesus' house. It takes place maybe around 20 A.D. in Israel. Some major historic events are Jesus' lifetime and the occupation of the Romans. One of places in Daniel's village is the blacksmith shop. It was stocked with bars of iron and hung with rows of tongs and chisels and hammers. It had a bench for the customers to sit on, a fire, bellows and an oven.

terrific

This story is about the Jews trying to fight off the Roman occupation. It's also about the different ways different people reacted to how the Romans should be gotten rid of, and the influence of Jesus.

The climax of the story is when Daniel decides to break away from Rosh. When he found out that Joel had been taken captive, he went to Rosh for help. Rosh said that every man was responsible for himself. Then Daniel realized that Rosh was wrong, that fighting and stealing from innocent people wasn't the only way to defeat the Romans. So he went off on his own with his band of 20 men. Daniel and his group attack Roman soldiers who have Joel prisoner. They free him, but two or three people die. Later Leah gets sick and is healed by Jesus. At the very end, Daniel invites the Roman soldier, who had been talking with Leah, into his house. I think he realized that not all Romans were bad, and it turned out that this Roman soldier wasn't even Roman. Daniel had also accepted Jesus' message of love instead of hate.

At the beginning of Chapter 22, Daniel goes to see Thacia, Daniel's friend, dance at a festival. But he runs away because he doesn't want Thacia to see him. She sees him anyway and goes after him. Without saying it directly, she asks Daniel if he will marry her. He says he can't because he has vowed to die for Israel if he must. When he goes home, he tells Leah about Thacia dancing. Then Leah sets out a meal, which includes fresh fruit. Daniel asks her where she got it, and she says "from the Roman soldier." Daniel starts yelling at Leah and she crumples and cowers from him. He goes and walks off his anger in the rain. When he gets back Leah doesn't even look up at him. This contributes to the development of the overall plot because Leah stops talking and working around the house, and Daniel thinks she is dying, which is when he goes for Jesus.

terrific summary of the highlights

A⁺ Excellent, well written paper.

5/12/98
DNP / NYLAND

THE WATSONS GO TO BIRMINGHAM-1963
Christopher Paul Curtis   (210 PAGES)

Kenny Watson is about 9 years old and is our narrator and the main character in this story of his family. They call themselves the Weird Watsons. He is very smart and a good student, but he tries to be a daredevil like his older brother Byron. Kenny is gullible, as is his little sister Joetta, and is easily fooled by his bully brother who is always trying to scare or excite him. He has a lazy eye so that his left eye looks towards his nose which makes him look strange. Byron suggests that he look at people sideways so his eye is less noticeable. He tries to be a good kid and listen to his parents and teachers.

Byron, the eldest of the three children, is constantly in trouble. He is the other main character. For most of the story, he is the bully, the bad guy, the mean, annoying poor student, rotten brother, etc. He hangs out with his friend Buphead who is as much of a trouble maker. Byron has been held back in school and is constantly angry and fighting any rules. Later in the story, Byron looses most of his meanness (Kenny thinks this is because of the Alabama heat) and becomes a protective loving brother.

The baby of the family is the only daughter, Joetta who is about 6. She is sweet, follows her parent's rules, and is a snitch. She is also protective of her older brothers and tries to keep them from being punished by their parents. Her mother says she couldn't ever tell a lie, she'd rather be dead.

The parents, Wilona and Daniel, seem to have the same opinions about the rules for their kids. Daniel, works very hard at a low paying job. He is a loving parent who likes to play and act funny. He likes living in Flint, Michigan even though it's freezing cold and the kids call their house an igloo. Wilona comes from Alabama and is miserable with the cold. She loves her children fiercely, and wants the best for them and is pretty strict.

Grandma Sands is Wilona's mother who lives in Birmingham. She's tiny, wrinkled, and looks like a nice old lady. But she is very strong willed, strict, and powerful in her manner. You can see where Wilona gets her tendency to have a strong sense of discipline.

The first half of the book takes place in Flint, Michigan where the winters are freezing. Then the family takes a trip to Birmingham, Alabama where it is extremely hot and humid. The time is 1963 when the Civil Rights movement is just beginning.

There was still a great deal of discrimination against blacks, especially in the South.

The first half of the book tells a variety of stories about the Watsons. They mostly have to do with what a problem Byron is. The parents decide to take Byron to stay with Grandma Sands for the summer because they think she can straighten him out. When they are in Birmingham two frightening events occur which are when Kenny almost drowns and Joey is thought to have been in a church that was bombed.

There are two climaxes in this story. One is when Byron tells Kenny about a "Wool Pooh" which sucks kids down under water and drowns them, but Kenny doesn't believe him and goes into a dangerous lake thinking that his brother is a lying wimp. This is where it gets exiting.

He goes into the beautiful calm water slowly, but sees fish swimming around in circles right in front of him. Kenny has no idea why, but they just keep swimming around and brushing against his leg. He loses interest in the fish when he sees a turtle. He wades out farther to catch it, but the turtle swims away. Kenny tries to grab it again, but the rocks crumble beneath him and he loses his footing. Then the whirl pool takes over, and Kenny thinks its the "Wool Pooh". He tries to swim out of its grasp but the whirl pool is to strong. His imagination makes him see a figure that Kenny will never forget keep pulling him down. Kenny fights as hard as he can and manages to get four short gasps of breath before he is forced to give up because of exhaustion.

Just as he is going to lose consciousness, Byron comes and drags him out of the water onto shore. As Kenny throws up "tons" of water and food, Byron holds him and kisses his head while crying "like a kindergartner".

The second climax follows quickly. Joetta goes off to Sunday school with some of Grandma Sands' neighbors. Shortly after, a huge boom is heard and felt in the neighborhood. They find out that there was a bombing at the church where Joetta had gone. Wilona, Daniel and Byron run to the church, Kenny follows separately. He goes into the bombed out church looking for his sister. He finds a shoe that looks like hers and grabs it. But he sees the same vision of the "Wool Pooh" holding the other end of the shoe. He grabs the shoe and it rips in half. He goes back to Grandma's house in a daze, thinking Joetta has been taken by the "Wool Pooh" to death. When Joetta shows up at Grandma's, Kenny expects to see the vision holding on to her. He finally looks at her and sees she looks normal and the shoe isn't hers.

Joetta tells Kenny that he should know why she is at home because she followed him home. She said she saw him standing across the street from the church, laughing and calling to her, so she ran after him. He tries to tell her he wasn't there, but she doesn't believe him. She thinks he's trying to scare her and goes to tell Grandma. He runs off to tell the family that Joetta is fine.

The resolution is that the parents and children return to Flint that same night, before Joetta can find out about the bombing. They even take Byron back home with them. The parents discuss how to explain the terrible hate crime to their children while

Kenny eavesdrops. Kenny becomes very upset and tries to cure himself of his sadness by going behind the couch and letting the magic spirits heal him. The kids always thought that spot was special because their pets would always go their when they were hurt. Kenny wasn't sure if he would get better, or if he would die like some of their pets had. Byron figured out his hiding place and helped Kenny by staying close to him. Kenny finally has a huge crying spell with Byron holding him in the bathroom and he seems to get over his distress about the near drowning and the bombing.

One episode involves Kenny and his dinosaur collection. LJ keeps stealing Kenny's dinosaurs and Kenny's mom doesn't like him. But Kenny figures it's OK that LJ steals a couple now and then, it's the price you pay to have a friend come and play. But during the World's Greatest Dinosaur War Ever, the boys buried all the "dead" dinosaurs. LJ tricks Kenny by taking him away from the war zone and while Kenny is gone, he steals all the buried dinosaurs. Kenny wasn't surprised to find the dinosaur graves empty, but he was mad. He was mad at LJ and at himself for being stupid and gullible again.

I think the message is the importance of family. Kenny's family cares enough about Byron to try to rescue him from his own bad behavior. Grandma Sands is willing to take on Byron at his worst. When Byron almost loses his brother and sister, it turns him around into a more responsible, loving brother. Kenny also is shaken by the near loss of his sister and himself.

The Watsons Go To Birmingham - 1963
By Christopher Curtis
210 Pages, April 7-May 1

Main Character:
     The main character is Kenny Watson. He has a younger sister Joetta and
an older brother Byron. Byron had just turned 13 and was officially a teenage
juvenile delinquent. Daniel Watson is the father and Wilona is the mother.
Kenny was a fourth grader at Clark school and his brother Byron was the "god"
of the school. Kenny had two things wrong with him that got him beat up and
teased. One thing was he was smart and a really good reader and the other
was that one of his eyes was cross eyed and looked at a his nose. Kenny got
along fine with everyone except Byron. Byron teased him and played tricks on
him.

Theme:
     The theme is about being a family and all the things that happen in a
family between the mother, father, sisters and brothers.

Setting:
     The story takes place in Flint, Michigan and Birmingham, Alabama in
1963. The Watsons live in Flint. Daniel, the father was born there and so were
the kids but the mother was born in Alabama. The Watsons leave Flint one
summer to drive to Alabama to see Grandma Sands, Wilona's mother.

Major Problem:
     The major problem in Byron. Byron was always causing trouble and was
a bully. Sometimes the stuff that Byron did was really funny and sometimes it
was really mean. Kenny would tease Byron when he thought that Byron couldn't
get him.
     Byron's lips got stuck on the rear view mirror of the car on a freezing day
and his mom had to pull them off. That's when Kenny could tease him and call
him the "lipless wonder". Byron beat up on kids at school including Kenny. He
told stories to scare Kenny and Joetta. Byron didn't listen to his mom and dad.
Byron played with matches, charged cookies at the store without asking, put
chemicals in his hair and was always in trouble.

Climax:
     The climax of the story is when the mother and father say they are taking
a trip to Alabama to leave Byron with his Grandmother. The dad fixes up the old
brown car and the mom writes everything about the trip in a notebook called
"The Watsons Go To Birmingham - 1963". They drive straight from Flint to
Birmingham and sleep in the car and eat at rest stops and go to the bathroom in
the woods. It takes 15 hours to get there.

When they get to the grandma's house two bad things happen. Kenny almost drowns because he gets caught in a whirl pool. Byron tells him it's a wool pooh like Winnie-the -Pooh only evil. Kenny is sick of Byron's stories and goes in the water and has a weird experience like he is dying and then Byron saves him.

Then a few days later someone bombs the church where Joetta is supposed to be. Kenny goes there and sees dead little girls and finds a shoe that he thinks is Joettas. Kenny is still freaked out from almost drowning and being attacked be a wool pooh and thinks it's happening to him again at the bombed church and that Joetta is dead. But Joetta is saved from the bomb because she wasn't in the church. She says she came out of the church and saw Kenny and followed him so she was safe.

Resolution:

The Watson Family came back to Flint. The didn't even leave Byron in Birmingham with the grandma. There was a space behind the couch that all the sick pets in the family used to stay to get better. It was where "magic" made them better. So Kenny just started staying behind the couch. Byron figured out where he was and started staying by Kenny and looking over the back of the couch to see if he was all right. Finally Byron got Kenny to come out and go into the bathroom. Byron made Kenny talk about the terrible things that had happened. Kenny cried and Byron helped him by listening and not making fun of him. Byron tells Kenny that he can't go behind the couch any more because there is no "magic" behind the couch to make him better.

Message:

The message is that no matter what happens in your family, even if your brother beats you up, that your family is really the "magic" you need to make everything better.

THE ONE - EYED CAT
Paula Fox
216 Pages

The main character of this book is Ned who is 12 years old and lives with his parents in an old drafty farm house that had belonged to his grandparents. His father is a Lutheran minister in the local town and his mother has rheumatoid arthritis and is unable to walk. Their town is in the Northeast and much of the story takes place in the winter. The year is sometime in the 1920's or 1930's. They have a housekeeper named Mrs. Scallop who makes Ned nervous and even his mom doesn't like her. Ned works for an elderly man who lives next door named Mr. Scully. Ned values telling the truth; he also doesn't want to hurt anyone or anything.

Ned's mom is sick and requires a lot of care from his dad and Mrs. Scallop. He has to be quiet around the house. But he enjoys talking with his mom and feels that she knows him very well. His dad is always very kind and thoughtful. Sometimes Ned wonders if he knows that he sounds like he is preaching even when he isn't. His father would never hit him, but Ned feels it is important not to disappoint his father. Mr. Scully is nice to Ned and Ned helps him around his old house, cutting wood and helping him sort through his things. Ned feels his company is important to the old man who has lived alone for a long time.

Ned's Uncle Hilary gives Ned a gun for his birthday, but his dad doesn't want him to have it, because he is too young and his father doesn't like guns. But Ned sneaks up to the attic where his dad put the gun, takes it outside, and shoots at a shadow. He becomes convinced that the shadow was a cat that he sees in the woods that has lost an eye. He believes that he shot the cat's eye out. He and Mr. Scully take care of the cat by leaving food and water out for it. But the cat is wild and they can't get near it. Ned becomes scared of all animals because he thinks they know he shot the cat and they are out to get him. His guilt is overwhelming him. He hates keeping his horrible secret from his parents, but he can't imagine telling them the truth. He feels guilty for disobeying his father, guilty for hurting the cat, guilty for lying to them.

One day when Ned went to visit Mr. Scully, he finds him face down on the floor. He runs to the neighbor Mrs. Kimball who is a practical nurse for help. She tells Ned she thinks Mr. Scully has had a stroke and has Ned run home to have his dad call the ambulance. Mr. Scully survives the stroke and is moved from the hospital to a nursing home. Ned goes to visit Mr. Scully in the home several times. Mr. Scully can no longer talk, but he seems to enjoy Ned talking to him. When Ned realizes that Mr. Scully may not live much longer, he confesses to him about shooting the cat. Mr. Scully reaches for Ned's hand with great difficulty and gives a little squeeze. Ned thinks that Mr. Scully has forgiven him for his wrongdoing and feels better. Ned gets sick and can't take care of the cat for several days and he is worried about him, but then he sees the cat with a mouse in its mouth and he is pretty sure the cat will be OK. He also tells this to Mr. Scully and he thinks Mr. Scully is happy to hear the cat will be OK. When Ned goes to visit Mr. Scully the next week, he is told that he has died. He feels very sad that his friend is gone.

Shortly after Mr. Scully's death, Ned's mother starts a new medical treatment for her arthritis which makes her much better. She is able to walk again. Ned doesn't see the cat any more and hopes that the cat has been able to hunt for itself.

The message from Ned is that if you keep a guilty secret inside, it will haunt you and colors all your thoughts. Once you tell one lie, it gets easier to tell more, but then you can't remember what lies you have told. I think Ned should have tried to see if he did indeed shoot something the night it happened. And I think he should have told his parents right away. They may have been able to help the animal and they probably would have forgiven him quickly so he wouldn't have suffered from his guilt so long.

3/25/98
DNP

KOKOPELLI'S FLUTE

WILL HOBBS
165 pages

Tepary Jones is 13 years old and adventurous. He lives on a farm with his parents where they grow rare plants. His father is a seed farmer and his mother is an archeologist. He has a dog named dusty that he takes everywhere. The story is told through Tepary's eyes and in his voice. He values beauty and honesty. He changes from a person who runs away from his fears to a person who tries to conquer his fears.

Tep's parents treat Tep like they treat their plants. They give the seeds love and attention but don't spoil them. They leave them on their own but don't let them die. They learn what their plants need to survive. It's the same with Tep. His parents love and nurture him but don't spoil him with stuff that he doesn't need. They let him be and go where he wants kind of like keeping him on a long leash. The way they treat him would probably be different if they lived in the city.

This story takes place in New Mexico at about present times where a small family lives on a little seed farm. It is near an ancient Indian cave structure with lots of paintings and carving. This part of New Mexico has a lot of wide open space and very little population.

The main problem in this book is that Tep turns into a wood rat every night from sundown to sunup. He has to take over his rat instincts with his own so that he doesn't destroy any more of his parents crops. That was the hardest thing for him. He has to escape his rat enemies and predators which he does with the protection of his dusty.

The climax of this story was when Tep's mom got hantavirus and only Tep could save her. He went to Picture house and turned into a rat on the way. He went into the rat's nests and fought off the pack rats to get to the medicine man's herbs and the flute. He found them and, using Cricket's advice of looking for the spiral pictures on the walls, turned himself back into a human. He brought them back to his house where Cricket showed them which special herb to brew into tea. This relates to the overall message of the story when he didn't give up fighting the other rats and didn't give up trying to get the code for turning back into a human so he could help his mother.

After the climax Tep's mother gets better with the help of the tea. They all find out who Cricket is (Kokopelli) and then Cricket leaves. The corn that Tep brought back from Picture House started growing on it's own. Tep's favorite thing that happened was becoming the boss while his dad became the manure specialist. The father finds that the ravens and coyotes don't eat any more of there crops and only Tep knows why.

The message that this story told its readers is that you have to keep fighting, keep going for your goals, don't give up. When Tep was born he weighed only 2 pounds but he kept going, he didn't stop thriving, he didn't let death overcome him. And another example was when he didn't let the rats instincts take over. Again he kept fighting the rat so that he wouldn't destroy any more of his parent's seed farm. In the end he won. This lesson is valuable to me if I were to have a problem like one of these. It tells me not to give up. That is what the whole story is about.

(B) Very good report

<u>KOKOPELLI'S FLUTE</u>
·Will Hobbs

① I think that the story was kind of a good story because it was like a story of a fantasy or fiction. I said this because the story wasn't true, but I liked it.

② I think Tep and Dusty was the most real character because he did real things like he watched the pot hunters steal pots and some ancient stories. He and Dusty did real things like they watched the eclipse.

③ I will say that the cave was a setting because once apon a time the people that lived In the town and there was this cave that has some gold and jewels and the sacred stone or wall for Kokopelli.

④ I think the author likes to write books about fiction or fantacy. I think the author was a good story writer.

⑤ What most interested me about the story was that when I finished the book, I said that it was a fantacy book.

April 30, 1998
DNP/Nyland

Tuck Everlasting
By Natalie Babbitt
139 Pages

Winnie is a ten year old child who is the main character. She lives a solitary life with her parents and grandparents in a cottage at the edge of town. As an only child, she has learned to entertain herself. But also she has become fearful of the world beyond the fence that surrounds their yard. Her family has told her how frightening the world can be and she watches from behind the fence. The toad that hops nearby catches her attention and sparks her imagination. She wanted to go play with the toad but she knew she wasn't supposed to leave her yard. But her curiosity became bigger than her fear and her desire to follow the rules of her home.

Angus Tuck was a man who should be about 130 years old at the beginning of the book, but he is only in his forties due to some strange properties of a nearby spring. He is uneducated, yet wise about the cycles of life. Probably because he's been living so long. He is kind, strong and sad about what he knows about his life compared to normal people. Tuck is important because he explains the painful side of everlasting life. We might otherwise have only thought of the good parts.

Tuck's wife Mae is also older than her she appears because of the waters. She is a warm, loving mother to her two sons who appear to be 17 and 22 but who are actually closer to 100. Mae tries to keep Tuck's spirits up since she realizes they have many more years to be together. She's very brave and protective of Winnie. Mae takes care of Winnie in a warmer way than her family and teaches Winnie about differences between families.

The younger son of Tuck is Jesse, who looks 17. I picked him because of his special relationship with Winnie. Winnie falls for Jesse and he also wants Winnie to grow up just enough so that they can be together. Winnie says he is beautiful. He's adventurous and love's life enough to love his very long life.

The older son, Miles, is old enough to understand the pain of living forever. He had been married and had children and then watched them grow older as he stayed 22. He looks back wistfully at the thought of his 80 year old children.

The Man in the Yellow Suit was the "bad guy". When he first meets Winnie in front of her house, he acts friendly. But he later shows his true colors, greedy, mean, and covetous. He shows us the greedy naive view of everlasting life.

Winnie Foster's cottage is across the road from a small, lovely wood that is the remnant of the large forest that used to cover the land that is now the small village of Treegap. The story takes place in the 1880's beginning in the hot August sun. Her family the wealthiest people in town and own much of the nearby land, including the wood. Surrounding the village are farms and fields full of cows.

Within the wood is a large old tree in a clearing with a small bubbling spring. When Winnie decides to leave the safety of her yard and go look for the elf music she had heard, she comes upon the tree and spring and Jesse. At first she watches him drink from the spring, then he sees her. She is embarrassed but she finds him "beautiful" and is not frightened. She wants a drink but he adamantly refuses to let her, even if it is in her wood. He tells her it's dangerous, but not why. When Mae arrives with Miles, they realize they have to convince Winnie never to tell anyone about the spring. They hurriedly decide to kidnap her and take her home with them about 20 miles away.

At first Winnie is frightened, yet excited. She'd been wanting to run away and find some adventure and now here it was. The first night with the Tucks she was uncomfortable and lonely for her family, but they were so kind and thoughtful, she came to care for them and know that they cared for her. She still wanted to go home to her family, but now she had friends also. Tuck explained to her about the cycles of life, how everything is meant to be born and to die, and that because of the water in the spring, he and his family had fallen off the cycle and were stuck where they would always be. He was sad and remorseful. He would like to grow old and die and in that way feel more a part of life. Mae was more matter-of-fact. She just lived her life and tried to make the best of it for her and Tuck and the boys, when she saw them every 10 years. Jesse asked Winnie to wait until she was 17 as he was, drink the water then and come live with him forever. This was pretty inviting to Winnie, a life with Jesse forever.

But the bad guy saw the kidnapping and followed them. The man in the yellow suit stole the Tuck's horse and rode back to Winnie's family. There he used his knowledge of what happened to Winnie to force them to give him the wood in return for telling them where she was. Surprisingly, this extortion worked. They gave him the wood and he set off with the constable to get Winnie back. But he got to the Tuck's first and told them of his plan to sell the water to those he considered "deserving" probably the rich. He wanted them to be examples for his sales pitch. When they refused, he grabbed Winnie and said he would take her and make her drink the water and she would be a wonderful sales tool. Mae had heard too much. She took the end of the shotgun and whacked him on the head.

The constable rode up just in time to see this. Mae was taken to jail, Winnie was taken home, the man in the yellow suit was taken into the Tuck's house to wait for the doctor. He died soon so Mae was held for murder and would have to be hanged. Which of course wouldn't work.

The climax comes as the Tuck's devise a plan with Winnie to help Mae escape. Winnie took her place in the jail cell while they rode away. She knew she probably would never see them again, and would be in trouble. But she loved them and wanted to help. She thought she just might drink that water when she turned 17 and find Jesse.

Winnie went back to her family, happier now and with much more freedom than she'd had before. Her family was letting her grow up. She decided to make the toad that lived near her cottage everlasting and sprinkled the water Jesse had given her on the toad. She could always go to the spring and get more when the time came. Since the man in the yellow suit died, her family still owned the wood and the spring.

The Tucks moved away and traveled and one day they came back to where Treegap had been in 1950. Tuck found Winnie's grave and said "Good Girl". He was glad she had chosen to live a normal life rather than an everlasting one.

Once, during a fishing trip with Miles, a mosquito landed on Winnie's knee. As she brushed it off she realized how awful it would be if all mosquitoes lived forever, constantly making baby mosquitoes. She realized that if people knew about the spring, they would all want to live forever and the planet would get very full very fast.

One awful thought is if you couldn't kill anything, what would you eat? Live food? At first the idea of living forever sounds great, but after you read about Tuck and his family, you realize that it has serious drawbacks. I just wish we could slow life down a whole lot, so we wouldn't have to rush and we could be young longer.

Tuck Everlasting

4-27-98

Optional: (A) Gutenberg pages 130, Natalie Babbit

Personal Response:

1. I really liked this book. The author does a lot of metaphors about life that paint interesting pictures in your mind. An example is comparing life to a river that just keeps flowing. The characters are strong and have conflicting, believable feelings. Winnie wants to run away from her family, but anything might happen to her; for a conflict example. The settings are well described.

great

Characters:

The main character in this book is Winnie. Winnie is a ten year old girl. She lives in a very clean and organized house. Her family owns a wood, but never goes there. Winnie can't stand being cooped up in such a tight household, and runs away to the wood. There she meets the Tucks, a family that can live forever due to magic water, and becomes their friend. The Tucks tell her their story, about being able to live forever. She hears the father's negative opinion on everlasting life and the son's, Jesse's more positive one. She however, does not form one herself until the end.

great

When Mae Tuck gets arrested for shooting a man who wanted to sell the magic water, Winnie takes her place in the jail. Winnie was brave and true to her friends. Her opinion of everlasting life is negative and she chooses not to drink the water and marry Jesse (the Tuck's youngest son) when she's 17 years old.

setting

This story took place in 1880. It takes place at Winnie's "touch-me-not" house, the Tuck's more comfortable house and pond, the wood owned by Winnie's folks and the jail house.

One of the most interesting places in the story is the Tuck's house. It has cobwebs and dust all over. A mouse even lives in a drawer! Odds and ends are everywhere and the dishes aren't stacked too neatly. Winnie thinks the Tuck's house is comfortable.

plot/climax/resolution

The plot of this story is having a family that lives forever. There is also a man who overhears the Tucks telling Winnie their secret. He offers to tell the

Fosters (Winnie's parents) where Winnie is (with the Tucks) in exchange for the wood with the magic water spring. Through the book you're wondering what will happen to him. (He dies.) You're also wondering if Winnie will tell about the magic water and/or drink it herself.

The climax of this story was when Mae shoots the man who knows about the water (he doesn't have a name. I'll call him Bob) and the constable shows up. Mae is taken to jail. If Bob dies then Mae is a murderer and must be hung. She can't die, however. This is a threat to their secret.

The resolution starts when you know Mae has safely escaped the jailhouse and Winnie takes her place.

episode

My episode is when Winnie runs away from home. This contributes to the story by having her meet the Tucks. If she hadn't run away she never would have met the Tucks.

Winnie slipped through the gate, surprised at how easy it was. She had expected it to be hard to run away. Winnie crept into the wood. It was quiet and cool. Squirrels

man in the yellow suit

butterflies toads and trees were all
there. Light shone green through the over-
leaves. Winnie came to a clearing in
which a boy sat. As Winnie watched he
uncovered a fountain with his toe. He
started to drink. Winnie realized how
thirsty she was...

4th Grade Reading List

Social Studies Curriculum-Related Books

*By the Great Horned Spoon

*Yang the Youngest and his Terrible Ear

*Zia

*Island of the Blue Dolphins

*Sing Down the Moon

*The Black Pearl

*A Jar of Dreams

*Journey Home

*Journey to Topaz

 *The Bracelet

*Desert Exile

*Weedflower

*Kira Kira

*Patty Reed's Doll

*Bound for Oregon

*Dragonwings

*The Rainbow People

*Seasons of Splendor

*Dear America: A Journey to the New World

*Grandfather Tang's Story

*Stone Fox

*Blue Willow

*Child Bride, by Ching Yeung Russell

*Buffalo Gal

*The Big Wave

*Maroo of the Winter Caves

*Bandit Across the Wide and Lonesome Prairie

*Earthquake at Dawn

*Treasures in the Stream

*Valley of the Moon

*Ballad of Lucy Wipple

*The Iron Dragon Never Sleeps

*Gary Paulson Books:

Tucket's Ride

Call Me Francis Tucket

Tucket's Home

Tucket's Gold

Fishbone's Song

Other 4th Grade Titles:

A Wrinkle in Time

How to Eat Fried Worms

Charlotte's Web

Charlie and the Chocolate Factory

Boyhood

Call of the Wild

White Fang

Riding Freedom

The Invisible Thread

Matilda

Boy

The BFG

The Cay

Tuck Everlasting

The Shakespeare Stealer

The Door in the Wall

Because of Winn-Dixie

Moon

The Great Gilly Hopkins

Esperanza Rising

One-Eyed Cat

Flip-Flop Girl

The Tale of Despereaux

Tales of a Fourth Grade Nothing
  and other Judy Blume titles

* I have placed asterisks in front of titles that are correlated with the social studies curriculum and that I encourage my students to read. Some of these the entire class is required to read.

5th Grade Reading List

Social Studies Curriculum-Related Books

*Sign of the Beaver

*My Brother Sam is Dead

*Sarah Plain and Tall

*In the Year of the Boar and Jackie Robinson

*Number the Stars

*Witch of Blackbird Pond

*Where the Red Fern Grows

*Incident at Hawk's Hill

*Return to Hawk's Hill

*They Led the Way

*Brother Eagle Sister Sky

*A Gathering of Days

*Prairie Songs

*Caddie Woodlawn

*Red Badge of Courage

*The Education of Little Tree

*The Friendship & the Gold Cadillac

*Let the Circle Be Unbroken

*Roll of Thunder Hear My Cry

*The Road to Memphis

*My Family Tree and Me

* Light in the Forest

*New England Journal

*On the Way Home

*The Red Rose Box

*Big Men, Big Country: A Collection of
   American Tall Tales

*Cut From the Same Cloth: American Women
   of Myth, Legend, and Tall Tales

*Moon Over Manifest

*The Witches

*Tall Tales: Johnny Appleseed, Paul Bunyan,
   Pecos Bill

*Jim Ugly

*Hattie Big Sky

*Day of Tears

*Dave at Night

*Journey to America

*Alan and Naomi

*Crispin: The Cross of Lead

*Our Wonderful World

*Around the Block, Around the Town

*A World of Many Cultures

*Prisoners of the Empire series:
   Under the Blood Red Sun
   House of the Red Fish
   Jump Ship to Freedom

*Hello, My Name is Scrambled Eggs

*On the Way Home

*Forge

*Sounder

*Something Upstairs

*True Confessions of Charlotte Doyle

*Constance

*Running Out of Time

*Witches' Children

*Blood on the River

*Mississippi Bridge

*War Comes to Willy Freeman

*Bud Not Buddy

*Saturnalia, Fleischman

*Park's Quest

*Johnny Tremain

*Slave Dancer

*Early Thunder

*Amos Fortune, Free Man

*Squanto, Friend of the Pilgrims

* Indicates books correlated w/ the Social Studies curriculum subjects.

More 5th Grade Social Studies Curriculum-Related Books

*The Terrible Wave

*The Girl Who Loved Wild Horses

*Old Yeller

*Annie Oakley

*Quentin Corn

*Return to Dies Drear

*Molly's Pilgrim

*Out of the Dust

*Boston Jane

*Rifles for Watie

*Dear America Series: Dreams in the Golden
    Country (many titles)

*The Seeds of America trilogy, by Laurie
    Halse Anderson

    Chains

    Forge

    Ashes

*Orphan Train Adventures:

    A Family Apart

    Caught in the Act

    In the Face of Danger

    Keeping Secrets

    A Place to Belong

    Circle of Love

*The Desert is Theirs – Poetry

*Escape to Freedom: A Play About Young
    Frederick Douglas

*The Gift of the Sacred Dog

*Hang a Thousand Trees with Ribbons: Story
    of Phillis Wheatley

*Ashanti to Zulu

*Good Night Mr. Tom

*Thought My Soul Would Rise and Fly

*The Story of Nellie Bly: Stop the Presses,
    Nellie's Got a Scoop

*Women Win the Vote

*Encounter, by Yolen

*Bull Run

*Lyddie

*I Heard the Owl Call My Name

*Annie and the Old One

*Saratoga Secret

*Moon Over Manifest

*Milkweed

*Hugh Glass, Mountain Man

*Sacajawea and the Journey to the Pacific

*John Henry: An American Legend

*Stones in Water

*Sarah Bishop

*The Good Liar, Gregory Macguire

*The Serpent Never Sleeps

*Streams to the River, River to the Sea

*Island on Bird Street

*A Picture of Freedom

*Let My People Go

*Wolf by the Ears

*Lizzie Bright and the Buckminster Boy

*The Cabin Faced West

*Traitor: The Case of Benedict Arnold

*Calico Captive

*A Long Way from Chicago

*A Year Down Yonder

*Sally Lockhart Mysteries:

    Ruby in the Smoke

    A Tiger in the Well

    The Shadow in the North

*Tituba of Salem Village

*After the Soldiers Were Gone

*Trapped Between the Lash and the Gun

*Countdown

*Orphan of Ellis Island

*Jip, His Story

*Star Spangled Secret

*Squanto, Friend of the Pilgrims

Other Fifth Grade Titles:

Gary Paulson Books:

    Hatchet

    Harris and Me

    The Haymeadow

    Masters of Disaster

    The River

    Brian's Winter

    Brian's Return

    Brian's Hunt

    Sarny

    Nightjohn

    Soldier's Heart

The Night the White Deer Died

Bridge to Terabithia

My Side of the Mountain

The Eye of the Amaryllis

Eyes of the Emperor

Afternoon of the Elves

The 13th Floor

Stuart Little

Rascal

The Trumpet of the Swan

Romeo and Juliet Together and Alive at Last

The Shakespeare Stealer

Anastasia Krupnick

Interstellar Pig

Eat Your Poison Doctor

Misty of Chincoteague

King of the Wind

The Giving Tree

Beauty and the Beast

The Ugly Duckling

A Friend Like That

A Day No Pigs Would Die

Dear Mr. Henshaw

Mrs. Frisby and the Rats of NIMH

The Prince of Whales

The Pigman

This Place Has No Atmosphere

The Josie Gambit

Do Animals Dream?

Wrapped in a Riddle

Shadow of the Wall

There's a Dead Person Following My Sister Around

Abel's Island

Greyling

From the Mixed Up Files of Mrs. Basil E. Frankweiler

Dominic

Invention Book

Junk in Space

50 Simple Things Kids Can Do To Save The Earth

It's Like This Cat

School Daze: Report to the Principal's Office

The Animal, the Vegetable, & John D. Jones

After the Goat Man

Pollyanna

Anne of Green Gables

The Industrial Revolution

Machines, Mind-boggling Experiments You Can Turn Into Science Fair Projects

6ᵗʰ Grade Reading List

Social Studies Curriculum-Related Books

*Dateline Troy
*Digging to the Past
*The Roman News
*A Fair Wind for Troy
*The Winged Cat
*Escape from Egypt
*The Golden Goblet
*The Egyptian Necklace
*A Place in the Sun
*The Greek News
*Tut, Tut
*The Trojan War
*It's All Greek to Me
*Your Mother Was a Neanderthal
*See You Later Gladiator
*Greek Mythology, by Ken Jennings
*The Egypt Game
*The Bronze Bow
*Stone Age Sentinel
*Homesick
*The Vandemark Mummy
*The Boy of the Painted Cave
*Return to the Painted Cave
*Seth of the Lion People
*The Day of Ahmed's Secret
*Pompeii: Buried Alive
*Adventures in Ancient Greece
*Hunt for the Last Cat
*Land of the Thundering Herds

Other Titles:

Crazy Lady
Night Cry, Phyllis Reynolds Naylor
Make Like a Tree and Leave
Sixth Grade Can Really Kill You
The Firebug Connection
Toby Scudder: Ultimate Warrior
Hummer
The Westing Game
Sixth Grade Secrets
Tree By Leaf
Anastasia at this Address
Under the Mummy's Spell
Ten Kids, No Pets
Of Nightingales That Weep
Lloyd Alexander, Chronicles of Prydain Series
Dawn Rochelle Series of Four Novels
   by Lurlene McDaniel:
      Six Months to Live
      I Want to Live
      So Much to Live For
      No Time to Cry
Monkey Island
The Pushcart War
On His Honor
A Girl Named Disaster

* Indicates books correlated w/ the Social Studies subjects

APPENDIX G
Language Arts and Writing

The Elements of the Writing Program for Grades 4, 5, and 6

Developmental Readiness: Building writing competence is a cumulative process. Skills are taught and applied, and writing tasks are assigned based on developmental readiness of the student and grade level goals.

Process: Writing is taught as a process. The writing process includes prewriting (mind mapping, listing, brainstorming), writing (drafting), revising (refining), editing (proofreading), and publishing (preparing a final product).

Format: Students use these processes to write in a variety of forms including stories (cartoons, short stories and novels), essays (five paragraph), book reports, research reports, poems, letters, journals, diaries, newspapers, advertisements, interviews, notes, outlines, plays, etc. The format of a piece of writing relates to its purpose.

Purpose: Students apply their developing writing skills for a variety of purposes. Writing is used to communicate information, thoughts, feelings, opinions; and to persuade, entertain, amuse, etc. Writing, as a critical thinking tool, is used to analyze and synthesize ideas, and to solve problems. Writing is used to clarify and refine thinking; and to communicate understanding across the curriculum in literature, social studies, science, and math.

Tools & Technology: Students are taught to use writing resources such as dictionaries, thesauruses, encyclopedias, and other resources. Students use spell checkers, and computers for word processing.

Mechanics and Expression: At the upper elementary grades, students receive instruction to increase competence in written mechanics and to refine and develop written expression.

(See reverse for details of Written Mechanics and Written Expression.)

Story Project Revision and Editing Guidelines

Dear Parents,

Students are writing a rough draft, revised draft, and final copy of their stories. <u>On rough and revised drafts</u>, write suggestions and corrections directly on them in ink. <u>On final copies</u>, write corrections in pencil.

<u>Revision</u> focuses on the elements of the story. The following are some things to look for when providing revision assistance:

1. Ask questions about story parts that are not clear or that could be clarified by adding detail. Suggest possible solutions.
2. Look for passages that could be shortened or expanded.
3. Look for passages that could be made more interesting through the addition of descriptions. Using words that "show" and "paint pictures," rather than "tell" has been one of our goals.
4. Even fantasies and science fiction stories need to create events that make sense and that are logical within the story's make-believe reality. If a story progresses as an illogical sequence of disjointed events, not held together by a clear context, provide suggestions to help fix the problem.
5. Each story should develop character and setting descriptions, a plot structure that leads to the climax, and a resolution.

<u>Editing</u> focuses on the writing mechanics of the story. The following should be included in editing corrections:

1. Write-in the correct spelling of misspelled words. Requiring students to correct spelling in a lengthy project is too time consuming and frustrating.
2. Mark incomplete and run-on sentences. Show what changes will correct the problem. For example: add a missing verb, or break a run-on sentence into two or more shorter sentences.
3. Provide assistance with capitalization, commas, apostrophes, and ending punctuation.
4. Paragraphing: Use editing symbol for a new paragraph whenever needed to break up long paragraphs. Editing symbol sheets are in story folders.
5. Dialogue: Each new speaker's words must begin a new paragraph. The proper punctuation for dialogue is as follows:

   "Let's go to the store," Kate suggested.

   Ben quickly responded, "Please wait until I finish making my list."

If dialogue dominates the story, suggest cutting dialogue and replacing it with narrative.

I know that providing revision and editing assistance on these stories is very time consuming. I greatly appreciate your help with this job!

Suggestions for Story Editing/Revising

Dear Parent,

Thank you for being willing to read and comment on student writing. You will likely see a very broad range of writing skills when looking at several students' work. Please try to focus your help in a way that addresses the skill level that you see expressed by each student. Every student should receive suggestions and ideas for story improvement. Write comments and suggestions in the margins as you go. At the end, write a brief overall comment about the story. Give positive, encouraging comments, as well as constructive criticism.

Thanks! Debbie

What are you looking for?

When reading and giving suggestions on student writing, focus first on the content. Content should be communicated clearly, in complete sentences, with regular paragraph divisions. Everything that a reader needs to understand the story must be written down. Frequently student authors forget this very important point.

Story Structure:

Even very short stories must contain all story elements. The basic elements of a story are: setting, character, plot (a problem with a sequence of events that develop the plot and move it forward), the climax (the high point in the plot/the problem is solved), and the resolution (the ending/what happens after the climax to wrap up the remaining unresolved story elements.)

Internal Logic and Believability:

Even a fantasy or science fiction story is required to present a believable reality. The author must communicate in a way that allows the reader to be drawn into the world of the story. The author must provide enough detailed information and description so that the reader can mentally follow the story events. The reader should be able to picture the setting and the characters. Characters' actions should be logical and make sense in the context the author has created.

Dialogue:

Frequently students will use dialogue almost exclusively to "tell" a story. To discourage this I have suggested that no more than six lines of dialogue be included in this story. Every time the speaker changes the author should begin a new paragraph.

What do you write on a student's story?

In the story margins, or within the text, write questions and comments that point out problems in the story. Your questions and comments should point to what the student needs to do to improve the story.

What about written mechanics?

The main goal of this reading is to help the student improve his/her story. But, in addition to revision suggestions, add a few editing marks to correct spelling, capitalization, punctuation, paragraphing, etc. Don't overwhelm the student's work with marks. Be as strategic as possible.

parented.doc

Name _____

EDITORS' MARKS

STUDENT PAGE

These symbols help editors make corrections on manuscripts.
You can use them to edit your own or a classmate's work.

Mark	Meaning	How to use
✐	Delete; take out	dining room room ✐
STET	Put back what was deleted	I'm really upset with you.
∧	Add a letter, word, or words	Please clean room.
#	Make a space	the kitchen table
⊂	Close up a space	story book
∽	Transpose; reverse letters or words	forever
⋀	Put in a comma	apples pears, and grapes
⊙	Put in a period	Susie went home⊙
∨	Put in an apostrophe	She wont come.
⸮ ⸰	Put in quotation marks	Ann said, Yes.
≡	Capitalize the letter	she won't come.
/	Make the letter lowercase	You hurt my Sister.
¶	Start a new paragraph	"Come," I said. "No," said Sue.

322

Guidelines for Correcting Written Work

Dear Parent,

Thank you for your assistance in reading, correcting, evaluating, and commenting on the students' writing. Direct, detailed feedback is the best way to provide students with guidance to improve their writing. I appreciate your assistance with this time-consuming task.

Attached are:

1. Proofreading Symbols: I have attached a sheet of standard proofreading symbols. You are free to use these symbols, or to adapt them to suit your own editing preferences.

2. The district's "Elementary Scoring Guide" used to evaluate the sixth grade writing competency tests. This can serve as a point of reference in evaluating student writing.

Scoring: If I want you to score a set of papers I will include specific instructions.

If I do not include specific scoring instructions, you only need to follow the guidelines below:

1. If possible, read the entire set in one sitting. This helps keep responses consistent.
2. Use a dark color of ink so that corrections show clearly.
3. Correct for writing mechanics errors in capitalization, punctuation, spelling, sentencing, etc. If you are unsure about making a correction, skip it.
4. Make two specific comments about the content. One, point out a positive feature of the writing. Two, suggest an improvement to the writing. Be as specific as possible.
5. Check off each paper on the class list.
6. If you have any questions or concerns about a paper attach a "post-it" note to me.

Again, thank you for your time and assistance.

Debbie

4th GRADE RUBRIC
for
WRITTEN LANGUAGE

4:    -Clearly defined paragraghs
-Intro and concluding paragragh
-Supporting details in the middle paragraphing
-Mechanics
-Expressive language

———

3:    -Shows some evidence of introductory and concluding
     paragraphs
-Shows some evidence of supporting details
-Shows evidence of paragraph definition
-Shows moderate evidence of expressive language

———

2:    -Shows some paragraph organization
-Lacks either introduction or conclusion
-Shows little evidence of supporting details
-Shows little evidence of expressive language
-Shows little evidence of mechanics

———

1:    -Lacks paragraph organization
-Lacks supporting details
-Lacks mechanics
-Lacks expressive language

5th GRADE RUBRIC
for
WRITTEN LANGUAGE

6: -Demonstrates a flair with language
-Clear sentence structure
-Correct paragraph structure
-Includes topic and concluding sentences
-Topic clearly developed with detail
-Uses expressive language and a variety of style types

5: -Correct paragraph structure
-Sentences are varied
-Sentences are descriptive
-Correct spelling and punctuation
-Appropriate use of tenses

4: -Clarity
-Develops several specific ideas
-More vague and non-descriptive
-Repetitive
-Few spelling errors which do not distract the reader

3: -Paragraph lacked development
-Run on sentences
-Lacks clarity
-Missing words
-Spelling interfered with communication
-Awkward sentence structure

2: -Incorrect word choice
-Grammatical errors
-Lacks clear paragraph structure
-Many run on sentences
-May have good content, but may have missing words
-Awkward construction

1: -Incomplete sentences
-Not true paragraph form
-Some spelling mistakes
-Lacks development
-Punctuation mistakes

6th GRADE RUBRIC
for WRITTEN LANGUAGE

SCORE OF 8 - A paper receiving an 8 will display most of the following characteristics:

-    Full development of the topic
-    Clear and logical organization
-    Relatively free of mechanical error, with no serious error which inhibits reader
-    Mature sentence structure; reads smoothly
-    Coherent, with clear transitions
•   Flair in diction
-    Uses topic to develop a theme or to make a point
-    Stylish

SCORE OF 6 - A paper receiving a 6 will display most of the following qualities:

-    Good control of the assignment with full, consistent development
-    Good paragraph development, with transitions evedent
-    Unified
-    Some sentence variety; sentence structure under control
-    Relatively few mechanical errors, generally of a non-distracting nature only

SCORE OF 5 - A paper receiving a 5 will display most of the following qualities:

-    Responds to the assignment, staying on the subject.
-    Adequate development of topic, organized into paragraphs with some transitional signals
•   Sentence structure generally in control, with few sentence faults
-    Mechanics support basic flow of thought with few spelling errors and few critical errors of punctuation or capitalization.

SCORE OF 4 - A paper receiving a 4 will display most of the following characteristics:

-    Partial development of the subject with some serious departure from the subject
-    May wander, showing lack of coherence
-    Shows some lack of control over language
-    Mechanical flaws evident, frequently as an impediment to communication
-    Organization not evident or clear
-    Spelling a definite problem

SCORE OF 2 - A paper receiving a 2 will display many of the following characteristics:

•   Very short, illegible, frequent misspellings
-    Serious underdevelopment or getting off the subject
-    Many sentence faults, some of which lead to confusion
-    Inappropriate or inadequate punctuation and capitalization, sometimes leading to misreading
-    Organization inappropriate or lacking

SCORE OF 0 - Writer:

-    Off topic
-    Inappropriate
-    Blank

Parent Volunteer
Mini-Workshop

Daily Work:

I.   Student Activities:

A.   Literature: Reading, Writing, Speaking, Listening
Discussion—Small group discussions - independent discussions with groups of 4 to 5 students.
   Vocabulary, comprehension, response
Discussion Techniques - Asking open ended questions.
Students write inquiries using Bloom's Taxonomy of Knowledge, Comprehension, Application,
   Analysis, Synthesis, Evaluation.
(Questioning levels/critical thinking)
Students use Jr. Great Books Program's "shared inquiry" technique to create questions about
   what they are reading.

B.   Word Work:
Notebooks—Correct all errors
Dictation—This is the only work that is evaluated for correct spelling. Circle misspelled words
   and write in omitted words. Students work in teams to correct misspelled words. Team
   scores for Corrections.
Studying—"Say, look, spell, check"

C.   Spelling:
Urge students to use invented spellings in their writing. This promotes spelling progress and
   writing fluidity.
Refrain from providing students with requested spellings.
When reviewing any written work, circle misspelled words, and write correct spellings nearby or
   at the bottom of the paper.
There is no penalty for misspelled words. Students should add these words to their personal word
   banks—"cursive cards."

D.   Writing: (Rough draft, revision, proofread for final version)
Basic Mechanics:
Capitalization, Punctuation, Grammar, Complete Sentences.
Paragraphing:
Clear organization.
Topic sentences, with supporting sentences giving specific details and using descriptive language.
   S-t-r-e-t-c-h-i-n-g Writing Skills
Always Required:
Complete sentences.

Answers that include the question being answered.

Cursive handwriting on all assignments, unless specified.

E.   Math: Lessons, assignments, self correction, chapter testing.

Manipulatives, games, Equals activities, problem solving.

II. Correcting Student Work:

Objective Tasks: Count incorrect items & calculate percent.

Written Work: Use holistic Marks - (+) (/ +) (/) (/-) (-).

Target comments: Make positive comment; suggest area for improvement.

Incomplete Work Book: Every student has a page of the spiral notebook for each subject where incomplete work should be noted. Enter date and specific details of incomplete assignment.

Assignment Notebooks: Check for completeness, and give holistic mark.

III. Record Keeping:

Folders—Label assignment & enter evaluative mark.

Student Records—All assignments done on binder paper (or other 3-hole-punched paper) are to be stored in student binders after teacher review. This work is intended to provide a chronological record of students' work and progress. Students are responsible for maintaining their binders. Usually corrected papers should be added to the front of each section, so that most current work is on top.

Binders—They are divided into five sections with the following labels:

Math Assignments & Tests; Language Arts; Word Work; Research/Projects/Social Studies; Literature.

IV. Working With Students:

Reinforce appropriate behavior.

Notice and comment on desired behaviors.

Take advantage of your time in the classroom to develop a personal rapport with the students. Get to know them, let them get to know you.

Correct undesired behaviors by giving specific redirections. Examples:

"James, now is the time for you to work on your ___."

"Judy, you are expected to work quietly and independently now."

"Joe, the other members of your group need you to participate, too."

"Susie, what could you be working on now?"

"Lucy, doing cartwheels in the classroom is dangerous. You need to move around the classroom in a way that is safe and is not disruptive."

"Charles, I would like you to ___."

Special Projects:

I have tons of things that need to be "packaged" or organized for student use. Let me know if you are interested in putting together these materials and activities. These are projects that can be done in the classroom or at home. I will provide the materials and directions.

1. Put together directions and manipulative items for independent use or for setting out at a station. EQUALS stations binder. SPACES book.
2. Make porta-folders to be equipped with directions and activities.
3. Create inquiry tasks to accompany social studies units or literature books.
4. Use Spectra Art guide to organize materials for art projects. Materials, supplies, art prints from library.
5. Listen to "Great Composers" tapes and summarize biographical information. Generate companion activities.
6. Use Science resource books to organize materials for "hands-on" demonstrations and experiments.

Many of the above activities can be done with a small group of children who are interested in the project. You can organize, supervise, and direct the children as a part of the project.

Other Ideas: You Tell Me!

I am very appreciative of any contribution you feel you can make to the class. I want your experience in the classroom to satisfy your own goals, too. If you want to do something that I haven't mentioned, please talk to me about it. If you take on more than you feel comfortable with let me know.

THANK YOU! THANK YOU! THANK YOU!

Pronouns

How to Use "I" and "me" Correctly

The pronouns "I" and "me" are frequently misused—so frequently that they began to sound correct. If students understand the proper way to use them, perhaps they will be less likely to use them incorrectly.

I—is used in the subject of the sentence.

I am going to the store.   Mary and I are going to the store.
I saw the movie.   Betty and I saw the movie
I hit the ball.   John and I are playing ball.

Common error: "Me and John are going to the game."
People say the above, who would never say, "Me is/am going to the game."

me—is used in the predicate of the sentence.

Mary is going to the store with me.   Sally is going with Mary and me.
John saw me in the theater.   Mary saw Tom and me in the room.
The ball hit me.   The teacher called John and me.

Common error: "The teacher called Mary and I to her desk."
People say the above who would never say, "The teacher called I to her desk."

Other Pronouns

It is also helpful to teach the various sets of pronouns.

Subject Pronouns:

	Singular	Plural
1st person	I	we
2nd person	you	you
3rd person	he, she, it	they

Predicate Pronouns

	Singular	Plural
1st person	me	us
2nd person	you	you
3rd person	him, her, it	them

Possessive Pronouns

	Singular	Plural
1st person	my	our
2nd person	your	your
3rd person	his, her, its	their
	mine	ours
	yours	yours
	his, hers	theirs

The possessive is built into pronouns, so you never need to use an apostrophy, as you do with nouns:

Your home   John's home

Common error: You're home. [You're = You are]
(You're home in your home.)

(con't)

Pronoun Chart

This chart might be helpful if you are asked questions by your brighter students:

Subject	Object	Possessive	Reflexive
I	me	my (determiner) / mine (pronoun)	myself
you	you	your (determiner) / yours (pronoun)	yourself
he	him	his	himself
she	her	her (determiner) / hers (pronoun)	herself
it	it	its	itself
we	us	our (determiner) / ours (pronoun)	ourselves
you	you	your (determiner) / yours (pronoun)	yourselves
they	them	their (determiner) / theirs (pronoun)	themselves

Demonstrative	Relative	Indefinite	Interrogative
this	that	something / anything / nothing (things)	who
these	who/whom	somewhere / anywhere / nowhere (places)	what
that	which	someone / anyone / no one (people)	which
those	when		whom
former/latter	where		whose
		(adverb/subordinate conjunction)	where
		(adverb/subordinate conjunction)	when
		(adverb/subordinate conjunction)	why
		(adverb/subordinate conjunction)	how

from *Wikipedia*

Banner in the Sky

Identify and label each part of speech in the sentences.
Also, underline the <u>subject</u> once and the <u>predicate</u> twice.

1. The crawling child slowly ascended the spiral staircase.

2. The ice chasm had grown because of the warm spring temperatures.

3. He sat motionless in the canoe because he was afraid of tipping.

4. The chocolate cake was incredibly delicious, and she wanted more.

5. A fortune of silver was veined throughout the Sierra Nevadas.

6. The bulging chipmunk cheeks told of a very successful nut hunt.

7. The menacing noise of the mosquitoes almost drove the campers crazy.

8. Her camping food supply was petering and soon she would be hungry.

9. The setting sun was absolutely beautiful.

10. She was prone to leaving her sweatshirt on the playground.

11. The taut rope was held by the grunting, pulling teams.

12. The improvised skit was very impressive and was enjoyed by all.

13. Swimming in the northern winter lake was indescribably cold.

14. The indescribable beauty of the sunset riveted their attention.

15. The hail pummeled the players before theyscampered to shelter.

16. Her aching muscles needed a hot soak to relax.

17. John felt like an imbecile for forgetting to feed his dog.

18. The rigid steel pole didn't bend the slightest in the strong wind.

19. The anchor bolts were embedded in the fresh concrete.

20. The watch dog bristled at the squeak created by the wooden gate.

Banner in the Sky

Name _____

Date _____

Complete each sentence with the best word from <u>Banner in the Sky</u>. Some words may be used more than once or in another form. Place the part of speech in the first blank.

1. _____Because they entered the stadium at the ground level and their tickets were in the sixtieth row, the group had to _____ the stairs.

2. _____Jim wanted to build a push cart from the materials in the junk pile so he knew he had to do some _____.

3. _____The deep ice _____ posed a hazard to the winter hikers.

4. _____The rope between the rescuing boat and the disabled craft was _____ as the towing began.

5. _____The paper liter lay _____ during the dead still day.

6. _____People with poor diets are _____ to poor health.

7. _____It is _____ hard to believe that some of the beauty of sunsets is caused by pollution in the sky.

8. _____The boy was _____ wrong for spanking the unsupervised little puppy for digging in the garden.

9. _____The gold was _____ throughout the mountains of the Sierra Nevadas, and the 49ers dreamed of finding just one seam.

10. _____A _____ shopping bag in each arm told the weary mall goers they were nearly finished.

11. _____Roots from the neighboring tree were becoming a _____ to the water supply of the surrounding plants and a danger to crack the sidewalk.

12. _____The flashlight battery's power began to _____ and the light faded.

13. _____Mary didn't like giving up her room and _____ at the idea of having her grandmother move in for two weeks.

14. _____The aroma of the warm gooey chocolate cake was _____, and all she wanted was a piece put on her plate.

15. _____She found a short nail _____ in her flat bicycle tire.

16. _____The pain of the injury was _____ so the patient needed to take some medication for relief.

17. _____The driving rain _____ the hikers as they struggled up the unprotected granite hillside.

18. _____After an hour of typing the lengthy report and being only one-third completed, the student stop to slowly _____ the tired fingers.

19. _____After two solid weeks in the mountains, the student _____ for a good milkshake, a basket of fries and a delicious hot sandwich.

20. _____The _____ steel post didn't bend the slightest in the strong wind.

21. _____Jon felt like an _____ because he forgot to take off his pajamas before getting dressed.

22. _____To hide from the "IT" in the hide in seek game, Hal lay _____ on the ground trying to be as flat as possible.

23. _____The captain wanted a _____ ship where everything was clean and in its place.

24. _____The little boy tried to impress his grandfather by _____, the biceps muscles.

25. _____The hairs on the dog _____ when the door bell unsuspectingly rang in the middle of the night.

26. _____Her parents were rather _____ with their rules and would not let her stay out past 8:30 or have any friends over on the week days.

Banner in the Sky

word	part of speech	other forms	definition	phrase
ascended 211	v	ing, s ascent ascend ascension (n)	to move up	the bellion ascended the stairs
chasm 212	n	chasms	- deep, wide crack in earth - great differences in feelings	chasm in the ice
motionless 212	adj	motion motioned, ing, s	no movement	lay motionless on the ground
incredibly 212	adv	incredible adj incredibility n	hard to believe	incredibly smart move
veined 212	adj	vein veinlike	to mark with veins, lines	veined with silver and gold
bulging 212	adj v	bulge bulged, s	to swell out	bulging pockets, cheeks
menacing 212	adj	menace n menacingly adv. menace, ed	a threat or danger	menacing underwater reefs Dennis the Menace
petered 213	v	peter, petering, s	to gradually diminish	battery's power petered out
absolute 213	adj	absoluteness n absolutely	complete free from all restrictions to fullest extent	absolute power absolutely beautiful
prone 216	adj	proneness n	- lying with front down - naturally inclined	- lying prone on ground - prone to illness
taut 217	adj	tautly adv tautness n	drawn tightly or stretched orderly, tidy	taut rope taut ship
improvised 217	v	improvise, ing, s improviser n improvisation n	- to make up on spur of moment - to make from materials on hand	improvise a skit improvised a table out of ...

indescribably 219	adv	indescribe	can it be described in words / beyond words	indescribably cold, beautiful ...
unendurable 219	adj	endurable / endurance	not bearable	unendurable pain
pummeled 220	V	pummel, ing, s	to hit again & again with fists	boxers pummeled each other
aching 220	V / adj	ache, ed, s / ache (s)	dull, continuous pain / long, yearn	aching muscles / ached to go home
flexed 220	V / adj	flex, ing, s / flexible (flexibility, ness(s))	to bend / to tighten, contract	flexed tired fingers / flexed muscles
imbeciles 221	n	imbecile / imbecility	- mentally retarded / - stupid or foolish	
rigid 219	adj	rigidity n / rigidly adv / rigidness n	not yielding, or bending / strict / fixed	rigid steel / rigid rules
embedded220	V / adj	embedding / embed, s	enclosed in surrounding material	- embedded in concrete / - embedded in his mind
bristling	V / adj	bristle n / ed	- to show anger / - to rise stiffly / - to have hair on neck / raise in fear, anger ...	bristled at that idea

Weekly Writing I
"The Pet"
Assignment given Monday, Oct. 16

Due Dates

Brainstorming and First Rough Draft - Weds., Oct. 18
Polished Rough Draft - Thurs., Oct. 19
Final Draft and Artwork - Tues., Oct. 24

Assignment

Essay: Write a three paragraph essay from the point of view of your pet or an imaginary pet.
1. Description of yourself as the pet.
2. Description of your personality as the pet.
3. Description of your feelings (relationship) toward pet's owner -- you!

Artwork: Create an illustration of your pet and you. Use white 9 X 12 drawing paper provided.

Evaluation

Standard Criteria: (For all essays, stories, and research writing.)
1. Neatly written in cursive or word processed.
2. Correct spelling, grammar, and usage.
3. Complete sentences, with varied beginnings.
4. Paragraphs are developed from topic to supporting sentences.

Special Criteria:
1. Use vivid verbs, adjectives, and adverbs.
2. Use three similes and metaphors.

Use your **Writer's Handbook** for help.

Do your best and have fun!!!!!

Math

House Design Project

This project involves planning and drawing the floor plan for a 600 square foot house. The house should be designed for one adult. It could be designed for you, another person you know, or an imaginary adult.

The plan must include spaces for living, sleeping, eating, and studying. You need a kitchen, a bath, and laundry facilities. You may add other areas as space and your imagination permit. You do not need a separate room for every use. You may want to combine uses to have larger rooms, within the 600 square foot limit.

The assignment packet shows a typical floor plan. You will use four squares to the inch graph paper, with one square equal to six inches. Draw wall thicknesses at 6 inches. Include windows, doors, closets, kitchen appliances, and bathroom fixtures. Show dimensions of all rooms as in typical floorplan drawing. Electrical symbols are optional. Add furniture after your plan is complete.

Phase I - Rough Drawing

Use scratch paper to work out the basic floor plan. Once you have developed a room arrangement plan that satisfies you, begin your final floor plan on graph paper.

Phase II - Final Floor Plan

Work in pencil only. Work carefully, using a ruler to draw lines.

Once your final drawing is complete, write a paragraph, or two, describing the characteristics of the person for whom the house was designed. Add any special information about the house's design.

Project Timeline:

You may work in class and at home on the project, but materials must be in class each day. Phase I is due on Tuesday, Phase II is due at the end of the day on Thursday.
Have fun!

Name _____ Number _____ Date _____

Math Concept Review

1. Explain the difference between perimeter and area, using examples to illustrate each.

2. Brainstorm words used to indicate units of measurement. After brainstorming organize the words into labeled categories.

3. Explain how the decimal number system is organized to indicate place value. Illustrate with at least one three digit number example.

4. In fractions, greater and greater numerals are used to express smaller and smaller quantities. Explain this apparent contradiction using at least two examples.

5. Explain what you know about prime and composite numbers.

6. Explain how to round a number to a specified place value. Give at least two examples.

APPENDIX J

Social Studies

Mesopotamia Test   Name _____

Use page 22 of your S.S. Activity Book to give two examples for each of the five achievements boxes.

Key Terms Matching

1. urban   _____ belief in one God.

2. alluvial plain   _____ a huge Sumerian mud brick temple

3. ziggurat   _____ low, flat land formed from silt deposited by rivers

4. city-state   _____ city

5. Code of Hammurabi   _____ spreading of new ideas to other places

6. empire   _____ the exchange of one good or service for another

7. monotheism   _____ a conquered land of many peoples & places
governed by one   ruler

8. covenant   _____ a special agreement

9. exile   _____ the Five Books of Moses

10. Torah   _____ a collection of laws compiled by the Babylonian
                                                   leader

11. barter   _____ independently governed towns

12. cultural diffusion   _____ being forced to live in another place.

A. Explain, in detail, why people chose to settle in the region known as Mesopotamia. Specifically mention the influence of geography.

B. Who was Sargon, and what role did he play in the rise of civilization?

C. Who was Hammurabi, and why was his innovation important to the rise of civilization?

D. What do you know about the story of Abraham, and his importance as a historical figure?

E. Where did the Phoenicians live? Where did the Lydians live? What innovations were contributed by these two peoples?

Mesopotamia Test   Name _____Key_____

Use page 22 of your S.S. Activity Book to give two examples for each of the five achievements boxes.
(Answers on page 22 of teacher's key book.)

Key Terms Matching

1. urban
2. alluvial plain
3. ziggurat
4. city-state
5. Code of Hammurabi
6. empire
7. monotheism

8. covenant
9. exile
10. Torah

11. barter
12. cultural diffusion

___7___ belief in one God.
___3___ a huge Sumerian mud brick temple
___2___ low, flat land formed from silt deposited by rivers
___1___ city
__12__ spreading of new ideas to other places
__11__ the exchange of one good or service for another
___6___ a conquered land of many peoples & places
         governed by one ruler
___8___ a special agreement
__10__ the Five Books of Moses
___5___ a collection of laws compiled by the Babylonian
         leader
___4___ independently governed towns
___9___ being forced to live in another place.

A. Explain, in detail, why people chose to settle in the region known as Mesopotamia. Specifically mention the influence of geography.
rich, fertile soil deposited when the Tigris and Euphrates Rivers flooded. The rivers provided water to irrigate their crops. They built their towns on the alluvial plain next to their fields and the river.

B. Who was Sargon, and what role did he play in the rise of civilization?
Sargon was a warrior who founded the Akkadia Empire, becoming the first ruler of the empire formed in the region of the fertile crescent, Mesopotamia. He unified the separate city-states of Mesopotamia under one empire and leader.

C. Who was Hammurabi, and why was his innovation important to the rise of civilization?
King of the city-state of Babylon. He compiled the set of laws known as the Code of Hammurabi. This brought order to the growing towns and cities where more and more people were coming together.

D. What do you know about the story of Abraham, and his importance as a historical figure? Abraham was the earliest ancestor of the Israelites, according to the Bible. He was the father of the Jews and the Moslems.

E. Where did the Phoenicians live? Where did the Lydians live? What innovations were contributed by these two peoples? The Phoenicians lived on the Mediterranean coast of the fertile crescent region and the Lydians lived in what is now Turkey. The Phoenicians found a purple dye from a kind of mollusk that lived off the coast. This dye was used to color fabric, especially royal clothing. The Phoenicians were known for simplifying the alphabet, thus improving written communication. The Lydians were the first to make gold coin money. They used the natural resource of gold that was mined in their area.

An open notes test.

Ancient Greeks Unit Test   Name ___Key___

Write the letter in the blank to match the word with the phrase describing it:

1. Phoenicia __N__

A. a territory, or distant community controlled by a distant government.

2. Peloponnesus __Q__

B. a large hill where residents of the city and surrounding lands could seek shelter in times of war.

3. Crete __O__

C. a marketplace and meeting place where much of the business of Greek society was conducted.

4. Parthenon __S__

D. a region just north of ancient Greece.

5. colony __A__

E. largest city-state of the Peloponnesus.

6. agora __C__

F. a powerful city-state known for valuing learning and the arts.

7. acropolis __B__

G. government is controlled by a few of the richest and most powerful citizens.

8. oligarchy __G__

H. government is controlled by the people.

9. monarchy __M__

I. Ancient Greeks believed gods and goddesses ruled the world and lived here.

10. Pericles __T__

J. protector, provider, known for her wisdom.

11. Sparta __E__

K. epic poet believed to have written the Odyssey and the Illiad

12. Mount Olympus __I__

L. empire to the east of Greece that made several attempts to conquer Greece.

13. Homer __K__

M. government is controlled by one person, usually a king or queen.

14. Athena __J__

N. an area at the eastern edge of the Mediterranean Sea.

15. Persia __L__

O. a large island where an ancient civilization flourished for over 1500 years.

16. The Iliad __P__

P. an epic poem about a ten year war.

17. The Odyssey __R__

Q. a large peninsula of Greek territory.

18. Macedonia __D__

R. an epic poem about a hero's 10 year journey back to his home.

19. Athens __F__

S. a temple dedicated to Athena.

20. democracy __H__

T. he led Athens through its Golden Age

Native American
Long Term Projects
December 6 - January 18

Overview: Over the last few weeks students have worked on an overview of the six major Native American cultures that flourished on land that is now within the continental United States prior to European settlement. The culture groups are: Northwest Coast, Plateau and Great Basin, Southwest, Great Plains, Southeast Woodlands, and Northeast Woodlands. The cultures of California have been omitted, as have the arctic and subarctic cultures of Alaska.

Five to six students are working on tribes within each of the six culture groups. Each student has chosen a tribe within one of the six culture groups to study in-depth. All research materials are being provided in the classroom from the Patwin Library, the California State University, Sacramento, Elementary Curriculum Library, and my personal library. These materials are sufficient to fully meet the content expectations of the projects. Both a written research paper and a model of a Native American village will be due on Tuesday, January 18.

General Expectations: Students will have 60-75 minutes per day in class, throughout this unit, to read and take notes, and to write rough and final drafts. The students and I worked out the following expectations:

Dec. 6-17: Read and take notes on one Native American tribe. Students are expected to produce about one page of hand written notes per day during this class time. If note taking is completed more rapidly students will begin to write rough draft of written project. During this period students need to begin to plan for construction, at home, of a model Native American village. Students can seek guidance during class for planning model.

Jan. 3-7: Write rough draft of written project.

Jan. 10-14: Write final draft of written project.

Part I - Notes: Students will be expected to make note of information from the available resources on the following topics: food, clothing, shelter, tools, beliefs & ceremonies, arts & crafts, games, stories, social & political organization, adaptations to seasonal changes, etc. I am teaching the students to take notes on these different subtopics on different pieces of binder paper or on note cards. Some of the books are short enough that students will read them from beginning to end, making note of information as they come to it in their reading. Other books will be too long to be read in their entirety. With these books students will use the table of contents and index to locate sections to read and from which to take notes. Students should not be concerned about subtopics on which they cannot find information. The available books have plenty of information for a thorough project even if the amount of information on individual subtopics will vary depending on the tribe and the books. Students will learn to skip over information that they have already noted as they cull various sources. Students will keep a bibliographic list of all of the books they use in their research.

Part II - Written Project Format Options:

1. Traditional Research Paper - Some students will prefer to write a traditional research paper organized around the subtopics found in the resources about their tribe.

2. Story - Some students will prefer to combine the researched information into a realistic story format. For example, "A Day in the Life of a Sioux Indian Boy," or "A Year in the Life of a Cherokee Girl," or "Life in an Anasazi Pueblo."

3. Create Your Own Format - Some students will think of another unique way to share their research. Students will need to get approval of their proposal for this option no later than Thursday, Dec. 16.

Part III - Model Village Project: Students will be expected to plan and build a model that represents the major aspects of the tribe they have studied, showing examples of shelter, food, clothing, and tools. Models should be no larger than the top of a student desk (approx. 18" X 30").

Model Options: Some students have expressed an interest in pursuing an alternate in-depth model project. Alternate model projects must be approved no later than Thurs., Dec. 16.

Extra Credit Options:
1. Teach a mini-lesson to the class about some aspect of your tribe.
2. Write an original story/legend/poem based on your research.
3. Tell a story from one of the resources, or an original story, to the class.
4. Create a craft project to illustrate information from one, or more, of the subtopics.
5. Create a musical composition and perform it for the class using a modern musical instrument, or an instrument you modeled after a Native American instrument.
6. Write and direct a play to be performed by you and your classmates.
7. Draw or paint a mural representing the life of your tribe.
8. Make food similar to that made by Native Americans to share with the class.
9. Make clothing that represents your tribe.
10. Make and demonstrate a tool similar to that used by your tribe.
11. Let your imagination and information guide your choice.

Summary of Due Dates:

Dec. 10 - Approximately five pages of notes.

Dec. 17 - Approximately five more pages of notes.

(My major criterion is not the number of pages, but the productive use of class time. Page number guideline is meant to encourage students to use class time effectively. You can help reinforce this by asking your child to share their progress with you during note-taking/draft writing processes.)

Jan. 10 - Rough draft.

Jan. 18 - Final draft and model.

Parental Assistance:
It is very important to me that the students have ownership of all of their work for this project. Parental support will be necessary to plan, schedule, and check-up on the sub-tasks of the project. Parental assistance will be needed to help find, or provide, the materials for making the model. Most of the materials should be readily available in nature. A family trip to the UCD Arboretum might be helpful. Parents are encouraged to work with their children to assist with editing and revising. When I have time to read rough drafts I do not hesitate to provide correct spelling, punctuation, capitalization, etc. Please feel free to provide this assistance to your child.

Computer Written Reports:
Hand written notes and drafts are required as evidence of appropriately used class time. Hand written notes are the only evidence that students, parents, or I have of on-going progress with this assignment. It would be unrealistic for students to expect to produce a word processed final draft by Jan. 18, without having completed a word processed rough draft by Jan. 10. Therefore, I will not accept computer written final drafts unless a computer written rough draft is turned in by Jan. 10. I do not object to parents assisting their children with word processing, but once a parent word processes a child's work the line becomes blurred on whose work it is. If you word process your child's work, please be sure that your child participates in the transformation that occurs between the child's hand written draft, the edited (marked up) hand written draft, any computer drafts, and the final version. The child needs to be directly involved in decisions affecting the final form of the written report.

Examples of Bibliographic Citations

Book with a SINGLE AUTHOR
Stauffer, Donald Barlow. *A Short History of American Poetry.* New York: Macmillan, 1976.

Book with an EDITOR instead of an author.
Gibson, James, ed. *The Complete Poems of Thomas Hardy.* New York: Macmillan, 1976.

Book with TWO AUTHORS
Link, Arthur S., and William B. Catton. *American Epoch: A History of the United States since 1890.* New York: Knopf, 1963.

Book with THREE AUTHORS
Adams, William, Peter Cohn, and Barry Slepian. *Afro-American Literature: Drama:* Boston: Houghton Mifflin, 1970.

Book with FOUR or MORE AUTHORS
Goldner, Orville, et al. *The Making of King Kong.* New York: Ballantine. 1975.

Book with CORPORATE AUTHOR
United Nations. *Statistical Yearbook, 1978.* New York: United Nations, 1979.

Book with NO KNOWN AUTHOR
Literary Market Place: The Directory of American Book Publishing. 1976-77 ed. New York: Bowker, 1976.

Book translated from a FOREIGN LANGUAGE
Solzhenitsyn, Aleksandr 1. *The First Circle.* Trans. Thomas P. Whitney. New York: Harper & Row, 1968.

Magazine: Woodward, Kenneth L. "Séances in Suburbia," *McCall's* (March 1970), pp. 70-71, 149-51.

Newspaper
Lucas, J. Anthony. "The Drug Scene: Dependence Grows," *The New York Times,* January 8, 1868, pp. 1, 22.

Encyclopedia: Driver, Harold E. "Indian, American." *Encyclopedia Americana.* 1969. Vol. XV.

Encyclopedia (Unsigned Article): "Ironwood." *Encyclopedia Americana.* 1969. Vol. XV.

Sound FILMSTRIP with an AUTHOR:
McDaniel, Marion and Michael McDaniel. *Redesigning Man: Science and Human Values* (Filmstrip). New York: Harper & Row Media Program, 1974, 6 rolls, col., with 6 cassettes.

Sound FILMSTRIP with NO AUTHOR
"Robert Frost" (Filmstrip). In *The American Experience in Literature: Poets of the 20th Century.* Chicago: Encyclopedia Britannica Educ. Corp., 1964, 5 rolls, col., with 5 cassettes.

ART PRINT: Monet, Claude. *Boats at Argenteuil* (Print). U.S.A.: Shorewood Press, Inc., n.d., col., 16½ x 25 in.

SLIDE: *Surrealism* (Slide). Stamford, Ct: Educational Dimensions, 1974, 20 slides, col., 2 x 2 in.

MICROFORM: "Watch Out for Food Poisoning" (Microfilm). *Changing Times.* Aug. 1975, pp. 36-38.

MOTION PICTURE: *The Food Revolution* (Motion Picture). New York: McGraw Hill, 1968. 17 min., sd., col., 16 mm.

Sound RECORDING or CASSETTE
Whitman, Walt. *Leaves of Grass* (Sound Recording). Ed Begley, reader. Caedmon, n.d., disc TC 1037.

VIDEO TAPE or VIDEOCASSETTE: Wolfe, Pamela. "Pam Wolfe Bakes Bread" (Videorecording). Presented at Greenwich High School, 1977, cassette, 30 min., b & w, ¾ in.

CD: Title of CD (Grolier Electronic Encyclopedia), Publisher, copyright date.

Internet: Author(s) (if given), type of internet program (Netscape, America On Line, etc.), Computer address (aol.com.chason,etc.).

Name _____   Date _____

Early Human Research and Report

Each student will organize and write a structured essay report on one of the following early humans: homo habilis, homo erectus, neanderthal, cro-magnon.

Materials provided: Social Studies text chapter 1, a summary sheet of research data on one early human group, "Early Human Report Outline" model, "Homo Erectus" model of entire essay report, a map outline, vocabulary list, video shown in classroom, and library/classroom resource magazines and other books.

Research/Report Process: Read, research using other media, take notes, outline, draft, edit/revise, redraft, final. Text of the report is about six paragraphs long (about two typewritten or word processed pages). See models provided above.

Report Text Format: Each paragraph needs to have a clear topic sentence and supporting sentences, organized according to the following outline.

    I. Introduction: Background information, including the topics of each of the subtopic paragraphs, and a transition sentence.

    II. Subtopic paragraph #1 - Appearance

    III. Subtopic paragraph #2 - Lifestyle

    IV. Subtopic paragraph #3 - Tools

    V. Subtopic paragraph #4 - Food

    ___ Additional subtopics may be added as determined by research findings.

    VI. Conclusion: Restate & summarize the main points (subtopics) of the report. Last sentence should be a general concluding statement.

(Each subtopic should be a minimum of one paragraph (five sentences). Some subtopics may require more than one paragraph. Each paragraph must have a clear topic sentence.)

Finished Report:

Bind report into folder including:	
Title page **Table of Contents** **Text of Report**- 6 or more paragraphs (about 2 pages double-spaced or 4 handwritten) **Illustration** - hand drawn in color **Map** - colored and labeled	**Glossary** - alphabetized vocabulary with definitions. **Bibliography** - minimum of four resources. **Notes** - outlines, cards, rough drafts, etc. must be turned in with the finished report.

Report Due Dates:

Subtopic paragraph drafts: _9/28_ #1   _9/29_ #2   _9/30_ #3   _10/1_ #4   _10/4_ # other (optional)

_10/5_ intro.   _10/6_ concl.

Edited/revised draft of entire report: _10/7_   Finished report : _10/12_

Parent Signature: _____Date: _____

October 8, 1999

Dear Students and Parents,

This letter reviews many of the instructions that have been given in class, or have been written on your directions or assignment calendar for the Early Humans Report. Please consult this letter as you revise and complete the elements of your report. **I must check you off for a draft of each element before I will accept a final report.**

Monday, Oct. 11 - Turn in a copy of every element of the report except the map and illustration (unless you haven't already shown me those.)

Computer or Hand Written: Students who have computers have been encouraged to use them since the edit/revise process is easier and less time consuming. If a student wants to turn in the final report written on the computer, I must see a draft of the entire report on computer before the draft is finalized. By final report I mean all the elements: title page, table of contents, text of report, glossary, and bibliography.

Elements of the Report:
Title Page: model given in class and copied into spiral notebook.
Table of Contents: (same as above.)
Text of the Report: This is the essay about the early human. Do not use headings for the text or any of the paragraphs. The heading is the title page of the report. Please double space the text of the report, indenting each paragraph. The vocabulary words are supposed to be underlined and explained as they are used within the text of the report. The organization of the text is supposed to follow the outline and the model, and should contain most, if not all, of the information provided on the data sheet. Each paragraph must contain an introductory and conclusion sentence, as well as clear detail sentences about the subtopic. Proofread all your work to correct spelling, punctuation, capitalization, etc.
Illustration and Map: The illustration and map are hand done in color. The illustration has a label indicating the name of the early human and a caption telling about the picture.
Glossary: The glossary is an alphabetized list of the vocabulary words with definitions placed just before the bibliography at the end of the report. Use the glossary in your social studies text book as the model. You will notice that the words in the glossary are not numbered, underlined, or capitalized unless they are proper nouns. Your glossary should follow this model. Your definitions should be complete, with details that clearly explain the meaning of the word as it is used in this report. In addition to the glossary you are supposed to use the vocabulary word in the text of your report, underline the word once, and explain its meaning within the paragraph in which you use it. This is, also, just like the model of the S.S. text book which uses key terms, highlights them, and defines them within the text of the chapters.
Bibliography: Follow the model on the back of this week's assignment calendar. Although you may add other resources that you used, I am expecting everyone to include the following resources listed in your bibliography: Armento, Cronkite, Reprint, and Boehm. These can be copied. Additions should be modeled after the examples.

Remember when you turn in the final report it must be secured in a report folder and must be accompanied by all of your earlier drafts, models, etc.

Hope this helps you to keep track of all that we have done for the last two weeks.

II Essay questions *Outstanding work!*

(1.) Three artifacts that archaeologists might study to learn about the past are tools, art, and fossil bones of early humans. They might study tools such as; flint burins, stones, iron ore, ect. They study tools to see what culture early humans had and they can find out where the early human lived where the remains of tools were found. Scientists can find that if the tools were more complex, they might to be able to find what the early human ate. They also might find how they communicated. Scientists could find a lot out about the early human's art. They could find out if they were musicians or if they had cave art, with the cave art you could see what food they ate and if they believed in a god. By finding a fossil bone, you could see the size of their skull and how big their brain was, if the skull was big or small. You could find the head shape, posture, ect. Those are three artifacts that scientists might study to learn about early humans.

(2.) Scientists think the Ice Age encouraged ancestrol humans to spread across the earth because the animals that the early humans hunted, migrated to places where they could find food. Land bridges were formed from the ocean's level dropping. Early humans needed food shelter, and clothing to survive the cold and hot

periods of the Ice Age so they follow
the herds of animals across the land
bridges into different continents that they
colonized. Now the early humans could
have food, shelter, and clothing if they
needed.

(3.) The development of tools allowed early
humans to take advantage of a wide range
of food recources. Tools made life easier for
early humans. They didn't have to kill animals
with their bare hands. With sharp stone
flakes, the people could butcher large
animals like, elephants, rhinos, mammoths, deer,
and wild oxen. With Sharp pieces of antler,
they were able to dig for all the
underground roots they needed. The early
humans could keep warm by fire
and sewing animal skins into shelters and
clothing, now that they had tools.

(4.) Two examples of how the development of
fire was important to early humans are protection
and warmth. Fire helped them with protection becau
if there was a wild animal near by and they
couldn't get to their tools, the fire would
scare the animals away. Fire would also
keep them warm on a cold night. Fire was

very important to early humans.

(5.) Evidence that scientists faced, gave the idea that the Neanderthals had a strong sence of community was because they helped one another and stayed in large groups (20 to 50 people) than the Homo Erectus. They all stayed in one place longer because burial grounds were Found near caves and shelters. Evidence in the Neanderthal's bones shows that some old or crippled skeletons would have lived when they were alive without help from the rest of the community. Some Neanderthals also had arthritis. They couldn't hunt or gather food but they were still important to their community and were taken care of by the Neanderthal's community. A Sence of community would have helped them survive the Ice Age because they stayed in groups and took care of each other. You can tell that they cared for one another because these are the first early humans to have burials. The Neanderthals had a strong sence for community

Outstanding!
answers!

Part 2

1. Three artifacts that archaeologists might study to learn about early humans are: old bone fossils to learn the age of a particular group of early man, tools they might excavate to find out how they lived and how they did certain things with the little variety of tools they had, and they might study art they find (that's from the past) to get an idea of that early humans beliefs. These are 3 things archaeologist might to learn about early humans.

2. Scientists think that ancestral humans spread across the world during the Ice Age. They think this because they've excavated bones that are from the Stone Age in Europe Africa, Asia, and many other sites. The Ice Age encouraged early humans to move because the glaciers kept the oceans frozen so land bridges open up. This allowed early humans to cross to new lands and follow animal there. This is why scientists think the Ice Age encouraged early humans to spread over the world.

3. The development of tools allow early humans to take advantage of a wider

Part 2 (continued)
Test

range of food because with tools
early humans could kill bigger animals,
scare away other animals from the pre
the animals and the early humans killed, and
5 to dig tubers up from underground. This
is how tools allowed early humans to
take advantage of a wider range of
food.

4. Three examples of how fire was
important to early humans are; with
fire they could stay warm during the
freezing hours of the Ice Age, fire scared
flesh-eating animals away so, early human
5 kept their food and lives, and fire cooked
the meat they killed so it would taste
better and they wouldn't get sick
or die from meat germs. This is why
fire was important to early humans.

5. Scientists base the idea that the Neanderthals had a strong sense of community
on the evidence of that they've
excavated graves of neanderthals that
had things that might have been important
to the person that died. This leads
us to believe that the family and friends
had had a sense of community towards
this person that died and had felt sorrow
when this person had died. This would

have been important for them to survive during the Ice Age, because without it they would die. They would die because without working together with a community, sick and old would die with out a chance. But with a community the sick and old would be taken care of and would live a longer life. This why it was important for the Neanderthals to have a sense of community during the Ice Age.

Country Report

1. **FLAG.** Color a 4" x 5" flag of your country. Glue the flag to a 12" x 18" piece of construction paper folded as a cover for your report. Write the name of your country above the flag. Write your name at the bottom of the cover.

2. **MAPS.**

    Draw a **full page-sized map** of your country. Locate and label the capital city and other major cities, the major river, and other rivers. Label all countries or bodies of water bordering your country. Label any other major features you think are significant. Put a compass in the upper right hand corner of your map.

    Draw **two other maps showing resources or products** of your country (e.g., farming, fishing, mining, forests, industries).

3. **INTRODUCTION.**

    Geographical location. Describe the geographical location of your country. Be sure to indicate whether it is located in the northern or southern hemisphere and whether it is in the eastern or western hemisphere. Indicate its approximate location in degrees longitude and latitude.

    Geography. Then describe the geography of your country. Tell its area; describe its location relative to countries around it; tell what continent it is on; give information about its weather; and name its major cities and geographic features (e.g., mountains, deserts, rivers, plains, jungles, etc.).

4. **HISTORY.** Write a brief history of your country. When was it settled? If someone discovered it, tell who and how. Why do you think it was settled? You can show these events on a timeline.

5. **A TRIP YOU TOOK THROUGH YOUR COUNTRY.** Write this as a journal as if you actually took a trip through your country.

    In an introduction, tell the **dates** of your trip. List the **clothes and other items** you packed in one suitcase and in your backpack.

    Then list a **day-by-day itinerary** of your trip (as you would have kept a daily journal):

    - Name cities you visited, sights you saw, events or holidays during your visit, and the weather each day.
    - Tell about the **food** of your country. Describe shopping in a local farmers' market, and tell about a restaurant experience.
    - Tell what forms of **transportation** you used. How did you get from California to the country and back? How did you travel once you arrived in the country?
    - Tell about any **souvenirs** you bought or found on your trip.

    In the conclusion, tell about the most interesting thing you learned about your country. Tell about the most enjoyable part of your trip.

6. **ILLUSTRATIONS AND PHOTOGRAPHS.** Include these throughout your report. All pictures must be accompanied by hand-written captions.

Enjoy your journey!

Fifth Grade Country Report

Statistical Information

People:

    Population - _____

    Population Density - _____

    Ethnic Groups - _____

    Languages - _____

    Religions - _____

Geography:

    Area - _____

    Location - _____

    Neighbors - _____

    Topography - _____

    Capital - _____

    Major cities - _____

Economy:

    Chief crops - _____

    Minerals - _____

Finance:

    Currency - _____

    Gross Domestic Product - _____

    Per capita income - _____

    Import partners - _____

    Export partners - _____

Health:

    Life expectancy at birth: male _____ female _____

    Infant mortality rate –

Education:

    Literacy rate - _____

Population 5-19 yrs. in school - _____

Teachers per 1000 students - _____

The Arts

Program for "A Midsummer Night's Dream,"

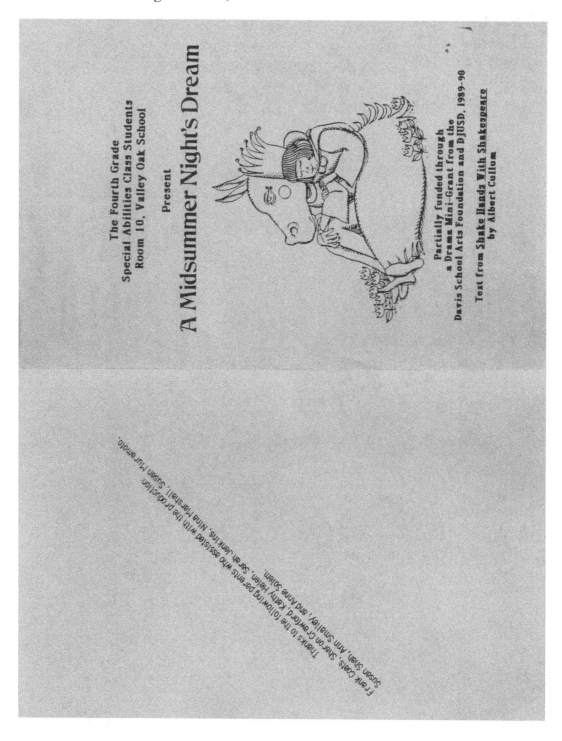

The Fourth Grade
Special Abilities Class Students
Room 10, Valley Oak School

Present

A Midsummer Night's Dream

Partially funded through
a Drama Mini-Grant from the
Davis School Arts Foundation and DJUSD, 1989-90

Text from Shake Hands With Shakespeare
by Albert Cullum

Thanks to the following parents who assisted with the production:
Frank Coats, Sharon Crawford, Kathy Helen, Sarah Jenkins, Nina Harshall, Susan Muranoto,
Susan Shah, Ann Smalley, and Anne Solem.

A MIDSUMMER NIGHT'S DREAM

Scene 1: The Palace of Theseus in Athens
Scene 2: The Magic Forest That Night
Scene 3: The Forest the Following Night
Scene 4: The Bower of Titania an Hour Later
Scene 5: Same Spot in the Forest a Little Later
Scene 6: Another Part of the Forest a Few Minutes Later
Scene 7: Titania's Bower in the Forest Early the Next Morning
Scene 8: Theseus' Palace That Evening

Directed by:
Morgan Jenkins
Eric Helen
Deborah Nichols Poulos

Cast
(In order of appearance)

Role	June 5	June 7
Narrator	Janice Nyland	John Adams
Theseus (Duke of Athens)	David MacKinnen	Timothy Natter
Hippolyta (betrothed to Theseus)	Sigrid Asmundson	Sigrid Asmundson
Philostrate (Master of the Revels)	Karen Kubey	Angela Kuo
Egeus (father to Hermia)	Mayura Obanaje	Jonathan Coontz
Hermia (in love with Lysander)	Heather McGee	Jennifer Muramoto
Demetrius (in love with Hermia)	Kellen Smalley	Walter Hickerson
Lysander (in love with Hermia)	Patrick Solem	Courtney Pasek
Helena (in love with Demetrius)	Emily Hodell	Laurel Crawford
Peter Quince (a carpenter)	William Marshall	Amanda Pittwood
Nick Bottom/Pyramus (a weaver)	Alyssa Nielsen	Ariel Reid
Francis Flute/Thisby (a bellows mender)	Amanda Pittwood	Morgan Jenkins
Robin Starveling/Moon (a tailor)	Jennifer Muramoto	Emily Hodell
Tom Snout/Wall (a tinker)	Qasim Shah	William Marshall
Snug/Lion (a joiner)	Eric Helen	Eric Helen
Puck (a sprite)	Angela Kuo	Molly Shannen
Oberon (King of the Fairies)	Morgan Jenkins	Mayura Obanaje
First Fairy	Evan Baker	Evan Baker
Titania (Queen of the Fairies)	Jenai Holland	Karen Kubey
Changeling Boy	Walter Hickerson	Kellen Smalley
Second Fairy	Laurel Crawford	Jenai Holland
Third Fairy	Courtney Pasek	Patrick Solem
Fourth Fairy	Molly Shannen	Echera Wong
Peaseblossom	Deven Coats	Heather McGee
Cobweb	John Adams	Deven Coats
Moth	Echera Wong	Janice Nyland
Mustardseed	Ariel Reid	Alyssa Nielsen
Oberon's Fairies	Tim Natter, Jonathan Coontz	David MacKinnen, Qasim Shah

An overview of the Davis Joint Unified School District's Self-Contained Gifted Program in 1991

The self-contained gifted program in the Davis Joint Unified School District is called the Special Abilities Program. This program began in the 60s, and has offered one fifth/sixth grade combination class since then. In 1982 the program expanded to include a third/fourth grade class. In 1983 it expanded to a third class and changed the format to a fourth, a fifth, and a fifth/sixth grade class. After this transition year, each class was made up of a single grade level.

The district has historically provided no special funding for these classes—we have had exactly the same budgets as all other regular classrooms in the district. However, this year, 1991, the district received funds from the state's new Gifted and Talented Education (GATE) funding. The district is using this funding to hire a GATE coordinator who will assist in developing a K-12 program.

One of the most difficult adjustments a gifted student in our program makes is from being in a situation in which she performs tasks quickly, easily, and well to a situation in which tasks require greater time and effort, and products are evaluated by different standards.

By the time students enter my class, they have usually spent four years in a regular classroom. Therefore, entry into the fourth grade self-contained gifted program presents many challenges for students, for parents, and for me. As we all know, it would be inaccurate to speak of their experiences in regular classrooms as if they have been the same.

Differences in school populations—and in approaches of individual teachers—account for great variation in the experiences of gifted children in regular classrooms. Even within my own community, it would be very difficult to generalize about the previous school experiences of the students who come into my classroom.

Our district schedules a group test for third graders in the late spring of each year. Parents have the option of having their students tested on this day. Students who score at or above the 97th percentile on either the quantitative or verbal battery of the Cognitive Abilities Test, a group test, are eligible for the program. Parents also have the option of having their children privately tested using individual tests at their own expense. The same percentile score is required.

After receiving notification of qualification, parents decide whether or not to enroll their children in the program. Students entering the fourth grade come from all six of the elementary schools in the district. The class is composed of gifted children of all descriptions. Some are highly motivated, high achieving successful students, while others are unmotivated, low-achieving unsuccessful students.

There are children with learning disabilities, and although uncommon, there are students with physical disabilities as well. Two years ago there was a blind student who entered the fourth grade. There are students from all socio-economic levels, and a variety of cultural, racial, and ethnic backgrounds.

There are children from homes in which English is not the primary language. Although the students are a homogenous group in terms of the entry qualification standard, the dominant characteristic of this class is its heterogeneity. Achievement and performance in the basic skills of language arts and math cover the spectrum from below grade level to high school level and above.

Although the program has evolved over the years, and the entry requirements have remained constant, the diversity among the students has increased. It is important for you to understand that because of the limitations of time for this presentation, I only discussed the major transitional issues of entry into this type of program.

My Students with Special Needs

Three special-needs students in my classes over the years

The three special-needs students in my classes were very different from each other. I think it is important for you to know about each one to better understand why I feel special-needs students can be well served in a regular class.

Christian

The first special-needs student was a fifth grader in a power wheelchair who had a full-time aide to help him with all the tasks he needed to do. I believe he had muscular dystrophy, but I am not sure. His aide also worked with other students in the class. She helped with reading groups and math, as well as assisted with a variety of other jobs throughout the classroom.

As it turned out, Christian was just as capable as any other student in the class—if not more so. He simply needed help with the physical tasks of learning. He was able to participate in all classroom activities, including playing a part in our Shakespeare play. And he also participated in some of our P.E. activities by keeping score and timing races.

Matt

A few years later, I had a sixth grade autistic student, who also had an aide. I had gotten to know Matt on the playground in the years before he was in my class—when I was on recess yard duty. I'd seek him out and usually found him pacing around the blacktop between games of foursquare and tetherball. I'd walk right alongside him, asking him questions and interacting with him, as if pacing on the playground were just an ordinary activity. When it was time for him to go to sixth grade, his parents requested that I be his teacher. He was a delightful student.

Autistic students have difficulty interacting with others, so they frequently stay isolated from their classmates. I explained this to the other students so they wouldn't be put off when he acted this way with them. I also said that just because he might not come up to them to talk, they should make a point of seeking him out and talking to him. They followed my suggestion, and by the end of the year Matt was participating in all of our classroom activities and had made tremendous progress relating to the other students.

Years later, I saw Matt a few times. Once I was sitting in a window seat at a local restaurant when Matt and his mom walked by and saw me. They came in, and Matt talked to me about what he was doing since graduating from high school, and he voluntarily gave me a hug. On another occasion, I was at the local lumber company where I was delighted to see Matt working on the retail floor helping customers find items they needed. Eventually Matt was able to live independently in his own apartment.

Dylan

My third special-needs student was Dylan, who had Down syndrome. He came to my class for math, and his aide came with him. Dylan was friendly and talkative. Though he soon became fully integrated with the class socially, he needed help with the work we did in math. His aide frequently led a small group of which Dylan was a part, and she would also respond to any other students who needed help.

Dylan did need help with socially appropriate behaviors, but because of our talk before he entered the class, the other students knew not to laugh or react to his misbehaving. Dylan did a good job of behaving more and more appropriately.

The benefits of this learned behavior

Frankly, it was a positive experience to have these special-needs students in my classes. My students were enriched by learning alongside them as they began to see how an accepting behavior could benefit the special-needs students.

And the special-needs students definitely were enriched by being a part of a regular classroom where—usually for the first time in a normal setting—they were not viewed as being different, but rather as simply a part of a whole. It had to have boosted the special-needs students' self-confidence to feel accepted. And it definitely was gratifying to see all the students learn to interact with each other as if there were no special circumstances involved.

Further, integrating the aides into the class reaped benefits all around. (Of course I asked each aide first.) Their working with other students when needed was a help to them, and, because of their wide involvement, they quickly became accepted as more than just a helper to the special-needs student. Indeed, each aide certainly was a tremendous help to *me*. And because each one became actively involved, having the special-needs student in the class became more acceptable; all the interaction simply became normal.

The aides told me that few other teachers used them the way I did, and that they also benefited tremendously from the experience—not only from the interaction with the other students, but because it made their days in class more diversified and interesting.

APPENDIX N
Common Errors in Written and Spoken Language

1. Correct use of "I" and "me."

"Mike and I went to the store."

"Mike went to the store with Sally and me."

The first example uses "I" correctly in the subject of the sentence. The second example uses "me" correctly in the predicate of the sentence. An easy test for what is correct is if you would use "me" alone, you would still use "me" if you add another name. For example,

Never say, "Me and Mike" went to the store. (You wouldn't say "Me went to the store.) Also, "Mike went to the store with me." (You wouldn't say, "Mike went to the store with Sally and I" just because you added 'Sally.") This is a common mistake.

2. Correct use of "fewer" and "less."

"Fewer" is used when referring to a counted amount. "Less" is used for aggregate, singular mass nouns. For example, you can have **fewer** ingredients, dollars, people, or cats, but **less** salt, pepper, money, equipment, or access. If you can count it, use **fewer**.

"There were fewer children in the class when several were out with the flu."

"There was less food available for lunch because one of the delivery trucks was in an accident."

3. Use of "and" when saying numbers.

"And" is used to signify the decimal point. For example, "the answer to the equation was one hundred twelve and seventy-five hundredths (112.75)."

On the other hand, for the year you would say, "Two thousand nineteen," not "Two thousand and nineteen." Also, you would say, "The house was listed at two million, five hundred thousand," not "Two million and five hundred thousand." (There is no decimal point in either 2019 or 2,500,000.)

(Even national news anchors and well-educated people make these mistakes, e.g., Anderson Cooper when speaking on 60 Minutes and David Bromstad when on My Lottery Dream House.)

It is the same when you write out an amount of money on a check: You write out "Two hundred twenty and 56/100" not "Two hundred and twenty and 56/100"

4. Use of 'unique.'

Unique is a stand-alone adjective. It means one of a kind—there aren't any more like it anywhere else; if this one disappears, then it will be extinct. You can search and search all over the world, but you won't find a second one. After they made this single one, they broke the mold and threw the pieces into 27 different trash cans so that no one would be able to make another one.

Therefore, saying "very unique" or "especially unique" or "quite unique" *is* incorrect.

5. Use of singular verb after a singular subject.

When the <u>subject</u> is singular, the <u>verb</u> must be singular. In the example under #4 above, the last sentence mentions three separate singular options: "very unique," "especially unique," "quite unique." Therefore, the correct verb is the singular "is," not the plural "are."

Similarly, you would say, "<u>Each</u> of the five women <u>is</u> dressed differently." (The verb has nothing to do with the **phrase "of the five women"** that precedes it).

6. Use of "both of us."

Some people say, "the both of us." This is incorrect. It is just, "Both of us went to the party," or "Mary went to the party with both of us."

7. Use of conditional

Say, "*If I had known* we were out of milk, *I would have* stopped at the market." Or say, "*I would have* stopped at the market *if I had known* we were out of milk." Don't say, "*If I would have* known we were out of milk, I would have stopped at the market."

8. Don't say, "these ones"

Say, "*These* are the *ones* I meant to give you." Or, "I meant to give you *these*." Don't say, "I meant to give you *these ones*."

About the Author

This photo was taken of me in front of one of my quilts.

Deborah Nichols Poulos taught grades one through six over 27 years, including eight years in a self-contained fourth grade gifted class. During her first nine years, she taught a different grade—often in a different school—each year. After those first years, she taught only grades four through six. She did most of her teaching in Davis, California.

As she gained experience and confidence, she started to develop her own strategies that she found yielded better results than what she had been taught—or, in many cases, had not been taught at all. Having experience in many different grades during her early years of teaching prepared her to be flexible—and to develop techniques that she could use with students of any age or ability.

Her husband has long urged her to write a book about what she had learned from teaching. More recently her memoir group advocated this as well, pointing out that they thought her teaching ideas were compelling with unique perspectives. *The Conscious Teacher* is the culmination of her efforts.

CPSIA information can be obtained
at www.ICGtesting.com
Printed in the USA
LVHW061109240322
714080LV00007B/339

9 781684 095582